MATTERS OF THE HOOD

To: Erin
Thanks for Your Support.

Richard Konrad

MATTERS OF THE HOOD

RICHARD KOONCE

RK Publishing Company LLC
935 Rockcreek Road
Charlottesville, Virginia 22903
richbooks3@gmail.com

Matters of the Hood © Copyright 2012 Richard J. Koonce III

All rights reserved. No part of this book may be reproduced without written permission from the publisher except for the use of brief quotations in a review.

This is a work of fiction. Any references or similarities to actual events, real people, living, or dead or to real locales are intended to give the novel a sense of reality. Any similarity in other names, characters, places, and incidents is entirely coincidental.

Library of Congress Control Number: 2012924203
ISBN: 978-0-9891306-0-8
Cover Design/Photography: Robert Banks RRBANKSPHOTOGRAPHY.COM
Author: Richard J. Koonce III
Editor: Rayshon Harris/ Richard Koonce

Copyright © 2012 by RK Publishing Company LLC. All rights reserved. No part of this book may be reproduced in any form without permission from the publisher, except by a reviewer who may quote brief passages to be printed in a newspaper or magazine.

Contents

Acknowledgements 7

Chapter 1 11
Chapter 2 29
Chapter 3 47
Chapter 4 59
Chapter 5 73
Chapter 6 91
Chapter 7 109
Chapter 8 123
Chapter 9 141
Chapter 10 161
Chapter 11 175
Chapter 12 185
Chapter 13 209
Chapter 14 233
Chapter 15 243
Chapter 16 273
Chapter 17 287
Chapter 18 309
Chapter 19 329
Chapter 20 353

Acknowledgements

As I sit here preparing to type these acknowledgements, my mind is all over the place. I'm unsure of where to begin, and who I'll unintentionally leave out. I'm sure it's going to happen, somebody is going to see me and say, "why you didn't shout me out in the acknowledgement," and my answer to that is two-fold. 1) I forgot! 2) Charlottesville isn't but so big and I have been all over this City doing whatever it was I was doing at the time and crossed paths with hundreds of people who are cool with me. However, just listing all those people, their attributes, behaviors, and all that is a great recipe for an entire book so I'll say to you, be careful what you ask for. This day has been a long time coming, I dreamed of this before I even wrote the first book. To let everybody in on alittle secret, I wrote my acknowledgements before I wrote the first words to my first book.

Fast forward 8 years later, five books in, everything changed. So please forgive me if I didn't mention your name or shout you out if you believe you should have been, I've made this spot for you.

_____ Put your name there and when you see me, I will put my name here *[signature]*

First, The Most High. To the ONE woman who has been a permanent fixture in my life since the minute I took my first breath, Sally D. Williams. It's easy for a mother to love their child when everything is going smooth and according to plan. Nevertheless, that's NOT the story between my mother and I. Even when I was knee deep in the lifestyle, throughout the highs/lows, her faith in me Never wavered, she never failed to love me, console me, and take care of me when I was unable to take care of myself. At the bottom of the barrel, I looked up and saw her smiling down with her hand reaching out and ready to pull me up out of the mess I created. For that single act of kindness, I am truly humbled and grateful. I now Crown my mother: The Greatest Woman on God's Green EARTH!

Khaelicia daddy loves you! K. Hassan daddy loves you! Alexis daddy loves you. Kayvon daddy loves you. My prayer, my sacrifice, my life, my struggle, and my death are for you. I never want my story to become your story.

To my City: Charlottesville, Virginia stand-up!! To my Hood: That almighty 10th Street stand-up, the Projects all day, all night stand-up. From Main Street to Madison Avenue. These blocks, corners, and alleys is where I learned to hustle, it's where I learned Brotherhood, and where I ultimately learned what Loyalty means. My little/big brother Hop the Don, straight-up you held me down, you believed and here's where your voice in my head got us. My brothers from another mother, Marcus (Capone) Jones, Twan (Antoine Davenport) I got you when you get home. Hank and Corey aka Albert. My M.F. partner in crime, Torri aka Roger Price, Squid aka Sherman Timberlake, let'em know what time it is behind the G-Wall for me. Fat in a half, Malcolm can't forget you homey. S.dot aka Sean, AG, Kenny Black (know I'm not putting your Government), JY you haven't cut my hair yet. Joe Mallory, I see your vision. Yo Rip aka Beatle, you read all the rough drafts while we were on vacation and I won't never forget how you ran across the yard laughing about how real the Book was back then. My man Skillz, Black Teddy. My barber Jamell and Bo-Bo. Martina Payne good looking out.

My cousin Pat, what can I say? Brother, you came through in the clutch for me. Brings Moms back and forth to those spots deep in the country on your days off, missing the big Football games for me and we all know how much you love your sports. You skipped going fishing on Sundays, all the stuff you enjoy you missed it because I needed to see Moms. Thanks Brother, I'm indebted to you. Danny, you got a part in every Book I wrote.

To the Koonce Clan: Carletta, you don't have to be scared to let me stay at the crib nowadays. Richard Koonce Jr., Richard Koonce the 4th aka Thriller, Liz, Damien, Richaun (keep your eyes open),Tammy Lee-Koonce aka Rock my M.F. Twin. Rip Tracy Carr-Koonce.

Newark, New Jersey, South Orange Ave. and Newton St. That corner belongs to the Koonce Clan and I dare somebody say otherwise. Over 30 years my Pops held that corner down. My New Community Family, Shaheed, Malik (damn it's been 20yrs. and I haven't seen you since that fateful night), Sheed, Feru, Junior, Ab (rip). My Baxter Terrace crew: My brother Rocky aka Rahman Muhammad Jenkins (the World miss you homey), Ron-Gotti, the Twins, I never forgot ya'll brothers. Martina Payne.

Those who helped make this Project possible: Rayshon Harris, my Editor and Partner. John Allen thanks for the support. Christel Webb, what can I say? To all my Matters of the Hood rough draft readers, I truly thank you for the support and love. Nicole Trice aka Litebrite, thanks.

Gotta shout out the ole' heads: Roland M. Johnson, New York Junior, you two brothers influenced my life and although ya'll not here, I've never forgot you guys.

RIP: My Pops, Richard J. Koonce Sr., Tracy Carr-Koonce, Lynn Shelton, Gene from D.C., New York Jay-Jay. The King of Northwest Benjamin Willis aka Mann and Ru. Amy Carter, China, Rocky (again).

Chapter 1

A few months had passed since the 752 gang had been taken off the streets of Charlottesville, Virginia, sidelined by the Federal Government with one of the biggest Drug Conspiracy case's in the area in some time. Every since, the Projects hasn't been the same. Gone was the open air drug trade that had become 10th Street's featured attraction. From Main Street to Madison Avenue, it was a ghost town. Usually, twenty or thirty dudes were out shooting dice, arguing, breaking bottles, shooting their guns all hours of the night, and causing major havoc on the streets of Northwest. Those who wasn't caught up in the ruckus with the Government, kept a low profile. It was widely understood, most of them only came outside when absolutely necessary. At the end of the day, they still had to get their hustle on and eat, despite what became of their peers, their motto became: The Show Must Go On! For Malik and his partner Joey, the timing couldn't have been any better.

Known mostly as the average young weed huslta during the height of the CRACK epidemic throughout Northwest, they stayed off the Government's radar, because they only sold weed and nothing else, nor did they run with that group who had that target on their backs and were known to be notorious CRACK dealers. They stayed out the way of the gun slinger's, the gambler's, and never disrespected anybody simply because they could. They didn't wear the famous White Tee-Shirts or don their necks with Platinum chains that cost more than most people's home. That wasn't their style, everything their peers done, they just did the opposite.

From the outside looking in, they moved different and for a reason. Their peers often laughed at them for giving them such a hard time whenever they wanted some weed from them. They met their clients in different spots every time, no matter how long they knew them or how long they had grown up with them; business was business for the pair. They belonged to the Projects' but they sold weed all over Charlottesville, to them, money was green and it spent all the same no matter who it came from. It wasn't anything to them to identify a good night for the CRACK dealer's because their phones wouldn't stop ringing. What separated them from all the other weed seller's was the fact they kept High Grade weed and was consistent with their flow. Money was coming in on a constant basis for them until the Government came into the City and snatched 98% of their clientele like a thief in the night. There one day and gone the next.

Malik was parked across town in the graveyard on 1st street in a secluded area, perched on top of the hill where he could see both ways in case he had to react to something quickly. He rubbed his hands together in anticipation! Beside him, sat a fly cutie from Prospect named Amanda. She was a small framed chick with a body to die for, nice tits and a round ass to match. However, that's not what set her apart from most chicks in the hood. The true beauty lied in those Hazel-green eyes of hers, one look and they demanded your full attention. In the hood, Amanda was considered to be a down-ass-bitch. She was about her business, her hustle was unlimited, if the money was right, the head was perfect! No shame in her game, either. Malik's new Range Rover was sitting properly on some 22's, chromed out, t.v.'s everywhere, she admired the truck but business was on her mind reminding her of why she was there in the first place. She was on her grind.

Malik had pure lust in his eyes as he glanced over at her, it took her all of Ten seconds to recognize that look, it was nothing to her; it's the same look she's been getting from the opposite sex her entire life. It was what's gotten her over on many males most of her young life, despite having to learn the hard way. Most men loved her exotic features and small frame and her funny colored eyes. Her long wavy hair didn't hurt either, accompanying all of that was her no nonsense attitude. In a different life, she could've easily become a top-flight fashion model; she had the whole package except she lived in the ghetto. However, in this life, Amanda was only a fly bitch from the hood who liked to get her nose dirty and party until the wee hours of the night. She was making an exception for Malik, it was still day light and she usually came out at night time, going against her normal routine. Only for him she thought. From dust to dawn was her working hour's but Malik was one of her biggest sponsors of the moment so whenever he called, she came running. She would stop doing almost anything for

him because if she c...   ...ng else, she knew fucking with him meant
big bucks. He never...   ...her service's and her time. It was during
times like this that he   ...anted to ask her, 'how did you come to
sucking dick for powd...   ...sn't scared to ask her, but deep down,
he felt-he already knew   ...own question, it was apparent to him.
He's seen it before, that   ...ive behavior in the lives of countless
men and woman. His s...   ...f experience after experience. The
hood has a way of taking   ...wn, chewing us up and spitting us
out piece by piece of what   ...ntimes, that process made the men
and women cold, bitter, ang...   ...hat's what he knew to be reality in
the hood but at the moment   ...'ered, he was there on a business
arrangement. Their relationsh... ...the God's, made only in heaven.
He got his dick sucked from...   ...Amanda, well; she got her fair
share of drugs and money. Bo... ...left happier than when they
arrived. This is what they did tw... ...week.

Stretched over the center co... ...as going to work; sucking
Malik's dick like her mind was ba... ...as, she loved sucking dick
probably more than he loved gettin... ...She was in love with the
power she had once she laid down ho... ...e started ringing bringing
both of them out of their zone, starn... ...ike it was a foreign item, reluctantly
he knew the ring, it was his partner Joey calling. He had to answer. Amanda
didn't miss a beat; clearly she could hear Joey's voice on the other end. Being
nosey was part of her job as she strained to listen and not miss a beat was a challenge. The only thing she heard clearly was Joey told him to meet him on 10th
street in fifteen minutes. On the low, she was hoping it was his CRACK-head
girlfriend calling so she could blow-up his spot. She couldn't figure out why he
was still dealing with the bitch in the first place. It wasn't anything for him to
get almost any chick in Charlottesville, he was already fucking enough of them,
and he could have any of them, including herself. She had always wanted to be
his wifey, the more she thought about it the more aggressive she became while
sucking his dick. It was killing her; she wanted to know what that CRACK-head
bitch had over her? It was a mystery to her but for the moment, that's what the
driving force became as she jerked up and down on his dick faster and shoved
his dick so deep down her throat almost chocking herself in frustration. "Damn!
Damn…That's right, suck this dick bitch…That's it, deep throat all this dick, you

pretty eye mutha-fucker," he moaned over and over! He was in a zone, knowing she loved whenever he talked mad shit to her. It seemed to drive her crazy. "Suck it bitch...Suck it."

He grabbed the back of her head as he barked order's, " show me them pretty eyes bitch...Look at me while you suck my dick," he demanded. Grabbing a handful of her long hair, he forced her to look at him," show me your eyes," he said with more aggression. With her eyes glued on him, he began thrusting his hips up to meet her mouth, his intentions were to shove his entire dick all the way down her throat, however, with each forceful thrust, Amanda relaxed and welcomed his manhood. The more she relaxed the more force he used, she allowed him to fuck her face as hard and aggressive as he wanted. She knew this was her opportunity to do her thang, she began humming her favorite song. Before she knew it he was begging her to stop. Malik didn't know what hit him, when he finally looked down at her, cum was dribbling out the corner of her mouth and she was smiling. She started smacking his dick against the side of her face as more cum oozed out. That's right daddy, make that dick cum all over my face...Umm, you taste so fucking good," she moaned as she continued jerking his dick. He forced his dick from her grasp, he couldn't take it any longer, " you love this shit, bitch," he laughed out of breath? Amanda used her fingers to wipe the corners of her mouth of excess cum. A glob of cum was hanging from her chin, she wiped that, put her finger's in her mouth licking them clean as she smiled back at him. "What," she questioned. "Yeah I love this shit just as much as your horny ass do nigga," she spit. "I'll tell you what Mr. Malik, let a bitch get paid and you can drop my ass off where you picked me up at since you seem to have a problem with how a bitch gets down," she said full of attitude.

Pulling his jean shorts up, he threw his tee-shirt over his shoulder. Her attitude was about to cause him to smack the dog-shit out of her and if he was going to do it, he wanted to be dressed first.

He continued staring at her the entire time he got dressed; for the first time he detected something in her eyes he's never seen before: Sadness. Knowing how rough the hood was, he related to her, even if for only a few seconds. He knew a little something about her, and Amanda's story wasn't that different than so many others in the hood. The one thing that separated her from the rest of the bitches in the hood was that she had some class about herself. She's been on his radar for a long time, even when she was fucking with an O.G. from the Projects. The nigga Safee' had the bitch looking fly everyday but since he was locked-up and everybody else from the hood had been sidelined by the Government, she was left to fend for herself the best way she knew how. Her little nose problem didn't help her situation none, she was known to be fucking with some of them little niggaz from Prospect from time to time. They had become her hustle, they supplied her with shit loads of powder for her time and she made the best of a fucked-up situation. 'Damn this bitch is freaky,' he thought. "Where you want me to drop you off at?" Amanda was looking in the mirror at her smooth brown skin and spotless face making sure she wiped the cum from the corners of her mouth. Pulling the sun-visor down, she relaxed comfortably in the plush leather seats dreaming what it would be like to by Malik's wifey. She sat up quickly examining her hair, "shit, you got cum all in my damn hair, nigga!"

Stealing a look at him, he was staring right back at her. 'Why is he looking at me like that?' She could see a concerned look in his eyes and it confirmed her assumptions. He cared. She really digged him, he reminded her so much of Safee' it was crazy, that's what scared her about him? She couldn't take another Safee' or could she? Without him knowing it, she could suck his dick everyday all day for nothing. She got drunk off the power she had over him when she made him cum in her mouth, the way he talked shit to her, the way he moaned from pleasure, the way he said her name, whenever she had him squirming and trying to get away from her, she knew she did the damn thang. That power made her drunk; it shot electrical currents throughout her body making her horny all over again. It was enough that sucking dick made her horny but it was something about the way he treated her, it made her feel kinda special. If she had more time; she would hop over the center console onto his dick and really show him the true meaning of how a real cowgirl makes her money. Instead, she settled on the ghetto in her, " what the fuck you waiting for nigga? Why the fuck we haven't left yet," rolling her eyes.

That was it, she went too far. "First off bitch, you never said where the fuck you want me to drop your dumb-ass off at...Second, if you keep talking that shit, I'm going to fuck you in the ass until you beg me to stop," he said seriously. Amanda giggled, pouted her lips and locked eye to eye with him. "Don't tempt a bitch with a good time...This pussy is already soaking wet, but I'm telling your crazy-ass now, ain't no way you're sticking all that dick in my ass. Nope! You can fuck this pussy for a month of Sundays if you want any which way you want but not in my ass...You trying to hurt a bitch," she said laughing.

She lifted her tiny skirt up showing off her freshly shaved pussy, spreading her legs wide open and eased two fingers into her love-tunnel. When she pulled them out, they were glistening from her juices, she put them in her mouth," ummm, she taste good too." She wiped her fingers across his mustache, "you'll taste her one of these days," she said playfully. "You crazy...You do realize that, don't you," he got more serious," so where to?"

"You already know...Prospect nigga," she smiled. "Prospect all day...All night," as she snapped her fingers together. He pulled out a baggy of cocaine from the console, "for you Miss Prospect all day and all night," laughing as he tossed it into her lap. "Seven grams for your work."

At the sight of the powder cocaine, Amanda's eyes became enormous and full of life. It didn't take a Rocket Scientist to figure out Malik was blessing her for her time and her services and not only did she need that look out, she believed she deserved it. Her wheels were turning, immediately she thought about what she would do with the work from him? Seven grams was a come-up no matter how you looked at it. "You gotta come scoop me more often if you're going to be this generous. You keep this up and I might just have to let you fuck me in my ass with that King Kong dick of yours," licking her lips thinking about his dick in her mouth. Raising a brow, "you sure you don't want me to hit you off again...I bet I can make you cum before you get to Prospect...You know I'll swallow every bit of that cum," she said laughing. Briefly, he entertained the offer. Getting his dick sucked on the way over to Prospect sounded really good, but, reality set in, he still had a console full of 8-balls and couldn't risk getting pulled over by the Jakes. "I'm going to take a rain check on that one, but I'll tell you what...Make yourself available for later tonight and I'll swing through."

Knowing Joey was across town and waiting for him on 10th and Page, this had to be something important. He made his way to Prospect as quickly as possible. He had every intention of fucking Amanda later, he wanted to fuck her in the ass some kind of bad! Amanda jumped out the Range Rover at the steps at the top of the hill. She peered through the open window at him seriously, "you better call me to... Don't have a bitch waiting on your ass all night either," she demanded with a smile. "I got you bitch. Shut my damn door before the Police come through this hot mutha-fucker...You know these niggaz over here are hot as fish grease."

    Winking at her as she walked off, he admired the way she was working that damn mini-skirt. She was fat to death and he was definitely going to be calling her later tonight. How could he not? He had plans brewing in his mind concerning her; he wanted to put her down with the CRACK game but his better judgment told him not to do it. He's been thinking about it for some time now, she knew everybody and their momma in Prospect. Then there was her little nose problem, that shit was bound to get her ass into something her head-game couldn't get her out of. Business was business and he was going to want his money no matter what story she came with, mixing business with pleasure always got people in trouble and he knew he was no different. He was cutting it close as he looked at the clock on the dash-board but Joey would have to sit tight; he was hungry and determined to stop at GoCo's for Chicken and Potatoes. He had the latest Mean-Streets CD blasting as he rolled down every window, the tint wasn't working for him at the moment, he was on the opposite side of town and wanted them dudes to respect his position and see him in the cockpit of the monster truck. All this paper was getting the best of him sometimes and it took him a minute to adjust to being the man and it was hard for him to check his ego at the door. Why should he? Showing off was what niggaz did from the Projects' and no matter what, he felt he deserved it for all the hard work he was putting in. His new Range Rover Sport was only a small testament of what he had in store in the month's to come. Since they made the transition from selling only weed to mostly CRACK, he stayed fresh to death. His crispy white ones, Rocawear jean shorts, his every other day haircut and his new 7 Carat Rolex on his wrist, he was doing the damn thang. From the outside looking in, by all accounts, Malik was no longer that little nigga from the hood selling weed, he was a man now.

    All eyes were on the Range Rover as he pulled into the parking lot of GoCo's, he basked in the attention. Refusing to smile even though he was smiling on the inside, he outlined his face with a mean-mug, serious, and attentive. He met every eye that starred at him with a menacing gaze of his own, it let everybody knew he wasn't to be fucked with or played. He enjoyed his newfound fame, he was already fucking bitch's from every hood in Charlottesville and getting more paper in a couple of days than he was seeing in a month's time selling weed. He was living the good life! Noticing a few familiar face's over at the gas pumps, he knew them to be from Garrett Square but he didn't fuck with them like that so he wasn't speaking. He kept it moving. Looking back over his shoulder as he entered the store, he noticed two of the four dudes were still staring in his direction. He quickly determined the two who were paying extra attention to his style wasn't from Garrett Square, they had to be from out of town and he could sense a bad vibe. Their attire and aggressive demeanor were different; he made a mental note of the pair and began placing his order for his food.

No matter what you thought you detected in Malik, he didn't have an ounce of pussy in his blood, his partner Joey had taught him a valuable lesson. He taught him what it really meant when they said" GANSTA'S MOVE IN SILENCE AND VIOLENCE! Had this been a few years back, he would have stormed out the store and approached the pair but the times were different, he was playing the game under a different set of rules, the stakes were too high to be bullshitting around.

Outside, he eased back into the truck, with his head halfway out the window, he laughed at the pair as he drove past as they were getting into a hooptie. 'I bet not catch none of them niggaz in the Projects'...Come over that way with that bullshit if they want,' he whispered to himself.

So caught-up in the nonsense with them dudes he forget to leave the lady at the register a tip. He turned around, ran back into the store," I forgot to leave you something," he said winking at the older lady. He pulled out a crispy fifty dollar bill," this is for your enjoyment and not that damn...excuse me, but this is for you and not them." He didn't leave her any room to protest because he was out the door just as quick as he came. Every now and again, Malik tried his best to balance his wrongs with doing something right and good for someone else. He made sure that most of the time that person was a total stranger, as was the case with the lady at the register. He knew his whole order was less than Ten dollar's but since he was making money over hand and fist, he liked to give some of it away. He was trying to remember where he heard that from but he couldn't remember he just did it whenever he got the urge. On look at his Rolex, he knew he had to get his ass back across town, Joey was out there waiting on him and he didn't want to keep him waiting any longer than he had to. 10th and Page Street was the heart of Northwest and Joey was making a rare appearance. He was patiently waiting for Malik, he knew Malik so well that when he urged him to meet him in fifteen minutes, he was still on his way from the County. Malik was always late and he knew it so he didn't bother telling him he was on his way; he wanted Malik to think he was on the corner waiting for him. They often joked that Malik would be late to his own funeral someday.

In the big scheme of things, Joey was quickly becoming the man to see in the Projects', ever since he met his new connect and made that decision to sell CRACK full time, his pocket's had the mumps. Malik wasn't only his partner in the CRACK game; they were more like brother's from a different mother. At 18, they've been homey's since way before they even started Elementary School... They played in the same Sand Box!

With that being said, Malik and Joey couldn't have been more different. Where Malik was loud and aggressive, Joey was more calm and reserved. Malik was the big spender, Joey invested his paper, and he never got into that long distance spending sprees Malik went on in most of the major cities. Malik was the ladies' man, a different chick every night, Joey on the other hand, he never was known to fuck any of the chicks in the hood. Many people made the mistake and asked the question, "Joey, why you fuck with Malik in the first place?' A few simple minded individuals had the courage to ask and were met with a vicious open-hand from Joey. It began to be understood that no matter what Malik got himself into, there was always one person on the entire planet he Knew he could count on to bail him out, if he needed to be bailed out of a situation. That was Joey! Joey was a regular type of guy, no flashy car, never wore jewelry in Charlottesville, didn't do the club scene, no bad habits, and he stayed to himself for the most part. His main function was to remain a free man and stack his paper; everything else was just a means to get to where he wanted to be in life. Their transition was smooth and the CRACK game had been kind to them thus far and he wasn't trying to fuck that up, he knew how fucked-up the CRACK game could get and didn't want any parts of that mess. He was certain to take a page out the playbook of his peers, most of them spending the better part of their best year's locked away in a prison cell or worse, some became snitches for the Government; neither of those situations sat well with him! He worked really hard to keep him and Malik as far away from a prison cell as possible. He would rather die before he became a snitch...No further explanation is necessary, is it? His new connect had become his mentor and he vowed to soak-up as much knowledge about the CRACK game as possible. He didn't want or need to see the inside of a prison cell and if he played his cards the right way, he wouldn't have to see one.

It's been a minute since Joey sat on the rock wall on the corner of 10th and Page Street, since their come-up, there was no need to be hanging on the block for no apparent reason. Checking his Iron-Man sports watch to check the time, he heard the music, the new 'Mean-Streets' CD, just recorded last night. It couldn't be anyone other than Malik; he didn't have to look up. Knowing his partner so well, Malik always made a grand entrance whenever he came around. For once, he was on time so there wasn't but so much he could say. Malik made a right turn onto Page Street and drove half-way down the block.

The weather was perfect for a mid-May day, it wasn't to cool or to warm, hustling weather is what they referred to how nice it was out there. For Joey, this was his time of the year; he hated all the bugs that came with the summer time, so a nice spring day was welcomed. Watching Malik as he exited the Range Rover, Joey picked-up on his walk, it was different. His walk was strong, confident, and demanded the attention of anyone within eye-sight. His gear was top-notch, clean and always color coordinated, his new sneaker's probably cost him an arm and a leg because he only order his sneaker's off the Internet. His jewelry was breath-taking; it went well with his Ninety Thousand dollar Range Rover. He was arrogant before they became the man in the hood, but now the paper only added to his already arrogant demeanor. You could tell he was living life and enjoying every minute of it. Was he unaware of the image he's created for himself over the last few months? Some thought he had lost his mind with his 'in your face mentality, 'and how flashy he's become but at the same time, they knew to keep their comments to themselves. It was widely understood, when it came to Malik, 'Keep your mouth shut and your opinion to yourself!' He wasn't the type you could approach on some bullshit. Joey couldn't hold his smile back; he was clearly happy to see his partner, "what's good fam?" "Same shit...Different toilet, homey," was his response as he gave Joey a hug and a pound. Their embrace was quick but strong. "What's so important that you had to drag me away from my busy schedule to meet you in the middle of the hood?" "Who's the flava of the day...I'm sure you were off somewhere tricking with one of your little hood-rats," said Joey poking fun at the way Malik got down. Malik looked up the block, turned away from Joey, "I don't have a clue as to what the hell you're talking about. All I know is, they say, it ain't tricking if you got it," he faced Joey and tapped his two front pockets. "And you already know, I got it!" Joey loved the fact they could go back and forth poking fun at one another and not have their feelings get involved, he also knew Malik had to fuck a different chick every day of the week. "When you said something about you schedule, now that, that was a dead give-away. You're a natural hustla, you make paper without ever having to try or put in a lot of hard work. You can do this shit with your eyes closed, I'll give you that much...If I can get you to use that same energy you use fucking these bitches out here, we'll be millionaire's in the near future. These bitches is scandalous, watch yourself...I ain't got time to be running your crazy-ass down to the free Clinic every other week to cool that fire off in the head of your dick. "We got jokes, huh? These bitches is feeling the kid out here. You know what it is...its supply and demand," he winked as he went on. "Let me break the shit down for you, there's a demand out this bitch for a dude like me, so you know I gots to supply these chicks with the dick because if not, Charlottesville will be the epic-center of World War Three," he said busting out laughing!

    They both fell out laughing at Malik's joke, their lives had certainly changed since they started selling CRACK, and everybody treated them different. Even the old heads in the hood was coming at them for a little help or advises when-ever their situation involved paper. Six months ago, they were two dudes who sold weed, fast forward, now they were easily the talk of Charlottesville, Malik's flashy ways didn't hurt their standing in the hood and throughout the City. Even the undesirables and clown-ass niggaz talked about the two. With each of them being totally different, their roles were important. Joey was the brains and Malik, well; Malik knew everybody and their momma in Charlottesville.

    Joey was the type to calculate every step he took and loved thought out plans. Malik was more so, the in your face type, he got it how he lived. Joey wasn't the boss, not officially anyway, they considered to be equals. Malik understood that more than anyone could have imagined. Joey was his alter-ego, and it served him and his style perfectly. Their bond was unbreakable. If it came from Joey, Malik took it as Gospel! Even if he was reluctant, all Joey would have to say was, 'Just Think about It!' "If you wasn't my brother and knew better, I'd think the only time your dick gets hard is whenever you're around dudes like, Benjamin, Jackson, or Grant. Won't you get your dick wet sometimes," laughed Malik. "Outside of finding new spots and counting paper, you don't seem to be enjoying yourself much these days...All work and no play, well, you know what they say," laughed Malik.

Malik always took advantage of having a moment of poking fun at Joey, it was rare because Joey was always on his grind and so serious. Nobody didn't need to tell him, he knew Joey was looking at the bigger picture and he knew he was supposed to be doing the same thing but when you have chicks throwing themselves at you day and night, it's hard to turn down free pussy. Ask any real nigga who was getting money. He left Joey to planning the future while he indulged in the Sins of the present.

"You got that one, but remember, you can work hard now and play later or you can play now and work hard later."

That was Malik's cue to end their conversation before it got into all that philosophical bullshit he hated listening to.

"A-ight Fam, you got it," said Malik throwing his hands up. "What's really hood with you, though?"

"Straight to business, huh? Perfect. I got some serious shit I have to run by you," he looked away from Malik for a second. "The connect met with me earlier this morning, we kicked it for a minute and now I have to run that same conversation I had with him by you. Let's walk up 10th street," said Joey looking down at his watch. "What does you meeting with the connect and you having me meet you in the middle of the hood?"

Malik didn't like being on 10th street in the daytime without his strap and he never really cared much about what the connect had to say. He never met with the connect and the connect rarely showed his face on the block. Even during re-up time, it was never the connect who showed up, he always sent one of his chicks to do the deed. Joey picked-up on the seriousness in Malik's voice, he had his attention and knew this was about the best opportunity to relay the message from the connect. "The connect said he saw you at 'Food-Masters' in the Range...He never said when, he just said he seen you there..."

"Aight, what the fuck do that have to do with anything, Joey? You're liable to see me anywhere in Charlottesville, I'm all over this bitch," returned Malik in frustration! Shaking his head, Joey whispered, "I know that."

He knew what he was about to say was only going to frustrate Malik even further but he had to say it, he didn't have much of a choice. There was a long silence; neither said a work until they turned onto Anderson Street. "Malik, he wants you to get rid of the Range Rover...He said it's too flashy and draws way to much attention to us."

Malik wasn't sure he heard him correctly and asked him to repeat himself. "I know I didn't hear you say what I thought I heard you say...Repeat that shit again." "He wants you to get rid of the Range Rover and the Jewelry." Not believing his ears, "you can't be serious, are you serious?" "I'm dead serious Malik! He went on and on about, how that flashy shit keeps getting dudes in fucked-up situations and to keep it One-Hundred, I'm feeling him on this one. It's not just the police or the Feds we have to stay clear of, it's mostly these pussy-ass dudes who don't know any better and try you on some bullshit and then we have to do something we'll later regret somewhere down the line." Joey was trying his best to break it down without offending Malik or his ego," all he's saying Malik is that there's a time and a place for that but right now, this isn't the time or the place. Charlottesville's definitely not the spot to be riding around in a Ninety Thousand dollar truck." Malik knew Joey was on his side and he also knew what he was saying was the truth but the fact of the matter bothered him. How can the connect ask him to get rid of the Range Rover? He barely knew the connect and now all of a sudden the connect was worried about him? "Whatever happened to asking me not to drive the damn truck in Charlottesville...What happened to that?" He shook his head," What about, park the truck Malik, that shit is hot," he looked Joey in the eyes," he don't even know me like that, homey!"

It didn't take long for Joey to figure out that Malik was pondering what the connect had said. It was written all over his face and Joey wanted to change the subject, something more serious and more important. Also, he knew how quick Malik was to say fuck it and refuse to listen whenever he believed someone was trying to play him. "Malik, let me ask you a serious question," looking directly in Malik's eyes?

"Go ahead, but I'm telling you now, I'm getting tired of all these questions and this bullshit about the connect...What the fuck? This must be fuck with Malik day," he said growing irate. "Ask me what you want to ask me?" "How much paper you got in the stash?"

Malik turned his nose up; he thought the question was offensive, "What type of question is that? That's like asking a nigga how long is his dick!" Perfect answer, thought Joey. Already knowing Malik wasn't going to be willing to answer the question, at least not without some resistance and he was already a step or two ahead of him. "For the record, that question has nothing to do with the connect...I doubt he cares enough about either of us to ask us something like that. He wouldn't concern himself with those issues. That's all me, homey." he peered into Malik's eyes. "Let me ask you like this then, if we both got knocked today and I was broke, would you have enough to bail the both of us out and get us a lawyer?" He shot Joey the craziest look, he seen the seriousness in Joey's eyes, he was sincere in his approach and he couldn't avoid the question. In his mind he knew what his answer should be, but the reality of the situation was that his answer wasn't what it should be. This was the moment he seen the light .For him, it was the gift of friendship. He knew Joey cared about his wellbeing when no one else cared. Joey seen right through his bullshit!

One thing Joey knew about his partner was that he never thought about tomorrow, as long as the night before was sweet! Paper wasn't on his mind, well, spending it as fast as he could make it but never the one to save much if any. To get him to see the bigger picture, he had to insert himself because Malik would do almost anything for him.

"Joey...I'm betting that you probably already know the answer. You're slick like that," laughed Malik.

"But, I'll answer it anyway for you...I got about Twenty-Five in the cut," he said with a beaming smile.

"That's more than I expected. Twenty-Five Thousand ain't bad for you. You spend a lot so I can live with that.

"Whoa...Whoa," said Malik waving his hands in the air. "I ain't say nothing about no Twenty-Five grand...More like Twenty-Five hundred."

Joey shook his head. He knew all too well, he had to choose his next words very wisely. "A-ight," rubbing his temples. "Listen, I know you're not the type to think about tomorrow or nothing like that. You simply live for the day and tomorrow will take care of itself. That was cool when we were selling a little bud and fucking bitches but right now, that's a huge problem. We're in a game of chance; this ain't no damn show-n-tell show out this bitch. Everyday could become our last out here and it's time you start approaching everyday as if it was your last. We can lose our life out here, Malik," he stated through clenched teeth.

"I'm feeling you. I never have a problem listening to you, especially when I know the shit is going to help us. I just never took the time to think about putting something away for a rainy day, even if we got pinched, I know ain't no need spending a Hundred thousand on no bullshit lawyer and still get a life sentence...So for me, I never saw the point."

"I know! None of us out here ever wakes up in the morning and say,' this is a great day to go to jail," he looked up the block and thought about what he just said. Not me and certainly not you! We're not the type of dudes to be sitting over at the jail talking about how we wished we had saved 10% of the paper we blew out here tricking and spending the shit all crazy. It's always a bad time to get locked-up, even if we're sitting on Millions. It's a lot more paper out here that we haven't even touched yet and I'm trying to put us in the position where we can get this paper. It's really important we start stacking all we can, who knows when the run will be over."

"What else did the connect have to say because I know, somehow, I can feel it, there's more to the story...Ain't it?"

"Basically that was it...Well, he did say he seen you selling Star a fifty at 7:52 last night." He couldn't help but laugh. He had to, to keep from cursing as they passed an older couple sitting on their porch. He whispered," this nigga following me or something?" Joey looked his dead in his eyes," yes! He follows me and he follows you.

He calls it looking out for his best interest, there's something else you'll find even crazier. He knows about both of your stash spots, the one at Tina's and the one on Rosser." "Joey...Straight-up, what type of dude is we dealing with?'

Joey exhaled," a-ight, here's the deal. I can answer that if you want me to but at the same time, "rubbing his temples."At the same time you have to get rid of the Range Rover and your Jewelry. If you're willing to do that, I'll answer every question you got to the best of my ability. "This wasn't anything light; Malik's decision could change the course of not only his life but Joey's as well. He beamed in on Joey and couldn't see anything but seriousness. "I'm running with you 100%, fuck the bullshit. If you say get rid of the Range Rover and the Jewelry, I'm getting rid of the shit. Period," spit Malik.

"Get rid of the Rover and the jewelry," was all Joey said. He knew from the way Malik was eyeing him that he was going to listen. Checking his Iron Man watch, he looked-up," we have to be on Paoli Street in Five minutes." Making a left off Anderson street, he was telling Malik the connect was going to be meeting them and wanted to talk to them together. Then he laughed because he had to correct himself, he didn't really know if the connect was coming or one of his people's, but it's all the same thing. As they were about to turn on Paoli street, a Black on Black 760 Li pulled over right in front of them as the back window went down. "Get in gentlemen," was what they heard barely able to see inside.

Their connect wasn't a big dude, probably the same size as Malik and Joey. The three of them fit comfortably in the back without having to bunch up together. The same new 'Mean-Streets' CD was playing and watching the underground movie, 'Matter's of the Hood!' Malik was trying his best not to ask the oblivious question, 'how did he get that CD because it was just made last night and he was at the studio.' The difference from the CD he had and the one the connect was listening to was the fact that the connects CD had an extra song on it. Instead of saying anything, he bobbed his head and listened to the new song. "I'm sure you guys know all about this music but what ya'll know about the dudes behind the music," laughed the connect?

"I grew-up with most of those dudes, I see them every day. I should be asking you the same thing," laughed Malik.

"Malik, pass the keys and the jewelry to the dude in the passenger's seat," said the connect side-stepping Malik's original question. "Once he gets out, you take his seat."

Malik was so busy listening to the music he didn't notice the BMW coming to a stop right after he handed over his keys and jewelry. Reluctantly, he gave in and something inside of him told him this wasn't the time to be asking no questions. The big Black dude with the African accent took the keys and got out. The Rover was Ten feet away from Malik and all of a sudden he felt like he was being torn away from his most prized possession. He settled in the passenger's seat and occasionally glanced in the side mirror to see the Rover following closely behind. He felt better knowing wherever they were going, the Rover seemed to be going to the same place. That was until they got to the Scottsville exit on Interstate 64. The Rover got off on the exit and the BMW kept going, that would be the last time he'd ever see the Rover again, he thought. Twenty minutes later, they were pulling into a gated community up on Lake Monticello. Easily they passed through the security check point, no identification was required. The guard apparently knew the big African driving. It didn't take much longer after that before they were pulling into a big circular driveway. There was a Lexus 430 parked off to the side of the driveway. Joey spotted it and thought he'd recognized it from somewhere but couldn't remember from where. Soon as the driver parked, the connect got out and looked back over his shoulder," follow me gentlemen."

Malik and Joey were dead on his heels," this shit is like a mini-mansion. I gotta get something like this one of these days," stated Malik taking in the sights. Joey shook his head in agreement," that's why we have to start saving all our paper!"

Chapter 2

ALL eyes zeroed in on Amanda as she exited the new Range Rover on top of the hill of Prospect, fixing her super short mini-skirt as she waved hair out her face. On her way towards the steps, she knew everybody was watching, not only because of what she was wearing but because of who it was that had dropped her off. Taking her time as she walked she made sure to add some extra flare to her stride as she switched her petite ass from side to side. It was in those exotic features of hers that made her the envy of most females and the fantasy of her male counter-part. Amanda was a straight-up chick, her self-confidence and sleek attitude separated her from most other chicks in her same situation. Clearly she paid no attention to all the cat calls and whistles, in her mind she was thinking,' you gotta come better than that if you want my attention!' At the moment she had other shit on her mind, like the work she had in her bag, she moved with grace and elegance maneuvering down the steps. Careful not to trip, her heels wasn't made for a lot of walking, maybe being fucked in but not for walking and she knew it that's why she took her time. The farther she got the more they whistled, hollered, and damn near begged her to stop for a minute of her time. However, the cocaine she had was calling her and that's all she really could hear, at least until she heard someone call her out of her name. Then it came again. Fuck you...You stinking, stuck-up bitch, yelled a voice! She put the brakes on those heels like she was rocking a pair of soft bottom Prada's.

Time seemed to stand still, it seemed everybody in Prospect knew one common little secret about Amanda except this little nigga because if he knew, there's no way in hell he would have made that statement. See, the other thing which made Amanda different from all the other chicks was her background and her personal struggles. The bitch was a certified gansta, she was known to fight niggaz, bitches, dogs, and anything or anybody whom she thought disrespected her. She had never once back downed from a challenge in her life! To her, she didn't mind all the cat call and whistles trying to gain her attention, that's a part of the game when you live in the ghetto. It's part of the hustle and bustle in the life of a hustla, she knew that much, she didn't need anyone to teach her that, again, she learned the hard way growing up. Every so often, Amanda would choose a lucky dude from on top of that hill and invite them into her apartment for a night they'll never forget. Her bedroom was legendary in Prospect, even though there wasn't many who could say they actually seen the inside of her bedroom but the   ones who seen it, couldn't seem to keep their mouths shut as to what she had done to them sexually. They always ran their mouths like little bitches and that's what she got a kick out of. Her dominance! She was known to do tricks only seen in a porno-flick, she was just that good. Her unique set of skills in the bedroom kept her pockets laced and her apartment stocked with the latest gadgets. Nevertheless, nobody dared to call her out of her name. Whore, slut, or even prostitute was something she was more than willing to fight for. To her she wasn't fighting for what they were saying, more so, it was her good name she cared about. The youngster never knew the mistake he made by calling her out of her name but she intended to make sure that the next time their paths crossed, he wouldn't dare call her out of her name.

From the bottom of the steps, she turned with fire in her eyes and screamed, " I got your bitch you little dick mutha-fucker," all the while she was easing her straight razor from the bottom of her bag ready for war. "I bet you won't bring your bitch-ass down here and say that shit to my face," she began to laugh." I'll tell you what; I'll make it sweet for you. If you come and say that shit to my face, I'll suck your little dick in the middle of Prospect for everybody to see," she said laughing almost uncontrollable. A short dark-skinned dude appeared from out the crowd, he had his arms spread saying," damn lil'momma, why you gotta act like that for?"

The dude figured, if he showed a little remorse and respect for what he just said to her it would gain him some points in the future, especially since what's he's been hearing about how she got down. He slowly made his way down the steps as he tried to console her attitude," my bad...My bad, lil'momma. You gotta know, I ain't mean nothing by that bullshit, I was joking with you, you can take a joke can't you?"

She knew what he was saying because Amanda couldn't stop smiling. His first glimpse into her beautiful eyes caught him off guard. He heard they were pretty but not like this, he couldn't stop looking at them. He was in a trance! She seen it coming, he was stuck and she's seen how she has that effect on many different men in her life. 'The eyes get'em every time,' she thought. Unbeknown to dude, he made his first mistake, and soon he'll live to regret it. He was about two feet away from her when her smile disappeared. Her hazel eyes seemed to turn green right before him and she had rage and anger filling those crazy green eyes. She made two perfectly straight passes with her razor down the right side of his face with lightning speed.

In his mind he was thinking,' I know this bitch didn't just slap the shit out of me and walk away?' All he knew was he seen her hand then he didn't and she was now turning and walking away. 'Damn, that shit stings like a mutha fucker,' he thought reaching for his face. When he pulled his hand away from his face and looked at it, it was dripping with dark red blood. He checked his shirt and it too was spotted with blood. 'Where's it coming from?' She watched as she opened the side of his face like a can-opener. It didn't start bleeding right away, she saw all the way down to his white-meat. She turned and walked away thinking,' he'll figure it out soon enough!' Five steps away and that's when she heard it, it was like a scream from one of those scary movies except this wasn't a movie, this was real life. Without even turning around she said over her shoulder," who's the bitch now," as she entered her building through the back door laughing again. She had one thing on her mind now, the cocaine in her bag!

Soon as she stepped into her apartment, White-girl was sprawled on the sofa in her panties sleeping like a baby. Other than family, White-girl was Amanda's only true friend. They grew very close in a short amount of time. They completed related to one another, neither of them had much of a family outside of the streets and they've been hanging ever since. White-girl was in Prospect looking for some powder a few months back and Amanda intervened right before them young dudes on top of the hill beat her for her money or have her doing God knows what for some cocaine. White-girl seemed relieved to be rescued by Amanda, she watched as Amanda busted through the crowd and ordered her to follow her. Right off the bat, White-girl was intrigued by the way Amanda was carrying herself. The confidence and her exotic features told White-girl that she should listen to this stranger. She's been in that apartment with Amanda ever since, enjoying the fast life. Smoking weed, getting drunk, sniffing powder, and fucking a different black dick every night. She was addicted to the good life of the Hood!

Sharing a favorite pastime, Amanda and White-girl made one helluva combination. They both loved sniffing powder cocaine and fucking like there was no tomorrow to put the icing on the cake, White-girl turned out to be a bigger freak than Amanda, they complimented one another nicely. Without knowing any better, it was easy to look at White-girl and think she was your average White chick by the way she acted but once you look closer you'll see how wrong you were. She was built like a sista, full lips, perfectly round-ass, nice thighs, and two huge grape-fruit sized tits. It didn't take long for the word to get out that Amanda had this badass White chick running with her, her cell phone couldn't stop ringing. She gassed it up by telling everybody the bitch White-girl was down for whatever and it was like she spoke the power to the truth because White-girl loved all the attention she was getting from the brothers. Amanda had to watch her because her biggest problem was that she didn't know how to negotiate. In the beginning, White-girl was sucking and fucking for a couple of dubs when she should've been easily getting 3to 4grams for the shit she was willing to do. Amanda put her foot down and took total control of what was going on inside the bedroom, the bathroom, or even the living room because there wasn't no cut cards. If a nigga was paying, they were fucking!

Her motto became: 'you wanna Play...Your blackass gotta Pay.' The funny thing about their relationship, no matter how many dicks they sucked, how hard a nigga thought he fucked them, or thought he had them doing, they always laughed. The biggest trick was in the fact that they loved to fuck, suck, and do all the kinky shit that came their way probably more than them niggaz who was paying the big bucks for their time. To them, they were getting paid to do something they'd probably be doing for free if only them niggaz knew how freaky they really were. The clearly lived for the moment and enjoyed every second of it.

Amanda eased right past White-girl being ever careful not to wake her, at least not yet. She wanted to make it to her bedroom and stash a little something for later because fucking with White-girl; she'd sniff everything and be thinking the shit grows on trees or some shit. One thing Amanda hated more than not being able to get high was running out of coke and not being able to get more. At three or Four O'clock in the morning, it's hard to get someone to get out their bed to bring some cocaine to you, she learned that the hard way. As if on cue, she located her favorite stash spot, nobody knew about this spot and she intended to keep it this way as she closed her closet. She peeked her head out the window to see if she could get a glimpse of the dark-skinned dude getting into the Ambulance, she seen the light's through the curtains. 'Pussy,' she thought to herself taking a huge one on one of the powder cocaine. She took a huge chunk of the powder and carefully placed it in a fifty dollar bill as she went to crush it into a fine powder and ready for sniffing. Before she realized it, the coke was over flowing from the sides of the bill, she had to get another bill to make due. A smirk spread across her face knowing anytime she needed two bills to hold the powder, she had enough to last a minute. This was now the official beginning of their day, that devilish smirk replaced her smile; her wheels were starting to turn as she wondered what the day would bring? Cradling the bills in her hands she made it back into her tiny dining room and set-up shop in her favorite chair and got herself a cold beer. Sitting one bill in front of her she took another sniff and inhaled deep, a second later, she exhaled the powerful white substance she loved with the bottom of her heart. This time, the cocaine went straight to her brain, she relaxed, closed her eyes and whispered to herself,' that's the feeling I'm looking for!'

Staring over at her road-dog, she knew it was now time to invite her to the party, "White-girl, White-Girl," she yelled louder. "Wake your crazyass up. Come over here and try some of this banging shit I got over here," she managed in between sniffs of coke. When they locked eyes, she knew White-girl was trying to figure out if this was real or was she in some crazy dream. "Come on girrrl," she said seductively.

For a second, White-girl could barely see, the sleep was in her eyes and clouding her vision. She wiped the sleep away and looked closer, this wasn't a dream, this shit was real. She smiled. Refocusing, she opened her eyes and saw Amanda sitting at the table with a beer in front of her that could only mean one thing: 'The day had started without her!' Steadying herself she jumped to her feet, eyes stuck on the two bills sitting on the table, nobody needed to tell her, she knew what the bills meant. Getting closer, she looked into the bills, to her, they looked like mini-mountains of cocaine...In other words, that's cocaine-heaven to her! She eyed Amanda seriously," I'm not even going to ask." she turned away. "I'll be right back, don't start the party without me. I gotta wash my face and brush my damn teeth," she hollered from over her shoulder as she disappeared in the back of the apartment. It didn't take White-girl long, all of four minutes and she was back. She couldn't stop smiling as she thought about how close she and Amanda had gotten in such a short amount of time. Amanda was her girl and it was times like this that proved it. She waved at Amanda like she was the main attraction in a parade or some shit.

"Sit your crazy-ass down somewhere and let's get high," said Amanda playfully.

"Girrrl, I know you didn't get all of this from fucking with that boy, Umm... Umm. What's his name? Malik."

White-girl's eyes rolled up in her head as she pretended to act like she didn't know who Amanda had been with but deep in her heart, she wouldn't never forget Malik or what he represented. Amanda picked-up on the bullshit and before she knew it, she held her hand up and cut White-girl off, "and what bitch? Damn right I got all this from Malik's fine-ass...I'm that mutha-fucking good," she fired back as she made her long tongue touch her nose.

Not wanting Amanda to get mad at her, White-girl smiled," I know that's right, girrrl. With that long as tongue of yours, I know you handled your business with that nigga," she said giving Amanda a high-five! Relieved, Amanda fell out laughing and White-girl joined right in. Just as she knew, Amanda began filling her in on the juicy details of her latest sexual conquest.

"I'm telling you girrl; I had his ass cuming all up in my mouth in like Two minutes flat," bragged Amanda. Pointing down towards her pussy, "and you know me....I was like, you got yours, now it's time for me to get mines. I eased that niggaz head right down here and he got busy," over exaggerating the truth. It wasn't a secret; Amanda was a bad bitch, mentally and especially sexually. She couldn't front, Amanda had taught her a thing or two about how to please a man and how to suck a dick the proper way. Amanda's body and facial features were very intoxicating; men fell at her feet and begged to be with her. She was known to have a hurricane tongue.

The more she listened, the more she focused on her tongue; White-girl imagined that long tongue running up and down her clit. She was wet! "Girl, you gotta spread that love...Put me down with that nigga. Let me throw this white pussy on his ass and let's see how he acts," she said smiling.

Amanda had stopped dead in her tracks once again. 'This bitch crazy?' "Put you down with what, bitch," she shouted with pure force? Her frown displayed her true thoughts and she wished she could turn it up-side down, she made a mistake. Her feelings were involved but she quickly recovered.

White-girl hadn't known her long enough to understand the history Amanda and Malik shared, much less, she had no idea that she had a thing for Malik that was bigger than getting drugs from him. Their history was long, they dated on and off throughout high school and even in the streets, they vibed on a level that wasn't easily explained. 'Shit, Shit,' she thought realizing her mistake.

She forced a smile, "you know what? I might just do that...I'd love to see Malik fuck you in the ass because that's exactly what he's going to want to do to your white ass," she started laughing. "I'm telling you now, he's got a King-Kong dick on him girl...You think you can handle all that dick," she asked raising a brow?

White-girl instantly picked-up on the way Amanda quickly shifted gears but she didn't do anything to allow her to know that she seen it. She had to give it to her, she was slick, as fast as that attitude surfaced, and it was gone, just like that. "For the right price, he can fuck me however, whenever, or wherever he wants to. He can fuck my face, my ass...I don't give a fuck, just tell him to pay me," she smiled but dead serious.

"We'll see...You over there saying that shit now but we'll see. Soon as you see that big-ass dick, I bet you'll think twice about all that meat going up in your ass but if you're serious, and I know you are. He's supposed to call me later and if he does, we'll put on a show for him because if we don't do it the right way, I'm telling you now, that boy will fuck the both of us silly, mark my word."

Amanda was already plotting a plan in her head as she watched White-girl from the corner of her eye. For some reason, White-girl was always talking about trying to fuck the same dude she fucked and it was getting on her nerves but since she thought she could run with the big dogs, she had something for her ass. When it came to sex, Amanda didn't have any limitations and she was going to push White-girl to her limit and fucking around with big dick Malik, she knew exactly what needed to be done.

"Won't you make yourself useful and go and get me another beer and bring the Hennessey too," said Amanda reminding her who the boss is!

With no hesitation, White-girl made her way to the kitchen and did what was asked of her. She didn't have a problem with doing shit for Amanda. Why would she, Amanda had saved her ass on more than one occasion and she's the one providing for her, making sure she eats, makes sure she gets high, and I she's the one providing a roof over her head. What's wrong with fetching a Beer or two? With both hands full, someone was knocking on the door. Briefly stopping to unload everything onto the table she made her way over to the door. The banging grew more intense, she was startled creeping over to the peep hole. She use to have a bad habit of just opening the front door for whoever knocked, that is until Amanda smacked all the living shit out of her. Now, she seen the importance of looking through the peep hole, this was the hood and anything could go wrong by opening the door for the wrong person. It's, It's your cousin Jazzy, you want me to let her…

Amanda had to cut her off before she finished her sentence. She already knew what she was going to ask her. "Open the damn door White-girl, you know damn well she's my fucking cousin…You's a silly bitch, sometimes. Common sense, you do know what that is don't you," laughed Amanda? Soon as she turned the lock, Jazzy busted into the apartment huffing and buffing. Completely out of breath, Jazzy quickly closed the door behind herself and almost knocking White-girl down in the process.

"Move your dumb-ass out my fucking way," shouted Jazzy as she violently brushed White-girl's shoulder getting past her. She went straight to the table where Amanda was sitting and when she turned back around, White-girl was still standing at the door like she was waiting for her to leave or some shit. "Bring yo simple-minded-ass away from that door," she looked over at Amanda. "Where you find this bitch," as they both laughed!

Jazzy had her back to White-girl and never seen the look she gave her. It was mean and disrespectful. She was mad now, anytime Jazzy came around, her mouth always got the better of her, meaning Jazzy's mouth. Jazzy clearly didn't cut the white girl any slack and dug in that ass every opportunity she got. Had this not been Amanda's cousin, she would have spoken her piece and kicked Jazzy's ass a long time ago but she knew there wasn't any win in that. Her and Amanda were first cousins and bound by blood. She peeped that a long time ago and she didn't want to fuck up a good thing, not yet anyway. Amanda didn't help matters; she was clear about whose side she was on in this on-going battle between the two of them.

"Bring your dumb-ass over here," she said strong and firm to White-girl. Amanda made it clear in her tone that she wasn't in no mood for the bullshit. Dropping her head in defeat, White-girl counted to Ten, calmed herself, because if she didn't, she knew what was going to come out her mouth in the next few seconds would fuck not only her plans up but she would be on the losing end of a fist fight. Plus, she wanted to get high and all that cocaine sitting on the table was enough reason to let that shit Jazzy was talking slide. A nice long night of sniffing cocaine for free outweighed getting her ass kicked by two cousin's any day of the week. She was smart enough to realize it and she knew it!

"My bad, girl, I...I was over there stuck for a minute," said White girl putting her stupid look on. "If ya'll ain't say nothing, I would've been standing all night," letting out a goofy laugh. Amanda and Jazzy looked at each other and busted out laughing at how goofy White-girl was. She always acted crazy like that once she got a little cocaine up in her, which was all the time. Focusing her attention back to Jazzy, Amanda asked her seriously, "why you all out of breath and shit?" Jazzy had dived into the bill of cocaine that was on the table. She wasn't paying

Amanda any attention as she seemed to be trying to stuff as much coke up her nose as humanly possible.

Jazzy was one-third of their crew and she was Amanda's cousin. They all hung together every day. She was fly as well. Tall red, and had big tits and a head game that was crazy. It was like that shit ran in the family. She always acted like she didn't like White-girl but on the low, she liked her, she liked her! However, oftentimes, she felt like she was fighting for Amanda's time and she didn't like that and that's what made her lash out at White-girl all the time. She knew before the night was over, she would be apologizing for how she was acting. Amanda broke her train of thought,"...bitch, I know you heard me," she shouted!

"Damn...This shit is proper," said Jazzy as she scooped her index finger into the bill and then rubbing the cocaine all over her gums. Instinctively, she emptied her purse onto the table. Looking over her shoulder, she winked at White-girl, "get a bitch a beer or something," she said fumbling through the contents on the table until she found what she was looking for.

"Where is it...," Jazzy whispered but no sooner she said it, a brown paper bag emerged from under some papers and lip-stick. Hoisting the brown paper bag in the air, she turned the bag upside down as everything fell out onto the table. She looked directly at Amanda," girrrl, look what I got?'

On the table were bags of CRACK, bags of powder cocaine, X-pills, and some weed. "Where the fuck you get all this shit," asked Amanda looking at her crazy?" I'm telling you right now...You might as well carry your ass right back out that fucking door because I ain't got time to have them niggaz running up in my spat over some bullshit your dumb-ass done went and done," she eyed Jazzy close. "I mean that shit, Jazzy...I ain't with no bullshit!"

Jazzy didn't move. She stood right where she was, she didn't say anything. She let Amanda get her piece out before she would say anything. She appeared cool and calm but her facial expression didn't match her thoughts. 'This bitch gotta be high,' she thought. This bitch is running around hitting niggaz pockets while they sleep, switching niggaz bags, cutting niggaz face's damn near off and now...Now she wants to be on some self-righteous bullshit. This bitch is cruddier than I am.' She forced her lips to smile and stay together because she almost started laughing right in her face. She waved her hands in the air after hearing all she could take," a-ight...A-ight, look damnit! I ain't rob nobody or no shit like that so calm your ass down...Gansta! Calm down, ain't nobody running up in here like that, at least not for something I did," she said with a wink. Her devilish smirk let Amanda know news still traveled fast in the hood.

"So where you get all this shit from then? I know damn well ain't nobody up and give your grimy-ass this shit. Where it come from? Even if you fucked every nigga in Charlottesville, you still wouldn't end up with this much shit, so tell me, where the fuck did it come from," she shouted! "Your pussy ain't fire like that so I know you ain't fuck for the shit," throwing a shot.

Even on the sidelines White-girl knew a shot when she heard it and she couldn't help herself as she let out a few chuckles of her own. It's a rare occasion when they go head to head and she intended to sit back and enjoy the show, especially after all the abuse she takes on a regular basis.

"Shut your stupid-ass up, "snapped Jazzy as she pointed her finger in White-girl's face. " Amanda...Get your little mascot before I serve her ass," she shouted.

"Jazzy, don't try to make this shit about-White-girl, we know you don't care for her in the first place and I'm not going to let you use that as an excuse. Tell me something I don't know...And you can start with that," she said pointing down at all the drugs spread out on the table.

Jazzy started laughing," a-ight gansta...Sit your ass down so I can tell Ya'll the story and exactly how this shit went down," pulling out a chair as she slide into it. Jazzy took two hefty scoops of the cocaine still on the bill in front of her and sniffed real deep and hard. When she looked-up, both White-girl and Amanda were staring directly at her like she was crazy. Again, she waved her hands in the air," a-ight...A-ight, listen...I was on my way back from Este's and as I was coming through the woods, I had to pee and I mean pee bad as a mutha-fucker. I was halfway through the woods and I couldn't turn around and my apartment was on the other side of the creek. Trapped. I couldn't take in any longer and I got off the main path and hid myself behind that old club house, I'm telling you, a bitch was nervous. I squatted and started pissing, I heard foot-steps and the first thing I thought was a nigga done caught me with my pants down. I couldn't go out like that so I cut that shit short and peeped around the side of the club house and when I did...I seen the young boy Jacob stashing this brown paper bag in a hollowed-out tree three feet from where I was. I knew he was up to something because he couldn't stop looking over his shoulder.

He looked right at me one time and I thought he had me but he didn't. I kept still, I didn't move, I didn't breathe, and I still had to pee but I knew whatever was in that bag had to be something special because he was going through a lot to hide it and my nosey-ass wanted to know what was in the brown paper bag so I kept my ass right there. I kept watching him, yep, my nosey-ass kept watching and when that little nigga left, I walked right over to the tree and pulled the brown paper bag out that tree and I turned around and started running all the way back towards Este's. When I opened the bag...Boom! This is what I saw. I caught a ride from the Exxon gas station and when I got to the top of the hill, that little nigga was right up there, for some crazy reason I started running all the way to your apartment." She folded her arms and looked back at them like they heard one of those, 'Matters of the Hood' true stories, now...If you want me to pack this shit up and carry my happy-ass down to my own apartment, I'll gladly do so, but I had a different plan," she said seriously. Bitches, we just hit the fucking lottery," she shouted.

Amanda was surprised and awed all at the same time. White-girl was over there glued to her chair as she took in every word of Jazzy's story, she was intrigued! She was in loved with everything that went on in the hood. She loved the hustle, the sex, the violence, the robberies, the date-rapes and even the murder's she found interesting. But for her, what was most interesting and grabbed her attention the most was the deceit, all the deceit in the hood, she loved it!

"A-ight, now what? What you plan on doing with all this shit anyway," asked Amanda? Jazzy shook her head in disbelief," it's not about what am I going to do. It's not me at all bitch, it's us...Didn't you hear me the first time...I said we hit the lottery bitch, not just me. We in this together, even her," nodding at White-girl!

"I ain't smoking no damn CRACK, Jazzy! I'll sniff coke all night long, but me and White-girl ain't smoking jack-shit. Nope. Fuck what you heard, we ain't with that bullshit...I know you heard what Whitney said about the shit...CRACK is Wack!"

"Amanda, what the fuck are you talking about...Ain't nobody asking you to smoke no damn CRACK. Who said that?" Jazzy threw her hands in the air, "you sound just like that stupid bitch over there," she said pointing at White-girl. "You really think I want any us smoking that shit...Get real, you gotta be kidding me." She got up from the table not believing what she had just heard. She knew her cousin was smarter than that, as she made her way to the kitchen all she was thinking about was a nice stiff drink. She poured a shot of Hennessey, looked over her shoulder after she downed the shot, took a deep breath and took her time with what she was about to say. "Ya'll listen to me...We ain't smoking shit... We're going to sell it. Me," pointing at her own chest. "you and that white bitch over there," she finished with a million dollar smile. Amanda's lips were pursed together, " like that makes it all the better.

What the hell we know about selling CRACK? This bitch here, she's greener than grass and I've never sold the shit a day in my life." Amanda started laughing, " this bitch barely know anything about the powder she sniffs every day, so tell me how the fuck we're supposed to be selling CRACK and none of us knows shit about how to do it...Tell me that?" All the while, Jazzy downed two more shots of Hennessey before she returned back to the dining room. Her wheels were turning and she was thankful that she knew this was going to happen when she first thought about the shit. She couldn't stop smiling," I guess that means ya'll some lucky bitches...Today is ya'll lucky day," she said taking a seat and eyeing all the drugs.

Jazzy was rubbing her hands together, "A-ight, I'm going to teach ya'll how to sell the shit and show you how this CRACK game operates." This was Jazzy's big opportunity to stay a-step ahead of her cousin. "All ya'll bitches know how to do is suck dick for a few grams of cocaine, if ya'll can keep your mouth shut and ya'll legs closed for ten fucking minutes we'll start seeing some real paper around this bitch," she said shooting Amanda and Whitegirl a devilish smirk. She focused her attention to White-girl for a minute, "I know your crazy-ass want some paper, don't you?" Still glued to her seat, White-girl had been sold on Jazzy's plan the minute she said something about selling some CRACK. That's all it took, she wanted in," and you know I do, girrrl," she said with a huge smile on her face. Nodding her head, Jazzy smiled," now that's about the smartest shit I've ever heard you say since you came around here!" "Bitch you're acting like I don't want no paper or something...I want to see some paper too," added Amanda feeling left out.

The Hennessey was starting to take its affect; it seemed to be giving Jazzy an added sense of power over her cousin who was normally in control of things like this. "Check it...I know if these wack-ass niggaz on top of the hill can sell this shit...I know damn well we can do it too." "I know that's right," chimed in both Amanda and White-girl at the same time. That's what Jazzy was waiting to hear," all I need to know now is...Are you two bitches ready to get down with me and get this CRACK paper?" White-girl raised her hand like she was a class or some shit," I'm definitely down with you," she said with a smirk on her face. At that moment, she knew she had found the right combination in Jazzy and Amanda to run with. "What about you Amanda? You down or are you going to keep sucking sweaty nuts and dirty dicks to get your sniff on or what?"

Having the upper hand was something Jazzy could easily get use to but she had to refocus because she didn't need either of them getting suspicious about her, especially since she was speaking from the position of power. This was rare and she didn't want to just yet give up her position, she was going to out-shine her cousin even if it meant having to share the wealth. She beamed with pride on the inside.

Amanda was tracing every inch of Jazzy's face as she listened and watched her every movement. Satisfied, she threw her fist in the air," yeah whatever just counts me in bitch," she said all the while staring into Jazzy's eyes. Agreeing to sell CRACK, she couldn't ignore her gut feeling, it was telling a story of its own but she continued to ignore it. Her mind was telling her that she just made the biggest mistake of her young life in a split second but she pushed it to the abyss of her mind. Her love and loyalty outweighed her common-sense, how did she come to agree to sell some stolen CRACK? The

closer she watched Jazzy, she swore she seen a glint of excitement in her eyes or was that that same look she got whenever a dude looked at her? That was it and she knew that look all too well, she's been seeing it since she was a little girl, no mistaking that look. Her desire to get some real paper and stop having to suck dicks to get high was saying something; clearly that's a step-up in the hood. Looking down at the floor, she whispered a silent prayer...

'Lord, please don't let nothing go wrong with this...Please watch over us girls Lord...Watch over us and protect us...'

When she looked-up, Jazzy was separating the CRACK from everything else. The powder was all in a neat pile, the X-pills were scattered everywhere, and the weed, well, from the looks of it, she was about to roll a blunt. Jazzy was caught off guard as to how much was actually there, it was more than she imagined. Sixteen 8-balls, Twenty-two X-pills, and over Three ounces of powder. There was only about a half-ounce of weed she thought, but when she moved the weed, there was more CRACK but it was already cut-up, she smiled.

Jazzy took a deep breath as she looked over the table, she took her time as she slowly began to speak, "okay...This is a lot of shit, ya'll...I think we can make a couple thousand off all this shit if we sell it right," she picked the powder up and smiled," ya'll know what time it is with this...We bout to come up," she said in a singing voice!

Again White-girl raised her hand to speak, "I...I...I'm not trying to sound all crazy , but don't ya'll think if we go out there on top of Prospect and start selling CRACK it's not going to be long before them dudes put two and two together," she looked sad. "I'm not trying to get my white ass murder over some fucking CRACK that ain't even mine...What happens when the boy Jacob come asking questions...What happens then?"

Jazzy nodded," point well taken! You're exactly right about all that. Niggaz will split your shit over some paper and that's why we're not going to sell shit in Prospect...We're taking our show on the road," declared Jazzy. "And what you mean by that," asked Amanda dumbfounded? Jazzy was loving this shit a little too much and she didn't know how long she could hold it back from laughing in Amanda's face. "Here's the plan... We're going across town to the Project's to sell this shit that way, we ain't got shit to worry about. Fuck Jacob and fuck the rest of them bamma-ass niggaz out there. You know his pussy-ass ain't coming nowhere near the Projects, he's scared to death of them niggaz over there...I know you remember what they did to him the last time they caught his ass over there. You remember, don't you Amanda?"

Amanda clapped her hands together as she thought about how dirty them Project dudes did Jacob, "I know that's right," as she gave Jazzy a high-five. She always thought he was stupid anyway; his dumb-ass went over there while 'Mean-Streets' were throwing one of their famous cook-outs, she was there and seen the whole shit first hand. Jacob was all drunk and she tried her best to calm him down but she couldn't. He disrespected Malik one too many times and Malik nodded his head as about 25 young niggaz from over there jumped on Jacob's ass. They had a field day with him; they beat him an inch from death!

"And might I add...What about all that fresh and untapped dick roaming all over that side of town? All them little niggaz over there be getting paper... Plus them niggaz is young," giggled Jazzy. On the low, she knew her cousin had a thing for them Project niggaz...First it was Safee', then it was Malik. She had taken all of that into consideration and from the look on Amanda's face, she knew she made the right call. White-girl eased back in her seat, she was all ears. Jazzy and Amanda went back and forth as to why the Projects would be the perfect spot to sell their stolen drugs and she liked what she was hearing. She realized something about the cousins but in order to see it, you had to venture past the surface and read between the lines. It was no secret, Jazzy envied her cousin Amanda, she wanted to be her and she was enjoying every minute of knowing something Amanda didn't know. She never said a word, she sat back, listen, watched, and observed everything quietly. Jazzy was going on and on about how they had to stay focused and take The CRACK game serious. She told them, one false move and it could cost them their lives. She thought it would be easy, especially since they were willing to fuck in the process but it was business, that's the price they intended to pay for stepping on anyone's toes. Small cost, since they were already fucking for free, right?

"Another thing...Everybody over there know your pretty-ass use to fuck with Safee', he's one of their own and not to mention Malik," she said pointing at Amanda. "That's the key right there...So tonight, tonight we're going to have a blast. We're getting high as the light-bill and in the morning we're jumping off the porch head first into this CRACK game. All this getting high shit every day, that shit is over," Jazzy starred at them and winked. "Ya'll bitches down with it or what?"

She knew that was a tall order but she intended to follow through with it nonetheless. She wasn't even sure if they were going to agree with it or not but she threw it out there anyway. "Slow ya roll, boss," said Amanda putting her index finger up. She took a shot of Hennessey then added," you ain't running shit just yet bitch...I'm feeling that no getting high shit because if not all we'll do is sniff all the profit and I ain't with that, it's stupid but...This shit is a group decision, we make decisions as a group and the majority rules. Period!" She looked over at White-girl and before she could say anything else, "I'm down with that... That way ain't nobody in control," she said with a goofy smirk on her face. Her smirk quickly turned to an evil sneer as she cut her eyes at Jazzy.

Over the last couple of month's all White-Girl heard over and over was about how those Projects niggaz went hard and chased paper even harder but they never went over there and this was her grand opportunity. On the low she had been tempted to step out and go over there on her own to see what all the fuss was really about but she didn't. Once she found out Amanda was fucking Malik, and he was the Man over there, she decided to play her cards as they were dealt. "Even though we're using them niggaz as a front, I can't wait to get my freak on...I heard them Project dudes really know how to break a bitch off something proper," she said eyeing Amanda funny!

Amanda and Jazzy looked at each other and damn near fell out their chairs laughing. Not only were they laughing at what she was saying but how serious she was while she was saying it. The entire house got extremely quiet for about
Ten seconds, it was so quiet they could hear the music on the Stereo. Each of them was locked in on their own thoughts. Everybody seemed to sense that going over to the Projects' was a big deal. For Amanda, that was Safee's old stomping grounds and it represented that whole 752 Gang, to this very day, everybody knew that hood belongs to them niggaz and they ain't been on the scene in a long time. There was still rumors and speculations as to who was really

running the Projects' and if you were in the 'loop' in Charlottesville and you would know that there's only one person who never went to prison and never snitched. He was way too smart for the Federal Government and none of them pussy niggaz knew his real name. For those of ya'll who know, ya'll know they call him the, "Quiet-One!"

All Jazzy was thinking about was this was her opportunity to get close to Malik's homey, Joey. She was well aware he didn't go for the average hood chick. He was always with a chick that wasn't from the hood and appeared strong, intelligent, and confidant, he liked them to be able to make a decision in a tough situation. If she could prove that she could get paper then he would respect her for her grind. White-girl was looking forward to all the guns, sex, violence, and the deceit. She wanted to experience it all, she could care less where they were going or who was running what, she wanted in and it was as simple as that. Her one advantage over Jazzy and Amanda was in the fact that she was really down with any and everything. She would be willing to do all the shit neither of them was willing or even able to do and she would use that to her advantage.

Jazzy had been gotten up from the table and went to the front door. She had thought she had heard someone in the hallway. She was super-paranoid by this time. Amanda and White-girl had to literally go over to her and pry her away from the peep-hole as she continued to stare out into the hallway. Nobody was there but you couldn't tell her that, she was determined. When they finally did pull her away from the peep-hole and looked at her, they both couldn't stop laughing. Jazzy had the peep-hole imprint on her forehead from pressing against it for so long. "Damn cousin, you high as a mutha-fucker," laughed Amanda leading her back to the table.

Chapter 3

AFTER having been locked in the mini-mansion with the connect more than half the night, Joey and Malik were about to impart on their journey back to Charlottesville. Refocused as a result of spending so much time with the connect, they were looking at the game from a different angle now. It wasn't just a game of chasing paper, this shit was a lifestyle and in this lifestyle there were peaks and valleys. Their connect had dumped an enormous amount of wisdom on them but what became more interesting was in the details about how much he knew about their personal lives. It came as a surprise as the connect went on and on about their stash houses, where they bagged-up the CRACK, who was selling it for them, shopping sprees in New York, all the way down to the bitches they were fucking. He knew it all! This shit was real, the connect wasn't just talking about the shit, he had picture's to prove his point. 'If I were the Federal Government, you two would be facing some very serious conspiracy charges,' that's what the connect told them and that shit was ringing in their ear's like none stop music. Joey was most impressed by the way the connect had been prepared and how precise he was. Back when he first had met the connect, he thought he was full of shit and just had a slick tongue, and an unlimited supply of CRACK. Now he knew better, the connect was definitely who he said he was. Proof was in the packaging!

He had no real reason to take the connect seriously until recently when they began talking more often. But tonight, the connect took shit to a different level, he poked all kinds of holes in his armor, life altering holes. Even though he destroyed their whole mind-state, he was careful in his approach while he rebuilt their foundation. He gave them a better way to hustle and he was receptive. The only bad thing he drew from their meeting was that with everything the connect had taught them in such a short amount of time, the shit gave him a headache. He literally took a couple Tylenol's before they were about to leave. On the other hand, Malik had gotten something totally different out of the meeting than had

Joey. It took him some time to warm-up to the connect, reluctantly, he came around but not before he damn near tried his best to bat everything the connect had said out the park. He was going for the home-run but he came up short every time. The connect's power is what intrigued him the most. Comparing his own version of what power consisted of, fucking a different bitch every night, spending out at the mall, and doing whatever he wanted to do whenever he wanted to do it; that's what he thought power was. He was wrong!

Three hours later, Malik had become the brightest student in the class, just like that, he couldn't front, even he was attracted to the connects power. Closely Malik watched how the connect interacted with those around him, it was like everybody in that house trusted in the connects judgment, when he thought power like that came from the use of force or violence, the connect was smooth in his approach and it was effective. That's when he realized that he had the game fucked-up; he was looking at it from the wrong angle. The minute he admitted his own character defects, he seemed to be able to breathe a little easier, literally.

The connect knew this was a delicate subject and he had to be very patient with both of them, but at the same time, he knew they were special, this shit was in their blood even if they didn't know it, he did. He didn't want them thinking they had to experience everything. He encouraged them to learn the mistakes of those who came before them. Hammering into their heads that they didn't have to fall by the wayside and become a victim of the Federal Government.

They needed to make smart choices and not become a victim of their own reality unless that reality involved walking off into the Sun with a Gang-of-Cash! Don't let your little head think for your big head," he said over and over. Why you think one head is bigger than the other one," he asked smiling? "Because, the big head has a brain, a mind, it's able to reason, the little head. Well, what can I say, It'll get you in all types of trouble if you let it," he reinforced!

He knew many dudes who fell victim because they couldn't determine which head they were supposed to be listening to and that mistake was fatal in some situations. Jealously was and will always be a mutha-fucker, you ain't shit to a nigga whose chick you're fucking. Remember that, remember it." He also showed them pictures of almost every detective in Charlottesville, he wanted them to know who had the real power and who was crooked. Making a comparison to 'Stick-up Kids and the Federal Government,' he knew they would like this one. "Everybody know how dangerous the Stick-up kids are, they run in your shit thinking about a robbery but oftentimes, they leave with a homicide. That's crazy! That's only half the battle, now you gotta worry about the F.B.I., C.I.A., A.T.F., and the local task-force, either of them will kill you while you're still breathing and that shit's legal. He needed for them to feel the sting of his words and from the looks on their face, they felt it. He wasn't lying to them, he respected them way too much to be bullshitting them and everything he told them was the truth. Look at how the Federal Government did the boy Roland. It's been Twenty years, where he's at? Not to mention all the dudes who came behind him, this shit was serious and the connect knew first hand, he's been around since the very first Indictments in Charlottesville and never been to prison. He looked Malik in the eyes and said, "the Range Rover...Well, we don't least, we buy the whole car! Consider it a learning experience, charge it to the game," then he reached in his pockets and tossed him a set of keys. "Outside waiting for you is a brand new Honda Accord, in the trunk, ya'll will find a Kilo of CRACK...It's time to step the game up," he said smiling. Then he turned his attention to Joey, "don't worry, I haven't left you out," he tossed him a different set of keys. "Parked in the back lot of the Holiday Inn at the 5th street exit is a brand new Toyota Camry...You'll need your own car to move all this work within 7 days." Malik and Joey looked at one another amazed; they couldn't believe what they were hearing much less seeing. He wasn't bullshitting, he was to smooth for that clown-ass shit.

When the connect stood to embrace them, he wished them both luck, turned and walked out the huge living room. And just like that, their meeting was over as the mammoth Black Africans escorted them outside. "All the paper-work for the cars is in the glove box," was all the African said in his broken English dialect. Without hesitation, Joey jumped into the cock-pit as Malik made his way to the passenger's seat with the Brick of CRACK sitting on his lap. Joey was weaving in and out of traffic on the Interstate as the Sun was barely peeping over the horizon. There was a sign that said,'Charlottesville Twenty miles,' Malik didn't know if he was happy or scared. "I can get use to this," said Joey full of excitement as he briefly glanced over at Malik!

Malik glanced at him like he was fucking crazy; the Kilo of CRACK was wobbling all over the place as he drove like a bat out of hell. "I'm sure you can get use to this...But, if you don't slow this mutha-fucker down, the only thing we'll both be enjoying for the next hundred years is Friday's Ju'mar in a Federal Prison! I suggest you slow this mutha-fucker down," he demanded. Joey shrugged his shoulders, "yeah...You right," easing up. At times, Joey could become as arrogant as Malik, but for the most part, he stayed in grind-mode he rarely had time to show boat. However, this was a special morning for the both of them, they had graduated. They were ready and willing to step their game up. Joey pulled into the parking lot of the Holiday Inn and circled around to the back where he quickly located what he was looking for. It wasn't hard, wasn't but two other cars out there, he parked right beside the Toyota Camry. They checked the trunk together, and what they saw, the shit was unreal, guns were everywhere. They had enough guns to start a war in a small Country.

Malik dipped his hand in the trunk and retrieved a bullet-proof vest, he's always wanted one and now was his opportunity," he ain't bullshitting, the connect is serious about us taking this shit to the next level," he said easing the vest over his tee-shirt and strapping in on. "Malik? You done lost your damn mind putting that shit on in the open like that," whispered Joey. "Wh...what... What you talking about," he asked looking at Joey like he was stupid for not putting one on himself. Then he shrugged his shoulders, " ain't like we ain't dirty, remember, we drove all the way back dirty and you wasn't worried about that so I know you ain't bitching over a little vest or are you," he laughed?

Malik wasn't finished with Joey, he liked having the upper hand and couldn't stop laughing but also recognized the seriousness of the situation, "tell me it ain't so, not the speed demon coming up the highway," winking as he looked around as reality started setting in. "Let's bounce!"

Joey stayed in the Honda and Malik hopped in the Camry, they were back to back all the way across town to Page Street. Their first stop was Auntie Pam's, she was Malik's favorite Aunt. One thing they knew about Auntie Pam was that she would be up doing her thang. They parked right in front of the house, the new cars were new and nobody knew about them so they didn't have to worry about hiding them as they did with the Range Rover. Their plan was to take the CRACK inside and let Auntie Pam test it to see if the shit was as good as the connect said it was, Malik opened the front door and they could smell burning candle's as they crossed the threshold. They could hear voices in the kitchen and as they made their way closer, they could smell the CRACK in the air. As they bent the corner, they knew the whole crew was there. Auntie Pam's back was to them as they enter the kitchen and she never turned around, " what the hell are you two doing up this early," she asked without looking at them? Malik couldn't take his eyes off of Tiffany but she avoided eye contact with him at all cost. Auntie Pam got up and hugged them both. Nobody couldn't deny the fact that Auntie Pam looked good for her age and to smoke CRACK every single day of the week. She's been getting high over the course of the last twenty years or so but she didn't look a day over thirty. Perhaps as they say, prison saved and preserved her body and her mind. She was sharp and on point. When she came home this time, she assembled an all female team and they had their shit down to a science. Of the few things she took seriously, her girls kept her on point. They even had a name for their crew, S.S., Inc. and it stood for: Still Smoking Incorporated! And she was the glue which held the shit together.

Tiffany was the youngest of the bunch, just eighteen when Malik brought her to his favorite Aunt to look after her. They had a very vivid history and he thought it was partly his fault why she was fucked-up in the game, especially since it was him who she called that night her parents kicked her out of their huge home after she stole everything that wasn't bolted down. He noticed how she put her stem away as he inched closer, she very rarely smoked CRACK in front of him and he couldn't figure out why. What she brought to the crew was something special; she had a glib tongue and talks a trick out his money without ever having to give up any pussy. Sometimes, and that's sometimes, she might let them play with her luscious pussy or suck her perfectly round tits but that was it. She was young, fly and still full of life and those tricks couldn't get enough of her but she had her eye on someone else and couldn't bring herself to sell pussy, at least not yet!

Brenda, she was the booster, one of the best in the entire city, that's when she's able to keep her ass out of jail. She supplied the young hustla's with the best high-end clothes money could buy. She was definitely that bitch in the hood to see if your paper was straight t. She and Auntie Pam grew up together; they came in the game together, considering their selves sista's.

It wasn't nothing to catch them arguing, fussing, and even fighting at least once a month. With over twenty years of hanging together, they seen it all, done it all, and was looking forward to doing more. Then there was Lee-Lee, she was the only white chick running around in the Projects' like she grew-up there. The thing about her was that she loved to fight and could really throw a punch. She was into the Plastic money, credit cards were her tool and she had that shit down to a science. Most of her orders consisted of sixty inch Plasma televisions, bedroom sets, kitchen sets, swimming pools, and anything else someone needed for their home. If you could afford to pay her half-price for her shit, she got it.

Auntie Pam was able to offer these ladies something someone has never offered them before...She offered Love-N-Loyalty! Auntie Pam was a street legend in her own right, it's rumored that she was the driving force behind Safee' and that whole 752 Gang. Although, she never got to see them take Charlottesville by storm or at their height but she was there during their climb to the top. She had caught a Four year bid and by the time she was coming home, everybody had caught cases. "Auntie Pam, let me holla at you a minute," said Malik nodding his head towards the living room.

She shot him a look that didn't need any words; it was all in her facial expression. They knew something she didn't, but if you could read her mind it would say something like this,' you must be crazy if you think I'm getting up away from this table with all this good CRACK'. That's exactly what she was thinking until she saw the serious look on both their faces, she knew something important was up and she couldn't deny her two favorite's," you know what," she said getting up from the table. "This shit better be important. Ya'll fucking-up my high...You know these bitches gonna smoke all my shit by the time I get back," she said laughing.

Walking away as Joey held her by the arm, "yeah, I love you to Joey but guess what? I love CRACK too," walking back over to Brenda giving her a high-five! They lead her up-stairs but half-way up, she bent over the banister and yelled," ya'll bitches better not smoke all my shit!"

Malik shook his head, "you crazy, you do know that don't you," he asked laughing? "You know they got big love for you and Tiffany will make sure they leave you something so don't sweat it!"

She kept walking up the steps, she wasn't really trying to hear that shit Malik was talking about even though she knew he was right. She led them into her bedroom and Joey locked the door behind them, she knew then, this wasn't anything small. Joey took the duffel bag off his shoulder and dumped the contents onto the bed. Auntie Pam's eyes were the size of quarters, she knew what she was looking at but then again, it's been so long since she's seen one she couldn't believe it.

"Ya'll know what that is," she asked smiling?

"We gotta know what it is, we got it...The million dollar question is do you know what it is," asked Malik seriously?

"You gotta be kidding me, right? You can choose any slang you want when it comes down to it...Some people call it a brick, a bird, a whole thang, but for me, I like to call them...Two-point-Two," as she reached down to touch it.

"Why you smiling like that," asked Joey? She put her hands on her hips and starred into his eyes, "you mean to tell me, you got me down there arguing with my girls' to save me what's left off the funky three grams we had and ya'll sitting up in here with all this? Ya'll could've said something."

"It ain't like that Auntie Pam. We couldn't holla all loud what's in the duffel bag. Don't worry about it, you know we got you. This a whole brick and if ain't nobody else got you, you know we got you....Matter of fact, get your stem so you can test it and tell us what we're working with," stated Joey.

"Yeah, what he just said," laughed Malik as he pointed at Joey! He seen she was stuck, she was watching but she wasn't moving. Since she didn't move, he made his way over to the bed and started peeling the duct tape from the package. He was having a difficult time maneuvering through all the tape.

"Boy, hand me that thang, you don't open it like that...This shit ain't no damn Christmas present. Don't watch me, watch my moves," she giggled as she comfortably in a sitting position. Reaching into her draw, she pulled out a shiny pair of sharp shears.

Easily, she went to work like a brain surgeon operating on a patient and the only thing that mattered was to get the job done as quickly as possible. When she was finished, all the duct tape fell from the brick all at one time in layers. The off white substance was the prettiest thing she's seen in a long time. Lifting the brick up to her nose she inhaled deep, there was a certain smell she was looking for." Ummm, smells good," passing it to Joey. Malik used his straight razor to slice a small piece of CRACK from the larger rock. Rolling it around in the palm of his hand, he was thinking, 'this is the beginning of real power!' "Try this," he said passing her the small rock.

Auntie Pam folded her arms and looked at him like he was out of his rabbit-ass mind," let me tell you something right quick....Giving me that little-ass piece of CRACK is like giving me none at all. The sooner ya'll realize that little advice you'll be good. Now, if you don't put something in my hand, you better," she said playfully. She made her way back over to her dresser as she pulled out a brand new stem. She rigged it to her liking and when she came back over; Joey put something in her hand that she didn't have to complain about. She laughed, "yeah, I got a stem in every room."

Malik looked at the size of the rock and had to say something," the connect said this shit ain't like the shit we've been having. It's supposed to be stronger so take your time," he said full of concern. "You know you're my favorite Auntie!"
She looked over at Joey, then back to Malik," I'm your only Auntie!

You must wasn't listening when I told ya'll that I do this shit right here," she pointed at the stem as she packed it. Joey fell out laughing, he knew she was right. Not to mention, she was stubborn and was going to do it her way or no way at all.

He watched closely as she packed her stem, tiny crumbs fell to the side and she swiftly scooped them up and placed them on the top of her stem delicately. When she was done, she used her odd hand to reach in her pocket and pulled out her lighter," that's what the fuck I'm talking about," as she rolled her eyes. Slowly, she ran the flame over the top of the stem melting the CRACK so that it wouldn't fall any more. She took one last look over at them before she tilted the stem towards the ceiling with the lighter blazing. Slowly, the stem began to fill with a thick cloud of white smoke. She continued to inhale, deeper, deeper. The more she inhaled, the bigger her eyes became. With her lungs at full capacity and unable to inhale anymore, she took the flame away from the stem. Momentarily she held the smoke deep in her lungs, and then in a split second, she began blowing the smoke out. The more smoke she blew out, the higher she got. Sweat beads formed on the bridge of her nose and her forehead, instinctively, she licked her lips. She looked down at the carpet, then she heard it; Bells were ringing deep in her ears and her eyes were the size of fifty-cent pieces.

"Is it good," asked Malik?

Wasn't nothing wrong with her ears, she heard every word but the CRACK had her, 'Scotty had her body!' For the life of her, she couldn't move a muscle. She couldn't open her mouth; her jaws seemed to be stuck. Her hands were stuck on her legs, clenching her stem; the highly addictive substance had invaded her body making her incapable of doing anything. She knew she was slobbering at the mouth but she couldn't stop it, then she heard them again, the bells, they were still ringing as loud as when they first started.

In her mind, she was telling herself to move, to say something but she couldn't. Nothing came out her mouth and her hands wouldn't move. As a minute went by, she was slowly regaining movement in her hands but her mouth still wasn't working just yet. She recognized this type of high so she knew in a few more seconds, she would regain her sense of direction but for the moment, there was nothing she could do to speed-up the process. All of a sudden, out of nowhere, she dropped to her knees and was moving all over the floor picking shit out the carpet. Everything white, she thought was a piece of CRACK, the only way she knew it wasn't CRACK was because she put every foreign piece of what she picked-up into her mouth spitting it out as she moved on. "Damn Malik, this shit gotta be a head-banger, I ain't never seen her ain't like this," said Joey looking at Auntie Pam like she was crazy.

No matter what they said to her or about her, she kept crawling all over the carpet like they wasn't even there. She went from one end of the bedroom all the way over to the other side never leaving her knees. They held back their laughter as long as they could out of respect for her but this was the funniest shit they've ever seen in their lives. Then she stopped crawling and jumped straight to her feet staring deep into their eyes but she never said one word. They both got nervous as they watched her grab her chest. Five minutes later, she said," damn! This shit will kill a bitch if she ain't careful," then she busted out laughing. Relieved that she was alright, Malik and Joey laughed along with her. They were happy she was back, for a minute there, they thought they lost her. "It's banging like that?"

"Shit, what you talking about? I told you this shit will kill a bitch if she ain't careful with it. Ain't no CRACK like this been in Charlottesville since Safee' and them got locked-up. If I ain't talk to him the other day, I'd swear he was still running around here somewhere on the low because this shit is on the cooker. Whoever cooked this shit, they cooked it just like the cooker Safee' use to use." Joey had heard all he needed to hear, "enough said, since this shit is banging like that, we're about to lock this bitch down...The whole City is gonna belong to us. We're taking this shit to the next level. We'll need all the help we can get because it's a time limit on this one...We got Seven days and the connect wants to have his paper. I ain't got a problem with it; I know we can do it if we put our minds to it. All we need from you Auntie Pam is your crew, do we got that?"

"Does a faggot suck dick," she asked with a smirk on her face. Her smile became serious," we down. Now, I need ya'll to understand something, I've been out here in these streets for a long time but I'm telling ya'll now, I'm tired, I can't keep doing this shit. When I was running with Safee', I didn't take advantage of that situation but now I am. Of course I'm still going to smoke my ass off but at the same time, I got my eyes on the bigger picture. I'm going to put something away for a rainy day and I suggest ya'll do the same, you know this shit doesn't last forever, especially you Malik," pointing her finger at him!

Joey looked over at Malik like he wasn't the only one who noticed how he never seemed to save a penny but he didn't say enough. If that conversation with the connect wasn't enough to do it then nothing would change his mind. Auntie Pam walked over to the window; the Sun was peaking over the horizon.

"I've made a lot of paper out here in these streets but it was always for somebody else and the only thing I have to show for it is this house. My last bid, I had to pull four years, if it wasn't for Safee', I would've lost everything. He finished the last three years of my mortgage for me plus he sent me two-hundred every month, faithfully. Twenty days before I came home, they took him and I was crushed! He's family and I make sure I talk to him at least once a week, do whatever he ask of me, but I still miss him and I hope everything works out for him. Speaking of him and his partner, ya'll remind me so much of them that it's crazy and it scares the hell out of me," she folded her arms and starred at them.

She took a deep breath,the difference now is I'm not going to miss my opportunity to make a difference, chase this paper, and ride this bitch until the wheels fall the fuck off!"

Malik was the first to notice a single tear run down the side of her face, he whispered," we know he was your people and all that, we got you! I'm focused. Joey's focused, so let's get this paper and make all of them proud of you. Be happy, Auntie!"

She was in total agreement, she felt lucky they included her in their plans. As she was listening to him, she noticed something in his voice. It was strong, and demanding when he spoke. He was sounding like a grown man; it was like he changed overnight because just yesterday, she was fussing with him over the bullshit he was doing to Tiffany. Also, she's seen it a million times; chasing paper had its way of changing a young man into a grown man overnight!

Joey started waving his hand in the air and laughing," a-ight ya'll, all this emotional shit is starting to get to me…Let's get down to business." "I know that's right," she high-fived Joey. "I gotta get back down-stairs and get my team on board with this new 'thing of ours,'" 'she said laughing. Nodding her head at the CRACK, "break me off an ounce of that," as she pointed. Joey didn't waste a second, he knew what she was about to do and didn't want to get in her way. However instead of breaking off what she asked for, he found the scale under the bed and weighed out 125 grams and gave it to her. "See if you can rock this by the end of the day," he said with a smile. She scooped it up in one swift motion," ya'll want to see some crazy shit, come down here and watch how these greedy bitches look once they hit this head-banging shit, ya'll think I was bugging out, wait until you see them." They followed her downstairs and back into the dining room. They were still smoking CRACK, everybody except for Tiffany anyway. Malik could feel her staring at him but every time he glanced over at her, she would look the other way. He wanted to say something to her but he decided against it, he knew he'd have time for that later. "' ladies...This is compliments of these fine two gentlemen," as she laid several grams of CRACK on the table. "Let's show these fellas how we gets down!" Everybody began filling their stems with the powerful substance and not thinking anything of it but Tiffany sat there staring off into no-man's land.

"Tiffany...Get over it girl, he know you smoke CRACK," shouted Auntie Pam. "He might know but he's never going to see me to it," she insisted crossing her arms over her chest in defiance. Malik walked out the room, he knew this was too much for her and in his mind, he respected her for her decision. "Joey, I'm out, call me later," he said over his shoulder walking out the front door. Joey nodded and stood right where he was at. He watched as all the lighters came to life at once, he took special notice how Auntie Pam was the only one who was taking her time. He laughed on the inside because he knew what that was about. The entire room was so quiet as they filled their lung's with the powerful CRACK smoke and soon as they blew the smoke out, all hell broke loose! It was like everybody was off into their own world, eyes big as quarters, and sweat forming on the bridge of their nose. They were stuck, nobody moved, nobody spoke, nothing...Joey knew they were on their way, this CRACK was just that good.

Chapter 4

WHEN Silas and Sosa got back to Garrett Square from GoCo, Sosa headed straight for Tasha's apartment. He wasn't in the mood to socialize and wasn't about to thank the youngins' for giving him a ride in that beat-up hooptie to a store all the way across town, as far as he was concerned he didn't owe them jack-shit. His only concern was that as long as that paper was correct that was all that really mattered at the end of the day. Silas could tell that something had to be on his homey's mind the way he stepped off because usually he would stand around and be all buddy-buddy with them dudes, but not him. Not today and not ever! As far as he was concerned, Sosa should act like that more often, they were in Charlottesville for one reason and one reason only--stack that paper. He loved to see his homey show them Charlottesville dudes no love. He walked in front of Sosa to Tasha's crib knowing she wasn't there, because if she was there he wouldn't go, he didn't care much for her.

Silas and Sosa were from Newark, New Jersey and had caught wind a few months back that Charlottesville was a sweet spot to stack your paper and after a few days of talking, here they were in the city of Charlottesville doing their thang. They did their best to stay under the radar and out the way; Sosa preferred it that way. Back home in Newark they made a name for their selves around elementary school. They had been thick as thieves ever since, growing up in a big city forced them to grow-up faster than most kids their age who hadn't been exposed to what they were exposed to. They learned how to survive early because the streets taught them that if they wanted to eat and stay health, they had to learn the game, and when they did they tried their best to turn Newark up-side down! They had been in Charlottesville only 2months and Silas was starting to get bored because there wasn't enough excitement out there for him. It was Sosa who kept telling him to chill...be patient! Silas wasn't trying to hear all that bullshit especially since Sosa been kicking it real hard with the chick Tasha. The paper was coming in steady but a little too slow for him and he wanted to branch out and see what the rest of Charlottesville had to offer. Charlottesville was way slower than Newark and he found it very hard to adjust without faking it, when they decided to come down South he didn't object one time and it was because the way they made it sound when it came to the paper and how much could actually be made out here. He bought the idea: Hook...Line...And Sinker!

The first week in Charlottesville they both fell in love with the city. They had no problem blending in with the local dudes from around there her wifey and the whole nine, that irritated the shit out of him and he wasn't for the bullshit. One thing he knew about Sosa was that he'd never allow a female to come between their brother-hood and the paper, but here recently he could barely tell the difference, the fog was too thick and his homey seemed to be losing his way. That left him only one choice and all the females were on their dicks and looked at them like fresh meat. Silas fucked a different chick every day of the week for the first 30 days or so, but Sosa was only concentrating on chasing that paper in Garrett 24-7. Once the paranoia went away because he had heard one too many stories about how up-top dudes get sent home in body-bags cause somebody caught them slippin' but Charlottesville didn't present itself to him that way and he got more comfortable with each passing day. By the time he ran through the whole Garrett he was bored out of his mind. With Sosa spending most of his time with the chick Tasha and her son he started bouncing all over Charlottesville. He found a spot that was more his speed. The Projects'! The Projects' was the spot to be, everything was going on over that side of town, The CRACK game was booming way harder than Garrett. His idea was to move their business over there so that they could get in hit it real hard and be ghost. They were down South to stack that paper, but when he brought his idea to Sosa he told him they were already good down Garrett. With Sosa acting like he was all in love with this country chick, starting to call.

Going across town to the Projects' was weighing heavily on his mind again and before he knew it he was talking to Sosa about it again, "yo, we gotta get across town, the Projects' is jumping, I'm telling you them dudes eatin' over there son!"

Sosa was going through the mail the same way he's been doing for the last few weeks because he wanted to save her a trip from walking all the way to the other end of Garrett to the mail box so he got the mail for her now. Her little boy Jay, he was so hyper he would bolt out the car soon as she parked and then she's running all around the hood trying to chase him and check her mail box. Instead of making her go through all that he just picked the mail up for her, plus it kept her away from all the rest of the young knuckle-heads' that be hustlin' by the mail box.

He heard Silas when he spoke about the Projects' but he wasn't feeling that idea. To him there was no purpose, they were eatin' right there in Garrett, why go across town and step on somebody else toes? "Word! I heard them dudes be eatin' real in the Projects'...But we ain't starving for nothing over here. The paper is good, we ain't hot or nothing, we got the youngins' out here doing all the dirty work for us and we don't ever have a problem with the count, it's always good. And all these chicks love some Silas, asking me all the time 'where Silas, Where Silas?' If we just maintain and keep doing what we're doing now, something like a half of brick a month and guess what? We don't have to sell shit unless we want to. That's the life right there homey, and you're telling me we should go all the way across town to the Projects' and start a war with them dudes for a spot in there hood where they grew-up all their lives? That's what you're telling me?"

Silas didn't like hearing what Sosa was saying because he thought that Sosa had got weak on him, "what? Fuck them dudes over there, they can get it--I bust my gun in case you forgot! You got your nose so far up Tasha's ass that you done forgot why the fuck we out here in the first place...So let me fuckin' remind you: To stack paper and bounce! Now what part does Tasha fit in all this? Let me know, because when we left Newark, I swear it was only me and you...Fucking with that bitch got you all fucked-up, you ain't thinking straight homey," said Silas!

"You're bullshittin' right, "was all Sosa could say? He knew that Silas was serious and he loved to be caught up in the middle of beef--major beef. He once told him that beef was what kept him alive so long in a city where you barely lived passed your eighteenth birthday. Charlottesville was to slow for Silas and Sosa knew it!

"I ain't bullshittin' homey, I'm dead ass! Did you see the little nigga pull-up at

GoCo... Umm, Umm, Malik, he was driving that brand new Range Rover? From what I been hearing, son just started selling CRACK around the same time we got out here. Before that, son was selling a little weed or some bullshit. Son came up out of nowhere! They say him and his man Joey got the whole Projects' on lock-down and to make shit even sweeter, neither one of them carry a hammer. Now you tell me why the fuck we shouldn't be over there getting that Project paper?"

Sosa knew this was coming it was only a matter of time, "Silas, you acting like we ain't seeing paper our self, the Feds ain't sniffin' around, we ain't gotta worry about the gun play, we're completely off the radar. It's like we ain't even out here, but I guess that ain't enough for the infamous Silas, huh? I'm telling you Silas, you gotta get off that bullshit, one slip out here and these crackers will have you and me up under the jail," reinforced Sosa!

"Fuck the police, fuck the feds, fuck them Project dudes, and right about now...Fuck you too, "said Silas as he stormed out the front door. Silas was mad as hell, Sosa had the game all fucked-up and he had to get away from him before shit really got out of hand. The way he looked at it, it was Tasha's fault, she was the reason Sosa was starting to get soft: 'his ass pussy whipped, that's what it is!' Since they got to Charlottesville it seemed like they have been growing farther and farther apart, it was like they were both starving and willing to do whatever it took for them to see some paper, that's when shit was smooth. Sosa's not hungry anymore, that frustrated him. The streets respected paper and that's it, fuck all the other up-top shit is played out. It's niggaz from right here in Charlottesville who are out here doing their own thang and they don't give a fuck where you from, those days are long gone and Sosa didn't understand that. They had started to blend in so well that now Silas was looked at as another nigga out there on the grind and that didn't sit well with him. In his mind he wasn't nothing like the rest of them dudes out there, whether from Charlottesville or anywhere else, he felt he should stand out! There were only a hand few of real dudes out there and he considers himself to be one of the few!

Without realizing it, Silas was becoming his own worst enemy, the very thing that had kept him under the radar and out the way was the very thing he desired the most: ATTENTION! With or without Sosa he was going to get the respect he believed he deserved. That's why he kept his own rental car parked by the grave-yard on 1st Street. He didn't let Sosa know about the rental, especially since he's been bouncing through the Projects' on the low. And that's exactly how he met Angie, and used her to learn all about Joey and Malik. He ran across her over on Charlton, she was looking for some dope and CRACK. What got his attention was that she didn't look like your average dope fiend or CRACK-HEAD, she had a pretty face and her body was still intact. Over the last month or so, he would go chill with her at her crib in the Projects' whenever Sosa was laid up with the bitch Tasha and he wanted to get away from the both of them. The pussy was on a thousand, and the head game was nothing to play with! The more he thought about her the more he knew he had to get over there. He took out his cell phone and dialed Angie's number to see what's up with her. "Yo, what up Angie? You busy? Good... Good, I'm on my way over there, 'he said hanging up the phone.

When Angie answered the phone she was still a little sleepy and ignored it for as long as she could before answering. Forcing her sluggish body to the phone was a task in itself, but once she recognized Silas voice, life sprang into her body. His voice was like wind in her lungs, "hey Silas baby, what's good with you? Oh, you just asked me that...I'm never too busy for you and even if I was I wouldn't be any more once I heard your sexy voice," she said in her most enticing voice.

I'm on my way...You hungry?" Umm...I'm hungry but not for food...I'm hungry for you sexy! She knew he was just as big a freak as she was and he loved to dominate her and she could tell in his voice he was frustrated and she wanted to make it easy for him. She turned on the charm and talked a little more shit to him about what she wanted him to do her before they hung up. Just hearing Angie's voice was enough to calm him down some so that he could focus on his own plans. If Sosa didn't want to leave Garrett then that would be his choice, as for him...The Projects' would be his next stop. He needed to be where the action was! He found a nice little spot on Main Street called Mels' where he often stopped to get something to eat. He knew Angie would go a minute without eating and he wanted to be sure she ate something that's why he stopped at Mel's, for Angie! The longer he thought about Angie and those long sexy legs of hers, his dick got hard, she was bonafide in the sheets and good in public, and he loved it.

Angie hung-up her phone and forced her feet to hit the floor as she lit herself a Newport and placed her cigarette in the astray after 3 long drags from the cigarette. The lack of dope in her body had every bone in her body aching. Her rig was on her dresser ready and waiting on her, she had learned to keep herself a good wake-up shot for the morning no matter what she did the night before. Waking up dope sick wasn't no joke, staying sick was out of the question for her, she couldn't start her day off like that! Despite having a monster CRACK habit, she kept a little something for herself, being cross-addict to both CRACK and DOPE wasn't a good look, but Angie managed to keep herself looking good. Even the young boys in the Projects' paid her top dollar for a shot of that warm, wet and tight pussy of hers when she wanted to get herself some of that young dick. One thing she understood was that the older she got there wasn't nothing like a good shot of that young dick.

She wasn't into the whole trickin' scene but when she wanted to be fucked, she figured she might as well get a few dollars' at the same time! A good shot of dope in her veins made her horny as hell and a good youngin would literally fuck the shit out of her. It was the best of both worlds for her: She got her freak on and made some paper at the same time! The one thing Angie liked the most about Silas was that he respected her, bad habits and all. It didn't hurt that he sniffed dope too and made sure she kept enough so she wouldn't get sick, that was a plus. With her being a natural hustla, he also gave her enough CRACK to sell and still have enough to smoke and all he required from her was a little bit of her time and attention. The thought of how good he ate pussy, she began to feel the moisture between her legs. Finding a nice vein in her left arm, she smacked it a couple times, tied her scoff around her arm as she slide the needle in her vein. She watched the dope as it disappeared from the needle into her arm and instantly felt like herself. When she pulled the needle out she used her index finger to wipe away a little speck of blood, she tasted the little bit of her own blood because it was always sweet and it was a habit of hers. She couldn't shoot dope in her veins without tasting it. She had to shower for Silas--he loved a clean pussy!

Sosa remained in Tasha's living room just staring at a blank screen on their 60 inch flat screen television after Silas stormed out the front door with an attitude. As he looked all around Tasha's apartment the more he felt like he had done the right thing by letting Silas leave.

He loved her taste in furniture; everything was perfect, from her color coordination of how it seemed to match. The living room blended in so well with the dining room and the kitchen like it was all one big room yet still managed to keep a separate look of its own. The plush red carpet set everything else in motion. 'How can Silas not get use to something like this?' Even though they were living in the hood, you couldn't tell from the inside of Tasha's apartment. She kept her shit laid to the nines, and to make it even sweeter, he didn't have to come out his pocket for nothing in the whole apartment. She had her shit together when he first met her; she worked 10 hours every day. She often told him she didn't want to struggle and her son was enough inspiration for her to carry herself to work every morning without any complaint. Letting him know early on in their relationship that she definitely wasn't out for his paper; even if he gave her paper she made it her business to pay him back when she got paid. He never asked her to pay him back, it was her idea and she told him that by her having to pay him back it kept her on her toes. It was clear that Tasha was a very independent woman who could hold her own without a man in her life! 'If I could only get Silas to see that Charlottesville is nothing like Newark and this could very well be a good spot to settle down and retire from the CRACK game.' But, Silas was stubborn and wasn't trying to hear nothing he had to say right now, that's just how he is; especially when he believes he is right. He knew he had to get Silas off of his mind because if he didn't. Well, you guys know the drill, Idle time is the devil's play-ground! He reached for the speaker that was sitting next to the huge entertainment system, with the flat screen on top. After he pulled the speaker close to him he got up and went to the closet to get a screw driver out his tool box. Sosa took his time as he unwired the speaker from the entertainment system. He took off the cover, turned the speaker around and began unscrewing the 8 screws one at a time. This was a specially made speaker and its contents contained his future, the two speakers were probably the only things in the entire apartment that was actually his and brought them with him once they got serious with each other. Nobody knew he kept his stash inside those speakers. He kept another set those same speakers at his cousin's house back in Jersey, another set at his Moms and nobody knew it was a stash spot; he made sure the speaker's worked.

Once he got the speakers open, he grabbed twenty-five thousand out one of the pockets of Tasha's winter coat. All the pockets were full of cash, he kept his paper in her coat pockets because if something bad really happened and the house got robbed or something, when they ran across the twenty-five thousand they would probably leave while the real stash was safe and tucked away in the speakers. He figured the best way to hide something was to keep it in an obvious spot, usually it would be in plain sight! He counted his paper once and then recounted it all over again, that was a sure way to get Silas off his mind! And it also served as a reminder of why he hustled in the first place. He packed the speaker with nice and neat stacks of paper back inside...He had over 5 stacks of twenty-five thousand dollar stack's and working on another one. He lost his count and decided to take out the entire stacks one more time, more so for his ego than anything else. He had 3 months' worth of work sitting in front of him, 'with a brick left, this ain't bad. In about a year or two I will be able to really retire and walk away with my paper and the woman of my dreams in Tasha!' Sosa decided to pop-off a few of the rubber bands he had on the paper keeping the stack's nice and neat and spread the paper out all over the red carpet. For him counting his paper was a stress reliever for him and not like most hustlas, he wasn't a big spender! He looked at his iron-man sports watch, knowing Tasha wasn't due back home for another 45 minutes; he had plenty of time to recount all his paper one more time. With half of the living room floor cover in paper, the front door busted open so hard the back of the door slammed into the wall. He jumped and reached for his gun, but it was Tasha's son Jay bolting through the door in front of her. Jay made a bee-line for all the money on the floor as he dived into the pile on the floor laughing and trying to play with him.

"Money mommy, money mommy, lots of money mommy, "said little Jay as he played with the piles of money on the floor. Tasha was struggling with the bags she had in her hand and wasn't able to see exactly what had Jay so excited until she was able to position herself to see what was going on. The smile she had on her face, quickly disappeared and was replaced with her face twisted and evil. Her beady eyes stared at Sosa hard enough to burn a hole through his soul. She was still staring at Sosa but speaking to Jay, "go up-stairs to your room honey, mommy will be up there in a minute."

Tasha never took her eyes off hit the whole time! He could tell something wasn't right the way she was looking at him but he didn't know why. The way she was looking at him he was wondering if Silas had caught her outside and said something stupid to her. 'I hope that dummy didn't do or say something stupid. He called her a bitch before he left!

"Nigga, have you lost your rabbit-ass mind? Oh, you bringing money and drugs in my house now? I have a son and you can't--" Sosa knew exactly where this was going so he stopped her mid-sentence "baby...baby, its only paper! I don't keep drugs' in your house; you should already know that by now. I respect you more than that."

Tasha didn't get the reaction that she thought she was going to get from him, but she wasn't finish quite yet with him either. More prying had to be done "oh, you super-nigga now, huh? Suppose niggaz run up in here with guns blazin' ready to rob you for some stolen money huh, what the fuck you gonna do then Sosa...What?"

Sosa got up from off the floor, "stolen money...What the fuck you talking about Tasha?" The closer he got to her the more she started crying, "go 'head take it--take it, I don't care about it, you're a thief. You're a thief, you're just like the rest of these good for nothing ass niggaz...I...I thought you were different," she said sobbing! The way she hit the floor it looked like she had fainted or collapsed. It scared the hell out of him, as he rushed to her side.

"Tasha, Tasha, you a-ight baby," he asked as he shook her? She didn't answer him she started crying all over again. All he could think about why she was bugging over some paper. True it was scattered all over the floor but she called him a thief? He was confused and had to get to the bottom of why she called him a thief!

He grabbed her by the shoulders holding her firm as forced her to look at him, "Tasha, talk to me, tell me why you're so upset about me having my money in the house?" He put his hand under her chin again having to force her to look at him because she kept putting her head down. "Tasha, will you please talk to me," he said as he wiped away her tears.

When she finally opened her eyes, there was a confused look on his face. He wasn't supposed to have that look on his face nor was he still supposed to be there. He was supposed to have taken the money, but he didn't. She turned away so she wouldn't have to look in his eyes.

He wouldn't let her off the hook that easy. "Look at me Tasha, you gotta tell me what's going on here," he was forceful but gently all at the same time. With his voice full of concern, she was beginning to get confused now. When she turned to face him, she saw something in his eyes that would forever change her life. He had several tears running down the side of his face and his eyes had so much love in them, she got scared. It was a look she had only seen on little Jay's Father! It told her everything she needed to know; Sosa wasn't the thief she thought he was.

"Tasha, talk to me. Tell me what's going on with you? Does the money bother you that much?" Barley above a whisper she said, "no, it's not about the money Sosa, that's not it at all." "Then why don't you tell me what it's about because you got me nervous right now?" She took a deep breath and began talking to him real slow,"this...this is... going to sound real stupid, but when I came in the house and I,I saw all the money on the floor...I...I...thought you found something of mines and you were stealing it." Sosa was now more confused now than he was at the start of things'. He watched her get up off the floor, "come with me, I need to show you something, "she said to him.

She stood up reached her hand out for him then said softly, "come with me, I want to show you something," as she lead the way up-stairs. Inside the bedroom she went to the closet and came back with a black suitcase with gold writing on the side of it. He could tell she was struggling with the weight of the suitcase but he didn't offer to help. When she got close enough to the bed, she threw the suitcase and its contents onto the bed. His eyes got the size of someone smoking CRACK! "There's three hundred thousand there and this," holding a large sandwich bag that was full to the top with CRACK.

"I thought you found Jay's money and was stealing it. I'm so sorry for not trusting you, I'm sorry baby." She sat on the edge of the bed and invited him to take a seat next to her, "come sit with me and let me tell you all about Jay's father."

He really didn't know what to do or say but he followed her eyes and found a seat on the bed next to her. She exhaled and began to speak slow and steady. "Jay's father was a hustler like you, the only difference from now and then, is that I didn't know the extent of how deep he was. Over the course of our 2 year relationship he bought a couple houses, some land in the country, and a shit load of cars. His family thought that I was after his money. Hold up, let me slow down, I'm getting ahead of myself. Well, the last time I saw him I was like 8 months pregnant, he gave me this suitcase to hold and made me promise that no matter what, that I wouldn't give it to anybody regardless of the situation, just hold it until he comes back. It wasn't anything for him to be gone a few days here and a few days there, I thought nothing of it. Back then we were staying at the house in the country with a lot of land on it, he used to say little Jay would need space to run around without getting himself in trouble…It was like he knew something wasn't right…"

Little Jay came and knocked on the bedroom door, "Mommy…Mommy, I'm hungry," he said!" Okay baby, mommy will fix you something to eat in just a few minutes, let me finish talking to Silas okay?" "Okay mommy but don't forget," said little Jay as he ran giggling out loud.

She took a deep breath and finished telling him the story behind the suitcase and the CRACK, "anyway, that next morning his sister called me from Miami and the funny thing about it was that I had been to Miami with him on several occasions, met his whole family and they all knew I was having his son. When she called me, all she said was that he was killed last night by his wife! I'm telling you, that shit blew me outta the fuckin' water; never in a million years would I have thought he was married to someone else. He had a wife! We spent so much time together I thought she was playing with my mind, but she wasn't. I forced myself to go down there that evening, and go to his funeral. I'm telling you, I never even looked in the casket; I refused to believe that he was dead, much less a wife. I just never believed he was dead, but I remember asking him what was in the suitcase and him telling me that I'll find out in due time and to just take care of little Jay! I've spent the last four years of my life waiting for him to come back and meet his son and get all this, now I realize he's never coming back...I realized that when I met you!" She handed him the bag of CRACK, "you take this and do what you do with it!"

"You been keeping all of this in the house?"

"Yes. Since I've been with you, it only confirmed that he's never coming back and I have to move on with my life no matter what. He had to know that eventually I would start seeing someone else and I believe in my heart he knew something bad was about to happen to him and this was his way of showing us he was sorry for how things had turned out. Not only was he sorry, he made sure that me and Jay had enough and wouldn't have to depend on nobody else. It's ours though, me, you and Jay!"

He was truly in love with her and the money or the drugs didn't have anything to do with it. All along he knew there was something different about her and now he knew what it was: her loyalty! She had her own paper, still lived in the hood, and worked her ass off every day like she was a damn slave and that impressed him. "Come here sexy!" He hugged and gave her a passionate kiss, "what am I supposed to do with all this shit here," he asked referring to the CRACK?

She playfully punched him in the arm, "I know you don't think that I don't know that you and your boy Sosa be having all them little boys out there selling that stuff for ya'll. Silas I'm not stupid or green. I guess you'll do exactly what you've been doing with it get rid of it. I just want you to be careful and don't trust none of these dudes, they'll stab you in the back in a minute."

"I can't take this...Jay's father left this for you and his son!"

Tasha looked at him with a dumb look on her face, "so you expect me to get out there and move this stuff with the rest of them dudes?" He shook his head because she had a point. "Listen, he knew, he knew one day I would be attracted to somebody like you and this was his way of making sure all of us would be alright. So you're wrong, it was mines, now it's yours, mister. Well, to keep it gansta with you, it's ours! If we're going to be together and we are, you're going to have to understand I'm not this little country chick who don't know nothing about nothing, I just act like I don't know nothing."

She stood up because she knew that she had to get downstairs to fix Jay something to eat. "Before Jay was born I was out there in them streets just like everybody else, I was that bitch to see in the hood so don't get it twisted. Are you still thinking about getting out the game?" Her last question caught him off guard, he had mentioned about two weeks ago about getting out of the game but because she never replied or said anything to him about it he thought it fell on deaf ears... What he didn't know was that she did hear him she didn't want that decision based on how she felt about him getting out the game, so she kept her thoughts to herself. She had been thinking about telling him about the money and the stuff but was afraid to say something.

"It might not be my place to say it but I'm going to say it anyway, your boy Sosa's been bugging recently, don't you think so?"

He knew she was dead ass when she said that, "you right! I know if I don't do or say something to him about it he's going to have the both of us in prison for a long time! Well, you already know that I love you, you got money, I got money. I say we just bounce. Leave Garrett behind and ride off into the Sun set before it's too late and something bad happens.

"I'm feeling you on that, to make matters worse, my gut is telling me to get outta dodge before it's too late!"

"My only condition would be that your boy cannot tag along with us! He can come visit once in a while, but right now, we have to make a decision based on our family." She started rubbing on her stomach and smiling.
"Tasha, are you pregnant?"

"No crazy! I'm not pregnant, not yet anyway, but once we get married I will be," she said beaming with pride.

They walked hand in hand together downstairs and he watched as she interacted with Jay and that's when he knew there was no way in hell he was ever letting this one get away. His mind flashed back to that big bag of CRACK he left up-stairs', "babe, I'll be back in a little while, I have to get you know what out of this house before I go crazy. I don't want to be hearing no bullshit out of you either when I'm out there doing my thang," he said poking fun at how she usually acted whenever he was gone away from the house to long.

"You ain't gotta worry about that, I'll be too busy trying to find us a house somewhere where it stays warm all year around. Somewhere far as hell away from CHARLOTTESVILLE! Between that and all of this packing, I won't have any time to be worrying about what you're out there doing in them streets. All I know is that as long as you take care of your business...In the house, and outside the house," she said patting her kitten!

"Tell you what then, go 'head and get Jay fed and to bed early, I'll be sure to be back in here soon, put that see through cat suit on that I love so much, then call me, I'll show you how to take care of business inside and outside!"

CHAPTER 5

THE next morning Amanda was the first to wake, in her queen size bed staring at the ceiling trying to make her mind recall the events of the previous night. Forcing herself to sit-up was a task all in itself; her head was throbbing and her stomach growling. She needed a cigarette! Fumbling through all the clutter on her night stand, debris and unused numbers she had collected throughout her travels, she thought she'd never find what she was looking for. Her lighter and cigarettes came into view after moving the clutter around.

Amanda's bedroom was laid to the nines; it wasn't trashy but messy at the same time, cut up pieces of paper with different dudes' number on them, lip stick, a comb, a brush, chewing gum, and her most prized possession, her famous straight razor was all cluttered together on the night stand. She had always been a little slow at putting her belongings where they belonged, after all, it was her bedroom and she made sure to keep it off limits to any and everybody. Including Jazzy and White-girl. Dropping a long ash on the floor, she watched as it fell on her beautiful carpet wishing she had the strength to stop the ashes from making a mess. Knowing that she couldn't, she focused her attention to the television catching an early talk show. Usually she wasn't much into all the gossip and hating that went on them type of show's but this day she used to television to help motivate herself and get moving.

The clothes she wore yesterday were still in a neat pile on the carpet at the foot of her bed, with her stomach growling she tried to focus and remember the last time she had something to eat... Was it before or after they started partying last night or was it before she had got with Malik's crazy ass? She couldn't figure it out to save her life, all she knew was her stomach was talking.

'a-ight Amanda get yo shit together.' By the time her feet hit the floor her head was pounding on the inside where she imagined her brain was. Opening the night stand, she grabbed herself two Tylenol Codeine, number 3's to be exact. Throwing the pills in her mouth she swallowed them dry. If she had been thinking properly she would've gotten herself some water because the chalky white pills left a bitter taste in her mouth and barely went down. They were stuck in the back of her throat! With no other choice, Amanda forced herself out the bed rushing into the bathroom.

She looked at herself in the mirror as she ran some warm water into the sink. Swishing warm water around in her mouth, she swallowed hard forcing the remaining pills down without a problem. It was a relief to feel the pills go down and not having that funny feeling in the back of her throat. She casually put her index finger under the water to check its temperature, getting the water to her liking; she sniffed water from the palm of her giving herself one helluva drain. Her nose was so clogged up from the previous night and all the cocaine she sniffed, the warm water was a blessing, so much so that she repeated the process three more times.

Satisfied with her drain and the pills beginning to kick in she headed into the kitchen to brew a nice hot cup of coffee. She walked by the living room, two figures caught her attention out the corner of her eye; it was her cousin Jazzy and White-girl on the living room floor asleep, naked as a Jay-bird. Their bodies were intertwined like one big human pretzel, she whispered to herself 'somebody got their freak on up in here last night!' All that shit Jazzy been talking to White-girl, I knew it, them bitches been bumping pussies all the fuckin' time. How can I have not known, this shit been right under my nose and in my house? There was a twelve inch white dildo lying in the open on the carpet beside White-girl's right hand, turning her nose up at the dildo, she grabbed her own pussy because of the size and thickness it looked like it would hurt a bitch. After putting the coffee on, she decided that she had time to shower; the pills had her rockin' she was ready now. Her whole body started to get real relaxed; she decided on a bath instead of a quick shower, she needed to soak her body. Gathering candles, bath beads, and her oatmeal for her skin, she was definitely ready.

An hour later, she emerged from the bathroom, looking, smelling, and feeling like a million bucks. To her surprise, White-girl was in the kitchen asking her did she want her to bring her coffee to the bedroom. "Yeah, but make sure you pu-." White-girl had cut her off and finished her sentence for her, "I know, I know, make sure I put sugar and cream in it. Two scoops of sugar and a dash of cream, little on the sweet side, just like you," said White-girl flirting with her a little bit.

Is this bitch down there flirting with me, Amanda thought to herself? This crazy bitch already know what it is with me, I'm strictly dickly! "A-ight, you can bring that shit back here bitch." Jazzy hollered from the living room, "Amanda, you finish in the bathroom?" She knew that Amanda was finished but she wanted to make the bossy Amanda feel good, being it was her apartment and shit. Without waiting for Amanda's answer she side swiped White-girl in the hallway making her spill little coffee on the carpet. Wanting to say something slick to White-girl but a thought in her mind, it was of White-girl eating her pussy, so instead of being her usual nasty self towards her she just said, "watch yoself!"

Satisfied with the outfit laying on her bed; Amanda began putting the finishing touches to her get-up, a pair of crisp, all white on white, Air Force One's, no socks today, she wanted to show off her ankle bracelet with the diamonds in it. "Jazzy make sure you hurry up too, I need you to do my hair," she hollered just as Jazzy closed and locked the bathroom door.

Jazzy did her thing in the bathroom and came out in no time with a huge towel wrapped around her body as White-girl slid pass her into the bathroom to get her shit together. She sat Amanda down on the floor in between her legs doing her hair. Amanda didn't care too much to be sitting between her legs but if she wanted her hair done the way she wanted, she would have to bite the bullet on this one. She could never figure out why Jazzy didn't like doing her hair in the kitchen like she did everybody else's hair, it was a mystery to her. It was well worth it because regardless of what you think about Jazzy, she was a hair doing bitch. Top-notch! "That should do it bitch" said Jazzy, well aware of her skills.

Amanda stood-up stretching and yarning, "damn bitch, this shit is tight! We should open your ass a shop so we can get some paper from your skill's, half these bitches out here that already got shops can't even fuck with you girl. To make this shit even crazier, you doing bitches hair out the damn kitchen," said Amanda looking at her new up-do in the mirror. White-girl came out the bathroom and took one look at Amanda's hair and all she could say was, "damn!" Then she looked over at Jazzy with sad puppy dog eyes and said, "I wish that you could do something like that with my hair." "Isn't nobody fucking with that big-ass dome you got on you, girl," said Jazzy laughing her ass off.

More so speaking under her breath, White-girl whispered, "you got a mean dome piece too and I ain't talking about the one on your shoulders either," referring to Jazzy's pussy eating skills. Their eyes locked for a second too long before White-girl and Amanda both started giggling together.

"Yours ain't all that bad either bitch," said Jazzy making it known that she heard what White-girl had said making sure it was understood that she wasn't the only one giving head last night. Amanda had thought both of them were funny enjoying the show. With Jazzy, Amanda always sided with her even when she was wrong, family came first in her book and she made it a point to show it.

"I know that's right Jazzy...You might not have put that pussy on nobody's mustache last night but you sure as hell put it on some damn Lip-Gloss," said Amanda barely able to keep her balance from laughing so hard. White-girl knew that both Jazzy and Amanda wouldn't stop clowning her once they had started so doing the next best thing; she went to the spare bedroom and finished getting dressed. She learned the hard way that she had to be really careful and pick her battles when it came to those two, "I'm going to finish getting dressed, ya'll crazy," she said laughing it off.

Since Jazzy's hair was always done and ready, it only required only minimum amounts of attention. It only took her a good 15 minutes to be ready to bounce. Amanda looking like the spokeswomen that she was, sat at the dining room table with a bill in front of her looking for something to scoop the cocaine in her purse. It was the cocaine that she had stashed yesterday after she got back from seeing Malik. Before she knew it, Jazzy had snatched the bill up off the table like a women possessed.

"Yo ass ain't even ate shit yet and you trying to get high, hold ya horses, you can't keep ya weight straight now but I can see the fuck why," blasted Jazzy! "We got one more thang to do before we bounce, get me a razor blade Please!"

Amanda went in the back to her Queen dome and knew exactly where to look for her razor blades she kept stashed away safely in her closet, tucked neatly in one of her show boxes. By the time she got back in the dining room White-girl and Jazzy had cleared off the dining room table as they replaced it with a huge chunk CRACK and a bag of sandwich bags. Amanda's stomach had started back talking to her, since Jazzy had taken away her little stash she was starting to feel some type of way about it because at the very least she knew a couple blasts from the bill the cocaine would curb her appetite. Throwing the box of razors onto the table with an attitude and frustration growing by the second, 'here bitch because I ain't got no time for this bullshit, I gotta find me something to eat."

Jazzy had gotten her hand held digital scale from out of her purse, her brother had told her that it would come in handy one of these days and she was grateful that day had finally came. "A-light, ya'll bitches sit back and pay attention, class is about to be in session. I'm about to show ya'll crazy bitches how to transfer this," pointing at the huge CRACK rock on the table, "into some hard earned cash broke down into dubs."

She was using the razor blade like a surgeon slicing and cutting from the larger rock and making smaller ones, "this shit shouldn't be all that hard Amanda, a dub of CRACK is damn near the same as a dub of powder and I know damn well you know what that looks like! The scale will make it even easier. Everything you put on the scale will weigh .2's and each one is twenty dollars, it's as simple as that," said Jazzy proud of her presentation. "Amanda, you'll do the cutting and use the scale, I'll eye ball some and White-girl, you put'em in the corners of the sandwich bags and be sure to snip off the ends, don't leave to much excess."

It took them another fifteen minutes to cut up two 8-balls which totaled just over six hundred dollars. "Amanda call the Korner and place our orders for some food," said Jazzy stuffing the CRACK into her purse. "White-girl, call us a cab, they'll know you're a white chick so we shouldn't have to wait all that long," said Amanda laughing. White-girl was well aware of the advantages of being in her regular life, but in the hood that shit didn't fly one bit, except for calling cabs.

She was now a minority! However, she was highly observant of everything around her, especially when it came time to watching what Amanda was doing.

She had to bite her tongue more than she liked to but she knew the only way to catch a sucka was to play the sucka. With them being on their way over to the Projects' and Amanda plugged in with Malik on the sex thang, it was only a matter of time before she either got Joey's attention, Malik's attention or got Amanda to get some CRACK from Malik. She considered this next move to be phase II of her overall game plan with the first being able to just get in the door with them. She had sucked and fucked her way in the door letting little niggaz run through her pussy like it was nothing. Nevertheless, she would have to play the whole 4 quarters if she wanted to win!

―――――――   ―――――――   ―――――――   ―――――――
―――――――

Joey and Malik was eager to get an early start the next day, after sitting down with their connect and absorbing all that knowledge he had to offer, they could think of nothing better than to implement some of that knowledge. Malik met Joey on West Street and talked him into riding with him for a while.

"I'm doing the driving today, come on homey, let's ride," said Malik gunning the engine a little of the Camry thee connect had provided for him. Having Malik doing the driving wasn't such a bad idea, Joey thought to himself. It gave him the time to sit back, relax and make a few important calls. Malik wasn't holding anything back as he constantly tested the power of the Camry in comparison to his Range Rover. "See you like your new toy," said Joey?

"Yeah, your whip is like your bitch, you know what I'm saying? If you don't know her limitations and what she's capable of then she'll get you into a whole lot of trouble down the line," said Malik laughing. "The power ain't the same as the Rover, but I can definitely get use to this!" Malik crossed over Main Street,"yo, let's hit the Korner for something to eat before we hit the barber shop. What you think?" "I see you still eating them cracker's food, huh?" They both laughed because that's what Auntie Pam always said to them whenever they mentioned eating from that spot, but they both loved the Korner food, so it has always been their joke whenever the Korner came up.

The fact remained, they cooked like some ole' black lady. "Man, I don't know why people still be bugging of that white people shit, the only color that makes a difference today is GREEN, all them dead presidents. Some of the same black people we deal with every day will be the mutha-fucker to testify on our black ass if some shit went down. As far as I'm concerned Joey, you're the only person I trust-Even Sammy-the-bull told on his right hand man, so what does that tell you," said Malik with a serious look on his face.

Joey looked over at Malik with a smirk on his face because he felt that he was just starting to come around and see the big picture of how things' really worked out here. Confrontation wasn't one of Malik's strong point's either but to see him battling with real idea's and willing to mentally fight the ways of old really made Joey feel good. His method's has always been violence, rather than use his mind, he would use violence to solve his problems. However, itf made their relationship a match of greatness. Malik was the killa and Joey was his alter-ego that made the killa think before reacting. Joey's job consisted of trying to get Malik to see that their goal could easily be achieved without having to put down their murder game and it's been working for the most part. Joey also knew that with Mo' money came Mo' problem's!

Malik eased the Camry into the parking lot of the restaurant, he saw three female's getting out a cab and noticed Amanda immediately in that tight fitting Pink Roca wear sweat suit. Joey tapped him on his right shoulder," yo, ain't that the shorty over there you be fucking with the pretty eyes...Ummm...Ummm! Amanda?"

Without taking his eyes off of the three females he parked the Camry right beside the cab," yeah, that's her...Let's go and checked these bitches and see what they talking about.

"Hey Malik," said Amanda as she eyed the Camry.

"What up with you sexy," fired Malik licking his lips. His little man was on the rise the moment he looked into those pretty eyes of hers but he still played it cool.

"What up sexy, nothing! Why you ain't call me last night like you said you were. That's what I want to know?"

He slowly walked over to her, she put her hand up to stop him from me a damn hug before I take it," he said laughing. He put her in the bear hug and made sure she felt what was growing in his pants.

She playfully pushed him away from her, "stop boy, I wanna know why you ain't call me last night? See, you missed out on something real special to," she said as she gave White-girl a kiss on the lips! Malik's eyes got big as hell because he knew she was referring to having a threesome with White-girl. He been asking about White-girl for a long time and every time all she would tell him was that she'll think about it. It was obvious that she had thought about it and was ready to make that move with him.

"My bad little momma, I got crazy busy last night, you know how that goes." "Yeah whatever. Anyway, this White-girl...White-girl, this Malik, the one I been telling you about, "said Amanda giving them a formal introduction to each other. "Yep, he's everything that you said he was and then some. I'm sorry you didn't call my girl last night, we had something real special planned for you big boy," added White-girl before she turned to walk away after giving her lips one swift lick. Amanda had to punch him in the arm because all his attention was focused on White-girls' ass and the way she was rocking her hips. "Damn Malik, if you thirsty like that we can go fuck in your car real quick. But don't be playing me out here for no damn white chick!"

The way White-girl was walking, her ass, demand some much needed attention and Malik couldn't do anything but stare at all that ass on that white bitch, "it ain't even like that shorty," he said flat! Amanda was nobody's fool; she knew Malik had a thing for White-girl because he's been asking to fuck her ever since she first came around. She couldn't front on him though because she knew that if he would've pressed hard enough he could fuck, but he kept it gansta with her. She respected the fact that he even would listen to her when it came down to it. "Yeah right! Where's the Rover at anyway?"

Joey was off to the side minding his own business thinking about different ways to move the work when he heard Amanda asking about the Rover. The one thing he hated the most was bitches getting all up in other people's business and he couldn't take it any longer, "damn shorty, you sure ask a bunch of questions that don't concern you...Malik you need to check shorty." Knowing that it wasn't but a matter of time before Joey and Amanda got into it, they always did. Their dislike for each other went all the way back to high school. Amanda always tried to tell Malik that Joey thought he was the boss of everything and everybody. Then he had Joey in his other ear telling him that Amanda wasn't nothing but a scandalous paper chasing bitch that had a nose problem. Back then, Malik use to think that it would be one of them who would eventually cross him but as the time passed neither did and he learned to keep them far away from each other as possible. "Ain't nobody even talking to your stuck-up ass Joey," said a frustrated Amanda as she palmed her straight razor and preparing for battle.

Joey easily peeped the move she made, "you know what Amanda? If you ever pull that rusty-ass razor blade on me, I can promise you this...Your peeps will be wearing your picture on the front of a fucking tee-shirt" There was a murderous look in Joey's eyes that Amanda had never seen before and it let her know that he was dead serious and she didn't want no parts of that.

Easing her hand back into her purse she said, "but wasn't nobody even talking to you Joey" "I know damn well that you wasn't talking to me bitch, and that's ya'll bitches' problem now...Ya'll be asking too many questions that don't concern you; you the police or something?" Jazzy was on the sidelines waiting her turn, when she heard the word bitch that was her cue, "who the fuck you calling a bitch Joey?"

Joey laughed out loud, "if the shoe fits then you better rock them shits... BITCH."

"Fuck you Joey...Fuck you," was all Jazzy could muster to say. She's been on his dick and sweating him for a long time. Ever since that one time he fucked her and blew her back out she's been trying to get back with him. Even now when she looked at him all she saw was his massive dick going in and out of her mouth down her throat, pass her tonsils. Joey knew Jazzy had been feeling him ever since he let Malik convince him to fuck her. They all got drunk together one night at Amanda's, and out of nowhere, Amanda started sucking Malik's dick. It didn't take long for Jazzy to join in trying to outdo her cousin. She was doing her thang for a minute that was until Joey's dick got all the way hard. In her mind she was saying she couldn't believe it and before she knew it she was gagging and begging him to take it easy on her throat. He slapped on a rubber turned Jazzy big yellow ass over and entered her from the back. He had her in the middle of the living room floor where she couldn't hold or grab onto anything. She didn't know it until later that it was all one big set-up. For almost an hour straight she begged, pleaded, cried and tried her darnest to get away from Joey and his massive dick. He wouldn't stop for nothing. He knew he was packing and he tried to warn her ahead of time, but she kept talking that shit to him. So when she wanted him to stop he didn't, but every time he got her on the verge of cuming he'd take his dick almost all the way out only leaving the head in her, then he'd ask her if she wanted him to stop.

She found herself begging for it, she was cuming so many times, she lost count after 10. Right before he got his, he said to her, "tell me you love this dick." With the pain and the pleasure so intense she did what he told her to do. She not only told him once, she told him over and over. What everybody else failed to realize was that she fell in love with Joey that night. She proved it when she pulled the rubber off his dick and rubbed cum all over her face as she whispered, 'not only do I love this dick, I promise that I will worship your dick forever, and I mean every damn word of this shit!

Joey got real close to Jazzy and said to her," been there and done that. I know that you remember how I beat that pussy up, don't you?" "You won't ever get another chance at this pussy again--that was then and thi--, "Save it Jazzy, just save it! Once you told me you'll worship my dick ain't nothing else you can really say. We both know what happened that night and if I ask for some pussy right now I bet you'll let me fuck your burning ass right here in this damn parking lot. If you think I'm bullshitting, just ask your cousin right there, she seen the whole damn thing, ask her if you don't remember how you was begging for it," then he walked off.

Joey went inside the restaurant to pay for their food, not only did he pay for what he and Malik had got, he also paid for Jazzy, Amanda, and White-girls' food as well. He figured that after putting both Jazzy and Amanda on the spot in one day and their business on blast the least he could do was pay their tab. He also had a soft spot for them because they were caught up in the ways of the hood.

The hustle and bustle of the drug game could take anyone down! When he came back out all he said to Malik was, "I'll be in the car."

Jazzy sucked her teeth as he walked past her, she wanted to say something but there was nothing for her to say to him. He was right, he fucked her so hard, long and in every position she could bend her body it didn't make any sense. It was all the truth, "let me go in here and get our food," she said. Once inside, she saw their stuff sitting on the counter next to the register so she walked over to pay the guy. He handed her the three bags and told her thank you and come again. When she inquired about how much it was he told her that the gentleman with the baseball cap on had just paid for their meal. Back outside she looked in the direction of the parked Camry but she couldn't see inside with the windows jet-black. She raised the three bags, nodded her head in that direction to thank him. She already knew that he was watching, he always watched, even when you thought he wasn't. Her mind started playing tricks on her again, she was telling herself, 'I knew he wanted some more of this sweet pussy. I let that nigga have his way with me the first time, he just didn't get enough.'

"Where ya'll headed," asked Malik?

"Over your way! We'll be in the Projects' later, why?"

He had to laugh, every since he's known Amanda he never caught her in the Projects', "not you miss Prospect all day...All night!"

"Everybody needs a field trip once in a while in their life," said Amanda reminding Malik of their high school field trip to King's Dominion where they fuck for the first time on the bus while everybody else was still in the park enjoying their selves.

"So you still remember that, Huh? How long you'll be over my side of town?"

Giggling, because she knew that he remembered the field trip just by the look on his face and the bulge in his sweat pants'." that's going to depend on you."

"What you mean by that? You know I ain't got time for no games!"

She started licking her lips letting him know what was on her mind. She couldn't front, when it came to his fine ass, friends or not, she wanted herself some Malik and made sure to leave the door open for him to decide what he was going to do about it.

White-girl came a little closer because she wanted to hear the plans for later that night. Realizing that both of them was playing around she had to voice her opinion on things, "if I were you Malik, I, would give my girl a call sometime after the sun goes down. You know what they say: Freaks come out at night!"

Amanda walked to the cab but turned around before she got in, "Malik you better call me tonight, too." Once in the cab, Jazzy told them all about how Joey had paid for their food after he talked all that shit to them and about them. "You know what? Joey ain't all that bad Jazzy, that nigga is strictly business, that's all. Even when it comes to me, I been fucking Malik's ass since before I really knew what fucking was and he's always been right there in the mix of shit. That's just his way of keeping Malik's head in the game. For real though, I respect that nigga Joey...A bitch wouldn't dare tell that nigga the truth, but I respect him all the same," said Amanda.

"I do too! I respect him, the way he carry himself and how can I ever forget that King Kong dick of his? I definitely respect that mutha-fucker!"

Malik and Joey drove the short distance to the barber shop on Cherry. He parked next to the pearl White SL600 Mercedes Benz that was sitting on some 22" deep dish chrome rims. "Those two still out here chasing that paper and getting it on the low," said Malik referring to the owner of the Benz and his right hand man.

Mann and Ru were legends in the hood, not only were they respected in the Projects, but all over Charlottesville as well. If you saw one, you automatically saw the other. Joey admired the love and loyalty the two shared with each other. It was the same way when it came to his homey. They walked inside and Mann was just getting out of the barber's chair. They spoke and gave each other a pound, showing their respect and love.

"Yo, What up Mann" said Joey? Mann got out the chair and gave Joey another hug this time he whispered in his ear, "you already know what's good with me, out here, chasin' that paper," said Mann laughing.

Malik went and took a seat next to Ru; neither of them spoke to each other verbally, but they nodded their heads in acknowledgement of the other. Ru was busy talking on his phone while Malik was checking a text message he just got from Amanda. The message put a smile on his face and he read what she wanted to do to him later that night with White-girl!

Mann's huge Platinum '10th & Page' chain was hanging damn near down to his nuts he said to Joey," I hear you and your homey right there is doing real well in the hood! Keep that shit on the best side: WESTSIDE 4 LIFE, and don't ever forget that shit...NO MATTER WHAT!"

Forty-five minutes later, J.Y. was done cutting both Joey and Malik's hair. Out the door and ready to officially start their day off, they got back in the car. Joey had slipped up and found a spot on 6th Street one day while he was as the Exxon Station getting some gas. One of the ole' heads' from the Projects' was out there sitting on the rail getting his drink on when he ran across a hundred dollar sell. The ole' head seen Joey and immediately approached him on the business tip. It was a lucky day for the both of them because Joey had some CRACK on him, and ever since that day Joey and the ole' head been hooking up every morning getting paper together. "Malik, pull over by the pay phone in the Exxon parking lot!" Instead of parking by the pay phone, Malik pulled behind the gas station.

Joey spotted the ole' head sitting there on the rail as usual, he got out the car and called him over. His next move caught Malik off guard, he pulled out a quarter ounce of CRACK from his nuts and handed it to the ole' head. The ole' head gave Joey two hundred and fifty dollars and walked back to the rail like nothing ever happened. They never said a word to each other, only a nod here and a nod there and the deal was complete.

The ole' head gave Malik a nod! "You getting paper over here too? I gotta watch you, you'll have spots all over the 'Ville'," laughed Malik happy to see his partner stepping outside of the Projects' for once.

Joey wasn't being secretive because they both had concealed certain things from each other and it was considered proper. There was no need for each of them to know the others moves all the time. As long as the major shit was discussed neither had a problem with the other when he did something on the low. Malik pulled off only to make a quick pit-stop at the park. He spotted one of his Chocolate deluxe female friends he's was fucking. On the low Malik had already known the park on Cherry would be flooded with young chicks. He'd made it a habit of his to stop by the park at least once a day, especially when he had the Rover. He loved the attention he got from the chicks when he came through.

Joey laughed because the instant Malik pulled into the parking lot next to the park, he knew what was up. With all them young chicks running around he knew Malik had to make his presence felt. "Yo, you see the chocolate one right there in the mini-skirt, she's going to be my new jump off, she just don't know it yet," said Malik as he got out the car."You just gotta show your face, that's what this shits about!"

"Sit tight, I'll be right back." Malik bounced straight over to the Chocolate deluxe and grabbed her in a tight bear hug as he kissed her on her neck.

"What up with you sexy?"

"You! You coming to pick me up or what," asked sexy Chocolate?

Before Malik could even answer the girl, Joey was out the car and on his heels, "homey, I just got a text, and we gotta get across town real quick!"

--- --- --- --- --- ---

Amanda, Jazzy, and White-girl got out the cab on the corner of 10th and Page Street, the trio walked the short distance to one of Jazzy's peep's crib like they owned the world and the streets was the cat walk for a fashion show. All of the younger dudes out instantly took notice of the trio. They made cat-calls, whistled, and some more shit to gain their attention. This was a normal everyday thing for Amanda, she was used to it. But for the first time all the attention wasn't just hers, they could hear the group commenting on White-girl and how fat her ass was. White-girl smiled as she absorbed all the attention which made her shake her fat-ass even harder, giving the young dudes something to really talk about and remember her by. "Ya'll chill on the porch a second and let me go in and holla at Auntie," said Jazzy.

Jazzy didn't bother knocking on the front door; she let herself inside the tiny house. The smell of stale beer and feet hit her soon as she crossed the threshold almost making her gag. The first thing she noticed in the house was a lot of empty bottles of that cheap wine the drunks be drinking outside the liquor store. Empty beer cans and bottles were all over the living room floor and every end-table as far as she could see. The lady that everybody in Northwest Charlottesville referred to as Auntie was still sleep on the couch with only her under-wear on and a blanket with so many holes in it looked like Swiss Cheese.

Something stirred her awake, and when she opened her eyes she saw Jazzy, "hey girl, whatcha doing over here?"
Jazzy almost turned around and exited the small house because she could see the effects of what CRACK had done to Auntie's fragile body. She wasn't so sure that she wanted to add to it with all that CRACK she had in her purse. She really didn't want to add to Auntie's misery by giving her more of the same highly addictive substance called: CRACK! 'Focus Jazzy, Focus,' she said to herself over and over again. Tell Auntie, I...I came to holla at you, I got something for you, but if you want me to come back at a better time I'll understand," said Jazzy showing Auntie two fat dubs. Jazzy was praying that Auntie would tell her to come back later so she wouldn't have to ever come back, she wasn't as sure about this as she was when she was back at Amanda's house. However, before she could say anything else, Auntie was up and off her couch with her stem and lighter in her hand like she had it under the blanket with her. Standing only inches away from Jazzy, Auntie said, "let me see what this shit is about!"

Jazzy had to turn up her nose because Auntie's breath was kicking like

Kung-Fu. That shit smelled like, ass, dick, feet and the sewer system all combined. She had to take several steps backwards just to maintain her balance. Even after taking several steps backwards, she could now smell Auntie's body odor. It not only invaded her lungs but now the entire little living room was on fire. "This shit bet not fuck-up my damn stem, either Jazzy. You know I don't be smoking no damn garbage," said Auntie as she carefully placed one of the rocks onto her stem. 'You might not smoke no garbage but your damn breath sure do smell like you brushed your teeth with some shit and rinsed your mouth out with some sewer water.' That's what Jazzy's mind was telling her but she had bigger plans and this wasn't the time to offend nobody; at least not yet! 'Focus Jazzy...Focus, she told herself once again. Auntie used her teeth to bite open the small plastic baggy that contained the CRACK. At first she put only one of the two rocks on her stem but after smelling the CRACK she decided to put both of the rocks onto her stem. Being greedy wasn't anything new to her! Using her lighter to melt the over-flowing rocks that sat unsteady on the top of her stem so they wouldn't fall off before she could enjoy the high, she was ready to smoke. She inhaled the thick white CRACK smoke as it sent a crackling sound and the rocks disappeared from the stem. She inhaled the smoke deep into her lungs before she removed the stem from between her lips checking it to be sure the CRACK didn't clog-up her smoking device. "Is it good Auntie, is it good, "asked Jazzy over and over? Auntie turned to Jazzy and put her index finger up, she wasn't quite ready to speak yet, the CRACK had her ears ringing but she got it together quick. "I wish you'd shut the fuck-up, you fucking up my high," claimed Auntie as the CRACK transformed her body from laziness to ready to get going. "It's a-ight...It ain't bad, how much you got?"

"Slow ya role Auntie, me and my girls need a spot to chill while we get rid of this package we got. If you look out for us and help us move the shit we'll definitely look out for you...You know I got you." Jazzy knew that the CRACK was already good by Auntie's own body reaction. "But before we come up in this bitch, you gotta clean this shit up!" Auntie didn't care anything about cleaning up her little house but if CRACK was involved, she would clean from the ceiling down to the floor." I gotta do that anyway, you ain't saying nothing slick. Where's your girls at anyway?" "They outside right now! Let me go and get'em before the sun cook they ass!" Jazzy introduced Amanda and White-girl to Auntie and they all talked for close to an hour as they finally pitched in to give her a hand in cleaning the tiny house. Jazzy had her right where she wanted her and now was the time to ask her what she really wanted to know, "Auntie, who getting that paper over here now?" What? You ain't heard? That damn bitch Pam down the other end of Page got this bitch jumpin' every fuckin' night. Her and her nephews....ummm...ummm, Malik and that damn Joey be hittin' her off, then she'll send them other bitches out to hit the streets all fuckin' night long. Them bitches like some damn Zombies, the way they walk up and down this damn street all night. And to make shit worse, the CRACK the got, it's like the CRACK they use to have out here back in 1988. Ain't nobody getting no paper out here once it gets dark and they come out here." "Auntie, me and Amanda about to take a walk up to the Projects'. I'm leaving White-girl here with you so she can finish helping you straighten this shit up a little more." Jazzy gave White-girl about 10 dubs so that Auntie can make some sells if any came through before they got back. 'White-girl, make sure you get the fuckin' paper first, this Auntie and I love her to death, but that damn CRACK is a mutha-fucker, it'll make you steal from yo' momma...So be easy!"

_____
_____

Chapter 6

SILAS was still frustrated by the time he got to Angie's. With Sosa and his refusal to get some of that Project paper, he couldn't understand how or why be a hustla and turn down something so sweet as getting paper in one of the most jumpin' hoods out here? It was mind-boggling to him, he took all of his frustration out on Angie, he was fucking her so hard and fast from the back every time his flesh slammed up against hers it sounded like a small caliber gun going off.

She was moaning and screaming at the top of her lungs and begging him to stop, slow down or go easy on the pussy, but he wouldn't listen. He moved his body like a man possessed! She pulled and tugged at the edge of the mattress trying her best to get a good grip so that she could force his dick out of her to stop the pain, she loved it in a sick way, but she much rather wanted to be the aggressor and she wasn't, so she had a plan. Silas was inflicting a tremendous amount of pain on her pussy but she had one trick up her sleeve to put her in a position of power instead of being dominating but make it easier for him at the same time. It would be quite some time before he even reached his climax so her little plan had to work for her. "Silas...Silas baby, stop...Stop for one second," she said as he slowed up and she twisted her body allowing his dick to slip out of her slippery pussy. She turned around and got on all fours, with his dick in her hand she rubbed it up and down the length of her pussy getting it as wet and slippery as possible, then she eased it in her ass, turned around to look at him and said, "now fuck me like I stole something from you!"

Three hours later, he woke up with a smile on his face, the last thing he remembered was fucking Angie in the ass and having her take his dick out her ass and put it in her mouth until he shot a load of hot cum deep down her throat. He had to admit, Angie was ranked in the top 3 females he fucked in his life. The pussy was always warm, wet and tight enough to know it wasn't every day she gave that pussy away, and not to mention the head game. She could give Superhead a run for her money on any given Sunday. He looked around the room and noticed she had left him a note on the night stand beside the bed.

It said,' Dear Silas, I'm on the block. There's paper to be made and I'm getting it for you Daddy. I also left some paper in the top draw for you, it's from yesterday! Oh, one last thing: Why'd you do that to me? I hope you liked it because...Because I LOVED IT."

He got out the bed and made his way over to the dresser to see how short the paper was, the bill was only a hundred dollars! When he opened the draw he saw well over two hundred, not bad for starters, he thought to himself. It felt good to know that even while he was sleeping he was still making paper. Now only if he could get Sosa to see the bigger picture. With his stomach growling only confirmed that Angie had gotten the best of him yet another time, despite how he started out, she always found a way to switch the tide and put his ass to sleep. He smiled because there was nothing better than coming in a close second in other than fucking! He was drained and now it was time to eat. Going downstairs to the kitchen to see what was down there to eat, opening the refrigerator,' Shit', he hollered and at the same time he heard 8 or 9 shots fired from a hand gun somewhere close to her apartment. He found himself on the floor taking cover reaching for his waist but he realized that he was butt-ass naked. The sounds of gun fire was one of the things he disliked most about the Projects because it reminded him of back home and to make matters worse, the dudes in the Projects' were trigger happy. It was a constant reminder to not leave the house without his gun.

They were country but they weren't scared to bust their guns. The single most important thing next to stacking paper was staying alive! With nothing in Angie's house worth eating he flipped out his cell phone and hit speed dial for Mel's. Mel's had excellent food and was only a short distance to walk from the Projects'. They told him that his food would be ready in about twenty minutes that gave him plenty of time to shower, brush his teeth, and get dressed. Before he left out the house, he made a mental note reminding himself to tell Angie she had to straighten up around the house and put some food in the box. Even though he was cutting the twenty minutes close, he took his time walking through the Projects', even the young boys who gave him funny looks didn't move him one bit, his P89 Ruger was on his side with the safety off!

For some strange reason, he respected the fact that the young boys was willing to hold down their hood in the presence of a stranger, it reminded him of how he and Sosa came up running around in the Projects' of Newark. His thing was, if you been in one Projects', you've been in them all. Some were more hostile than others but the bottom line was, if you showed a weakness inside the concrete jungle that was your ass, simple as that. He walked with his head up as he met each pair eyes with a murderous look of his own. He walked like he was supposed to be there and it was enough to earn an undisturbed pass through the hood. He almost walked through the tunnel because he didn't want to scuff-up his new boots, but said fuck it and went through the cut because it was shorter and his stomach was growling. There was no way in hell he was walking all the way around, through the tunnel, up the steps and across the little parking lot just to get Mel's when he could cut across the train tracks save himself 8 minutes.

One of the first things he did was learn all the short-cuts and exit routes there was to know. He would get Angie to walk him all around the Projects' late at night until he was comfortable enough to go through any one of the numerous cuts. His only adjustment came as he had to lift his New York Yankees fitted cap so that he could see better. If it had been dark out, he would've had his gun in plain sight and ready for battle. He scanned the area and proceeded across the tracks to get his food. It was on his way back through the cut he saw Angie in what appeared to be a heated argument with some dude he never seen before. She wasn't screaming or yelling, what caught his attention, was the fact that she had both arms raised over up high over her head, as if she was being robbed. He slowed his pace and took in the features of the dude who was standing in front of her. He was definitely a fiend, CRACK head or DOPE fiend, which one was the question? He saw the knife in the fiend's right hand as his left hand was patting Angie's pockets. Silas had a grin on his face! In a wicked way he wanted to see how Angie would react to the situation under pressure. Would she give in easily or would she force the fiend's hand? Silas slide his gun out his waist band, and balanced the food in the bag in case he had to handle his business.

The facts still remained; if Angie got robbed it would be the same as him getting robbed, it would affect his pockets', after all, Angie had his package and it was his paper He wasn't willing to let this greasy, crusty fiend takes away something that was his directly or indirectly. The smile turned into a frown the moment he personalized the entire situation with her. He had to intervene!

The fiends' big Rambo looking knife was only inches away from Angie's stomach as he shout to her," bitch, where's the rest of it? I know you got more than one fucking dub on you...Where's the paper?" Angie gave a weak but convincing, "I, I don't have anything else, that's it right there!"

"Bitch, you think I'm stupid or something? I saw you not even five minutes ago with a bag full of CRACK, seen it with my own eyes. Matter of fact, strip bitch, take them damn clothes off," demanded the fiend.

That was Silas cue; he didn't have to hear anything else because he knew what would come next. She would be violated and he wasn't going for it. He took a few more steps in their direction and said," yo Angie, what up?" He looked directly at the fiend, "you a-ight?"

Before Angie could respond fiend said, "go 'head young blood. This shit here don't concern you, I'm about to run this bitch pockets', so why don't you mind your own business!"

Silas flashed the gun, not necessarily pointing it at the fiend but just enough so the fiend could see it before he started speaking again, "see that's where you're wrong! Normally I don't show mines unless I'm ready to use it, but today is your lucky day, everything she got is mines and I can't allow you to take something from her, it's like you're taking something from me. Now, I'm only going to ask you this one time: Do you still want to rob her?"

The fiend looked confused because he had watched Angie hustle for a couple of days and never linked her to anyone out there. He even asked around to make sure he wasn't stepping on anybody's toes he would later regret, the answer always came back the same: Nobody! The murderous look in Silas eyes told him that he didn't want to fuck with him and he was as serious as serious gets. He cursed himself for not looking into it further, he had to figure out a way to stay alive.

"Yo man, I'm sorry. You too shorty, shit is really fucked-up for me right now," he lowered the knife. He looked defeated, he inhaled and exhaled, "young blood, I wouldn't dare take nothing that belongs' to you!"

"I know you wouldn't, I couldn't allow that to happen. Something in me is telling me to spare your ass, but if I do, that ass belongs' to me. Your ass belongs' to me," said Silas.

"Man, you can go ahead and kill me now, I ain't nobody's faggot…Fuck that, kill me," said the fiend closing his eyes bracing for the impact.

Angie even looked over at Silas with a confused look on her face," I know you ain't gonna fuck him? Just shoot the mutha-fucker and get it over with. If you don't do it, give me the gun, I'll do it. This mutha-fucker was going to violate me!"

Silas raised his gun to gain the attention of both Angie and the fiend, "Ho… Ho…hold the fuck up. Angie shut the fuck up. Ya'll got me fucked up, ain't nobody on no homo shit, I said that today is your lucky day dumb-ass so that should tell you something. What I need to know is why you out here trying to rob a helpless female? I want to hear your story and that will determine the outcome."

The fiend lowered his head because he knew he was dead wrong trying to rob a female, his life depended on what came out of his mouth. "Young blood, I'm out this bitch greasy as a mutha-fucker, I'm trying to rub 2 nickels together, I ain't got shit. I lost my way; I'm way off my pivot." He looked directly in the eyes of Silas," if I was fucking with somebody like you, I wouldn't have to be out preying on weak females. You said it yourself, today is my lucky day, right? I know it wouldn't be nothing for you to put 2 in my head and not miss a beat and go about your business; I can look in your eyes and tell you that much. But we both know I'm worth more to you alive than I'll ever be dead!"

"What's that shit supposed to mean to me," asked Silas?

"Like I said, I lost my way. If given the opportunity I could be of some help to you out here...I'm a hustla, been doing this shit since before I can even remember, if you give me the chance I won't disappoint you. All I'm asking for is a shot?

Somewhere in Silas sick mind something clicked and he started believing in his own vision of taking over the Projects'. He would use the very people who really make the CRACK game go around: The fiends'! "Angie, give this nigga 2 dubs' for me."

"What?" Angie shot Silas a look that said fuck you I ain't giving his ass shit. She knew that she was walking on thin ice by questioning him or his judgment, knowing the consequences of that; she decided to just do what he asked her to do. Reaching in her bra, she retrieved a bag full of CRACK, she saw the fiend watching her closely," what the fuck your dumb-ass looking at?" She took out her frustration on the fiend because she knew she couldn't take it out on Silas. She threw the 2 dubs at his feet.

Silas asked the fiend his name and where he was from, finding out that he went by the name Philly and that's where he was from, he felt some type of Kin-ship with him since they both were from up North." Listen, go do your thang and come to this address once it gets dark and I'LL hook you up then," said Silas. Philly looked at Silas," I'm saying, you already know what time it is with me, ain't no need in me going somewhere else. If you let me use your bathroom I could do my thang and we can get busy right away, we don't have to wait until it get dark. This shit is a once in a life time type of thang and I ain't trying to let you out my sight, for real." Angie looked over at Silas like he was crazy, just five minutes ago this nigga was about to violate her and now Silas is offering him my address. If anything, she wanted to kill this nigga herself, but she took it in stride. The three of them walked back to her house and nobody said a word. Angie walked way in front of them, the moment she heard Silas agree to let him use her bathroom, she walked off! "Smart man...Smart man," said Silas, as they walked out the cut together. Putting his gun back in his waist band Silas asked him," you been getting paper over here?" Philly didn't mind all the questions from Silas, he actually welcomed them he needed to Silas to believe in him because he'd stopped believing in himself a long time ago." I'm a hustla homey, I go wherever the paper takes me and right now it's a lot of paper over here. The problem is the youngins' though, they out here on some bullshit. It's straight cash-n-carry with them. That's why I was on that bullshit with shorty just now."

Silas was shaking his head in agreement to let Philly know that he understood where he was coming from. "So, it's safe to say your problem is that you don't have to work to hustle with?" It was like Silas had been reading Philly's mind because that's exactly how he felt. The young boys out there was scared to death to trust him with a package in his hand, thinking he's going to walk off with it and leave them with having to pay the bill on it. Since his pockets were empty it was damn near impossible for him to eat out there unless he put the bullshit in the game like he did with Angie." You hit the nail on the head! That's exactly my problem, now if I had somebody like you in my corner that wouldn't be my problem anymore." Silas started laughing out loud, "a-ight...a-ight Philly, I told you today was you lucky day, so you can go 'head with all that ass kissing. It is what it is. I'm definitely going to put you on; we both can help each other. Now, that shit with Angie, consider that you're first and last pass with me. If you fuck my paper up and I have to come looking for you, I'm going to put so many holes in your ass you ain't going to know where the fuck the blood's coming from. You don't have no room for error...You want a shot? This it, the rest is up to you!" "Bet. All you gotta do is keep the work coming and I'LL be out here on these streets, 24-7, point-blank...Period. Just to let you know, I understand your point completely, not only did you spare my life today, you're also giving me a job and for that I'm grateful." Silas looked Philly up and down for the first time and he was slightly impressed. He could tell that at one point in time that Philly had taken pride in his appearance because even though the sneakers' he had on were old, they looked like he's been spending some time trying to get them to look like something. His jeans were ironed and his shirt was neat, and the smell of cheap cologne reeked from his body." At least you're half-way clean. You could stand some new sneakers and a few pair of jeans but other than that, you'll make it."

By the time they crossed over the middle driveway, Angie had disappeared. There was a bunch of youngins' out there and they were talking to two females that Silas had never seen before in the Projects'. The taller of the two gave him the eye, he didn't pay her any attention, and he could tell what she was about with one glance. She wasn't about shit, but the other one, well she wasn't shit either but she still caught his attention. "Hey Philly, What's good, won't you come and holla at me, I got that fire" said the taller of the two?

"That's good to know Jazzy, I might just do that. What you doing over here, I ain't never seen you over here; you're usually over Prospect, What's up with that?" He knew that Jazzy was a stone cold freak from experience, she was down for whatever, especially if that paper was straight. A few months back he had caught her out there on the late night, she had some fire CRACK and he was broke. She presented the opportunity of a life time; he could still here her voice, 'Philly, I'll give you this fifty if you come in the house and eat my pussy until I cum.' She was talking to him from the up-stairs window, he agreed and when she opened the door all she had on was a towel and her body was still dripping with water like she just got out the shower. He came in, sat her big yellow ass right there on the kitchen table and ate her pussy like his life had depended on it. By the time he was leaving out of Jazzy's house, he not only had the fifty she promised him but another one to go with it because not only did he eat her pussy he fucked her all over that house that night. He looked up at her and she was still looking at him but not at his face, her eyes were glued on where his dick would be if he was naked.

"You know me Philly, a bitch out here trying to make a few dollars," said Jazzy talking to Philly but staring at Silas the whole time. "Philly, who's your people with you? I ain't never seen you with him before!" Silas knew she was sizing him up the whole time but he wasn't paying her any attention, he knew her type. She had trouble written all over her face, but the other chick with her, she could get it. His focus was on those exotic features and her tight waist. One look in the other girls' eyes and he couldn't help but stare. Luckily she was too busy engaged in another conversation to notice he was staring; he made a mental note to ask Philly about her later. "You can ask him yourself," said Philly with a slight attitude. This was one of the things he hated most about Jazzy, she would front like she didn't really know him all that well in public or ignore him all together but behind closed doors and a nose full of powder cocaine, she be begging him for the dick. Silas had detected something in Philly's voice and his body language that told him it was more than meets the eye when it came to him and Jazzy.

He didn't say anything, took one last look at the chick with the exotic features and started walking back towards Angie's apartment. He did catch a glimpse of Jazzy's ass, she was holdn' to, but too much baggage came with her, he could tell. His aggressive nature started to take over when he had to force himself to keep walking because shorty with the exotic feature's was calling him, at least in his mind she was, but he didn't know who she was talking to so instead of possibly getting her in some bullshit he kept it movin'. He formulated a new plan in his head within seconds: Philly would put him down with her A.S.A.P.

When Silas felt they had gotten far enough away from everybody he began to question Philly about the exotic chick with the funny colored eyes," I can see that you and the tall chick got a thing going on with each other, so I know you already know her, but what's good with the other chick...That's what I need to know?" Had she not been involved in a conversation with the young boy already he would've pushed-up on her, but he didn't want to get shorty in any trouble, dude could be her boyfriend or anything, so he would let Philly tell him the story on shorty. Philly could detect the eagerness in his voice and knew that Amanda had captured his attention the same way she does to any man she comes across for the first time." Yeah, I use to cop from the chick Jazzy at one point and time, but the other chick...Amanda, they both from Prospect! They like that nose candy too, and from what I been hearing: Amanda go like that for that nose candy, Jazzy to, but they say Amanda is the one," said Philly trying to throw salt in the game. By the time they got down to Angie's apartment, Silas didn't want to go inside; instead he sat outside on the porch. He could still see the chick Amanda and Jazzy up near the first driveway still talking to the youngins' out there. His mind was locked on getting to know who this Amanda chick was, from looking closely at her body he couldn't tell she had a problem with her nose, it hadn't affected her body. It didn't surprise him one bit, now-a-days' everybody and they momma messed with that nose candy, but he needed to find out on his own and that meant he needed to speak with her one on one! When Angie came out on the porch and saw Philly sitting there like he owned the damn place she almost went on him again.

She looked over at Silas with much attitude and said," so what's up with this," pointing at Philly? "This bastard wanted to rape and murder my ass not even twenty minutes ago and now you got this greasy mutha-fucker sitting on my damn porch. You must've lost your rabbit-ass mind just like his dumb-ass!" Silas didn't pay Angie no attention, he looked over at Philly and said,"yo the bathroom is at the top of the steps, you can't miss it...Go 'head, take care of your business," now focusing his attention back to Angie. When Philly went up-stairs and closed the bathroom door, Angie whispered,

"Silas, are you that crazy? We don't know this nigga from a can of spray paint and you already got him roaming all through my damn house...What's wrong with you?" "Be easy baby-girl, I got this! Bring my food out here for me. By the way I got something for you too," he said easing the tension between them. "Won't you come out here and eat with me?" "I'm good, I ate something before I left, plus I already got my daily requirement of protein for the day, if you know what I mean," said Angie equally as playful as he was. For some reason she really felt safe when he was around. Silas had got real serious and wanted her to know how serious he was so he stared deep in her eyes, "come closer," he said pulling her by the arm as she landed on his lap." I might not know this nigga Philly personally but I definitely know his kind. He'll swallow blood and lose his life before he ever cross either of us again, baby the man needed a chance and we're going to give it to him. We'll give him the chance that nobody else is willing to give the man and for that he'll forever be grateful, just trust me on this one. I know it's hard for you but you gotta trust me on this. Do you trust me?" Of course I trust you, I trust you with my life even though you told me the game wasn't meant for trust, I trust you, though, she said giving him a quick peck on the cheek.

Jazzy had noticed how intense the conversation had gotten between Amanda and the young boy out there, but she remained focus on Silas and Philly as they walked off. Even though the young boys out there wasn't the kind of hustla she wanted, she did enjoy their company, they had her cracking up laughing, but if she wanted an average around the way lil' nigga, she could've kept her ass right over Prospect and scooped one of them little niggaz up in no time. She was actually wanting to stand there and talk because she seen some dude with Philly who she never seen before and she knew it was only a matter of time that he would say something to her, but he didn't and when she looked back up he was gone. She knew right off the bat from his matching Prada sneakers, shades, and the way he walked that he was from out of town and that's what caught her attention. And the one thing that intrigued her most, was the fact that the Project dudes where very selective as to who they let in the hood and wasn't that kind to out of towners. Malik had flashed across her mind while she was observing the dude with Philly but soon as dude smiled, Malik went out her mind, that fast. There was adventure in the dude's eyes, but she could tell that his soul was troubled but she was drawn to him nonetheless. Her mind kept telling her to speak to him but the words wouldn't come out; she couldn't fix her mouth to say what her mind was thinking. She just starred on the low, but lost focus when the young boy made her laugh. It was one of the young boys talking to Jazzy who broke her attention and forced her out of her dream when he said," you Jazzy, when you gone let me hit that?" Extra diva style, Jazzy rolled her eyes at what he just said because she wasn't really interested in none of the young boys since Silas had walked pass.

"Let you hit what? You must be talking to somebody else because I know damn well you can't be talking to me on no bullshit like that." She had called his bluff, hoping he would back down. "I'm trying to hit that just like I said, don't act like you don't get down like that either, and "he said busting her out." So what's up, "he said full of confidence? Jazzy was growing frustrated by the second because the young boy was taking focus and time away from Silas." Oh, you trying to hit this," she said pointing at her own ass? "Fo' sho'! I'm definitely trying to hit that ass," looking Jazzy up and down. Cutting through the bullshit Jazzy was ready to let the young boy know exactly where she stood since it was no big secret how she went." Fuck the bullshit, if your paper is correct, we can fuck, all that other shit is in the way. So what I need to know, is your paper straight little boy, because I'll damn sure take it?" He stepped so close to her that she thought he was going to hit her, invading her space, he said," baby-girl, my paper is right and best believe that my dick game is all that!" "Let a bitch hold something then?"

The young boy already knew Jazzy's bio and how she got down, he knew she was trying to put him on the spot. His response would depend on whether or not he was going to get the pussy. He took a deep breath and relax himself, looked at everybody who had gathered around, choosing his words carefully he said to her," I'm trying to fuck, take this," throwing two-hundred to the ground. "I want the pussy so I don't mind paying for what I want. What's up?"

Jazzy had called his bluff hoping that when she mentioned the cash that he would back off. She knew them youngins' in the Projects' didn't mind pushing that paper out there for some weed, powder, or some drinks and possibly a hotel room, but straight cash usually pushed them away. This nigga is unpredictable, she thought to herself. She was thinking on her feet," you sure you can stand to lose your paper? Don't fuck around and fuck-up your re-up," she said trying to get him to change his mind. "For that pussy, this paper is yours! I look at it like this; it's an investment to me because once I beat that pussy up the first time around; you'll be paying me the next round. I can see your sexy ass now running all over the Projects' looking for a nigga like me with a flash light in the day time." Everybody who had gathered around listening to one of their own go head to head with the infamous Jazzy from Prospect started laughing. She gave him her best shot when she mentioned the cash but even that didn't budge the young boy, now the joke was on her. Needing to get the crowd back on her side she pulled out four hundred of her own paper then told him," put two more to what you already got and I'll make you a deal. I'll bet you that I can make you cum in 2 minutes flat, winner takes it all, now put yo' paper where yo' mouth is," she said grinning like she won the war.

The young boy gathered the other two hundred quick; everybody wanted to see how this thing was going to jump off." Here is mine, now when you want to do this, tonight?" Jazzy looked at the young boy like he was crazy, "tonight? Naw little nigga I'm about my paper, my shit is already on the pavement, whip that little dick out right now and get ya boy right there to time the shit. You'll be cuming in 2 minutes flat so don't waste my time," she knew if nothing else the young boy was going to respect her after this one way or the other.

Everybody out there knew the young boy was packing and could hold his own, everybody except Jazzy. He didn't hesitate for one second. He knew he was hung like a horse and now it was time to show this bitch what time it was with him. By the time he pulled out his horse dick, Jazzy and Amanda both looked at each other in amazement. His shit wasn't even hard yet and that shit was bigger than any dick she's ever seen in real life. The young boy smiled and said," ladies, meet horse. I call him horse because when he's hard he's like 13 inches, give or take an inch. This shit looks just like a horse dick don't it Jazzy? Now bring that yellow ass on over here and let me see what you working with girl, "he said while he stroked his massive dick in front of everybody out there. Jazzy was hesitant but she eased over in his direction. Out of nowhere somebody yelled out, "Po-Po!" Two marked police cars and one detective car was coming up the driveway. Since mostly everybody out there was dirty they scattered at the sight of the unmarked detective car more so than the regular police car. It was the Detectives everybody was concerned about and that's why they broke camp like that. All the detectives in Charlottesville were well known and had no problem setting you up setting you up if the situation called for it, so nobody was standing around trying to figure out what they were going to do whether they were dirty or not, situations like this called for you to be on your A-game and nothing less.

"Shit," said the young boy as he pulled-up his pants and snatched the paper up from the ground. "Ya'll better bounce-these mutha-fuckers don't play fair over this way," he said handing Jazzy her half of the paper that he picked-up. He was gone before they had a chance to say anything. Amanda with her slick-ass had already picked-up over a hundred dollars the instant everybody looked down the driveway. When they hollered Po-Po she grabbed the paper and that's it. Jazzy counted her paper and saw that she was short, when she turned to call youngin back Amanda grabbed her by the arm, "come on here girl, I already got your paper right here!" They walked back towards Run Street not worrying about the Po-Po because for them to come after them they would have to get out of their cars and walk and that just wasn't happening in the Projects'. "Bitch, I know you wasn't going to suck that boy dick right there in the middle of the driveway, was you," asked Amanda unsure of how far Jazzy was willing to go for the cash? "And you know I was! At least that was before that nigga pulled his pants down and pulled out that King Kong mutha-fucker out. Hell no! That little nigga fuck around and bust the back of my throat wide open with all that meat he had on him. Did you see that shit girl," giggled Jazzy happy that she had been saved by the police.

"Did I, what type of question is that? That thang was fat as a mutha-fucker and long as 2 city blocks...He should have his ass up in one of them porno flicks or some shit. I'm saying though, his little ass would've torn your ass up and not to mention if you gave'em the pussy... Your ass would be up in the emergency room for sure," said Amanda cracking up.

"Yeah, he probably would've got the best of my ass on that one, but best believe, I would've sucked the skin off that big mutha-fucker for that cash girl,

I don't know what you talking about. I would've been right there down on my knees choking and all but I bet I would've got that paper. That nigga was cumimh in 2 minutes regardless, even if I had to get you to help my ass!" "That's crazy," said Amanda looking unsure of helping her in that situation. "Amanda, let me put a little game in your life, I know you already know this shit but I'm going to tell you again just in case. Niggaz all over Charlottesville know how we get down for ours, this shit ain't no fuckin' secret. But what I learned a long time ago was to never let them niggaz get the chance to say shit about Jazzy. Shit, if that paper correct fuck it, I'll be a whore, a slut, a dumb bitch, freak and whatever else they want to call me; I'll be that for that occasion but when I'm done, I'll look that same nigga in the eyes and say to him real slow: PAY ME NIGGA! That's all a bitch like me gotta say and guess what? Those niggaz love that shit just like I do and they pay me, so don't get it twisted girlfriend." "I can feel you on that because when I'm in my zone, I could care less what a nigga gotta say about me or how I get mines to be real with you. But right there in the middle of the driveway; Bitch you got balls!" They slowed their pace as they got farther away from the action of the police and encountered another group of young boys who was posted up, down by Run Street, they did everything to gain their attention but they kept it moving.

Amanda saw Silas on the porch eating some food and she remembered catching a glimpse of him in the 1st driveway, he looked like he didn't have a care in the world. She tapped Jazzy on the shoulder," yo, you know dude right there?"
Jazzy sucked her teeth because she knew Amanda was about to throw some salt in the game with the new playa on the scene. "Naw, I don't know dude, matter of fact bitch, won't you go over there and put your gansta down…See what's really good with this clown ass nigga," she said knowing that Amanda rarely ever approached dudes. She always thought she was too fly for that, but Jazzy knew otherwise "I ain't going over there…He could be at his girl's house or anything. I'll catch that nigga around, from the looks of it, he ain't going anywhere. He got hustla written all over his face "You want to wait on that fine ass nigga, hoping you'll see his ass again? Don't you know, weight broke the wagon and tomorrow ain't promised to any of us?" Who the fuck you calling a stupid bitch anyway," shouted Amanda? She stopped dead in her tracks because Jazzy been throwing shot's at her all day long and she wasn't going for it cousin or no cousin. She was ready to dig up in Jazzy's ass now. Jazzy had known that

Amanda's weak spot was to call her a stupid bitch because her mother use to verbally abuse her and constantly called her a stupid bitch like it was her first and last name. Her mother always blamed her for stopping her life because she got pregnant at the age of fifteen. Amanda would fight a bull for calling her stupid! "Girl, I ain't mean nothing by that shit, stop being so up-tight and just go over there and holla at dude," said Jazzy trying her best to soften up her cousin because she knew if she said the wrong thing that Amanda would dig in that ass.

If it hadn't been for Silas winking at her and making her focus all of her attention on his fine ass instead of Jazzy, she would've punched her dead in the face. He had her complete and undivided attention without saying the first word to her; it was like his eyes kept drawing her into his gaze. Her mind was telling her to speak but she couldn't bring herself to make the words come out her mouth. She couldn't make a sound! He never said one word either, he only stared and smiled after winking at her several times to let it be known that if the situation was different he would holla. At that moment she made a promise to herself that if she did see him again and he wasn't with a female that she would holla at him without question, and that wasn't even her style. "AMANDA... AMANDA...AMANDA," screamed Jazzy from a distance. She could hear her name being called and knew that it was Jazzy calling her but she couldn't take her focus off that fine ass nigga sitting there on that porch, Bitch, where the fuck you going? W&W Market ain't open no damn more!" That was it and Amanda couldn't take it no longer, she came out of her trance with fire in her eyes and a chip on her shoulder. "Why the fuck you keep calling me out my name and screaming like you've lost your damn mind for," question Amanda? "If you were paying attention to where you was going I wouldn't have to be out here hollering and screaming your name like I'm fucking crazy!" Amanda looked where she was standing and how far away Jazzy was, they were clearly going in opposite directions," shit, my bad, bitch! You still don't have to be hollering like that." Amanda had to walk back up the little sidewalk and pass where the guy was still sitting on the porch eating his food. He looked to be observing the whole situation because he kept staring at her. The closer she got the more nervous she became. What his cool and calm demeanor didn't show her was that he was just as nervous as she was when she started walking back in his direction. He had to coach himself to even holla at her, but he was cool about the whole thing. He made his move when she was directly in front of the porch ready to make the left, "excuse me sexy, but can I holla at you a second," he asked nervously? She put her index finger up to her chest, "who me?" "Yeah you...You the only sexy thang around, hold-up a minute, if that's alright with you?" She was blushing hard and loved the way his voice was sounding, it was like sweet music to her ear's and she stopped dead in her tracks, "you can come holla at me, but what I want to know is why you only want to holla at me for a minute," she said raising her eye brow?

When he stood up her attention and focus was where his dick print was in his pants and she liked what she saw. When he got close enough he asked her, "so, what's your name sexy?" "Amanda!" She kept is short and sweet, "and yours?"

"My name is Silas, nice to meet you. So, Amanda, you from around here or what, because this is my first time seeing you and I'm usually very observant? I could never miss such a beautiful face as yours." "No. I'm not from this side of town, and that makes two of us because you're not bad yourself and I know that I wouldn't forget such a handsome face as yours. I'm from Prospect...And you, where you from?" "What you mean that makes two of us," he asked? "I haven't seen you either before today and I don't miss a handsome face for nobody. But I just told you that so why you gotta ask me that all over again you ain't paying any attention to what I'm saying are you?" Silas was falling and he was falling fast. This has never happened to him before and he was feeling like he was losing his breath and he couldn't say what was on his mind. It took him a full 30 seconds to gather himself and a few deep breaths to relax his mind." So what you doing on this side of town if you're from Prospect?"

Jazzy was already tired of the bullshit they were playing with each other and decided they both needed some help getting the party to second base. She had the perfect opportunity to add her two-cent, "she'll be doing you if that paper is straight!" He looked from Amanda to Jazzy and then back to Amanda asking her, "Who the hell is this?" That's my nosey-ass cousin; don't pay her crazy-ass no attention. This bitch certified for-real!" "Oh, believe me, I wasn't!" He gave Jazzy that murderous look that said to her 'stay out my way'. 'What kind of terms she on anyway, talking to you like that?"

Amanda rolled her eyes and said to him," I don't wanna talk about her, but what's good with you, though? Where you from anyway?" With a straight face he simply said, "Louisa!" She didn't know if he was serious or not, he had a good poker face. Her smile quickly disappeared and turned into a frown," we gonna start this off with lies right off the bat, huh?" She looked him dead in the eyes then said, "I'm going to ask you this one last time. You got an up-top accent so I know damn well you ain't from no damn country; so, if you want to continue this conversation with me I suggest you be honest. You acting like I'm the mutha-fuckin' FEDS or something, you need to go 'head with that bullshit!" Silas knew she wasn't green and that there was no need to be playing around with her but at the same time there was no need in telling her all his personal information on the first day. What if he never talked to her again? So he did what any playa in his position would do, he changed the subject,' how about we talk about where I'm from over dinner or something?" "You asking me out?" Placing both of her hands on her hips, ghetto style. "Ain't no question! I'm definitely asking you out," he said with confidence as he took his Prada shades off to get a better look." And I'm not taking no for an answer, so give me your cell number." Taking his own phone out his pocket and scrolling down to his phone book, he stored her number into his phone under Sexy. Then he hit the send button just to make sure she didn't give him no bogus number. When he heard her phone ringing he was satisfied," I'll call you tonight! Don't get too busy where you can't answer your phone either," he said laughing. "I got some business to handle right now."

Amanda took one last look at him from head to toe and was happy with what she saw and was already looking forward to his call; " you do that!" She took notice of everything he had on, from the Prada shades to the Prada sneakers. That was a dead give-away, she knew he was from either, Philly, New York, or New Jersey. Just as he was about to enter the apartment Amanda said out loud, "take care of yourself out here Silas!" When she looked up to see where Jazzy was she was nowhere in sight, she was long gone, all the way at the entrance of the Projects' making the left turn onto Page. By the time she finally caught up with her she was already in front of Auntie's house. And the first thing out of Jazzy's mouth was, "what's up with him? He ballin' or what?"

"He ain't talking about shit right now, he's supposed to be calling me later tonight and soon as I talk to him I'll give you the report; would you like that report to be written or typed," said Amanda letting Jazzy know that she was close to crossing that line. She was still a little pissed that Jazzy had called her stupid earlier anyway. "Where that nigga from anyway, he looks like one of them Brooklyn dudes... Those niggaz keep a fresh pair of Prada sneakers on their feet." Jazzy's mouth was going faster than her little brain could go but she never once took the time to see that Amanda wasn't even paying her any attention no more. Then out of nowhere Amanda screamed at her," bitch, if you wanted to know where the nigga was from you should've asked him yourself, you was standing right there all in his grill!" Jazzy lowered her head as they walked in the house together! Jazzy was feeling some type of way about how Amanda always got all the attention from the guys and her ego got the best of her. What pissed her off the most about Amanda was that when she wasn't even trying to get attention she somehow seemed to get it and Jazzy hated her for it. She looked over at Amanda and that happy look she had on her face made her even madder," Amanda, don't get this shit fucked-up, ain't no knight in shining armor in the hood for us, the only mutha-fuckers who sweep you off your feet around her is the police. This the Projects' so you better keep your mind on this paper because that's the only thing that matters in the hood."

"So what the fuck all that supposed to mean? Bitch, don't try to play me just because you know a little something about this CRACK shit and you supposed to be teaching us how this CRACK shit go. Don't worry about me, I got this pussy game down to a science so miss me with your bullshit, you fuckin' hater!" Amanda walked over to the sofa and sat beside White-girl, "hey bitch, you sleeping on the job on the first day," joked Amanda? White-girl took out a wad of paper and threw it on the little end-table, "Auntie went up to Grady or some shit, but she made this before she left. Damn Jazzy, your big mouth will fuck-up a wet dream." Jazzy picked the paper up and put it in her purse and didn't say anything else about the paper. White-girl made a mental note of that because she was expecting her to break bread with them. Amanda slide up the step's because she had enough of Jazzy's big mouth, plus she couldn't get her mind off of Silas. She locked herself in the bathroom and took her cell out and dialed the last number that called her phone. "Silas, this Amanda...You busy?"

CHAPTER 7

THE next morning Joey was awaken by the sound of his phone vibrating on the night stand right next to the bed, remembering that he was still in the hotel room, he had to check his watch for the time and not the night stand where a clock would have been had he been in his own spot. It was 7:30 in the morning, he answered, "yo what up?" Knowing that it could be only two people calling him this early in the morning and he was certain that one of them was still sleep.

'Yeah...Yeah, I'm awake now! Half an hour...I'll be there," he said before hanging up.

Instead of getting out the warm bed, he laid back down resting on the King size bed staring at the ceiling and thinking about what the connect could wanted with him this early in the morning? The connect wanted him to meet at the Villa, a small breakfast spot near the University of Virginia---It was going to take him a little longer than 30 minutes to make it all the way down 29 South from the Double Tree Hotel. What the hell was I thinking? The only way that he even stood a chance of making it to the Villa in 30 minutes was he would have to leave right now, no shower, skip brushing his teeth, or taking care any of his hygiene the proper way and that was out the question for him. He had to call the connect back, "make that an hour," he barked into the phone and hung-up before the connect could protest. This mutha-fucker is crazy, he knows damn well that I never make it in before the sun rise and he's wanting to have a damn meeting? He looked back at his cell phone noticing the connect had called him back, however it wasn't the same number he had just called from a few minutes ago. He's definitely slick as oil! This mutha-fucker got six or seven different number's he used to call my phone but as for me, I can only reach his ass at one particular number....He got game.

Looking over at the other side of the bed, he saw the world's most beautiful woman that God has ever created. She looked very peaceful, even after their early morning sexapade, she was still radiant. Her name was Terri and she meant everything to Joey! They meet the summer before last in Virginia Beach during beach week. She was fresh out of High school and on her way to attend the University of Virginia. It took him all of 24 hours to figure out that she was the woman of his dreams. Not only was she beautiful but she was extremely intelligent. Over the course of their week in Virginia Beach they did everything together, they racked up hundreds of hours of pure conversation. He wasn't nowhere near the caliber of hustla he is today.

With a dream and a plan in his own mind to become a millionaire, and it was Terri who convinced him that he could be anything he wanted to become, she never knew he wanted to become the biggest Drug Dealer in Charlottesville. She was going to the University of Virginia to pursue business and he wanted to further his business in the streets. He made sure that her money was no good as long as he was around and he never once got the impression that she was a gold-digger or a shiesty female. It was just the opposite for him when it came to Terri. On like the third day, he found out that she had never even dated a guy like him, she usually dealt with the nerds because they kept their nose in a book and not between her legs as she said her mother warned her about.

That was well over a year ago and here they were, still together, still having wonderful conversations, she was the best and to top it off...She played her position to the T !She never meddled in his affairs and the conversation never came up as to what he did to earn his money. To her it didn't matter because she would tell him that once she graduated from College that she would be making enough money to take care the both of them. He loved to listen to her when she talked about her future.

Another thing that really impressed him about her was the fact that everything she learned in school from her Professor's she would teach it to him, even testing him on the information she taught him. She made certain he read all the text books she got from her classes' even when he wasn't interested, he did it because she asked him. It was her Tax code book and operating a legitimate business in the cut throat world of business. She wasn't stupid, in her mind she really knew what he did to earn his money.

He was a street dude and he had to get his money the same way most street dudes get theirs and that was another reason why she stressed so hard that he become familiar with all the different Tax codes and what was considered Tax evasion. She noticed in Joey a few months back, she believed it had something to do with that drug-dealing gang from the Projects'. Even her Professor held an entire class on illegal drugs and how to track their money so that the Government could build a case against them. What impressed her most was the fact was that her Professor told her, that most street dealers wasn't very smart when it came to managing their money; they showed it rather concealing it. No matter what her Joey done out in the streets to earn his money, she knew deep in his heart that he was a good guy and not the monster her Professor tried to make every drug dealer out to be.

He didn't deserve to be used or tricked by the Government as her Professor had said, and so it became her passion to teach Joey the rules the government played by so that he wouldn't allow himself to be trapped by their wicked ways. Their conversations increased more when it came to money and thus they came up with a plan. Instead of her taking on an internship with a big Corporation in Maryland for the summer, she would instead intern for Joey using real money! She had taught him so many different ways to build Capital but it was always on paper using the DOW, Real-Estate, and the New York Stock Exchange.

This was around the same time Malik bought the Range Rover; he tried to talk some sense into him. He wanted the both of them to put up twenty-five thousand and let Terri go to work with the money. He had to convince her to put the portfolio in her name, but she came up with a dummy corporation to build up. As we now know, Malik never got around to putting up his share of the money, he wasn't too keen on giving no female that type of money and he wasn't the one fucking her. He bought the Range Rover and Joey was the CEO of a successful dummy Corporation, he had a variety of stocks: high end yield stocks, stock index, government T-bonds, Exxon, and the construction company that was also a dummy corporation. Nobody knew that Joey was in this relationship with Terri, except of course Malik.

The connect had his own way of finding out as well. Joey was very careful to keep Terri as far away from the hood as possible. The day she taught him the difference between what an ASSET is and what is considered a Liability, he knew she was an ASSET and knew he had to keep her away. That's one of the very reason's they were in a hot right now, he tried his best not to stay in the same spot twice with her. With her still living in her dorm he was a nomad! And that's the way he wanted it to look on paper, no apartment, no house, no car, he owned nothing that could be tracked back to his government name. Everything went through the dummy corporation; there was no link between him and her either. It was all a part of their plan, if they could hide information at this stage it would be nothing when it was really time to hide things.

Joey got out the shower, threw on some black nautica sweat pants, black tee, and some black on black ones. His Fendi shades completed his attire; he opted not to carry his gun since it was so early in the morning.

When he leaned in to kiss Terri, she woke-up at his slightest touch, "where you off to this early?"

"I have something to take care of, won't you get some rest, I shouldn't be too long. When I get back we'll get breakfast," he said as he kissed her good-bye.

She giggled like a school girl on the first kiss," after what you done to me last night...I mean this morning, I'm definitely need a few more hours of rest. Make sure you are careful out there and hurry up back to me--I miss you already," she whined playfully!

"You know I will." When he got in the hallway he had to turn right back around just as the elevator came. When he inserted his card into the door he told her," babe, come put the safety latch on the door!"

Reluctantly she forced her tired bones to move so that she could put the safety latch on the door because he wouldn't leave until he actually saw her get out the bed. "Always worried about your wife, ain't you? Don't nobody want me but you baby, now give me another kiss for making me get out the bed----PPPLLLease!" Satisfied that the room was locked and secured he made his way back to the elevator. Terri was his priceless jewel and it allowed him to relax knowing that she was safe and out of harm's way. A smile crept across his face just thinking about how lucky he was to have her in his life. Outside, he admired Terri's Triple-Black Infiniti G37, with the very expensive 20" inch chrome shoes. The car came to life as he cranked the ignition as it seemed to purr as it idled. Lauryn Hill's unplugged live CD was playing; he knew she was one of Terri's favorite artists, because she had forced him to listen to it with her on more than one occasion.

She was more into that conscious, positive and liberating music, he likes it as well, but right now, this occasion called for something different, something more up-tempo. He found his B-Stacks CD and lifted it out of its case, replacing Ms. Hill with one of Charlottesville's own! Every time he listened to one of B-Stacks songs he couldn't help but wonder about the impact he would have certainly had on the Rap Industry. He was extremely talented and had a gift; however, it was his realness that was his curse because it led to his down-fall. With Government Henchmen, the trap was laid and B-Stacks became one of the worst so-called Drug Dealers Charlottesville has seen in the last 20 years. The heavy bass, and his lyrics forced Joey to bob his head to the beat, 'Damn, homey, is life in prison the cost we really have to pay for playing this game called: HUSTLIN"?'

Weaving in and out of the light traffic all the way down 29 South, he pulled into the parking lot of the Villa before he knew it. Looking at the clock on the dash board, he still had five minutes to spare. He gave the entire parking lot the once over wondering which car was the connect in today? It was pointless, because the connect drove a different car every day, so he was wasting his time trying to guess what he was driving. He sat back in the seat and closed his eyes as he listened to B-Stacks for another minute or so before getting out the car and heading into the Villa to meet with the connect.

Soon as he entered the Villa the connect was sitting almost directly in front of him facing the door. The connect stood as soon as Joey got close, giving him a firm hand shake and a warm embrace.

"Joey, how's life treating you these days?"

"Everything is good...Chillin' as usual," said Joey as he eased away from the connects embrace as he felt the Cannon on the connect's waist. He cursed himself under his breath for not having his. The connect had a pleasant smile on his face and his eyes were very tentative as he looked out towards the parking lot, "that's really good Joey! How's Malik doing these days?"

"Actually, Malik's doing very well; he's even slowed down a notch or two." He eyed the connect, exhaled slowly before he began speaking again, "it's crazy early, what do I owe this pleasure," he said cutting through the chase?

"Have a seat Joey!" The connect kept looking out the front window as if he was expecting someone or something to happen.

"Infiniti G37, right? That's you right?" Joey hated it when the connect ignored his questions and there was no use in asking again, he was more than certain he heard him the first time. He went along with the connect and his games because he knew that was the only way that he'll figure out the real purpose of this meeting.

"Naw, that ain't me, that's the ole' ladies, too rich for my blood!"

"Ole' lady, huh? I see you're very careful when it comes to your ole' lady, you keep her as far away from the excitement as possible. I do notice that she has great taste," said the connect with a devilish grin.

"What's that supposed to mean," asked Joey with anger in his voice?

"Ease-up, Killa! Ease-up, you have to recognize a compliment when one's thrown at you. My point being, I've seen a lot of guys who use to be out here like we are now, but in their travel they took a liking to the wrong female and now they're no longer with us. Catch my drift? But you Joey, you'll never make that type of mistake, will you?"

Joey thought this was the perfect time to play the connect's little game, perhaps he could even beat him at it. He decided not to give him any feed-back about his choice in women. He just sat there across the booth staring at the connect, not even blinking.

"Joey, there's a new face in the hood, do you know anything about it or who this guy is?"

"Should I?" Joey thought to himself, that if the connect knew that much then why the hell was he asking him all the questions?

"Of course, you should definitely know Joey! Of course!" The connect began shaking his head," it's still your hood, ain't it?"

"Haven't nothing changed with my numbers, matter of fact, we're doing even better that what we were doing awhile back. So tell me, why should I even be concerned about a new face it the hood," Joey fired back at the connect?

"You may very well be correct about that Joey. However, it's not always all about the paper, sometimes, just sometimes it's about staying alive. Point in case: Where's your gun?"

"I left it at the spot, so what?"

"Any one of these days could be your last, you have to understand that it's real out here in these Mean-Streets and your gun is like you're sneakers, if you have to put them on, then your heat is also required Joey!"

Joey always frustrated whenever he felt the connect talked to him like he was a little child. "Man, I ain't got beef with nobody out there, I can go to anyone of these hoods in Charlottesville and niggaz show me love. Why the hell should I be carrying a gun everywhere I go? To me, that's like asking for trouble."

The connect knew that if he wanted Joey to see the big picture that it wouldn't be wise to meet Joey's aggression with the same aggression. Allowing Joey to even think that he was frustrated would be an understatement so he spoke real slow and calm, "understand this Joey, A nigga will murder your ass over five funky-ass dollars, now sit back and imagine what they would do to if they really knew what you were worth. Remember, the streets talk, you don't have to have beef in order for a nigga to put 2 in your dome. What the fuck is that? A nigga could have beef with you for nothing; he might want what you have.

Fuck the Police. Fuck the F.B.I. and Fuck the D.E.A., you got mutha-fuckers in your hood right now hunting your ass and you don't even know it. The time will come, and trust me, when mutha-fuckers know what I know about you, you'll wish you had your gun. Joey, you don't have to experience everything...Your gun is and will always be the great: EQUALIZER! Don't let me have to remind you of this again," said the connect in a tone that let him know he was very serious.

As odd as it sounds, at that moment, Joey felt the brotherly love he knew the connect had for him." I feel you man. I feel you. But you do know that you be getting under my damn skin, that shit be bothering me how you be talking, but I have to remind myself that you're only trying to help me and not harm me. Just know, I got it!"

"Now, that's the Joey I know and admire." He leaned closer as he whispered in his ear, "it's time that you step-up your game...I got 2 bricks for you and I need for you to get back with me in Seven days," said the connect as he slid a duffel bag from his side of the booth to Joey's side.

"Seven-day's? I'm barely doing one in Ten days, now you want me to do 2 in Seven days? You gotta be kidding?"

"Absolutely Joey, seven-days it is. You're going to have to learn how to expand your real-estate. Charlottesville has much more to offer than just the Projects'. It's not always about the paper, Love N' Loyalty," said the connect as he stood to leave. Instead of leaving out the front door like everybody else, he went out the back through the kitchen. Five minutes later, Joey was on his way back to the Double-Tree Hotel with 2 bricks of Cocaine in the trunk. Just as he passed the Cook Out, he changed his mind. No way was he going to drive all the way back out to the Double-Tree with all that Cocaine in the trunk and have to turn right back around and come back to the city. In his mind he was saying,' I ain't fucking with Albemarle County like that!'

Jumping on the 250 By-pass, he decided to take care of his business while he still had a chance to do so. Taking the By-pass exit would give him a straight shot to where he was going, the stash spot on Madison Avenue. He learned from the connect to have 4 or 5 different stash spots all over the city. Once he got on

Madison, he drove the entire length of the block, passing the stash spot as he scanned the area. With Madison being a chill spot, he had to make sure no one was e lurking. Satisfied that the coast was clear, he parked across the street from the stash spot and sat there for a minute. He was thinking about the Cocaine in the trunk. He looked around again before he got out the car and went to the trunk. He jogged across the street with the duffel bag in hand as he disappeared into the woods. Four huge pickle-jars' were already buried in the ground spaced out perfectly. He filled the jars' with the individual ounces of Cocaine and put the loose dirt back over the Pickle-jars' leaving the area as he found it to the best of his ability.

It didn't take him very long to get back to the car where he exhaled; stashing Cocaine could become hazardous to your health if you're not careful, and he knew it. Briefly, the thought of calling Malik crossed his mind but he figured that he was still somewhere laid-up with some chicken-head from around the way. He then decided to call Terri. She answered on the first ring," Hey, beautiful, you ready to get some breakfast?"

"Almost, I just got out the shower; all I have to do is throw something on. If you hurry-up you'll catch me in my birthday suit," she said giggling into the phone. Giving it some thought, he knew he couldn't make it all the way out there before she got dressed but he decided to play along with her game, "I'll try to make, see you in a minute," he said maneuvering the G37 through the side streets as he took the back way, coming out by Squire-Hill. Making it back to the Hotel in record time, he took the steps up because the elevator was taking too long. The thought of catching her in her birthday suit was all the motivation he needed. When he shoved his key-card into the lock, the resistance he met surprised him, then he remembered telling her to put the safety latch on the door when he left. "Babe, you forgot about the safety latch, huh," she asked smiling?

She had on a super-tight mini-skirt, with the matching silk button-up and she looked drop dead gorgeous. With her hair in a pony-tail, she was still very beautiful to him, he looked her up and down as he stepped in close to give her a passionate kiss on the lips. The kiss was long and sweet, letting her know exactly what was on his mind. Playfully, she pulled away from his grasp," can I please have my tongue back...Aren't we supposed to be on our way to breakfast," she asked with both hands on her hips?

"Yeah, but, what happened to the birthday suit? I was pushing the car to get here, the traffic was heavy; I thought I'd make it?" His eyes were full of sadness.

"You're soooo predictable...Food baby...Food! I'm starving like Marvin up in here. Get your girl something in her stomach and you can see me however you want." She turned around right in front of him giving him a good look at her big round ass, then said to him," You know, if you want your baby to stay looking like this," pointing at her ass," then you're going to have to feed me. So, what I need to know is: Where are we going to eat?" When she turned back around to face him they both were smiling and said in unison: Golden Corral!

Smacking her lightly on her ass and he said," hurry-up and put some heels on them feet...I'm ready!"

She backed away from him just in time to avoid the next smack on her ass, "I'm almost ready but I have to show you something before we leave." She walked over to her lap-top hit a few buttons as the screen came to life. There was a huge logo with two different stacks of money appeared as her screen-saver with the words. RK Publishing.

"Come closer so you can see." Slipping on her heels as he got closer to see the computer she said to him," our broker e-mailed this." There was a picture of a 30-unit apartment complex, "we can get it for next to nothing, babe!"

"Alright, so what's the problem," he asked?

"They're asking one-hundred and twenty-five grand and it's ours'. It was 330-grand, it tanked with the economy."

Joey had to cut her off because he knew if he didn't she would go on and on forever. He simply said to her, "Buy it! Now, let's get out of here and get something to eat."

She whispered, "It's in Atlanta, Georgia...Buckhead to be more precise," she said with caution in her voice.

Taking two quick steps in her direction and his face like a statue, he said, "buy it baby! I wouldn't care if the shit was in Mexico, Atlanta is perfect, we'll probably end up down that way once you graduate anyway."

She made the proper transition's on the spot as she confirmed to her broker that she would buy the apartment complex." It's done babe, you know you're my King, right? I just sent all the confirmation forms to her, we should be hearing something back from her by the time we're done eating, if not sooner. Just remember, we have to go down there and sign some papers in person."

Joey gave her a crazy look, " you know damn well that I ain't signing no damn papers for nothing. All this stuff is yours and yours alone, I won't be connected to any of it, that's best I could ever do for you. If I sign anything it's setting us up for failure and failure isn't an option for us!"

Knowin the history of the government and how they would try to link this to that with nothing to support their theory. The Feds will go all the way back to when they believe you sold your first rock to build a bogus case. God-forbid, if something bad did happen to him, she would be straight for the rest of her life. That was his mission, he would do any and everything to protect it. He rarely spends any of the money he's made from selling CRACK, it was used for investments and nothing else. The rest was kept locked away for a rainy day. He grabbed her by the hand as they walked out the room hand in hand all the way to the car. He never let her hand go until he heard her say, "you're driving!"

He threw her the keys as he opened the driver's side door, "no, you'll do the driving today," he insisted. She started the car and had to cover her ears. The hard beats and witty lyric's from B-Stacks singing...'WEST-UP...WEST-UP,' proved to be a little too much for her ears.

He laughed because he knew she wasn't into Rap like that, however, she would listen to it if he was around, just not that loud. He teased her playfully, "you know you love this hard-core gansta shit," bobbing his head to the beat.

"This stuff will make you go deaf, keep listening to this stuff all loud," she said lowering the volume. "Now, that's more like it, I can hear what's he's actually saying now...Yeah, I like this one anyway," she said now bobbing her head right along with him. It didn't take them long to pull into the parking lot of Golden Corral, she parked right next to a big pretty white 600 BENZ. She looked over at him, "I'm going to buy you one of those one of these days," she said pointing at the Benz.

He turned around to see what she was pointing at and a big smile broke out on his face, he knew the driver of the Benz and his partner. Mann and Ru were legends in the Projects'. Young, rich, and fresh to death every single day. Mann waved Joey over to his car. "What's hood homey," asked Mann? "Ain't shit, about to grab something to eat, that's it."

Mann embraced Joey and whispered in his ear, "the word in the hood is that shit ain't looking to good... New faces, new questions, you better start keeping your heat on your hip!"

Joey stepped back because he was stunned, that was the second time today that someone close to him had advised him to keep his gun on him. 'Good lookin' to, I'll do that." He didn't bother mentioning what the connect had said to him about the same thing. Joey was fucked-up in the head now and he couldn't think of nothing but getting back to the hood and run this shit by Malik. He was hoping that Malik knew what this was all about being that his face is seen in the hood more that his.

They walked into Golden Corral and got their table," Joey, you never answered my question about the Benz, did you like it?"

Not paying much attention to what she was saying, he devoured his food in total silence. He didn't look up from his plate one time. She had to poke him with her fork just to get his attention, and when she did he had a distant look in his eyes.

"Joey, I see that you have something on your mind other than where we at right now. Your mind is someplace else; perhaps you should go and take care of your business. I can't stand that we're together but we're not together." she said pointing her index finger at her temple. She grabbed his hand and kissed the back of his hand, "you know I love you, but since you talked to them guys outside you haven't been the same...You haven't said 3 words to me. I would much rather you go and handle your business."

He looked at her and didn't have to wonder why he loved her so much, because it was times like this where she read him so well. He knew he was mentally somewhere else. From what the connect and Mann had said to him, had him really thinking about what could possibly become a huge obstacle for him and even his gut confirmed it for him." You know me so well, don't you? I have a few things on my mind. It's very important and I have to get back work before to long," pulling his out phone calling a cab.

Terri reached across the table and snatched his phone as he was in mid-sentence, "cancel that please...Sorry!"

She looked him in the eyes and started laughing," I know I said I would much rather you go and take care of your business, but not so fast Mister. Now follow me!"

She stood up and looked over her shoulder winking her eye and nodding her head in the direction she was heading. She stopped momentarily to fill a tiny cup with warm chocolate. "This will work perfectly, come on," as she made her way to where the restrooms were.

Joey didn't know what she was up to but he knew she was up to something because she had that smirk on her face. When she dipped her finger into the cup with the chocolate and licked all the chocolate off he knew what was on her mind. Leading him into the men's restroom, she headed to the largest stall, "come on baby, let momma relieve some of that stress you got on your mind!"

She sat down on the toilet and pulled down his sweat-pants as she spread the warm chocolate all over Joey's dick as she slowly licked it off. She knew that next to money, Joey loved to have his dick sucked and to make it a match in heaven, she to loved sucking his dick. It didn't take her long to have him begging her to let him fuck her because her head game was that serious. "Babe, I want to fuck you right now," she said seriously. Standing up she turned around lifted her mini-skirt up for him, they didn't have to worry about her under-garments because she didn't have any on. She bent over and slid his dick into her already soaking wet pussy.

"Mmmm Joey fuck your pussy!" Fifteen minutes later they came out of the restroom, she was happy and he was feeling like he could take on the whole hood if need be. "I'll drop you off; you don't have to call a cab. I have to go downtown anyways," she said. With him leading the way out, they left the same way they came in: hand in hand!

Chapter 8

AMANDA and White-girl decided to take a stroll up the block to the store on Grady as the evening began to set it. They knew that once it got dark all the paper would be redirected down the block to the other end of Page where Auntie Pam and her crew would be serving 'monkey-nuts' for dubs. They had a pretty good run with Auntie, they made good paper for a couple chicks from across town, now it was time to sit back and unwind, relax some. Amanda had already asked Jazzy to come and walk to the store with them and when she didn't want to Amanda called her a lazy bitch! "Since your lazy-ass doesn't want to walk to the store with us, give me twenty dollars," asked Amanda?

Jazzy looked at her like she couldn't believe that Amanda had even fixed her mouth to ask her some shit like that, "twenty dollars?, what the fuck? You plan on buying the whole damn store or something? Matter of fact, use some of that paper ya'll got from sucking all that dick ya'll be sucking out there in the streets," she said with her hand draped on her hip. "Don't forget, we're supposed to be stacking our paper and not spending it as fast as we get it," said Jazzy making light of the situation.

"Bite me bitch," spit Amanda with her voice loaded with venom! Amanda walked off with White-girl pissed the fuck-off. It wasn't about the twenty dollars, because she did have her own paper to spend if it came down to it, but they were supposed to be a team. And the fact that Jazzy had the balls to even talk to her like she was some bum bitch out there in the streets had her pissed." I can't stand that yellow bitch sometimes!" Right on cue, White-girl chimed in, "don't even sweat that shit, you know she petty as hell, come on girl," said White-girl grabbing Amanda's hand as she lead the way up 11th Street on their way to Grady.

Amanda couldn't help but laugh at what White-girl had said trying her best to cheer her up, she really appreciated it too. "At least I know you got a bitch back...Fuck Jazzy." "And you know it girrrrl! Jazzy don't half-way like me no way. She only deals with me because of you, I might be slow when it comes to all this street shit, but a bitch ain't stupid. Believe me when I tell you, I'm very observant, you're the only family I got out here. Don't worry, shits going to get better I can feel it," said White-girl real serious. It didn't take Amanda long before she snapped back to herself with that inflated ego of hers'. "I know it's going to get better. Jazzy thinks that she got all the sense holding all the paper like we stupid. For-real, fuck this CRACK shit, because if all else fails we're already sitting on a fuckin' gold mine," said Amanda as she patted her pussy laughing. White-girl knew this was a good opportunity to get some things off her chest, so she shot her shot, "let me ask you something?" "Go 'head, speak yo' peace, this me and you girl," said Amanda.

"I. .. I. .was just thinking about all the paper that Auntie has made and been giving it all to Jazzy in the last two days since we been over here. I know Auntie made a good twenty-five hundred at the least, but Jazzy keep fronting like Auntie been smoking all the stuff and messing up the paper. Jazzy know we don't know all that much about this CRACK thing and that's why she's keeping all the paper to herself," she said giving Amanda a very concerned look.

Amanda was listening very close to what White-girl was saying, she was fighting against herself trying her best not to be having those same thoughts about her cousin. "White-girl, I know it don't look right with Jazzy, but I don't think that she'll be that grimy towards me...Especially behind some bullshit CRACK, she's still my cousin," said Amanda sounding less convincing than she wanted to sound. Nevertheless, the more she thought about it the more it seemed that Jazzy was beating them in the head over this CRACK paper. Her last silent thought was, 'when is she going to break bread with us?'

They walked the rest of the way to the store in complete silence, Whitegirl was thinking of ways she could get Amanda to resume her relationship with Malik and keep her away from Jazzy all at the same time. The only problem with that was Malik had been hard to catch up with and his partner Joey was impossible to deal with if he didn't fuck with you.

Amanda was deep in thought as well, for the first time she was questioning herself and thinking about going back across town and say fuck the CRACK game. And to make it even worse, she had yet talked to Malik. She was in his hood and couldn't catch up with him, she felt some type of way about it because everybody else was seeing him and his name was buzzing but she had yet to see him. Then she was thinking that he was feeling some type of was because they was hustlin' over there getting paper in his hood. She thought it was odd for a second because everybody accepted them in the hood without question. She made it her business to ask all his little workers about him and she knew they told him. Finally making it to the store, Amanda walked to the back where they kept the beer saying to White-girl," I'm getting 2 forty's...What you getting?"

Without hesitation, White-girl grabbed herself 2 forty's as well," I don't know about you but I'm getting fucked-up tonight," she said smiling. "I'm with you on that...Fuck the bullshit. We might as well get a couple grams, some smoke and do it how we do it," added Amanda!

Neither Amanda or White-girl had sniffed any powder cocaine since they had been across town hustlin' CRACK, they barely took a drink of beer. With all the bullshit and the stress with Jazzy, they wanted to sit back and enjoy themselves either with or without Jazzy. "Don't forget the Newports'," added White-girl.

"You know a bitch ain't gonna forget them...Matter of fact, I'm getting us both our own pack, I got that feeling tonight will be one for the books." Knowing the best way to influence Amanda was to make sure she was good and high, that kept her more in her own element, so she thought. She also knew that Amanda would do just about anything if she was high enough, smiling to herself, White-girl knew that she would do everything in her power to get Amanda as high as she's ever been tonight.

When they got outside there was a pretty white Cadillac DTS pulling up, Amanda noticed the Caddy had Jersey plates. She walked by only to hear her name being called, she turned around to see who was calling her and had to do a double-take. It was the guy she met the other day in the Projects, Silas! She walked back towards the Caddy as he was getting out to meet her, and to her surprise he didn't look at all the way he was looking the other day. He looked like a major heavy-weight in the CRACK game. The first thing she noticed was his huge Jesus piece and the yellow gold chain holding it in place. Diamonds were everywhere in the chain, on his left wrist sat a Presidential Rolex complete with diamond encrusted face, the watch had her in a daze like never before. The type of jewelry he was wearing, she only seen in the Rap video's she watched on television or seen in a magazine. To say she was impressed would be an understatement. What really got her pussy wet was his smile, his whole grill was Platinum. It was so bright that the sun reflected off of his grill making her have to adjust her eyes. His blood red Gucci sneakers, Gucci jean shorts and the enormous pink earring in his ear took her breath away.

"What up stranger, "he asked? She could hear him talking to her but she was stuck in a trance. Her mouth wouldn't move she couldn't form the words that her mind was processing; she just stood there staring at him like he was the star he was to her. Again she tried to say something but nothing came out of her mouth. Silas had to lightly grab her by the arm and ask her, "you a-ight, shorty?"

Amanda had to shake her head to bring herself out of the trance she was in, "yeah...Yeah, I'm good. I was just thinking about something that's all," she said looking at him.

"Where you headed," he asked looking deep into her eyes?

"You mean we, don't you," she said nodding her head in White-girls' direction? But, since you asked, we're on our way back down Page, Why?"

Silas loved the way that Amanda was looking, she was sexy as hell. Now he was the one in a trance as he starred into those green-eyes of hers. "Ya'll walking?"

Amanda smiled, "well...we were walking," she said as she made her way to the Caddy. She nodded her head to White-girl to let her know to come on with her.

"That's what I'm talking about! I love a woman who can recognize an opportunity when she sees one." He looked over at Philly, "yo, grab 2 boxes of baking soda!" Philly got out the passenger's seat to go into the store for the baking soda and Amanda took his spot sitting in the front passenger's seat like the seat was made specifically for her. "Oh, you riding shot-gun, huh," asked Silas?

"No doubt! I can tell you're not use to letting no female ride shot-gun when you got your boy with you. You don't seem like the type to have a female as shot-gun," she said real serious. She wasn't necessarily talking about riding in the passenger's seat as she was more so talking about life. Her eyes were drawing him in. He was forced to turn his head in the opposite direction. However, Amanda had seen that look a million times in different guy's when they looked at her and saw something they like so she had to ask, "what's the problem, you see something you like?"

She caught him and he did his best to laugh it off but he was caught out there, "you damn right I see something I like," he said looking out the driver's side window.

She started rubbing his thigh, "I can't tell, you ain't called a bitch yet," she said as she answered her phone. 'Yeah, this her. Hey Silas, of course I would love to see you today,' she said playfully into the phone as if he had really called her.

She was instantly comfortable in his presence and started joking with him." Now, that's the conversation I should've been having with you if you really like what you seen the other day!"

Before Silas got the chance to respond to her jokes, Philly came back and got in the back-seat. He brushed against White-girls' big titties. She started laughing because she knew what he was up to but she didn't mind one bit. Philly eyed her seductively, he knew from Jazzy that she got down with whatever, but since she never introduced him to any of her friends, she didn't really know nothing about him as he knew exactly who she was. He had plans for White-girl!

After some small talk, Silas got down to business," I see Jazzy got ya'll out here stacking that paper for her."

Amanda was caught off guard by what he just said and shot him a deadly look. 'How the fuck he know about that,'she thought to herself? She figured that

Jazzy had known him all the time and it confirmed what her and White girl was just talking about while they walked to the store about what Jazzy was trying to do to them. "What you mean by that," she asked?

"I'm saying...My man Philly introduced her to me the other night, she wanted to get some work and she got what she was looking for, you feel me? When she told me she had ya'll out here on the grind for her...That's all it was."

"Oh yeah, she said all that to you? I guess that's why you never got around to calling a bitch, huh, "said Amanda bitterly! "You're too busy up in that bitch face to call me, right?"

Silas got the point real quick and it only confirmed to him how Jazzy put herself on a pedestal whenever it came to Amanda or White-girl, and his conclusion was that she was using the both of them to do her dirty work. "Amanda, let's get something straight, whatever is going on between you and your peeps Jazzy that's between ya'll, I ain't got shit to do with it. My understanding was that ya'll was hustlin' for her, now I know she never told you that I was asking about you, I even told her to tell you to call me. It's obvious that you never got my message, but fuck that I'm trying to holla at you now on some other shit," he said squeezing her thigh.

Amanda starred at him for what seemed like an eternity, it was one of those rare occasions where she saw in him more than him just wanting to fuck her because she was fly and had pretty eyes. She saw something else in his gaze, all she could hear him say was that he was trying to get with her. There was a constant battle within herself and it had everything to do with him! She couldn't fix her mouth to say what her mind was thinking. All she saw was how sexy he was, but her mind wouldn't allow her to believe it was anything other than game to get some pussy.

He had to call her name twice and grab her thigh again just to regain her attention as he brought her out of the trance she was in. He parked the car and left the music playing, everybody in the car had their eyes on her.

"Amanda, you alright," asked White-girl with her voice full of concern? She came out of her trance again and looked around the car and noticed they were already parked in front of Auntie's house back on Page. She couldn't remember the ride back from the store or which way they went to get there. Whenever Silas said something she was captivated by his intense stare and it lulled her into a trance, the sound of his voice scared her to death. There had been only one other man on the Planet that had that type of effect on her was Safee'. There goes mixing business with pleasure, she was gone and there was nothing she could do about it, not that she wanted to either. "I'm good ya'll, this Jazzy shit got me bugging," she said lying.

"Can I holla at you later tonight," asked Silas as he watched her get out the car?

"You said that same bullshit the other day...Miss me with that bullshit," spit Amanda. Fighting what was in her, she didn't smile or even look at him, those feelings scared her and she didn't know if she was ready to deal with some shit like that.

White-girl was the last one out the caddy and she said to him, "Silas do me a favor, my girl is feeling you and it's bigger than you'll ever know so if you're trying to fuck let it be known. Miss her with all the bullshit, just like she said. She don't need the bullshit in her life, the end result will be the same, she ain't no whore or nothing like that but I know she's feeling you and she would fuck you so leave all that other extra shit on the sideline. Play the game the way it's supposed to be played. And it was nice meeting you!"

Silas watched how Amanda had went from hot to cold in a matter of minutes. He could tell that she was running from something and all he wanted to do was to protect her from the harsh realities of the hood. He knew all the signs all too well, it wasn't really that hard to recognize when a person was carrying a heavy burden. For a second, he put the car in park and was about to go chase after her but he also knew that if he was correct, he needed to give her some time to think things through and sort out her feelings. If it wasn't for him having to get down Garrett he doubted that it would have been easy to let her walk away. The ever presence of business had forced him to pull off and get to it. "Philly, we gotta get at them chicks."

Sosa had been on his grind getting it in around the clock, chillin' with the youngins' as he watched them shoot dice and chase paper. It was Dre', another Jersey dude who was now a permanent fixture in Charlottesville who questioned him first, "yo, what's up with your man Silas, where he been?"

Not taking his eyes off the dice game, "he's chillin' why," he said not giving Dre' too much information? He was going to keep his conversation about his homey short and to the point. Shit could easily get fucked-up talking about another man when he wasn't there to defend himself whether good or bad. Since he hadn't spoken to Silas in a few days he intended to keep Dre' and anyone else out of their business, even with Silas M.I.A., he still had Silas, half of the drugs stashed away. With his half and what he got from Tasha, he flooded Garrett with CRACK! Once Silas comes down off of his ego-trip, he would then tell him of his future plans of going legit. Not so sure if he wanted to tell Silas that him and Tasha was getting married soon, that's a bit too much for Silas and he knew it, just the fact that he was going legit would kill him and he didn't want to lose his best friend totally.

Silas had let it be known on more than one occasion that he was perfectly comfortable dying in the CRACK game, he had no intentions of ever getting out and nobody knew more than him how serious he was about his stance. Sosa had gotten a little bored watching the dice game; since he wasn't playing he knew he had to get gone. He was testing his own patience, he loved to gamble and with Dre' trying to ask questions he had to go. He caught Star out the corner of his eye coming in their direction he knew that could only mean one thing. He made a bee-line catching her soon as she came through the gate. 'What up Star, holla at your boy, " he said to her.

Star flashed a few bills before she started talking as she nodded her head for him to follow her, "look, before I spend my paper with you I want to know if you got some of that fire you usually have? I don't want nothing that's just a-ight, I need something that's going to make my bell ring in my ear."

Sosa reached in his pocket and gave Star a dub, "this you! Try it, if you like it spend your paper with me...If not do you," he said to her maintaining eye contact with her to let her know he was serious.

She took the dub from," a-ight, now let me get 6 for seventy-five. This shit gotta be good if you're willing to let me walk-off with my paper. Look though, this dub you already gave me don't count for one of the 6 you're giving me for my paper," she said smiling.

"You good, today's your lucky day Star, I'm feeling generous," he said dropping 6 dubs in her hand to seventy-five dollars. She knew that she made the correct decision by dealing with him instead of one of them young boys out there. She knew he was the man to see down Garrett, "where you gonna be later? Dude I got with me got more paper and I'm going to milk his ass dry," she said winking at him.

He pulled out a piece of paper with his number already written on it and handed it to her, "take my number, when you call me I'll come and meet you somewhere so you won't have to come back down here." He smiled because of the way she was holding her hand, with the CRACK in the palm of her hand and her fist balled-up in a tight fist, that was a universal sigh and he recognized it.

She nodded her head and began walking off, before she got out of the gate she turned back around and looked at him from over her shoulder, "good looking out...I'll be calling you in a little while," she said as her ride pulled-up to the curve. The white guy in the pick-up truck was urging her to get in. Sosa decided to take a break and go inside to see what Tasha was up to, but before he could to that, a pearl white Cadillac pulled-up and caught his attention.

His homey Silas was getting out of the Cadillac, his signature smile was radiant, "yo what up Sosa," he asked as Philly was dead on his heels?

"You know the drill, same shit, different toilet," replied Sosa. He was surprised to see Silas but didn't want to let him know he was surprised. He was equally surprised to see him driving the Cadillac that was a sure sign that the time had come to where that inevitable conversation he's been contemplating in his mind for the last few days had to take place. With Silas right there in front of him, still he knew it had to happen but he was still unsure how to compose the words to his best friend, brother, and business partner? How could he tell him that he was through with the CRACK game? Silas gave him a hug and a pound, that let Sosa know that there was no love lost over their conversation from the other day. He exhaled and said," I need to holla at you about something," but he wasn't looking at Silas but Philly. From his tone, Silas knew he meant business.

Silas looked over at Philly who had a perplexed look on his face and said to him, "sit tight, I'll be right back!" Silas and Sosa walked off together in silence, each was deep in thought about how to convince the other of their next move. It was Silas who broke the silence, "the work still straight?"

Sosa stopped walking when he thought he was out of hearing distance of the stranger Silas as had with him and looked at him as if to ask ,'are you serious?' But, he didn't speak what his mind was thinking, there was more pressing issue's to deal with, "no question! Why wouldn't it be straight? Your half is where it supposed to be, plus there's a little less than half of mines there as well. That's what I've been wanting to talk to you about, anyway!"

"Word! You're back, huh? Ain't nothing more important to talk about out here other than chasing this paper homey. Why we need to talk about that?" Sosa eyed him even closer, and what he saw in Silas's eyes was the destruction of man, GREED! Then he asked him, "damn homey, this what it all comes down to?"

Silas laughed it off not yet realizing the seriousness of the situation, "what's all that supposed to mean?"

"All you seem to ever think about is chasing paper, fucking bitches and nothing else. There's gotta be more to life than that."

"Here we go with the bullshit! Look homey, we're 400 miles away from home and you mutha-fuckin' right...Chasing paper is the only thing on my mind, just in case you forgot why we're out here in the first place, let me remind you: To get paper and fuck bitches! From the sound of it, yo ass got shit twisted not me.

We out here to chase that paper nigga, don't get this shit fucked-up, one mistake and it's over, or have you forgot?"

"It's more to life than."

Silas cut him off mid-sentence, "Naw bro., that's where you got shit twisted. That bitch you out here fucking with got your head all cloudy and shit. The next thing you'll be telling me is that your stupid ass is ready to marry this country bitch and stop chasing paper all together so you could go legit or some shit. You out this bitch trying to be something that you're not, you ain't no damn family man, nigga, you're a cold blooded killa and a hustla; you can't never be on that Will and Jada type shit because it ain't you," fired Silas steaming mad as he talked!

There was so much venom in his voice that the once inseparable brothers, has now caused a riff as big as the Atlantic Ocean. Sosa wasn't willing to argue with Silas, he already knew that once his mind was made up there was nothing he could do or say that could change what he was thinking. He stood inches away from Silas face and starred at him like he wasn't his brother and said, "I'm done... The work is where it's always been, do you!" With no explanation or nothing he turned and walked away, Silas would swallow blood before he would swallow his pride, so all was said and done.

With Sosa walking off, Silas said, "ain't no question about it, I'm definitely going to do me." He wasn't feeling Sosa no more, in his mind it wasn't him who changed but it was Sosa. He was ready to go check the stash spot, and if it wasn't what it was supposed to be he had no problem putting 2 in Sosa's and Tasha's head and that'll be that. By the time he got back to the car, Philly was sitting on the hood, "get the fuck off my fuckin' hood nigga," spit Silas! Philly knew not to test him, he had that same murderous look in his eyes the day he met him. It was written all over his face that he was pissed-off. Before Philly could get in the car good, Silas was already pulling off, "let's bounce," was all Silas said before driving the short distance from Garrett to the near-by graveyard. Once at the graveyard, Silas got out and was gone only 2 to 3 minutes before returning with a plastic bag full of CRACK. He threw it in Philly's lap, "hold that!"

Sosa knew he had just closed a chapter of his life that has been going on and on ever since he was a child. He wasn't sure if he was supposed to be angry, mad, or glad with his choice as he walked into Tasha's apartment. When he walked in the front door, Tasha was sitting in the middle of the floor in the living room. Sitting Indian style, surrounded by empty boxes and things of hers that needed to be packed, he made his way over to her and fell back onto the sofa exhaling loudly. She immediately picked-up on the vibe and knew that something was bothering him. Clue number one was that he never came around her without kissing her and telling her how much he loved her, so she knew something was wrong. "Babe, what's wrong?" He laid back on the sofa as he pulled his New York Yankee's cap down over his eyes, she got up and sat on his lap. Slowly lifting his cap so that she could see his eyes, with her right hand, she placed it under his chin, raising it up to her, she whispered, "talk to me baby. Tell me what's going on," she pleaded with him? Knowing that she was concerned about him, but he wasn't ready to talk to her about what had just happened between him and Silas just yet. His mind was saying to leave, walk out, but that's what he was used to, he fought the temptation.

The old Sosa would've been walked out and been done with the situation, however, he was trying to do something new and that meant, he would eventually have to talk to Tasha about what transpired. Leaving nothing to chance, he looked at her and said, "I just talked to Silas!"

Tasha's eyes got big because she was unsure what happened so she asked, "what happened, did you tell him?" The look on his face told her that he said something to him but she just didn't know what he said. Knowing they were more like brothers and his loyalty to Silas was one of the things that attracted her most to him. Regardless how things went, she knew it was hard for him to walk away from Silas like that.

Her job was to show him their lives were going in opposite directions. "Do you want to talk about it?"

"Not really, there's really nothing to talk about. His only concern is chasing paper and mines is trying to make a better life for you and lil' Jay!"

She leaned in and kissed him as if her life depended, in her mind, what she heard him saying, he was putting childish things aside to become a man. She had to take into account that Silas and him had been together almost every day of their lives since the 1st grade. She knew it was a hard task, but her duty as a woman and a mother was to convince him that the decision he was about to make was the best decision for all of them. "Sosa, make love to me. Right here and Right now," she begged with tears in her eyes.

Sosa said to her as he was shaking his head," I can't let him get the both of us knocked or even killed out here," with one single tear running down his cheek.

Tasha wiped the tear away with her thumb, "baby, me and lil' Jay love you so much, and we need you!" She unzipped his zipper as she sat in between his legs. Knowing she couldn't take away all of his pain but she was willing to give it her best try as she started sucking on his dick. Before it was all over, she had fucked and sucked him to sleep in each other arms.

It was about 2 hours later when he woke-up to the sound of Tasha's heart beating in his ear. He tried to ease his arm from up under her without waking her, but to no avail, his movements woke her anyway. She had a devilish smirk on her face as she asked, "and where are you off to mister?" He managed to get himself up and on his feet, "to the bathroom if you don't mind," he said to her holding his dick.

She laid back and closed her eyes as she thought about him, she knew for a fact that he was the man for her and she was willing to do anything to keep him happy. She recalled her old motto from when she was out there running the streets herself 'If you won't...Some other bitch will!' She had done things sexually with him that she had never even considered doing with a man, let alone actually doing those things. It was something about him that made the animal in her come out, and the craziest thing was...She absolutely loved it! The best thing for her was she knew she wasn't the only one willing to do anything to make this thing work between them. He's proven himself time and time again to her, and this last episode with Silas, that's the icing on the cake. Her intention wasn't to break-up their friendship, rather, she wasn't willing to lose him to the federal government as she's seen so many other's in her life.

When he came out of the bathroom, she handed him his ringing phone he answered,' hello? Who this? Oh, what up Star? Where? Yeah, stay right there, I'm my way right now!"

There was no reason for Tasha to have any worry as to who this Star chick was, knowing she just put down her gansta and was certain whoever this Star was she wasn't nobody that important and second, she had given him the green light to handle his business. All she wanted to do now was get their belongings packed and there was no way she would be able to get that done with him hanging around the house. The thoughts in her mind, forced a smile on her face, she was thinking that there was no way she could keep his dick out of her mouth long enough to get the things packed.

"Why you smiling," he asked?

Giggling, she said, "you!"

"And what about me?" She pointed towards his dick, "that! I'm in love twice....You gotta goooo."

"Oh yeah, why I gotta go?"

"With you here I can't get shit done, maybe with you gone something will get done around here," she said still giggling.

Sosa made his way up to Food Masters' in record time, all the while thinking about moving out the hood for the first time in his life and having a normal life with Tasha. Also taking into account that it was only a matter of time before 'them-people' would show up at the door with a bogus ass arrest warrant, complete with all the dirt he's ever done, just the thought of that came crashing down on him at one time. Retiring from the CRACK game without a scare was damn near impossible or unheard of, and for some, just walking away from the lifestyle could make you an even bigger target. Thinking of himself becoming a target forced him to touch his chest because the only comfort he was seeking was that of the 40.Caliber in his shoulder holster. That was the reminder that shit was real.

Walking up the hill from the high rise, he spotted Star standing on the side of Food Masters' next to the pay phone with her back to him as he approached. She was just about to drop more change into the pay phone to call him back but when she finally turned around, she saw him walking up the hill.

"Damn, it's about time. You slow as hell," she said laughing!

He knew that he was already rushing to make it there as quick as he could, so he played along with her game, "you should consider yourself lucky, it usually takes me anywhere from 30 to 45 minutes, so be happy that I'm here."

She met him on the side and handed him two hundred dollars, "that shit you got is some 'head-banger', but let me get something with a little weight to it. I'm telling you, dude got two other people at his house; they got like 2-grand, easy. Probably more, but you know I'm going to work they-ass," she said with a serious look on her face.

He wasn't into the whole selling weight thing, he was straight off the block, he flat-footed everything. However, he wanted to get rid of the CRACK he had and quick. Putting the paper in his pocket, he said," hold-up a minute, let me grab some cigarette's," as he walked into the store. He wasn't gone a hot 2 minutes and when he came back out, Star was standing at a Camry talking to somebody. Sosa decided to take a closer look and noticed that she was talking to the dude, Malik who drove the Range Rover!

He wasn't paying much attention to what they were talking about until he heard Star say, 'damn Malik, I would've hollered at you first but you don't be answering your phone when a bitch be calling you...Plus, he already got my paper!'

Even though Star was referring to him, he walked past them, eyeing Malik. Then he heard another smart comment, 'I see you like fucking with out of town, niggaz...Your lost.' Malik was holding CRACK in his hand and saying to her, 'this close to 5 grams, this what I'll give you for your paper.'

He knew what he was showing her would make her want to get her paper back from the out of towner and that was his plan. He didn't like none of them dudes anyway! He wanted to kill 2 birds with one stone. Star found herself in the middle of a bidding war and she didn't like it one bit. She knew if she swayed one way or the other it could prove to be hazardous to her health. Nevertheless, she weighed her options carefully; business was business so she was always told.

"Hold-up Malik," she said grabbing the CRACK out his hand. She walked over to where Sosa was standing and showed him the CRACK that she had gotten from Malik," can you give me more than this for my paper? If you can't, well I gotta spend my paper where I'll get the best deal. It ain't personal Sosa, just business!"

In that instant, the old Sosa took over, "I gotcha paper right here, I've been playing fair with you the whole time, no games, no bullshit. Now you coming at me sideways on some bullshit, if that pussy ass dude want your paper, tell him come get it. He can't dictate how I do mines...Ya'll got me fucked-up!"

Before Sosa could make it out the parking lot good, Malik had got out the car with a Mac .90 at his side. Scanning the area, he knew this was it as he slipped his own gun from the shoulder holster. "You need to mind your own business," said Sosa as Malik got in hearing distance. "And stay the fuck out of mines!"

Joey walked out the store just in time to see Malik and some dude he didn't recognize engaged in a hectic word exchange. The Mac.90 by Malik's side is what alerted him to the possibility of danger. "Yo Malik, what the fuck's going on out here," he asked but keeping his eyes trained on the dude he didn't know?

He knew Malik was trigger happy and the dude didn't seem to be too worried about the Mac.90. The dude seemed just as ready for battle as Malik, he threw his hands up in the air, "yo...yo... Let me holla at you a second," he said talking to the stranger. "Malik put that shit away!"

He walked over to Sosa, calm and non-threatening, "let that shit go, it's mad people out here. This can't turn out good for none of us," he said barely above a whisper. He looked at Star and asked her, "what's going on?" It was evident to him the stranger wasn't backing down and that only meant one thing, he was strapped as well. When he looked at the stranger closer, he could see the tip of the barrel sticking out from the lining of his hoodie, "you need to put your shit away too before somebody up here call the Jakes."

Sosa didn't move, his least worry was the police, "you need to be hollering at your man and make sure you get him some business because right now he's over stepping his bounds." Logic kicked in and the mention of the police brought him out his zone. Star took her time explaining to Joey what happened between Malik and Sosa, it all made sense to him now. Malik was dead wrong so he decided to be the bigger man, "my peeps was dead wrong, we don't want business that way...We good," asked Joey?

Sosa nodded his head in agreement, "I'm good, but let your man know that everybody out here ain't pussy so he should be more conscious of who he tries to disrespect" he said right before walking off leaving all of them standing there.

Star apologized to both Joey and Malik then made her way out the parking lot following Sosa and her paper. He was moving so fast that it was difficult for her to catch up to him but he finally stopped at the bottom of the hill by the high rise. "Usually I would just keep your paper and tell you that's the price of doing some bullshit during a business deal, but today's your lucky day." He reached down on the ground beside a parked car and handed her a huge CRACK rock, double that what Malik was going to give her, and then he said to her, " lose my fuckin' number," and walked off.

When Star went to put the CRACK in her pocket, she realized that she still had the 4 grams from Malik. She smiled as she thought about what she should do with it? She knew the best thing for her to do was to call Joey and tell him because he was easier to deal with and hopefully he'll tell her to keep it. Sosa took his time walking back to Garrett; he had to calm himself because he almost lost it all in one second. If it wasn't for Tasha and lil' Jay, he would've put 2 in Malik's head the moment he got out the car. Going legit was going to take some getting used to, it wasn't everyday he let somebody pullout on him and be able to talk about it later. He had to get away from Garrett and Charlottesville all together.

He didn't care about the CRACK he had left, he needed to get away and fast. When he walked back in Tasha's house, Tasha was sitting on the sofa, he asked," are all the clothes packed?"

"Yeah, most everything is packed, why? I still got a few things that need to be packed."

"Is lil' Jay still at your mom's?"

"Yep, and he'll be there all weekend long," she said licking her lips getting ready for round two.

Sosa called a cab on his phone and in 5 minutes he was in the cab with Tasha directing the cab driver to Baker Street. They got out next to a beautiful Black on Black Mercedes 600 Benz V12. Her eyes were stuck on the car, he watched as she looked from the corner of his eyes. Then he hit the switch and the trunk opened, "put your bags' in here!"

She looked confused because he just opened the trunk of this beautiful Benz, "whose car is this, "she asked?

He smiled, "it's yours if you want it, but right now we're going to Jersey for the weekend. Can you handle all this power?" Tasha jumped in the driver's seat as he threw her the key's, "you damn right I can handle all this power, you'll see, come on get in, "she said excitedly like a school child!

CHAPTER 9

WHEN Joey got back in the car he was fuming mad with Malik, "have you've you lost your fucking mind? You running around this bitch pulling out the Mac. 90's like we in the wild, wild, west...Don't you know these same people who seen you pull out will be the same people who will be testifying against us!"

"Ain't shit happen...Joey, dude over-stepped his bounds and I was ready to bless'em...I'm letting them out-of-towner's know that shit is real in the field down here," said Malik as if this was just another day in the life of a hustla.

"You mean to tell me that you're willing to catch a body in front of one of the hottest spots in Charlottesville because you're saying somebody over-stepped their bounds with you?" Joey had to laugh because the shit was so stupid, "and another thing, who's to say that son wouldn't have bodied you?"

"He wasn't trying to bust his gun...that's the fuck why! He out here pump-faking."

"Don't be so stupid Malik. You ready to throw all this away over some chump change, huh? From what I seen, son wasn't looking like he was backing down, matter of fact, to me, it looked like the boy had murder in his eyes."

"That shit might've scared you but I wasn't impressed at all. More than likely, he was just as scared as your soft-ass," said Malik laughing. "That's probably why it was so easy for you and him to reach an agreement!"

Joey drove in silence, in his mind, he was thinking about what the connect was telling him about these types of behaviors and that he needed to stay away from them. The more paper Malik made, the more arrogant he became. Joey didn't know what he could do to get Malik to see the seriousness of the situation; he did the next best thing: he stayed silent. All of a sudden Malik turned down the music and asked," yo, where you going, I need my V?"

Not uttering one single word, Joey pulled the car over and got out. He was directly across the street from the bus station on Main Street but if he looked to his right, there was the big Federal building where niggaz got life sentences. Briefly looking in both directions, he shook his head at the way Malik was acting but he was still reluctant to argue with him, it would be a total waste of his time.

Malik didn't bother getting out the car, he climbed over the center console, and once he was back in the driver's seat he pulled off. In his mind, he was thinking about how Joey had just handled that situation and wasn't too sure if his homey understood the CRACK game and how real it was to him, real niggaz died every day in these 'Mean-Streets'. What really had him heated was the fact that Joey took it upon himself to apologize for what he did to some pussy-ass-out-of-towner at that! He was so vexed he began beating on the steering wheel in frustration as he screamed out loud, 'fuck them out-of Towner's, they can get it too! This my fuckin city." Bending the right turn soon as he passed Mel's, through the tunnel and on to Auntie Pam's house on Page.

He parked across the street, sitting on the hood, he fired up a blunt of some sweet smelling Loud to ease his mind. He wanted to get super-high, that way he wouldn't have to worry about nothing. Knowing the Loud would do the trick, he smiled inside! Unsure if he could take the whole blunt to the dome since he wasn't an everyday weed smoker, usually the purple-haze was reserved for the chicks, however, this occasion called for it.

Tiffany and her goofy-ass was peeping out the window watching Malik the whole time, she knew right away that something was wrong by his movements, watching him roll a blunt only confirmed it. Stopping herself from rushing to his side, she wanted to give him a few minutes so that the blunt would relax him a little bit before she ran out there asking what she could do to make his day better. The blunt was her way in and she knew it, so if she gave the weed a minute to settle him down she wouldn't have to worry about him dissing her. Quiet as kept, Tiffany loved herself some Malik, love with a capital 'L'. In her head, she could just sit there staring out the window looking at him and be content, but at the same time she wanted to be close to him. She dressed herself in some really tight and really short shorts and a wife-beater with no bra. With a devilish grin on her face, she knew the wife-beater without the bra would certainly gain his attention. Looking at herself in the mirror, she knew she still looked good, her long legs' and round ass was still intact, her firm titties sat at full attention. She was giving the CRACK she smoked a run for its paper! Snatching her sun-glasses off the table she headed out the front door. She walked slowly across the street making sure she switched her ass extra hard as she licked her lips. When she got close enough, she said to him, "what you doing out here so early? Why you ain't come in the house, it's hot out here?"

Having to do a double-take as he looked at her, he didn't know if it was the weed or if Tiffany was looking like something to eat? For some reason, he couldn't take his eyes off of her, her long sexy legs, her titties, and that ass of hers had him going. His head was bouncing up and down watching her titties bounce as she walked closer to him. He could tell she wasn't wearing a bra and his eyes were locked in on her growing nipples. They looked like elevator buttons begging to be released from the tight wife-beater.

She was switching so hard that he thought she was going to break her hip, then she broke his train of thought, "Malik...Malik, I know you hear me talking to you, she asked as she purposely brushed her ample breast against his arm as she sat next to him on the hood of the car! "Huh, what you say Tiff," he asked with his eyes locked in on her nipples?

She sucked her teeth making a hissing noise, "I said, what you doing out here so damn early?" Still staring at her nipples, he made a feeble attempt to pass her the blunt, "here, hit this!

"You know I don't fuck with no wacky-tobbacie, if you're in such a giving mood then give me some of that hard-white you got in your pocket." She started licking her lips and looking down at his dick letting him know exactly what was on her mind without having to say it, "like I said, since you're in the giving mood, give me some of that while you're at it," she said pointing down at his dick.

The powerful Loud invaded his blood stream and he was high as the light bill, laughing at everything Tiffany was saying even the way her mouth was moving while she was talking was funny. He already knew that she wanted to fuck him, that wasn't nothing new to him but this time he wanted to hear her say it. "Give you some of what," he asked? Reaching in his pocket to pull out the four grams he had but he realized that he had never gotten it back from Star.

"You know what I'm talking about Malik, so stop playing with me! You know I'm talking about that dick, it's been a minute since you let me taste it," she was saying while getting even closer to him. "I want this in my mouth right now," she said grabbing a handful of his already hard dick.

Without any hesitation, he got off the hood of the car and lead Tiffany into the back seat, she followed with a huge smile on her face. The windows of the Camry had that limo tint so there was no need for them to worry about anybody seeing what they were up to. Malik laid his body across the back seat as Tiffany eased down his sweat-pant' down to his ankles. She ran her tongue the length of his erect dick as she moaned in delight. Her moans let him know that she was enjoying herself just as much as he was enjoying himself. Using her tongue to make wet circles on the head of his dick before she attempted to deep throat his dick in one swift motion, she gagged a little but she made herself relax allowing her throat to take the entire length of his enormous dick down to the bottom of her warm mouth. She knew he was into it from the way he grabbed the back of her head and started pumping up and down harder and faster like he was fucking her pussy but he wasn't, he was fucking her face and she loved it, it drove her crazy! She started moaning from the pain he inflicted on her throat.

Anything for Malik so she accepted the pain but it wasn't long before the pain turned into pure pleasure, while she was ll sucking his dick, she managed to slip out her shorts. She inserted 3 of her fingers into her pussy, looking up at him, she said, "I'm getting this pussy ready for you daddy!" Taking a second to withdraw her fingers, she put them in her mouth licking all the juices from her fingers, "daddy, fuck me, please fuck this pussy, I need you inside of me" she begged him.

This is one of the main reasons that he loved fucking her, she knew exactly what to say and do to gain his attention. He switched positions with her as he got on top. He bent her small frame like it was a pretzel as he inserted his enormous dick into her tight pussy inch by inch until he was deep inside of her. He could hear her gasp for air. He didn't waste any time before he started pounding her pussy hard and fast, he was looking down at his dick as it went in and out of her pussy, it was soaked with her pussy juices and it turned him on even more. The loud smacking sound of their bodies banging together was music to his ears'.

He was killing her and he knew it, "Malik...Malik, let me ride you, please let me ride you, your dick is too big...It's in my stomach," she begged! He knew he was hung like a horse so he eased out of her slowly allowing her to switch positions with him, but before she got on top, she started sucking on his dick some more. Leaving a long trail of spit on his dick, she straddles him as she inserted his dick into her asshole. She knew that if she could take it in the ass that it would drive him insane so she took a deep breath and slid the head in as she eased down on his dick. She was careful to go real slow because he could already feel her asshole stretching, she bit down on her bottom lip determined to get in all the way in.

A soft moan escaped her lips, "oh...oh, uggg, Malik go real slow, slow please," she begged. Tiffany started moving up and down slow, once Malik started playing with her clit it was starting to drive her crazy as she began riding his dick like a professional jockey.

He grabbed her by her tiny waist as he forced her up and down even harder on his dick. She was moaning and screaming at the top of her lung, "oh shit daddy, fuck meeee," she moaned over and over. What she didn't realize was the more she bit down on her bottom lip the more he wanted her so he fucked even harder. "Daddy, why, why you doing...Ahhh, why you doing this to me. Stop. Stop. Please stop, daddy I--I--can't take it no more, please stop," she begged him.

He didn't stop, it was more fuel for the fire, he just kept fucking her as hard as he could, since he could tell that she was on the verge of cuming, he played more with her clit encouraging her to rock her hips to the beat of their song, and she did. "Oh shit daddy...I...I...I'm fuckin cu---cuming right fuckin' now," she screamed as her body shook uncontrollable. It didn't take her long to regain her composure; she started sucking on his dick again.

Before he knew it, she had him cuming down her throat and all over her face, "yeah baby, cum in my mouth," she said to him. There wasn't a man on God's green earth she loved more than her Malik and she was willing to do anything to prove it, the pain she endured was nothing. She found a towel and began wiping off his dick, when they made eye contact the both of them started laughing out loud.

"That was right on time" he said wiping off the sweat from her forehead. "This could be everyday if you wanted it like that," she said reminding him of how she really felt about him.

Malik didn't like when Tiffany started talking like that, it was too much of a reminder of how things use to be. He was forced to look away reaching into the center console and pulled-out a nice size rock and tossed it over to her, "this for you Tiff," he said watching the rock land in her lap.

She looked at him like he was crazy, "Malik, I didn't just fuck you for no damn CRACK, I gave you a shot of this pussy because I like being with you! If you're trying to give me something, give it to me because you want me to have it and not for any other reason because I feel like you're treating me like a CRACK whore!"

She was pissed off by the way Malik was trying to play her and had to let him know just how she felt. "We're bigger than this Malik, have you forgot? I ain't no CRACK whore so don't treat me like one and the last time I checked you wasn't no damn trick," she said throwing the CRACK back into his lap as she got out the car. With tears streaming down her cheeks she took one last look back at him before saying," you keep that shit, if that's all I'm worth to you, keep it." Slamming the car door as she closed it, she headed back into Auntie Pam's house still crying.

Very few people knew the history the two shared and they both preferred it that way, however, it was no coincidence that she found her way to be living in

Malik's Aunties house, it was by design. He sat in the back seat watching her as she crossed the street and went into the house, he knew how she felt about him but there was nothing he could do to change the fact of who they were. It felt to him like he was in between a rock and a hard spot. Tiffany smoked CRACK and he sold it! She made her choice to smoke CRACK all by herself and there was nothing he could do to take their relationship back to where it was when they were back in high school and all in love. They were going in opposite directions and there was nothing he believed that he could do for her, let alone be the man he used to be to her, so much has changed since back in the days.

Since he switched from weed to selling cocaine he was so busy that he rarely got the chance to see Tiffany anyway. To him they were growing apart naturally, what he didn't know or understand was it wasn't so much of what he was doing; it was more she had decided to fallback. She didn't want him seeing her like that so she avoided him every chance she got. If it hadn't been for him, she would've been a hot-mess, but the love and the hope she held onto was the driving force that kept her on her grind. She felt that if she stayed away and stayed decent that one day he would see her for who she was and not for the drugs she was using, that and that alone, was enough to keep her weight intact.

Malik played a bunch of sick little games with her mind, he knew he could get away with it. If he told her to jump, she would ask him, 'how high,' she loved him like that. Her feelings where never a question for him, it was the fact she smoked CRACK that bothered him the most, but from what he saw from her today reminded him of the old Tiffany. The Tiffany he used to be madly in love with, the Tiffany that wasn't going for nothing. Looking down in his lap at the CRACK, he put it back in the center console and pulled out another bag with more CRACK rocks that the single rock. He put everything in his pocket and headed towards Auntie Pam's door, he wanted to talk to Tiffany and he needed to do it right now!

Auntie Pam was coming out the door just as he made it onto the porch, "boy, what you done to that poor chile' now," she asked looking him directly in the eyes? Now, Auntie Pam was one of the handful of people who knew the true history about Malik and Tiffany, after all, it was her idea to allow her to stay with her at her house and she became use to them going back and forth with one another. Tiffany had spent many nights telling her everything about the love of her life, so she was well aware of mostly everything that made them tick, but today, something was different. She decided to use this opportunity to have a real talk with Mr. Malik, because the boy was getting beside himself. Trying to bump past Auntie Pam, Malik asked, "where she at?"

"Up-stairs taking a shower and crying her eyes out over your crazy-ass. Why you asking anyway?"

"Because, I got something that belongs to her, that's why," he said pulling out the bag of CRACK.

She looked at him like something was really wrong with him," boy, that chile don't care nothing about no damn CRACK, Malik! That chile want you to see her and stop looking at her for what she's out here doing in the streets." She took the bag of CRACK from his hand and asked, "how much is this?"

"That's a G-pack, why?" Auntie Pam had an idea," hold-up a sec," she said before running up the steps two at a time. She went into the bathroom with Tiffany and made her get out the shower, "take this girl, it's a 60-40 deal between you and Malik, you pay him six-hundred and keep the other four-hundred for yourself," said Auntie Pam smiling at her. When she came running back down the steps she went straight out the front door yelling over her shoulder, "come on Malik, I gotta go to the store!"

In hot pursuit, the only thing on his mind was the work," where's the work Auntie Pam?"

"Come on now...I told you that I gotta go to the store right quick; now come on, will you." Once they were situated in the car, she looked over at Malik with the most serious look he's ever seen on her face and said, "drive!" He didn't want to ask any questions, that look she gave him was serious and he decided it best to pay attention to whatever it was that she had to say.

"Joey called me not too long ago and told me what happened at 'Food-Masters' and how you put him out the car on some damn Main street. You crazy, he's your brother? That's some bama-shit you pulled. He's going to be the only one who got your back out here when everybody else is going to be against you, trying to testify an all that bullshit, and no not to mention Tiffany! How the hell do you manage to disrespect two people who care the most about you? Either of them would gladly die for your crazy ass in these streets' and you're running around here disrespecting them, what type of bamma-shit is that Malik? I'm telling you know, ain't many people out here in this lifestyle who'll have your back the way them two will, this paper got your head all fucked-up. You need to find a way to mend this shit, and poor Tiffany, everything that chile do out here is so that hopefully one of these days you'll began to see her for who she is and not the trick your mind makes her out to be. I gave her the G-pack and she'll be giving you six-hundred, I'm willing to bet my life that she pays you!"

"Auntie Pam, she's going to smoke that shit and you know it. I can't believe that you gave that girl all that CRACK," said Malik shaking his head already counting that G-pack as a lost.

She could tell that he wasn't buying what she was saying so she had to do something to stop the bleeding, "I'll tell you what, If she mess up one penny, I'll pay you back double what she owes you myself, you got a lot to learn. This CRACK shit is highly addictive but that shit ain't got anything on LOVE and Tiffany worships the ground you walk on. She'd kill somebody before she let your paper get fucked-up," said Auntie Pam as she looked over at him to see if he was buying what she was selling. So far, so good! "Malik, have you ever heard of one single person that Tiffany has tricked without here? Believe this, that girl could have anyone one of these silly lil' dudes out here with that body she got, but she don't fuck around. You so stupid, you can't even tell that you're the only man hitting that pussy because you're too worried about how much CRACK she's out here smoking. What you need to realize is that she's an asset and not a liability to you...The sooner you realize that the better off you'll be."

She folded her arms over her chest and spoke almost in a whisper," Malik, never make the mistake of judging a person just because they smoke CRACK... Shit, I smoke more CRACK than the average human but I don't see you running around here disrespecting me...You know why? Simple, I demand your respect and that shit ain't got anything to do with me being your Aunt either so don't get that shit twisted!"

He knew that Auntie Pam was dropping jewel' and the story was right an exact, and all that knowledge at one time was a bit much for him, it gave him a head ache. He needed some time and space to process all that shit she was kicking to him, plus the weed still had him going. For a split second he thought about how much Tiffany cared about him, but he still couldn't get past the fact that, to him, she loved CRACK more than she loved him and he didn't want to have to deal with it right now, maybe later. As for as Joey, he was definitely wrong for putting him out the car on Main street, especially with that little beef, how can he know for certain that dude really squashed that beef? He doesn't! To add injury to insult, there would be nothing he could do to help him, and the icing on the cake is that Joey saved him from a very long and lonely prison sentence.

"Malik, all I want you to do out here, is realize who's who, you can handle the rest on your own, you feel me?" "I hear you Auntie Pam, I can't help but hear you," he said smiling. "Now take my ass back home, I don't need to go to the store, I just needed some time alone to speak with you and since now that's out the way, you're keeping me away from my stem and a good time," said Auntie Pam.

After speaking with Auntie Pam and telling her about what happened at 'Food-Masters', Joey decided to give Terri a call and have her meet him at Mel's. Anytime he found himself stressed out, he liked to surround himself with people who he knew for sure had his best interest at heart, so this couldn't have been a better time than to call his baby and spend a little time with her! With Malik over Auntie Pam's with Tiffany, he knew that he could relax a little, if nobody else, Malik would listen to Auntie Pam. He made all of his calls while strolling down Main Street and by the time he got to the parking lot of Mel's, Terri was just pulling in. The G37 Infiniti was looking immaculate, but the best was yet to be seen in all of its glory, Terri.

She looked fabulous standing beside the car, just the sight of her brought a huge smile across his face, not wanting to prolong it any longer; he walked straight over to her and gave her a long and passionate kiss. "You hungry, babe," he asked? Terri loved for him to show her attention and especially in public, and he wasn't afraid of showing his weaker side, if he even had one. But, for her, spending time with him was something that she took very seriously, and not to mention that he's allowing her this close to the hood, she was going to take advantage of every second with him.

"I can always use a bite to eat, especially when it's with my king," she said giggling. When she looked up and looked into his eyes she could sense that something wasn't right with him but she couldn't put her finger on it right away. She was going to make it her business to figure out what exactly was the matter with her king, and she was determined. "Babe, I've never been inside, can we eat here?"

Joey grabbed her hand and led her into Mel's, trying to be funny, "thank-you, sir!" As she passed him while he was still holding the door for her he smacked her lightly on her round ass. He knew it wouldn't be a good idea to deny her one of Charlottesville's best kept secrets in Mel's, he had some of the best food in the entire city and he wanted to share that with her. It was usual practice for him to eat at Mel's as often as possible, that way he was guaranteed a full course meal. Most hustlas didn't pay much attention to how or what they ate.

"What's happening Joey," said an older voice from behind the counter? "Haven't seen you in a couple of days, where you been?"

"You know me Mel, I stay on the low and out the way of these sucka-ass dudes, I know you can feel me on that," said Joey. Mel took one look down at Terri and said," oh, I can tell."

"Let me get two of your dinner specials to go," said Joey as he winked over at Terri. He made it his business not to introduce Terri to the ole' time gansta. He dropped a fifty on the table and walked with Terri over in the opposite direction so that they could sit in the corner and wait on their food out of sight of the ole' time gansta.

Using Mel's wandering eyes as his excuse not to have to sit in there and eat, he made small talk, but for her, this was something like a field trip and she was soaking up every minute of it. She decided to talk to him about the closing on the Atlanta Complex they bought and to mention the nice little house she wanted to buy them in Albemarle County.

"Joey, I thought we were going to eat here," she said instead of what she really wanted to say?

As if he was reading her mind he said, "So how's the business thang going?" Before she got the opportunity to answer his question, the older guy whom she now knew as Mel told them their food was ready.

Joey took the food and nodded as he gave him a little wink, by the time he turned back around, Terri was standing at the door with it wide open waiting on him as he did for her. Just as he was about to step out the door, in came Silas and Philly slamming into his shoulder. The bump seemed to be on purpose but it didn't register with him right away, he was about to say, pardon yourself, but Terri snatched him by the arm pulling him out the door.

Her eyes locked in on the pair, she knew enough about the streets to know something wasn't right, this was one of those times. Instincts took over, if she could tell that move was well calculated, so should Joey. She didn't want him doing nothing to put him or her in danger.

From Joey's recent moves from not carrying a gun to having a gun and a vest at all times was enough to let her know that shit was real out there in the streets and just because she was from the suburbs shit didn't mean nothing when someone that you loved seemed to be in danger! Taking into account how the stranger was staring back at them and mouthing something only confirmed that he and Joey were far from friends. She managed to read his lips and he was saying, 'I hate pussies,' and what surprised her most was the fact that she wasn't even scared. She knew that Joey would protect her with his life and quiet as kept, she would do the same for him.

"Come on baby, let's get out of here," she said calmly. He didn't hesitate getting in the car at her request but not without comfortably palming his gun and knocking the safety off. The pair was still staring out the window at him and it took him all of 2 seconds to put 2 and 2 together; the guy who bumped him was Sosa's partner from 'Food- Masters'. Sosa must've called his partner and told him about the incident at 'Food-Masters'? With Terri with him, there was no way he was going to let these dudes get the best of him much less put Terri in an uncomfortable situation, so leaving was the best thing he could do.

Excited, Terri was running her mouth hundred miles a minute with question after question but he wasn't really paying her any attention, he had to get to the hood to get some background information on these dudes Silas and Sosa.

"Drop me off at my car on West Street," he said not even looking over at her.

"I thought we were going to the room and relax a little bit, "she asked?

"I know that's what you thought; I thought the same thing until that little run-in back there."

"I know, I know, business is business," she said giving up the thought of changing his mind; his eyes told her all she needed to know. "You know them guys', don't you?"

Joey leaned over the console and kissed her on the lips as she double parked beside his car," you know I love you right?" Knowing that his calling to the streets was something she never wanted to compete against she made sure that he had his food and made him promise to be in as soon as possible.

"Call me when you get a chance," she said.

"I will! Hopefully I'll be done early and we can spend some time together," he said winking.

"Please do," was all she said as he closed the door and she pulled-off not even looking in her rear-view mirror.

_____ _____ _____ _____ _____ _____
_____

Silas was fuming with anger because Joey wouldn't engage into his bullshit. Since he had heard him and his man Malik was pussy, he's been itching to get at them so that he could have a reason to really push their shit back. He felt all that paper they were making should be coming his way, they didn't deserve it, he did.

Later that night, Jazzy came strolling in Auntie's house switching her ass off as if her shit didn't stink in her brand new Prada mini-skirt, her oversized Coach bag, the official Gucci pumps with the silk blouse to match, complete with the Gucci scarf around her neck. She started twisting and turning like she was in a runway model contest in the center of the living room.

"What's good with ya'll bitches," she asked smiling as her speech slurred?

Amanda looked over at White-girl as if she couldn't believe this bitch; she couldn't believe that Jazzy had the nerve to come up in there flaunting her shit like that. After a few blunts, beers, and more lines of cocaine than a broke down television in the Projects', she was a bit off her rocker as well, but she wasn't stupid! The only thing on her mind was how Jazzy had left them in Aunties house since yesterday and nobody has heard from her since. The last time they had seen her when she handed over 2 ounces of CRACK and was like I'll be back in 2 hours!' She's been M.I.A. ever since!

"White-girl, look what the wind finally blew in," said Amanda with anger.

"Oh, Don't hate bitch," said Jazzy as she turned one more circle so that everybody could get a good look," You like?"

Amanda rolled her eyes and began putting all the CRACK they had just finished cutting up into one bag instead of doing what they were about to do with it. She no longer felt like bagging up. Then she turned to face White-girl, "come on, let's bounce...This drunk bitch think we stupid!" All the alcohol Jazzy had consumed had taken control of her best judgment and Amanda's little comment brought her back to reality.

"What the fuck you mean by that," asked Jazzy?

"Bitch I ain't got time to be sitting here talking to your drunk-ass when it's evident," said Amanda pointing at her new designer clothes.

What you better be doing is telling me something since you're putting my shit all in your bag and talking about ya'll leaving...Bitch, ya'll got the game fucked-up if you think you're going somewhere with my shit. That's my CRACK and paper you got in your bag in case you forgot...You must have bumped your head," slurred Jazzy.

"Don't be stupid bitch," said Amanda barely above a whisper and just as calm as ever as she stepped so close to Jazzy that they were nose to nose.

Jazzy balled her fist-up real tight because it wasn't like she didn't know who she was dealing with, but the alcohol had already got the best of her, she knew that if she was going to strike she had to strike first. Amanda has been fighting most of her battles for her since they were in elementary school; nevertheless, Jazzy swung a lazy right hand at Amanda's head. Amanda didn't have to even duck, she just calmly took one step backwards watching the tail end of the punch travel to where her head would have been had she not reacted. It took Amanda all of a second to jump into action on her cousin as a 4- punch combination found its intended target, Jazzy's face! Her punches were lighting quick and powerful.

Before Auntie or White-girl had a chance to get off the sofa Jazzy was laying on the floor out cold and snoring from the damage. She had a deep gash above her left eye; her nose seemed to be crooked as the blood flowed freely out of her mouth and nose at the same time destroying her beautiful silk blouse.

"I told you don't be stupid, didn't I," yelled Amanda as she stood over her cousin as she whipped out her favorite straight razor. She had to smack her couple of times to wake her back up, with the straight razor only inches from Jazzy's face, she began to speak," bitch, I don't care nothing about us being family...Get yo' stupid-ass up!"

Jazzy tried to blink her eyes to focus but it was no use, her whole face felt like it was about to explode and she had a head-ache from hell. At the sight of Amanda's straight razor, she seemed to be able to focus a little as she listened to what Amanda was saying to her," bitch, like I said, I don't care nothing about us being family, you crossed me and I'd be damn if I let that shit happen again. If I didn't love your mother so much I would've been sliced your ugly face wide the fuck open, but I know you'll go running back telling everybody how I did you dirty, just know that you played yourself."

Taking her Coach bag and dumping the contents all over the rug until she found what she was looking for; a fat wad of cash was rolled-up in a sock," I guess this belongs to me since you already got your cut!"

Amanda and White-girl was on their way out the door when she turned back around and said to Jazzy," Oh, you killin' dat outfit, girrrl," she said laughing her ass off. White-girl fell in stride right behind her, although she didn't have to say one word, she already knew that Amanda would play fair with her, Jazzy was dead weight as far as she was concerned!

Auntie tried her best to try and get Jazzy to go to the Emergency room because her face was battered and bruised and she thought she could use a couple stitches to close up the gash over her eye. She knew that Jazzy's pride was bruised along with the rest of her body but she had to somehow get her some help, "Jazzy, you gotta go to the hospital."

All Jazzy wanted to do was lay down, it's been a long day, she'd been drinking all day long as she rode up to D.C. and back. "I'm good! Just get me some more ice; I'll be a-ight."

"I took and told you about being grimy to them girls," said Auntie as she walked back in the kitchen for the 10th time to get more ice. "In this game you have to let the people that's the closest to you know that they can trust you, whatever move you made without including them really fucked Amanda up. That shit had her fucked up all day long, and who the fuck is this Silas character you supposedly got some weight from yesterday?"

That was all it took for Jazzy to snap out of her daze, at the mention of Silas and weight in the same sentence it all began to make sense now," what you say about Silas," she asked?

"Girl, have you been listening to me? Any who...The guy Silas told Amanda and White-girl that you got some weight from him but you failed to mention that to either of your so-called partners. All they kept saying was how ya'll was supposed to be partners in this shit but they have to learn about your moves, second-hand. Amanda didn't want to believe dude, it wasn't until you came in here strutting your shit like your shit don't stink all up in their face. Them bitches been in here rubbing pennies together to get their little drink on being careful not to dip in the paper from the CRACK sales until they talk to you , and you turn around and come up in here like that talking sideways to that girl, you know she crazy just like her damn father."

Auntie put the ice-pack on the table and continued talking," those girls are green when it comes to this CRACK shit Jazzy but that damn Amanda. Her heart is as big as Texas with the attitude to match. All I'm saying is if I were you, I would've carried that shit totally different, you carried that shit ass backwards. You hurt them girl's feelings!"

She made Jazzy look at the whole situation differently and she wanted to tell her that she didn't know what the fuck she was talking about but she couldn't. Every time she went to cut Auntie off, she said something that made a lot of sense. In her best attempt to do as she's seen her brother Blacko do over the years with his team, she failed! If he could work his team 24/7, she figured she could do the same thing with Amanda and White-girl. He never paid his guys, where did she go wrong, she thought? Not realizing his secret, because it was in the fact he made sure to keep his soldiers satisfied: plenty weed, bitches, sneakers, and out of town trips to compensate for their lack of income. "Auntie, help me move the sofa," she asked?

Under the sofa was a huge bag of CRACK she hid in the springs of the sofa for a rainy day. Breaking off a small piece from one of the larger rocks, Jazzy snatched a stem from out the ash-tray and placed the rock on the stem. She took her lighter and put the stem to her lips as she took her very first blast of CRACK cocaine.

Auntie couldn't believe her eyes, Jazzy sucking a glass-dick! Part of her wanted to rush over and stop her, but her eyes were glued to the huge bag of

CRACK and her own deadly addiction. Her own desire to get high forced her to keep her mouth shut and sit back and await her turn at the stem because she knew it was coming, that bag was enough for them to smoke on for a while. With Jazzy just embarking on her first mission on her way up to see 'Scotty', she would need some assistance and she'd be right there to help her every step of the way. Her wheels were already turning as she thought about all the fun times that lie ahead. Jazzy blew the smoke out real slow and she was hooked the instant the thick cloud of white smoke left her lungs. She heard bells ringing in her ears and she had a euphoric feeling that took over her body.

The highly addictive drug had paralyzed her body but she loved how it made her feel in a strange way. She wanted to move her body but she couldn't! She wanted to say something, but she couldn't! The only thing on her body that seemed to listen to her commands were her eyes as they darted from left to right and then back left again. Even the pain in her face was long gone, that was the best part, a true pain reliever she'd found in CRACK cocaine. Her body was numb, even the thoughts in her head seemed not to be of any importance and she loved it. Deciding to sit back and relax and let the CRACK do its job as it continued to invade her system. There was one thing that she noticed from the high that was similar but way more intense from sniffin' powder, she couldn't close her eyes and it seemed like she could hear a mouse pissing on cotton.

"Auntie, you hear that, she asked? Auntie was watching her like a hawk from out the corner of her eye and that huge bag of CRACK was something to stare at. She knew Jazzy was starting to get paranoid. "Make sure the door is locked," said Jazzy.

This was what she was waiting for, eyeing the bag of CRACK, she figured that it was at the least 5 ounces or better, she got up to show Jazzy that she was locking the door even though the door locks on its own once it's closed. Jazzy put the bag of CRACK on the table and ran to the window saying," you hear that?"

Auntie didn't say one word, she walked over to the bag of CRACK and decided to bless herself with 2 huge rocks, 'she won't get me like the rest of them,' stuffing the CRACK down her pants. There was no need to second guess herself for stashing the CRACK to the side, she wouldn't wait on Jazzy to do it, she couldn't afford to.

For the next day and a half, Jazzy and Auntie smoked CRACK like their minds were gone bad. They talked, smoked cigarettes, and drank cheap wine. Auntie noticed that Jazzy couldn't get enough of the CRACK, every time she took a hit; Auntie stole rocks dropping them in her purse on the floor. It all came to a head two days later when she noticed Jazzy going through a mini-crisis over the CRACK because it was all gone.

"I know we ain't smoke no damn 5 ounces in 2 days, did we?" In Auntie's head this would become Jazzy's very first lesson in the smoking game, so she decided to hold out and see exactly what Jazzy would be willing to do to get her hands on more CRACK, Auntie has seen some crazy shit over the years.

"Don't worry about no more CRACK, you gotta get some rest," she said looking into Jazzy's eyes.

"I...I can't...I still owe Silas like three-thousand, I paid him half when I got that weight from him and he fronted me the rest. Shit! Shit! What am I going to do? Fuck it, I'm going to call him, I need more CRACK," she said pulling out her cell phone.

CHAPTER 10

BY the time Amanda and White-girl had made their way back across town to Prospect, she was feeling some type of way about what she had done to Jazzy. All night long they went back and forth about what Jazzy done to them and the more she listened to what White-girl had to say; it began to make more and more sense to her.

"Amanda, don't sit here blaming yourself for what you had to do to Jazzy, she had that shit coming. She did that shit to herself! What you should be doing is looking at the bright side; at the very least, you found out what type of chick she is now rather than later, you feel me," asked White-girl?

"I know that's right, but still, I didn't have to fuck her up like that," said Amanda as she looked-up into White-girl's eyes. Then she busted out laughing," yes I should have, I gave that bitch just what she was asking for...I guess it's just me and you now, huh?"

"It's always been me and you Amanda! Jazzy just happened to be your cousin, since you're so loyal she tried to use that shit against you and use me at the same time. The good thing about this is we learned how cruddy she really was, the flip-side is that we learned how to hustle this CRACK shit. We can use what we already got and get our own thang going right here in Prospect! We got options baby, we got options, that's all I'm saying."

She knew she had Amanda's attention and it was time to prep her for the next phase of her plan. "I'm saying, fucking with Jazzy like that you know on that CRACK shit: We know how that shit works and we can get our own paper," she said looking over at Amanda. This was the moment she was waiting for, she stared in Amanda's eyes and said it again," we can do our own thang. Your boy Silas is already feeling you and he got that weight. What? You're going to fuck him anyway, so why not use that to our advantage. Let's kill two birds with one stone!"

With her mind going a hundred-plus miles an hour, Amanda was surprised and caught off guard at the same time by White-girls' straight forward and blunt talk. It was as if White-girl was directing a movie or writing a book or some shit, for once she seemed to have all the answers and know all the moves to make.

"I'm feeling everything you're saying girl, but on the real; we're not fucking with Silas on that level and that's the end of that!"

White-girl's smile quickly turned into a frown as she sat back and listened to what Amanda had to say. " Don't be turning up your damn nose at me like that," said Amanda with much attitude. "I know somebody else that we can holla at and I know that he'll look out for us. My cousin Blacko, that's Jazzy's brother and you're absolutely correct, I'm going to fuck Silas in due time so there's no need in mixing business with pleasure."

That's what she wanted to hear from her comrade, the smile slowly started coming back to her, "you had a bitch scared there for a minute. I ain't know what was going through that head of yours! Call'em, let's get this shit jumping," insisted White-girl.

Amanda fell out laughing at how White-girl was urging her to hurry up and get down to business," this'll be good, plus, I want him to hear what happened between me and Jazzy from me first, that bitch will fuck up the whole story. Not to mention it's early and I get to wake his ass up because I know he's still in the bed sleeping," she said grabbing her phone to call her favorite cousin, Blacko! It didn't take him long to answer, he answered on the first ring, "yo' talk slick and make it quick..."

" Blacko, what up? This Amanda, where you at right now...You still sleep?"

"I know who this is, I do have caller I.D.," he said laughing at her.

"I'm at my spot right now but I'm on my way out the door as we talk...Why?"

She hesitated, "I'm...I'm saying...I...I need to holla at you about something."

"Go 'head and holla then! I don't have much time, I got some business to handle so talk fast."

"I can't! I need to holla at you face to face, it's not proper to be on the jack like this," she said giggling.

"Yeah a-ight...Meet me at McDonald's downtown in thirty minutes and don't be late," hanging up his phone before she had the chance to respond. He knew that Amanda wanted to talk to him about something that could get him in a situation that he didn't want to be in so the best thing he could do was to get off the jack as soon as possible. It had to involve the lifestyle; Paper, Drugs, Sex, and Violence. He had already heard that she and his sister had been posted-up over on Page Street chasing some paper so he quickly put two and two together. He was thinking Jazzy had got her to call him because she knew that he would do shit for Amanda before he would his own sister.

He smiled at the thought of Amanda stacking her own paper, after all, she was a natural hustla and she got it honest...Her pops blood was definitely a gift and a curse for her. It didn't hurt that she was his favorite cousin and she reminded him of his new connect, he looked forward to seeing her after not seeing her for a couple of weeks and didn't mind having her meet him at McDonald's. His new connect was mad cool and fly as hell, never in a million years would he have thought out of all the connects he's had on his journey, the best of all them would be a female. For the last 8 month's he's been dealing with Karma. From the jump all he wanted to do was to fuck her but she was only interested in the business, she never gave him her cell number, never talked about anything outside of business and he didn't know nothing more than her name. Since she gave him all the CRACK that he could handle, he learned quick to adjust to her ways of doing business and there was no argument in that.

Blacko pulled into McDonald's and parked his little hooptie right next to a Lexus where Karma was waiting; he got in the car with her. Soon as he sat back in the seat, Amanda came strolling out McDonald's staring at his car, it was evident she was looking for him as her eyes scanned the parking lot. They stopped at the Lexus, she smiled and started walking towards the Lexus. She figured that the fly chick sitting behind the steering wheel was the business he spoke about having to handle, and she couldn't blame him, if she was into girls, then she would have one just as fly as the female sitting in the Lexus, she thought to herself.

He put his index finger up trying to stop her before she got to close to the Lexus. "Blacko, who's that girl," asked Karma in high alert?

"That's my little cousin Amanda," he said beaming with pride because Amanda had a certain swag about herself!

Pulling the Mac.90 from the floor board, Karma said, "and you told her to meet you here?"

It didn't take Blacko long to realize what she was getting at as he watched as Karma had the Mac.90 trained on his rib-cage, "it..it ain't like that Karma!"

Her and my sister been trapping over on Page street and she wanted to holla at me as I was leaving to come meet you here. She's probably looking for a deal or something, my sister got her to call most likely, usually she's late all the time so I thought by the time I finish with you that she'll be here...I...I can tell her to bounce and I'll holla at her later if you want," he offered?

Without ever taking her eyes off of Amanda or the barrel of the Mac.90 away from his rib-cage, she began talking to him real calm and slow, "won't you go over there and tell her that I want to talk to her myself." There was something about Amanda that she couldn't deny, she reminded Karma of herself and she wasn't going to waste an opportunity meeting another female who had the potential as she has, Girl-Power! Blacko waved her over.

He got out the Lexus and embraced his cousin Amanda and whispered in her ear at the same time, "yo, get in the car, somebody want to meet you."

Playing it off, Amanda said, "hey Blacko, haven't seen you in a minute, by the way, you're getting fat," she said punching him softly on the arm. "But, I need to holla at you about Jazzy, we got into a fight!"

"Don't worry about that right now, I'm sure she deserved the ass kicking that you gave her, she's always trying to be slick and she thinks everybody else is stupid, so don't worry about it, this is more important," he said nodding his head towards the Lexus. When Amanda got in the car, the stranger nodded her head and gave her a pleasant smile," come on get in, Amanda, right," asked the stranger?

Looking confused, Amanda nodded her head, "yeah, it's Amanda, but who are you," she asked back as she eased her slender body in the soft leather seats comfortably?

Blacko detected the feisty attitude in Amanda's voice and said, "cuzo, be easy, this is a very good woman, you want to get to know her...Trust me," he said walking over to the driver's side window. Karma couldn't help from laughing as she hit the button to let her window down, "Blacko, go check the trash can in the men's bathroom over at Wendy's, you'll find what you're looking for there."

She focused her attention back to Amanda without even taking her eyes off the rear-view mirror as her eyes followed Blacko across the parking lot to Wendy's. "So, what you wanted to holla at Blacko about?"

Amanda couldn't believe her ears, the first thing that she thought couldn't be the truth, was this Blacko's connect? It had to be, why else would she tell him to go over to Wendy's and look in the trash can? She could hear his voice in her head, 'she's somebody that you need to holla at,' she trusted him with her life so she decided to just go with the flow. Amanda decided not to beat around the bush and for some strange reason she started feeling more comfortable in the stranger's presence.

"I, I was going to see if I could buy something from him. You know that way, I'd know that everything is legit."

"Good!" That was all Karma said, she took out her cell and called Blacko she seen him was coming out of the Wendy's parking lot," yo, you get straight," she asked. Shaking her head up and down, she broke her cell phone in half and threw it out the window," can't be too careful these days," she said with a grin on her face as she put the car in reverse ready to leave.

"Karma, my girl is still in McDonald's, I can't just up and leave her in there," said Amanda. "Go tell her to meet you later, I like you and all that but I don't like you enough to be meeting your girl, this is between me and you and nobody else."

There was no way in hell that Amanda was going to fuck this up, she wasn't getting out that car, she took her cell out and called White-girl, "yo, meet me back at the crib, I got something I have to take care of ....Yeah, you be careful too," she said hanging the up.

"I hope that your girl is very patient? You'll be with me for a while, hope you don't get home sick or nothing," said Karma poking fun at Amanda." You can handle that can't you?"

The Lexus eased out the parking lot, Amanda just nodded at her, she was a big girl and she could handle just about anything the hood had to offer, she's proven that over and over again in the past. The Lexus didn't stop until they got to the Burger King at Zion Cross Roads. This wasn't new to Amanda, she knew exactly where she was, smiling on the inside!

"You hungry," asked Karma?

Amanda turned her nose up because she hated Burger King, "naw, I'm good, I don't eat here," she said seriously.

That didn't stop Karma from placing her order and pulling out the parking lot as she headed back towards route 250 back towards Charlottesville. Amanda was thinking to herself that they had just ridden all the way down the country just to stop at Burger King. It wasn't until Karma made the left turn onto 676, the country roads didn't have names only numbers and that's what Karma said and laughed at her own joke.

Amanda caught the accent and she figured Karma was either from New York or New Jersey, somewhere up north. Karma eased the Lexus into a long driveway of what appeared to be a brand new house that had just been built there. "Come on," said Karma as she removed the towel from her lap revealing the Mac.90 for the first time.

Amanda wasn't moved by the sight of the Mac.90, that was the life in the hood, at the same time she had slide her straight razor out the minute she seen the towel on Karma's lap, she was good, she thought! She got out the car and followed Karma towards the huge house, and then all of a sudden Karma stopped dead in her tracks and turned to face her. She smiled once again at Amanda and then said to her, "oh, by the way Amanda, you can leave your straight razor behind; you won't be needing that around here, girl!"

Instead of going in the front door, Amanda followed Karma in through the 3-car garage, down a flight of stairs, around a corner, and into the basement of the mammoth house. It looked even bigger from the inside! While she followed Karma she got a good look at her stylish form fitting True Religion jeans, the matching tee-shirt, down to her Gucci sneakers, however, it was the huge Presidential men's Rolex on her tiny wrist that really caught her attention. The last time Amanda had seen one of them outside of watching television was when Safee' was still on the streets, and if she wasn't mistaken, he had one just like that. The basement was well decorated and very spacious. The 60-inch flat-screen was mounted over the fire place and surrounded by 5 or 6 big lazy-e-boys, a pool-table, ping-pong table and a small kitchen off to the left of where they were standing. They took a seat in front of what appeared to be a fully stacked wet-bar, "Have a seat Amanda, I'll be with you in just a minute," said Karma.

Grabbing a walkie-talkie from the end of the wet-bar, she began speaking in fluent Spanish into its receiver and 30 seconds later, two other Spanish ladies entered the basement. One of the Spanish ladies walked right over to where Amanda was sitting, almost invading her personal space, she looked Amanda up and down and then turned to leave the basement without saying a word to her. However, it was the other Spanish lady who spoke and confused her," take you clothes off, please," she said to her!

"What? Take my clothes off?" '

'Well, yes! Take your clothes off, in order for this to go well, you'll have to do as she says, there's no compromise, if you don't want to take your clothes off, I can take you back to where I found you, but ummm, you know by now we can't be too careful," smiled Karma.

Amanda didn't have time to respond, the other Spanish lady who invaded her personal space was back and she dropped a brand new Gucci sweat suit on the chair beside her," oh, you want me to put that on, huh? Why you didn't just say that," said Amanda?

She nodded her head and changed her clothes, she got naked in front of the 3 ladies as if this was something she done on a regular basis. Satisfied with Amanda's new outfit, Karma dismissed the other two Spanish ladies and spent the next 2 hours explaining the rules and regulations to Amanda. The do's and the don'ts as well, and she explained the purpose of changing her clothes, because the Feds will bug any and everything, if she was in her birthday suit and was willing to have her clothes taken then everything was on the up and up between them.

Amanda couldn't believe that Karma had agreed to become her new connect and she was loving everything Karma was telling her. Even though she was new to the CRACK game, the numbers she was hearing sounded crazy, she thanked her cousin Blacko on the inside because she knew he'd given her a new life! After all the listening she only had one question and that was, "so why are you doing this for me?"

Karma turned very serious as she answered the question, "don't look at it like that at all, because really, I'm not the one doing anything! This is all you, you're taking all the risk, so be very clear as to what's happening here. You could very well spend the rest of your life in somebody's prison if you were to slip one time, Amanda, this is a serious game and I don't have to remind you of that. You have to have skin of leather and be able to think on your feet, if you can do that, you can get in and get out a very rich woman, and last but not least, you remind me of a young girl that I once knew," she said staring intently into Karma's eyes.

Amanda had a lot on her plate to weigh, there were a lot of things that came with the drug game she had to consider, things like; Prison, Death, and being robbed! She wasn't naive by a long shot, she knew firsthand the havoc drugs could reek on someone's life, whether that person's a user or a seller, at the end of the day it was always the same; Prisons and Death! In her mind the risk was worth the reward, she quickly thought about her life and how she was always surrounded by the bullshit. She found out a long time ago she wasn't College material, barely wifey material after all the dicks she's ran through, either sucking or fucking it was all the same, and when you combine the things she's done for powder cocaine, it was ugly.

The only logical alternative for her and having a better life was for her to come up in the CRACK game. Karma made her swear to secrecy and the penalty would be death and she agreed. Six hours after meeting Karma, she was back at her apartment in Prospect with 18 ounces of CRACK, nervous as hell but eager to get the ball rolling. When she walked into her apartment, White-girl was stretched out on the sofa watching television.

"Damn girl, your cousin really loves you, doesn't he? He must've taken you shopping or some shit," said White-girl realizing that she didn't have any shopping bags.

She couldn't help but laugh at White-girl's happiness for her even though she was dead wrong about what took place between her and her cousin. "No silly, he ain't take me shopping, but what I can tell you is that he introduced me to somebody special," she said dropping the 18 ounce's onto the living room floor!

After bringing White-girl up to speed and without having to tell her all the information recalling her promise to Karma, the both of them started exchanging ideas about the best way for them to get the ball rolling and see some major paper. They were on the same page, they both wanted lots of paper and with the new CRACK connect on their side reality began to sit in.

"What the hell are we going to do with all this damn CRACK," asked Amanda?

"Girl, don't punk-out on me now! We're going to sell the fuck out this shit, that's what the hell we're going to do," said White-girl full of excitement.

"I already know that much, smarty. At first, we had Jazzy here to help us and put us in the right position with the right people like Auntie, but who's going to help us now...We gotta find somebody to help us move the shit," said Amanda!

"How about we go outside and holla at your boy Jacob and his crew...They out here 24/7 selling that shit Amanda, it only makes sense to get shit moving through the dudes who be out here anyway."

In the back of Amanda's head she could hear Karma's voice saying, don't sweat the small stuff...Get rid of the work in weight, its less trouble to move. She walked over to the window and sure enough, Jacob and his whole crew out there selling CRACK and shooting dice. She looked over her shoulder at White-girl and said, "you're starting to sound like you've done this shit before. Everything you've been saying lately has been making a lot of sense. Are you sure you're not an under-cover Queen-Pin or some shit," asked Amanda laughing.

"For real though, you're going to be the brains behind this shit we're going to do, can't anybody say you're green now," she said hoping to boost White-girl's ego.

One thing that White-girl found out the day she started hanging with her was the hood had big respect for her, regardless of what she done to get her hustle on, the hood maintained a certain level of respect for her and now she had to remind her of that.

Having her tag along with her while she went to holla at Jacob wasn't a good look, "Amanda, I think you should go and holla at Jacob by yourself. You don't need me tagging along, that's not a good look right now, maybe later, but not right now!"

"You right! I don't want none of them thinking shit is sweet...You know how I gets down, I'll cut one of them in a New York minute," said Amanda laughing at herself as she flashed a new straight razor.

"Sounds like a plan. Let's weigh out two quarters and you give one to Jacob for G.P., from there you should be able to gain his attention, he's greedy anyways." She was really feeling what White-girl was saying and trying to do, however, she had a little something to add to it," I'll give him one of the quarters, but I want to give the other one to somebody who gets high, that way we can see paper from both sides of the coin."

"Fuck it then, we can sell weight and open a CRACK house, we'll have that bitch jumping all day and all night long," said White-girl giving Amanda a high five.

Amanda left her apartment and walked up to the top of the hill and spotted Jacob by his loud mouth bent down on one knee in the middle of the dice game shooting dice. He was saying out loud, "that's right, four brings ten every time… Big Ben bitch," he continued to yell.

She walked in the middle of the circle and dropped a crispy hundred dollar bill. Two roll's later and he crapped-out just like she predicted. He rolled his eyes at her and said," you's a bad luck bitch!"

"First of all, only bitches roll their eyes and second, today's your lucky day. Come with me, and keep the paper, but I gotta holla at you right now in private."

Jacob knew that this day would come, in his head he was thinking she needed to get her nose right and was willing to come up off some of that good pussy of hers. With his wheels turning, he didn't waste a second getting up and following right behind her as she walked out of hearing distance of the other hard-heads out there. White-girl watched patiently from the window as Amanda led Jacob towards the park. She's a natural leader, she whispered to herself! Amanda didn't look nervous or scared one bit and she admired her for it. Her dream was to one day be able to be just as bold and forth-corning as Amanda, and when she seen that Jacob couldn't take his eyes off her round-ass she again whispered, that's going to be his down-fall one day.

When she made it to the park, she went and took a seat on the swings with Jacob almost tripping over her as she suddenly stopped. When she turned around she had to laugh, his eyes were still glued to where her ass was but now he was staring at her pussy like a dog in heat. 'He thinks he's going to get some.' However, she had different plans and a different agenda! Not wanting to come off too hard or too cold, she had to refocus her attention at the task at hand and remember what Karma had said. It was already in her head, 'in this game, you have to boost egos not tear them down and those same egos will boost your paper flow.' "what's up with you Jacob?"

"What you mean by that? You already know what's up with me, but the real question should be, what's up with you sexy," he asked making it clear what was on his mind from the way he was looking at her.

Putting on her game face, Amanda began by making him a business deal that he wouldn't be able to turn down or walk away from. The one thing that she knew about him was the fact that he was still trying to get back from when Jazzy clipped him for his package. "I'm saying...I know you're out here chasing this paper, so here's the deal. I got 8-balls for one-twenty-five and quarters for two-fifty," she said as she reached in her pocket and tossed him a quarter. "This you, if you like it then holla, if not...Do you nigga!"

He rolled the quarter around in the palm of his hand and looked at the CRACK, he was eyeing the crystal-like features of the CRACK, "I'm saying, you got these for two-fifty, right?"

"That's what the fuck I said, ain't it," she said with a helluva attitude. She caught him off guard and she knew it by the stupid look on his face.

He fished into his pocket and pulled out two-fifty, "let me get another one of these since you said this one is on the house." She put her index finger up and turned around walking away from the swings, she pulled her cell called White-girl, "yo bitch, get me one more of them ready and meet me by the steps in about 3 minutes."

Not wanting him to know that she already had another quarter on her, it was best that she took control of the situation and when she finally turned back around to face him, she once again caught him staring at her ass and was about to tell him, that's going to be your down fall one of these days but decided against it, she let him enjoy himself. "We gotta bounce," is all she said and began walking away.

He followed closely behind her asking her a stupid question," yo Amanda, how much work you got?"

Again she had to laugh at him, for the first time she realized he wasn't nowhere near the gansta he portrayed. In fact, he was weak and looking for a wing to get up under, she decided to play him for what he's worth, "you know, you can't be asking a bitch like me no stupid-ass questions like that nigga," she said with authority!

"I'm saying," was all he got out his mouth before she cut him off," nigga, you ain't saying shit, if you're trying to fuck with me, then fuck with me, but don't be asking no questions like that no damn more!" She had his undivided attention and she knew it was time to go in for the kill, "listen to me Jacob, we can work together on this and both see a lot of paper. I know you're down to get paper, I've been watching you for a long time, together, we can become rich out here...Are you with me," she asked?

CHAPTER 11

BY the time Malik and Auntie Pam had got to Page Street two hours later and a trunk full of groceries for the house. She fooled him when she told him that she really didn't have to go to the store, she got him good. When he parked he noticed that Joey was sitting on the porch, a slight grin formed on his face, he was happy to see Joey and be able to get away from Auntie Pam!

"Where ya'll been, I been out here like two hours or more waiting for ya'll," said Joey grinning?

Auntie Pam had talked Malik's head off about loyalty, friendship and the CRACK game, he was no longer mad at Joey, more like a breath of fresh air to see his homey. She put everything in perspective and he appreciated it, looking at it from her angle, he really needed it.

"Joey come on down here and help with all these bags...She went and wiped out Food Lion." Auntie Pam sat back and watched her favorite two nephews and happy that her talk with Malik had worked because all the tension was gone. "Well gentlemen, I see that ya'll can handle this here, I gotta run down the block and holla at Auntie. She called me earlier and told me to stop by. Oh, by the way, ya'll make sure to put that milk and stuff away for me before it spoils," she said laughing as she walked away.

"You want us to put all this stuff away," asked Malik making a sweeping motion with his hands over the bags?

"And you know it! Yo' ass ain't too good to be putting away no groceries... Don't let this paper get the best of you, make sure you get the best of it. Remember our conversation," she said with a nod and a wink.

They eyed her as she made her way down the block towards Auntie's house. Joey walked over to Malik and asked him, "so what's good homey?"

With that mad-dog look on his face, Malik took a step in Joey's direction and embraced him, "we're brother's for life, you know that right?"

"Ain't no question about it, brother's for life, this one and the next!" Auntie Pam looked back over her shoulder just in time to see them embrace, she whispered, ' thank-you lord!' The importance of them staying focused and on the same page was something she was determined to see through and that's why she tried her damnest to beat it into Malik's head and it seemed to be working. She understood the streets were mean, with all that paper going through their hand's it was only a matter of time before the real goons came lurking and snooping around, they could smell the paper in the air. She could only pray and hope they would be ready when that day came. It's going to take the both of them to be on the same page in order to survive the storm! Once all the groceries were put away they decided to sit down and talk, but Joey almost forgot what he had for him, "oh shit, I almost forgot, Tiffany told me to give you this," he said tossing Malik three-hundred. "She said she'll have the rest for you later tonight."

It was evident that he had caught Malik off guard because he had that stupid look on his face as he stared at the paper on the coffee table. From the looks of things, Joey figured that whatever he had going on with Tiffany outside of their love/hate relationship, the paper had stagnated him. He knew she was special to him, he decided not to try an figure them out, that would be a waste of time.

Malik snatched the paper from the table and didn't waste his time counting it, she already proven him wrong! He shoved it in his pocket and looked over at Joey who was watching him closely," yo, good looking out!"

Joey wanted to shift gears; Malik wasn't talking about the paper between him and Tiffany, he pushing for answers, it wasn't his business. "Yo, you know son who be with the boy Sosa, the one from 'Food-Master's'?"

"Who? Silas? Yeah, I heard of dude, why?"

Joey took a second to get focused, "yeah him... I had a little run-in with him at Mel's a few hours ago."

"What you mean a little run-in?"

"I was thinking, you know, after I got out the car with you, I went to meet Terri at Mel's and when we were leaving out, son kinda bumped me on his way in!"

"What you mean he kinda bumped into you; he either bumped you or he didn't, you're confusing me."

"I'm thinking that the one from 'Food-Master's' told him what happened, know what I'm saying?"

Malik's eyes got big as he listened to Joey tell him what happened at Mel's, "I'm telling you Joey, those niggaz got a problem. First of all, how you think them niggaz even know who the fuck you are for him to be calling him homey and they have him bumping into you at Mel's? Those the same niggaz who was eyeing me all funny when I was at GoCo's before I got rid of the Range...What else happened? You were strapped, right?"

"Yeah I was strapped! It happened right after I got out the car with you so you know I was strapped, Terri was with me so I had to chill. I couldn't let nothing jump-off with her with me, but I got a funny feeling...These niggaz gonna be a problem," said Joey.

"If you think that, what the fuck we're going to do about it then?"

Joey stood-up and went to look out the window, "I ain't sure yet, but what I do know, the boy Silas be in the hood, and he ain't got no business in the Projects'. He be Angie's house all the time, something's up with that! That's too close for comfort if you ask me," said Joey firmly!

"Beef, they can get it, that ain't nothing to me. You already know how I feel about them niggaz, just know and understand, killaz move in silence and violence," said Malik grinning.

Joey couldn't keep from laughing at how eager Malik was but it wasn't really funny. It was more so the brotherly love that Malik had for him that made him get so serious at the mere mention of someone harming him, he had to fuck with him.

"What the hell you know about killaz son," asked Joey laughing?

"Oh, you got jokes, huh? Fuck the bullshit Joey, ain't no nigga gonna disrespect my brother out here. Ain't shit sweet with us! I'm telling you, them bitch niggaz can get it. I hate them up-top niggaz anyway," spit Malik almost out of breath.

"I'm feeling you on that homey. Mutha-fuckers been dropping little seeds on us for a minute about niggaz in our hood, but we didn't see it then. Them ole' heads seen this shit coming way before we did, but best believe, we'll be the ones addressing this shit. For now though, we'll just stay low and see how this nigga Silas is moving over here."

"You know what? Tiffany was saying something to me about that CRACK head nigga, Philly, from what she was saying, she thinks he's getting his work from the boy, Silas. The boy Silas be sitting on Angie's porch all night long while Philly hit the block and the bitch Angie hustle in the daytime.

Joey exhaled because he knew a decision had to be made. Mentally he was well prepared for this day to come, but the reality of it was overwhelming but he forced himself to remain focused and in control. As for Malik, that was another story, "fuck the bullshit, this our hood, that nigga Silas eating under our nose, He gotta go!"

Joey knew the most important thing was an effective plan, they couldn't just jump out there like this was the wild-west or some shit. "You're exactly right, Malik! We definitely gotta address this shit with the boy Silas before shit gets out of hand, however, remember, control is everything in the hood without it, we'll fail. With him in the hood, he's disrespecting us and getting paper that belongs to us and we can't have that, not in the Projects' anyway. Don't think for one second we're gonna sit back and take this shit, we have to be smart about it, you know?"

Malik stood-up, "now that's what the fuck I'm talking about Joey! I'm with you 200%, all we gotta do now is keep the attention off of us, when we push this niggaz wig back, ain't nobody gone know shit," said Malik with that devilish smirk of his.

"Tonight, tonight we'll post-up in the Projects' so we can see what we can see. We'll take it from there; nobody's seen us posted-up like that in a minute, we shouldn't stand out too bad. I want to see his reaction once he sees both of us together, we ain't gonna do nothing hot, we ain't trying to go to prison before the beef get-to-cookin', all we need to see is his reaction."

"Another thing, Tiffany said he be shooting dice with the young-boys, so we know he ventures off the porch sometimes, and that's a positive for us. I've never walk away from a good dice game," said Malik.

Joey knew Malik was up to no good but at the same time he didn't want to spoil the moment, "snatch-up 5-stacks, we'll take it to the dice game, I'm sure that type of paper will bring your boy off the porch once he hears about the game. If that doesn't catch his attention, he's harmless, which I doubt!"

Malik visualized himself walking into the dice game and dropping 5-stacks and calling for the bank. "You already know what it is with me, ain't shit getting pass me, call me the fucking bank-stopper." He was excited at the chance to be back in the Projects doing what he loved to do outside of hustlin' CRACK, Gambling! Since getting rid of the Range Rover, the connect had urged them to stay out the Projects, and ever since, they spent 98% of their time down on Page.

However, anybody who was anybody knew all the action was in the Projects' and he missed it. The connect was right about keeping a low profile. With Silas in the Projects getting paper, they had do something, or else control would be lost and they wasn't having that. The Projects' was known to keep out-of Towner's out, unless they were crazy-cool, and nobody could vouch for Silas. That was something that just didn't happen in Northwest Charlottesville; the Projects' grew and produced their own Gansta's, ask B-Stacks! Malik had every intention of keeping in line with the legendary ganstas who came before him. There was no way he wouldn't protect not only his life or that of Joey's, but the whole hood as well! The Projects' was off-limits to out-of Towner's because the control of the Projects' has always been in the hands of one of their own and Malik was determined that things wouldn't change on his watch. This was a huge test for them, and they wanted it, so they thought!

Joey glanced over at Malik and knew that he was deep in thought, the CRACK game was serious business, so he decided to change the subject," yo Malik, what's the deal with you, Tiffany and this paper? You making side deals that I need to know about?"

Malik shrugged his shoulders and said," I don't know what you're talking about," but the smile that was plastered all over his face told a different story!

Auntie Pam was growing more and more frustrated knocking on Aunties door. She knocked three different times already, so she decided to yell, "open this damn door with your crazy-ass, I know you in there!" She had a funny feeling that she was in the house, probably peeping out the window, paranoid and high as a public works light bill. Just when she was about to say fuck it and leave the front door flew open. Auntie Pam didn't recognize the younger chick who opened the front door. However, what she did recognize about the young chick right off the bat, was that she had the look of someone who hasn't slept in a couple of days with her puffy eyes and matted down hair. All that and her wrinkled clothes told a whole story.

"Hey Auntie Pam," said the young chick opening the door wide enough for her to follow her in. She nodded at the young chick and walked right pass her and stood in the middle of the living room. Quickly she made a mental note of the messiness and the foul smell of stale beer in the air. Putting two and two together, she could see why Auntie had called her asking for a helping hand, from the way they were living up in there, the little house was screaming: Help! If it wasn't for the fact that her and Auntie went so far back, she would've been turned around and left. They been down for each other since back in the 80's, at one time, they were partners in crime and couldn't nobody tell them different. Despite going their own ways and doing their own thang in the hood, their friendship remained intact, when Auntie called her, she came without question. She didn't have to think twice about it either; she made it her business to get there! "Hey bitch," said Auntie Pam as she strolled into the kitchen where Auntie was sitting at the table. She noticed a small pile of CRACK on the table next to her as she took a seat next to her.

Auntie sucked her teeth and shot Jazzy a crazy look, "girl, sit down so I can tell you what's going on. Oh, that's Jazzy…Jazzy, this Auntie Pam."

Auntie Pam reached into her purse and pulled out her stem. She didn't bother to ask, she put the small pile of CRACK on the table on her stem and took herself a mega-blast, not once taking her eyes off of Jazzy." This ain't bad… Not bad at all, where you get this," she asked as she blew out a thick white cloud of CRACK smoke?

Auntie nodded her head in Jazzy's direction, "ole' gal done got herself into a bind behind this shit…That's what I needed to holla at you about."

Jazzy sat there in silence as the two older ladies talked and seemed to kick her name around like she wasn't even there. Auntie was the one who was really shittin' on her, but Auntie Pam, she didn't say much, she just listened and kept smoking CRACK. It didn't sit too well with her either, plus the fact that Auntie Pam had smoked the rest of the CRACK they had left, after that was gone, they were out-back! How was Auntie Pam going to help, when she done smoked the last of the CRACK? That last half of ounce she got from Silas had her five-hundred dollars down, Auntie Pam wasn't helping matters none by smoking the last of it.

She thought about calling her brother to get a loan from him but the fight between her and Amanda stopped her from doing that, she knew Blacko and Amanda were closer than they were, that was out of the question. Her best option was to sit and wait patiently and see what Auntie Pam would do, but from the looks of it, it all went up in CRACK smoke. Why she staring at me like that, she asked herself?

Auntie Pam listened closely to what was being said, but her real focus was on the young chick Jazzy. Then when she saw what she was waiting to see, she dumped a plastic baggy from her purse and poured the contents onto the table.

It was 50-fifties, and then she asked, "you smoke Jazzy?" She already knew what the answer would be; she just wanted to ask anyway.

Jazzy's eyes got the size of half-dollars at the sight of the CRACK on the table, she licked her lips and responded, "yeah, I smoke," barely above a whisper.

"Go 'head then, help yourself, do you girl," said Auntie Pam still not taking her eyes off of Jazzy. Jazzy didn't waste too much time making her way closer to the pile of CRACK on the table.

She slowly put a huge rock onto her stem as she inhaled real slowly, and smooth allowing her lungs to fill to capacity with CRACK smoke. When she was sure that her lungs couldn't take no more smoke, she eased the stem out of her mouth still holding the smoke in her lungs a few more seconds before blowing it out. Immediately she heard bells ringing in her ears and her heart felt like it wanted to jump out of her chest, she even rolled some! This hit of CRACK was more potent and intense than her very first blast had been and she then found out the difference between; a-ight CRACK and some top-notch CRACK! She continued licking her lips, she couldn't stop even if she wanted to, her tongue seemed to have a mind of its own.

Auntie went on to tell her what Silas was going to do to Jazzy if she didn't pay him his paper. It didn't sound nice either; Auntie Pam rocked back in her chair and asked, "how much?" She heard the total but focused her attention back to Jazzy, "I'll tell you what...I can't tell another man how to run his business but I do know that having a young black sista sucking a dog's dick because she owes a bill ain't right. The flip side to that is, at the end of the day, the only thing that matters is that bill, so a nigga will do whatever he has to do to get that bill paid. If you was grown enough to take that man's shit, you should be grown enough to pay the man what you owe him. Since you can't pay the man, then you should be able to take whatever comes down the pipe. You do know this game comes with consequences, don't you? When you make your own bed in this game, you have to be woman enough to lay in it."

She smiled," however, today is your lucky day. Me and this lady here, we go way, way back and since she's the one who believes in you, I'll help you out on the strength of her. Don't get it fucked-up though, you will pay me back, with interest, so that means your ass belongs to me do I make myself clear? So, if you want me to pay your bill, I suggest you get on that phone of yours and get that nigga down here," said Auntie Pam with fire in her voice. Auntie exhaled loudly, "good looking out girl, I could've smacked the living shit out this dizzy little bitch for that stupid-ass move she made," she said taking another shot at Jazzy's ego!

"Hold-up, hold-up a minute, don't be going on her like that! You know damn well both of us have done the same foolish and stupid shit she's done, probably worst. What? Taking a package from a nigga and knowing you can't or even won't pay the nigga, yeah, we did that too! Playing with our lives all in the name of getting high, just like she did, I can remember days and nights if we didn't have each other's back, who knows where we'll be today? So, don't be so quick to judge Jazzy, the girl just has to learn the game the right way, that's all and from the looks of things, it's your job to teach her. Either you're going to teach her the game the way you know it's meant to be played or get out the young girl's way," fired Auntie Pam!

Twenty minutes later, the exchange between Auntie Pam and Silas was complete. She needed to see Silas face to face, she had heard about him being in the Projects' on Angie's porch, but she didn't really know what he looked like, plus the little situation at 'Food-Master's' with Joey and Malik, she wanted to get a visual on the dudes right hand man. She wanted to look into his eyes and see if she could judge his character and what she seen in her eyes didn't surprise her at all. She knew right off the bat that in due time something bad would happen between this guy and her nephew's, when she looked deep in his eyes all she saw was, DEATH! Auntie Pam threw 6 of the 50's on the table, "ya'll split that, I'll get with you later Jazzy! So, be ready for whatever," then she was gone.

CHAPTER 12

SILAS and Philly had just left house down on Page with the paper Jazzy owed and was on their way across town to Prospect to meet up with Amanda. He was excited to finally be able to get the opportunity to see her after a weeks' worth of playing phone tag with her. When she called him a few hours ago he was in the kitchen cooking and getting their next package ready so he had to make her wait awhile. The last time he saw her it was on Page when he dropped her off, but since then her name been ringing bells in the streets, especially in Prospect!

The streets was saying that she was the chick to see for that hard-white, it was hard to picture what he was hearing, he was looking forward to seeing it for himself. Even from Page, he was aware she was out there chasing paper, but not to the extent he's been hearing, they were saying that she had whatever a nigga needed and then some. It puzzled him but at the same time it made him smile because he believed nothing to be sweeter than seeing a female in the hood getting paper. He put everything else on hold and made Philly drive him over to Prospect.

"She said she'll be standing out across from the bus stop and we shouldn't miss her," he said barely above a whisper as his eyes scanned the area. Philly was feeling some type of way about driving the Caddy over Prospect since the last time he was over there the youngin's carried him, he was hyped to but for a different reason.

"Yeah homey, they say that bitch be out there all night on her grind!"

Silas shot him a murderous look and then said very calmly," watch ya mouth and you'll save ya teeth."

"It's like that, dog?" "It's like that! Shorty good people, it's dudes like you who be wanting to see her fall flat on her face out here," returned Silas with the same venom in his voice that matched his look. Philly realized that he'd struck a bad cord by talking reckless about Amanda and he could've kicked himself in the ass for it. He should have known better, she's the only thing Silas been speaking on other than paper for a minute now, he decided right then and there that the best thing he could do was to keep his comments to himself.

If he had a thang for Amanda, then who was he to question that? It made no sense for him to become involved because right now the paper was coming and he got high at will, and nothing was worth risking that, he thought. "Shit, there she go right there, that's her right there," said Silas excited to see her. "Yo, park right there!"

Amanda across the street from the bus stop like she said she would. She looked beautiful to him in her tight fitting pink sweat pants, the V-neck tee, which made her titties look like they were begging to be released from captivity, he licked his lips. He looked down at her feet, he had to smile again, she had on a pair of construction Tim's with the strings untied, that set it for him, he was hooked and didn't even realize it, or did he? Even at the distance, he could see her nipples were hard, they looked like elevator buttons on her round titties and he wanted to take a bite.

They made eye contact, she waved him over, directing them to park in the driveway of the yard she was in. She was up and out of her chair in no time, nobody knew it, but she was just as eager to see him as he was to see her, but she remained cool, she had a new image to protect and any sign of weakness didn't play to well with the new image. She walked over slowly towards the Caddy as it parked and stood over to the side to give them enough room, but once Silas stepped out the Caddy, she was all smiles and couldn't help it if she wanted to.

"Hey Silas, it's about time you got here, for a minute I thought you forgot all about me," she said still smiling. In her mind she was saying to herself,' damn he's fine,' but her pussy was singing a tune all of its own. She was forced to cross her legs for a second to stop the moisture from flowing. With matching goofy looks on their faces, he went to embrace her as if she was his long lost wife he hadn't seen in like forever, but it was the other 7 or 8 dudes looking at him like he was crazy that brought him back to reality.

"What up sexy," he asked but looking away briefly? After giving the dudes the once over, he determined they were harmless and went about his business with Amanda like they didn't exist.

"I'm chillin', Chillin'! About time you came to see me...I was beginning to wonder," she said giving him a warm embrace of her own. She wanted to touch him! With her perky titties pressed hard against him, she whispered in his ear," I want to fuck you right now," as she put her tongue in his ear making a circle. When she was done, she took two steps away from him and winked," what about you?"

With her standing some distance away from him, he really got the chance to take in her complete beauty, and the eyes, they had him stuck! She wasn't just a chick with a pretty face, she had the body to go right along with it, her body was fine-tuned, he wondered if she worked-out? When he went to open his mouth and respond to what she said to him, no words came out, she caught him totally off guard and for the first time in his life he was speechless. He did the next best thing, he nodded his head yes! He definitely wanted to fuck her, any man or better yet, she was every man's dream fuck and now it was his time!

She grabbed him by the arm and said, "Come on, follow me, please," then she winked again. "I need to holla at you in private," she said giving the other dudes that,' get out my mouth look'! When she felt they were at a safe distance and no one could hear them she asked, "Why it take you so long to come see me?"

"I've been a little busy, that's all," he said shrugging his shoulders at the same time.

"Yeah right! You wasn't too busy to go and holla at Jazzy," she said raising a brow! He knew exactly where this was going and intended to put a stop to it right away.

"Yo fuck Jazzy! Real talk, kill that Jazzy shit, you've been on my mind so much that it ain't even funny." His intense stare reinforced his words, they made them have meaning.

She reached out," give me your hand," kissing the back of it, she placed it on her heart. "Can you feel it?" It took all the power and control he had in him not to cuff her titties, they were firm and round just like he liked them," yeah, I feel your heart beating, why?"

Her face got real serious," that's what I'm talking about, my fucking heart beats all out of control whenever I'm near you and this shit is scaring the hell out of me, I don't like it. The crazy thing is that I know you're special, I can feel it and that's why I'm going to fuck you to get it over with. Come on, let's get it over with then you can go about your business," she said walking off down towards the baseball field at the bottom of the park.

He grabbed her by the arm stopping her in her tracks and turned her around to face him," get what over with Amanda?"

"This," she said touching her own heart. "I'm, I'm not supposed to be having these types of feelings for you. I don't even know you but you make my damn heart skip a beat every time you come near me. If we go ahead and fuck and get it over with, that will be that and I will look at you like just another nigga I gave some pussy to, when I said that I wanted to fuck you...I meant it, let's get this shit over with," she said snatching her arm away from him.

He starred at her so long and hard it forced her to break her eye contact, she could feel his eyes penetrating into her soul, and that was something she usually done to someone. He was using what she used on other dudes on her and she didn't like the feeling. The more he looked into her eyes the more he realize her problem, she was a victim of the environment she lived in. He also knew at that moment that everything that he heard about her was probably true, she was all those things people said about her, but now he also knew why. She was a pro at hiding her true feelings by saying fuck it and having sex. Sex on the first date almost always sealed the potential of a real relationship.

He had to ask, "are you afraid of me Amanda? Do you think I'll hurt you or something?" Her eyes were glued to the ground and she was listening to what he was saying, to make matters worse, everything he was saying was her greatest fear: Someone Who cared about her!

For him to want to know more about her than her pretty face and thin waist was too much for her, that's why she wanted to get this over with, she wouldn't have to worry about having these feelings for him. If she could just fuck him, suck his dick and maybe even let him fuck her in the ass and all her feeling would go away.

For the life of her, she wanted to strip down out of all of her clothes but she couldn't, she wanted him, unsure if she wanted him like that? She looked at her Tim's and realized that she forgot to tie them up, that made her smile for some reason. He walked closer to her, they were so close he could smell her breath but he still had to put his hand under her chin and lift her face up to him so that he could look into her eyes.

"Tell me why you're so afraid of me?" His voice was sincere and his eyes let her know that he wanted to know more about her. Her pains, fears and life's lessons were tucked away safely in her heart and she didn't want to let them out just yet, or if ever. With more than half of the pain she had ever felt came at the hands of men one way or another and she did her best to look at him like he was just another man to her, at least that's what she kept telling herself in her head. "Amanda, talk to me, all I want you to do is talk to me…Will you just talk to me, tell me what's on your mind?"

She felt like her head was starting spinning and she was getting dizzy the more he talked and stared into her eyes. Forcing herself to take a deep breath to relieve some pressure on her brain, she suddenly felt a sense of calmness come over her and began talking to him. "Silas, I umm umm, brought you here, to the park so that I could go ahead and you know, give you some pussy, I knew if I just went ahead and fucked you that would make you just like everybody else that I've ever met in my entire life. It wouldn't have meant anything to either of us, you know? It's just a fuck and then all these feelings that I'm having for you would go away. That's the only way that I know, that's the only way these feelings can go away. I'm not wifey material so I'm not going to fool myself into thinking otherwise, but it's something about you that I can't bring myself to do it," she said looking into his eyes.

When she really looked into his eyes, he turned his head so fast that she swore she saw a tear streaming down his cheek. "You think I'm crazy, don't you?"

He shook his head no because he didn't think she was crazy, bold, but not crazy. It took a lot of power to admit your fear's and he respected her for it, he grabbed her and hugged her until she could barely breathe again.

"I...I can't breathe," She managed to get out.

"Sorry, Sorry, my bad, I didn't mean to hurt you. Did I hurt you?"

Amanda put her index finger up to stop him from talking and gave him a very passionate kiss. They played chase with each other's tongue for close to 5 minutes before either came up for air, then she said, "that's the shit I'm talking about right there!" She was serious but the grin on her face told another story. "What you mean by that," he asked?

"It's like every time I'm close to you my mind goes blank and I can't think straight. My emotions take over and my body starts doing its own thang. I can't control myself and that shit scares the hell out of me."

He would do anything to put her mind at ease because he was feeling what she was saying," I'm feeling you on that. I know that feeling, this is all new to me too, let's ride this thing out and see where it'll leads. I barely know you just like you barely know me, but I can't get enough of you. I could stand here staring into your eyes for all eternity that is the affect you have on me. And, not to mention that kiss, I wanted it to last forever."

"It can! If you really mean what you're saying, make it last forever?" He smiled," it's going to take more than me to make this thang last forever...I'm going to need help from you as well, I can't do it alone but I'm willing to try."

"I'm definitely willing to do my part," she whispered to him.

"Good! I'm willing to do my part as well but I have one last request: Tell me how I can make you the happiest woman under the Sun."

"It doesn't take much, just be true to who you are, but you can start by being my best friend. Oh, yeah, and respect me, can you handle all of that," she asked giggling? He grabbed her and pulled her close to him this time he was extra careful not to choke her, he was gentle with her. "I got a plan, what's on your agenda for the rest of the night?"

Mentioning he had a plan it caused her to raise her brow, in her sick mind, she was hoping that he was going to ask for the pussy now that they got the other stuff out of the way, because she would definitely agree with him, but she decided to play it cool. "Not too much, I have a few loose ends to tie up and that's it."

"Let's say I pick you up in a couple of hours and we go and get something to eat, do a little talking, lay down some ground rules, you know and just get to know each other better," he said laughing at himself by the way he was talking. Her emotions got the best of her once again, she broke down and started crying, everything that he said to her was a bit much and she was overwhelmed but she managed to shake her head yes.

He hugged her again and asked her, "Why you crying Amanda, I'm here for you and I'm not going to hurt you…I promise you that!"

Wiping her tears away and composing herself, she said, "the crazy thing is that no man has ever been able to turn me down sexually and it means a lot to me knowing that you want more from me than just sex. It fucks my head up that you want to take me out and just talk, I don't want to wait to later, I want to be with you now, I'm ready now."

They walked back to Prospect together and with very few words between them, each was locked into their own thoughts. So much was going on in their minds and the pace they were moving at was incredible. Philly was still there sitting on the hood of the Caddy talking to White-girl. They seemed comfortable together as well, laughing and joking. "Hey sista," said White-girl looking at Amanda with a huge smile and raised brow.

"Come here, let me holla at you a second," said Amanda leading her back across the street and into their building. "I need you to stay out here and take care of thangs for the rest of the night; you think you can handle that?"

There was no doubt in White-girls mind that she could handle the business out there for the night, however, she didn't know if that's what she wanted, but what choice did she have? Exactly, for her plan to succeed, she had to bend a little, so she agreed to take care of their business in the streets for the night. With all the dudes doing all the selling and moving the product, all she had to do was to sit back and count the paper that came in. With Amanda making it crystal clear that she wasn't taking any shorts that she didn't have to worry about nobody not paying her what they owed, so she was ready. Between having Jacob and Philly out there with her, it was bound to be smooth sailing. "Ain't no question sista, I got this! Just make sure he leaves the dude Philly here with me. Between him and Jacob, who knows what may come my way by the end of the night," she said with a devilish grin.

"What you mean to be saying is that either of them might get lucky with one, remember, we them chicks to see out here ain't shit moving without our blessing, and that includes who we give the pussy to," said Amanda reminding her of their new status when it came to 'MATTERS OF THE HOOD.'

Silas peeped over at her and smiled as he went about changing the CD. This wasn't the time to be listening to no Rap music so he put in Keisha Cole's, 'Just like Me.' Amanda started bobbing her head to the sultry voice of Keisha saying out loud, "I love this CD, she's a boss-bitch if you ever seen one. She be killin' it, that Rap shit be in the way," she said giggling.

"Don't be hatin' on my Rap music," fired back Silas playfully.

Amanda gave him a funny look then said to him, "let's get something straight,

I don't hate on nothing or nobody and believe that. It be mutha fuckers out here hatin' on me; niggaz and bitchez alike Recognize!"

"People tend to hate on that which they don't know or understand," said Silas very calm and serious.

"How can they not understand? When I was out here fucked-up in the game they use to talk major shit about me but now the same mutha-fuckers be up in my face begging me for change like I'm a fucking ATM machine or some shit. But you know what I do? I look out; I give them a few dollars here and there and send them on their way. When I was fucked-up, ain't nobody look out for me, but I'm bigger than that bullshit. I keep my head up and still look out." He knew she played the game from a different angle and was happy to know that she did recognize the bullshit but didn't let it become her. She also confirmed that she wasn't fucked-up in the game no more, so it must be true that she's getting major paper now!

"You ain't gotta worry about all that bullshit now, I ain't one of them fucked-up dudes you're talking about. I keep it one hundred, if you hang on long enough, you'll see for yourself." "Is that so?" "That's right, baby-girl." "Oh I like that!" "You like what?" "That baby-girl thang...Is that who I am now to you," she asked batting her eyes at him? "Anyway, do you remember the first time we saw each other in the Projects'? I knew you were special then, even then I knew! You had a bitch walking the wrong way and everything, I was stuck on stupid there for a minute staring at yo' fine-ass." While he was stopped at the red-light, he looked over and admired her beauty," why you ain't say nothing then?" Not wanting to spoil the moment because the instant she recalled him sitting on that porch, she learned later that it was a female who lived there and she didn't want to ask something she wasn't ready for, so she switched the subject. "So, what about you Mr. Silas, tell me something about you that nobody else out here in these streets know about you?" Rubbing his chin and buying himself some time, he asked," where you want me to start?" "First, you can't answer a question with a question and second, how about starting at the beginning, silly." This wasn't the conversation that he was looking forward to or ready to have with her so early. What he did like about her was that she was straight forward and to the point.

She seemed to have a good sense of what she wanted to know and how to go about getting it. Straight from the source!

He pretended to be in deep concentrate as he swerved in and out of traffic on Interstate 64. He was headed east from Charlottesville with intentions of getting off and turning around in a couple of exists, in his head, he was debating with himself as to what he wanted to say to her. It forced a smile, because he knew she wasn't the average chick, and if she was, the average chick would have never asked no personal shit like that. There were things about his life that he would never reveal to anyone, so he had to take his time and be able to choice the juicy shit that she wanted to hear and all without lying to her at the same time. Still unable to make his mind up, he decided to just let it flow, if he said something that didn't sit well, he could always use the,' I'm joking,' line to protect his image. "Oh, I guess the cat got your tongue, huh," she asked playfully?

Her eyes were very penetrating, he had to take a deep breath and then he turned down the music as he prepared himself. He knew his next move would have to be his best move!" My mind keeps telling me to keep my mouth shut, but my heart is telling me something totally different. I know for you and I to gain each other's full-trust, we're going to have to reveal who we are as a person, unfortunately, you asked me before I got the opportunity to ask you, so that means I have the honors of going first. This is very hard for me because, the only other person who even comes close to knowing my secrets is my homey, Sosa, and you haven't met him yet." She reached over and touched him lightly on his thigh to encourage him to continue," you mean Sosa from down Garrett? The one who fuck with Tasha, right?" "And just how you know Sosa," he asked with a slight attitude? "Ease-up play-boy! When I was trying to find out more about you, my investigations lead me to Garrett and ya'll names came up. I was only trying to find out if you had a girl. "So, tell me what else you find out about me that I should know, little miss detective," he said with a grin on his face? She smacked her lips together before she started talking to him" ummm for starters, you don't have a girl. A main chick anyway…You're from New Jersey…And you've been in Charlottesville only a couple of months. From the sound of your bio, I can tell that you're only out here for one reason and one reason only. You're out her chasing that paper real hard!" She was accurate and on point about what she was saying about him and it impressed him, but since meeting her things were starting to change for him and change fast. "You're absolutely correct, that is up until the day I met you. You seem to have a way about changing a nigga."

A warm feeling came over her and her heart was beating a little faster than normal. In her mind, she couldn't believe her luck, he was definitely a topnotch catch, he was fine, thugged-out to the max, and made her laugh and the most important thing she thought was the fact that he seemed to care about her well-being just as much as she cared about his. These were plus signs for her and it was written all over her face by the huge smile," a'ight, but finish telling me more about you, please," she begged playfully. He was so deep into their conversation that he missed the exit he was supposed to take and he grew nervous by the second. He'd never been that far down the Interstate, and only heard stories about the country cop who will literally hang a nigga if he got caught slippin'. "Shit, I missed the damn exit; I ain't trying to get lost out here in these fuckin' sticks. These cracker police will lynch our black-ass from what I've heard," he said patting the handle of his .40 Caliber that was tucked away in his shoulder holster. His eyes began scanning his surrounding even in the pitch black dark, he was alert and attentive.

Amanda wanted to laugh but she didn't, she kept her comments to herself. One thing she knew and understood about thugs was that they were willing to go to war with an entire hood, with one pistol and 6 bullets and not think twice. Take that same thug ass nigga and put him out there in the country where there are no street lights, just the blackness of the country night and they'll be scared to death. She let him out of his misery," take the Zion Cross Roads exit, it's the next one coming up, darling," "You been out this way before? What the fuck can be out here in the country?" She took this as an opportunity to let him know a little more about the woman she really was. "You'll be surprised what I know about this area and more, if you stick around long enough that is! I'm much smarter than I look." "For your information, I already knew that you were a smart woman. I figured that out 5 minutes into our first conversation... Thank-you very much," he said seriously. "That's the exit right there. Go right when you come to the stop sign, there's a McDonald's on your left down the road...Pull-in there, I'm hungry," she said smiling. "McDonald's? That's not how I planned our first dinner date."

She looked over at him and stared into his eyes and said to him," don't worry about where we eat at, that shit ain't important to me, fuck all this materialistic bullshit. I'm comfortable being in your presence and it makes me feel good, let's not sweat the small stuff, okay? Just remember that and we'll be good. He did as she asked and pulled into the parking lot of McDonald's and headed for the drive-thru and placed their orders. She then directed him to park in the back with the big-trucks. "A'ight, go ahead and finish telling me about you," she asked?

Taking a huge bite of his burger, he wiped his mouth and took a sip of his drink before he began speaking. "Well, I'm from Newark, New Jersey, better known as 'Brick-City', I'm seventeen and my birthday is…" she cut him off.

" hold-up! That's not what you were about to tell me the first go around. You was about to tell me something deep, so miss me with all that other stuff, that shits public information, I can find all that out on my own. That'll only take a couple of clicks on my computer and all that shit will pop-up."

For some reason, he decided not to beat around the bush with her and began telling her the story of his life as he knew it. "When I was growing up I had the unfortunate luck of having a CRACK head for a mother and a dope-fiend for a father. Life was anything but sweet for me, it was very hard and difficult for me because I just didn't really understand it all at the time. But, the one thing that I did understand and care about was being poor, I didn't like it and I was determined not to stay poor. I was about seven or eight when I started fighting any and everybody because the kid's at my school would tease me all the time. If it wasn't what I was wearing it was what I wasn't wearing, back then I didn't know what a pair of new sneaker's felt like. There was no Christmas for me. No birthday's either, no Easter-egg hunts, or the Easter Sunday outfit that went along with it. I had nothing and when I say nothing, I really mean nothing. Since I was so small, I rarely won any of the fights but that didn't stop me. I got my ass kicked every single day and on one particular day, I met Sosa. He was the complete opposite of me and who I was. He was popular and always had on the latest outfits with the sneakers to match, but what made him different than everybody else was that he never once teased me like the other kids or tried to fight me for whatever the reason was for that day. Then it all happened, one day, I got into it with the school bully and Sosa stepped in and punched him in the face and we kicked his ass all over that school. We got suspended but they couldn't locate my mother so she could come and pick me up from school and Sosa convinced his mother to check me out of school with them and she told the principal that she would take me home. We went around my way on Newton street we ran right into my mother soon as we bent the corner and I almost didn't tell them that she was my mother but something in me yelled out, there she go! Sosa's mother started laughing and I thought she was laughing at my mother but when she parked the car and my mother saw me getting out, her and Sosa's mother hugged each other. As it turned out, they use to be running partners way before either of us was born. They were super-tight! She convinced my mother to let me stay with them at their house for the night and after that night, I never went back to live in my mother's house again." When she looked over at him, he was staring out the window in his own zone and she whispered," so, you moved in with them after that, huh?"

He shook his head up and down, "it had to be a blessing because Sosa'a pops was seeing major paper in the dope game and he was rarely home. His moms would keep us up late at night telling us story after story about how her and my moms use to get down until they lost contact with each other. She treated me just like she treated her own son, when he got new sneakers, I got new sneakers. If the store was selling it, she got it for us. On my birthday's she would take me over to my mother's and hang-out, just like all the rest of the holidays and on my mother's birthday, she would give me paper so that I could go downtown to but her something. All that lasted up until I was about thirteen. Shit changed after that."

Amanda was on the edge of her seat and hanging on his every word and deep down inside, she could feel his struggle and pain in her heart. From listening to his story, she now knew their connection and what they had in common. They both were wounded souls, "so what happened when ya'll turned thirteen?"

The emotion was a bit much for him, he had to put his head down and close his eyes to regain his focus as he mentally replayed that fateful night they learned of Sosa's fathers' death. He struggled to get the words out, but he fought it because he wanted her to know who he was and where he came from. "

"He was murdered, shot in the face a bunch of times over in this project's called Baxter Terrace in Newark," he whispered. "Life ended as we knew it. Everything changed at that point, especially the paper, it was all gone and every day when we came home from school, Sosa's mother would be sitting in her favorite chair crying her heart out because she missed the man of her dreams so much. To make matters worse, his father's partner was indicted by the federal government no long after the murder and nobody knew where the real stash was so we had to eventually pack-up and move out of our big house and back to the projects' and welfare became a common way of life for us."

He took a deep breath before he continued his story, "by that time, me and Sosa was so spoiled that we couldn't understand life without having the best of everything and refused to accept the fact that we were living in a roach infested tiny apartment in the middle of a concrete jungle. We quickly devised a plan to get up out the projects' by robbing dudes in the hood, to us it made no sense standing on nobody's corner all day long to make a couple of dollars when we could skip all that non-sense and rob the source and that's what we did. We got started right away because we already felt like time wasn't on our side, so we watched and observed everybody and everything moving in the hood, and we would rob 2 or 3 dudes every night. After a while, we became notorious stick-up kids in Newark, robbing and jackin' niggaz all over the city and we were barely fifteen at the time!"

Amanda slid as close to him as possible and held his hand to let him know that she was feeling his pain and his struggle. She wanted to jump over the center console and hug him until the ends of time but she couldn't, not just yet anyway.

"For the first time in my life that I could remember my mom came to me with some real help. Sitting in a CRACK house she caught wind of a plot to have me and Sosa murdered. Over-hearing some dudes talking about how we were responsible for robbing one of their spot's and put a dent in their pockets, so the only thing they could do was to have us murdered, and they were bragging about how they had already paid some other dudes to do it, and it was only a matter of it. Nobody at the time realized that she was my mother at the time; I've been living with Sosa and his mother for so long that by the time we moved by into the projects' everybody assumed we were brothers and we liked it that way. That's the night we became men hiding in a child's body! We had to get them before they got us and we came off sitting pretty good, we didn't get the main dude but we got the dude next to the dude, we had so much drug's and paper that we moved Sosa's mother out of the projects' the very next day and sent her down to Atlanta. We still had enough paper for ourselves, but the one thing we didn't realize at the time was that the guys we robbed were fronting because they worked for someone even bigger than them. These dudes were connected because they had the type of pull to put the detectives on our ass real hard and another hit on us. Just when we was about to get moms out the hood, she was found in her bedroom with a needle in her arm, dead from a dope over-dose! She was never into heroin, she was a full-blown CRACK head. Even though she wasn't there for me physically, she was sick and they murdered her. I went ballistic, I started killing everything moving in Newark, if I thought you had something to do with her death you was gone.

I was on the verge of getting me and Sosa pinched, I was so reckless with my shit, he convinced me we had to bounce. We went down to Atlanta with his moms for close to two years before we resurfaced. From there we went from State to State getting paper and so here I am in Charlottesville with you."

Amanda had an abundance of emotions going through her head as she listened intently to his story. She felt, mournful, despondent, fortunate, and delighted all at the same time. The more she heard the more convinced she became about him being the one for her. No man has ever made her even entertain that thought, let alone it actually coming to pass. She decided she needed one more approval to make it official, her grandma would either seal or break the deal for her. "So, it's safe to say you came up guarding your heart, huh," she asked curiously?

"That's definitely the case with me. Especially when moms was murdered, that shit showed me these Mean-Streets will take the worst of us the same way it'll take the best of us. Anybody can get touched out here and that's why I keep my circle close and no friends, if it ain't family it ain't right."

Trying to change the subject and steer it away from all the murders and bad times, she couldn't take another death right now, "since you and Sosa are so tight, why I haven't seen him with you yet?"

He shook his head from side to side thinking about the only real family he had left. He wasn't about to admit that he'd ran him off with his thoughts of greed and jealous of the relationship he had with Tasha. He made a mentally note to call Sosa and apologize and let him know that he understood where he was coming from. With only a couple of hours under his belt with Amanda, she had him feeling and looking at life differently and he could only imagine how Tasha made Sosa feel.

Now he knew what them ole' heads were talking about when they use to say a good woman can make a man walk away from the life style that deals the cards from the bottom of the deck. Not only are the cards dealt from the bottom of the deck, all the cards are already marked with: DRUGS.ALOCHOL.DEATH. PRISON.LONELYNESS.NO LOVE.NO LOYALTY.NO HONOR.

That's what he was up against and at the moment, he wasn't sure if he was happy or sad shit started making sense? His loyalty to Sosa wouldn't allow him to discuss his business with her at the moment, not yet anyway. Nor was he ready to admit that he was self-centered and it was his own actions that ran Sosa away. He looked into her penetrating eyes and simply said, "he's good. Him and Tasha took a small vacation while I'm out here holding down the fort."

To him it was partly the truth, it was only in his own self-centered mind that distorted real life and it took one conversation with Amanda to open his eyes to see the true light. She collected all the trash and got out the car, looking back over her shoulder, "be back in a sec., and don't try to leave me either," she said sticking her tongue out at him. He managed to grab her by the forearm before she got all the way out the car and said to her in the most serious voice he had," hey, you don't ever have to worry about me leaving you!" The serious tone of his voice made her heart beat a little faster," that's good to know."

After throwing all the trash away and using the bathroom, she returned back to the Caddy only she was at the driver's side window. "Let me drive this machine; let me see what's all the fuss about the new Caddy," she demanded. She followed her demand with a silly smile because she knew that she couldn't force a dude like Silas to do something he didn't want to do. "Please!"

Matters of The Hood

The first thing he realized about her once she jumped into the cock-pit of the Caddy was that she was a great driver. He learned the difference between country driving and city driving. She was hitting curves on those back roads at 65 mph like it was nothing. No street lights to help guide her and she used minimum brakes, she was handling the Caddy like a Nascar driver with no signs of letting up. The area was quickly changing, they were in the sticks and she kept pushing the Caddy, the only time she showed signs of slowing down, was to allow a pack of deer to cross in front of her. He couldn't figure out for the life of him how she knew when to slow down for the deer, being in was triple-black-dark out there? On both sides of him, he could only see blackness and sights of deer rushing across the road occasionally. The roads were so curvy that the headlights seemed to be useless. He was lost. In his mind, he was wondering if they were still in Virginia. As they made their way out of the curvy roads and onto a straight way, she slowed down, which was unusual to him, but he found out why, deer were everywhere, even in the middle of the road like they owned it. He also noticed the corn fields on both sides of the road and that was all he could see! "You do have a license, right," he asked half joking and half serious? She knew that he was referring to her driving, but what he didn't know or understand was that she could drive those roads with her eyes closed. That was her little secret and she wasn't going to tell him how she knew those roads so well, at least not just yet.

"Yeah I got a license. I just got it yesterday from Walmart, they had'em on sell for half price," she said unable to conceal her laughter. He glanced over at her just to see the look on her face and what he saw in her eyes made him happy to be there with her.

She pulled the Caddy into a long driveway and a double-wide trailer came into view. There were at least 5 dudes standing out in the yard and for some odd reason, it reminded him of dudes standing on the corners in the city chasing paper. They were complete with the baggy jeans and fitted caps down low over their eyes. Two of the guys approached the Caddy trying to see who was driving; he unsnapped the button on his shoulder holster preparing himself for war.

Amanda reached over to stop him, "it's a-ight, these my peeps!" She rolled down the window and hollered," where's grandma nigga? Is she sleep yet?"

Parking the Caddy a little closer to the double-wide, they got out. One of the dudes ran over and hugged her," what up cuzo, what brings you down this way," he asked with a huge grin on his face? "What you mean? I can't come home now or something, where's grandma anyway...I hope she ain't sleep yet." She turned back to Silas," come on baby, I got somebody I want you to meet," she said grabbing him by the hand and leading him into the house.

The first thing Silas noticed about every one of the dudes out there was that they all had 40. Caliber Dessert Eagles on their hips tucked away safely in their holsters. The guns weren't concealed or nothing and that blew his mind. It was like he was in the wild, wild, west or something. Not to mention the love they were showing Amanda, like she was a rock-star or something. She lined them all up and went down the line introducing him to each and every one of her cousins. After that, she led him into the house to meet the most important person of all, her grandma!

He took a seat on the sofa while she went in the rear of the house to find her grandma. She found her still in the kitchen cooking. Silas was staring out the large bay-window looking at her cousins. In a little less than 10 minutes he counted 7 cars pull in the driveway and one of her cousins approach the car, hand the driver something and then the car would leave, just like that. It wasn't hard for him to figure out what they were doing out there. One of her cousins came into the living room and sat across from him, taking out several wads of cash out every pocket down to the cash he had in his socks. He lined the small coffee table with 5 stacks of paper; each stack he counted out was a thousand dollars. The cousin yelled out Amanda's name. It didn't take her any time to emerge from the back of the house with a grin the size of Texas on her face at the sight of the cash neatly stacked on the coffee table. "That's me?" She took a seat next to her cousin and kissed him on the cheek," I knew you could do it," she said putting the paper into a brown paper bag. "I'll call you tomorrow afternoon so be ready!"

Her grandma came out the back not long after and sat in her favorite chair, all her attention was on Silas. She made small talk and asked a few questions and then nodded her head at Amanda with an approving smile.

Amanda took one of the stacks back out the bag and handed it to her grandma," this should hold you for the rest of the month...Make sure you get all your medicine to, don't make me have to drive all the way back down here," she said pretending to be giving the orders. "Bless your heart sugar," said grandma kissing her on the cheek. She looked over at Silas and said to him, "Silas, take care of her, it's not often I get the pleasure of meeting her friends," she got up and disappeared into the back of the house.

He looked back up, her grandma had two plates of food. She put the food on the table in front of him and whispered, "she's fragile but sturdy, you have your work cut out for you, Silas," she said laughing.

She led him back out the house, watching the traffic come and go. The food smelled so good he had to ask the question," do you cook too?" It was on his mind because of what he heard about country girls, she was starting to appear to be too good to be true for him.

"I'm a country girl at heart, so of course I know my way around a kitchen. If you stay around long enough, you'll see," she said giggling.

"You getting paper out here too?" She laughed again because she knew the big misconception up-top dudes had when it came to the country. "Believe it or not, they get major paper out here in the country. You city boys got the game twisted, people smoke CRACK everywhere, even in the country. Don't sleep because these country dudes will shoot a tick off a dog's dick out here!" She maneuvered the Caddy out of the driveway and back onto those curvy roads at top speed," where we headed now," he asked? Without taking her eyes off the road, she said, "it's a surprise."

Neither of them said much, they were lost in their own thoughts. Everything was happening so fast, they went from zero-to-sixty in a matter of hours. His nose was open and he hadn't even smelled the pussy, let alone get it. The strange part about all of this was he openly welcomed those feelings for her. He wanted to take his cell out and call Sosa and tell him about Amanda, but since it was damn near midnight, he thought better of it and plus, he didn't want her to hear him talking all about how his nose was all open for her.

For Amanda, each move she just made was a well calculated move for her. She wanted to see her grandma's reaction to him and what she thought about him at first glance. And for two, she needed for him to see how country niggaz got down first hand, she had witnessed on way too many occasions where dudes from up-top made the fatal mistake of sleeping on dudes from the country and get sent home in a body bag. She didn't want him making that same mistake; she cared about him too much already! Knowing that it was his first time out to the real country and with her crazy-ass cousins, the memory of guns and chasing paper would be implanted in his mind forever. She felt that if he was going to be her king that it was her duty to school him on all phases of the CRACK game and that included the country as well. Fifty minutes later, she was pulling the Caddy into the parking lot of the Omini Hotel in downtown Charlottesville. He looked over at her with a strange look on his face," you got business here too?"

"As a matter of fact, I most certainly do have business here...Tonight you're my business," she said getting out the car. It was closer to 2 A.M. before they got settled into their room after stopping at the bar and having a few drinks. Silas was starting to feel a little ill, he looked at his watch and realized that he hadn't sniffed any dope since like Seven that morning. Amanda attributed his sluggish movement and his distant look in his eyes to the alcohol. She had no idea that his body was beginning to break-down due to the lack of dope in his system. "I'll be back in a minute, I gotta use the bathroom," he said making his way into the bathroom.

Amanda took the time to call White-girl to see how things were going while Silas was in the bathroom. Her conversation with White-girl lasted only ten minutes, with Silas still in the bathroom she knocked on the door lightly. Getting no answer, she turned the door knob, finding the door unlocked, she opened the door making her way inside. Silas was sitting on the toilet hovering over a Twenty-dollar bill with a straw in his left hand taking scoops of the off-white substance and sniffin' it.

"What you doing," she asked making her way closer? He had a dumb look on his face and he didn't know what exactly to say to her as to what he was doing. He not only got caught with his pants down by his ankles, but with his hand in the cookie-jar as well. He cursed himself in his head for not locking the door!

When she opened the door, she startled him causing him to spill some of the dope on the floor.

"You ain't gotta hide nothing from me, everybody sniffs a little from time to time," she said picking up the straw from off the sick. She grabbed the bill that was next to the straw on the sink and took two huge sniffs of the off-white substance showing his that everything was cool.

"Amanda, that ain't," was all he got out before the off-white substance disappeared into her nose. He knew she thought that she was sniffin' cocaine, but this was a whole new ball game; heroine wasn't to be played with and he knew it. She started sneezing off the bat," what the fuck is this," she managed to ask between the sneezing? It only took a couple of seconds for the dope to make her body relax and she suddenly felt a sense of calmness come over her body. "Baby-girl, that ain't what you think it is! That's dope, Heroine."

Not one to be outdone, she dipped her pinky nail back into the off-white substance, however, the difference this time was that she was much more cautious and only snorted half of what she snorted the first time around. "So, what it do to you? I feel like I'm sleepy already, am I supposed to be feeling sleepy?"

He knew where this would go if he didn't put a stop to what she was doing. He snatched the bill from her and folded it up and put it back in his pocket," this shit ain't for you Amanda! Don't let me catch you fucking with this shit again… You hear me, 'be asked with force in his voice? Nodding her head up and down, she followed him out of the bathroom and took a seat next to him on the huge bed.

Before he could say anything to her, she had his dick out of his boxers and in her mouth making circles around the head with her tongue. He moaned from the pleasure but then he thought about what she had said to him in the park earlier about how she used sex to hide her true feelings for someone. He put both of hands on her shoulders forcing her to stop as he pushed her away from him. When she looked up at him with those beautiful eyes of hers, he almost told her to continue sucking his dick, but he didn't. "You're supposed to be telling me your story now...Tell me something about Amanda that nobody else knows," he said rubbing her gently on her head.

"I want all of you, I can't do nothing with pieces of you," he declared. He completely shattered her theory that love wasn't meant for people like her. Not finding the words to express her feelings, she just laid back on the bed next to him. She had to fight to keep her eyes open and she was losing that battle quickly. He took one look at her and knew the dope was taking its effect on her system. He propped her up so she would be more comfortable on the bed and he began taking off her clothes. With the body she had, he was tempted to take a taste of her goodies but he promised her that he wouldn't never take advantage of her, especially in the state she was in now. She was out for close to 2 hours straight before she opened her eyes. "Is that the right time," she asked through her cracked voice?

"Yeah, that's the right time; you went out almost 2 hours ago. No need for you to ask about what dope does, now you know. I don't want you to ever touch that shit again, promise me that you won't ever touch it again!" He hugged her tightly just to reinforce how he felt about her. She looked down at the floor as she was sitting herself up in the bed and noticed all her clothes were on the floor next to the bed.

"You could've taken all my goodies if you wanted to, huh," she asked? He stood-up beside her on the bed," yeah, if I wanted to I could have but I wouldn't never disrespect you like that. That's why I'm still fully dressed, I thought you were out for the night and I wanted you to be comfortable." Silas licked his lips letting her know just how bad he wanted her but was willing to take his time and wait until she was ready to give herself to him on her own terms. However, he wasn't hiding the fact that he wanted her and would be willing to do just about anything to have her. Patience wasn't one of his strong points but she made him feel that if he waited, it would be worth his while all without uttering one single word. It was the way she looked at him!

She jumped out of the bed and went to use the bathroom, but there was no way she was prepared for what happened to her the moment she entered the bathroom. She called Earl! Silas didn't bother to go and check on her, he knew it was only a side effect of the dope. Moments later, he could hear the shower running. She stepped out the bathroom 10 minutes later still dripping wet from the shower. Her body was glistening!

Coming closer to the bed, she dropped her towel revealing her naked body to him. "Silas, I don't want to talk anymore, I don't want to play any more games with you, I want what I want and I want it right now. I want you inside of me, I need for you to make love to me." She leaned over and kissed him on his lips. "You're unlike any man I've ever met in my entire life and I'd be lying to you if I said that I didn't want you to make love to me because that's the only thing on my mind. Lord knows how bad I want you inside of me!"

He didn't give her a chance to have to repeat herself, he jumped out of his clothes in record time and pulled her down on the bed close to him. As she lay on her back, he ordered her to stand back up in front of him. He put her left leg up on the bed while the right remained on the floor. His tongue found a nice warm and wet area between her legs. He began licking and sucking on her swollen clit. She was forced to grab the back of his head to keep from falling onto the floor, the pleasure she was feeling was like no other and that was all she could do to brace herself. He slid 2 fingers into her wet pussy and she let out a soft moan," oh shit, shit baby, I'm...I'm...Cu---Cuming right fuckin' now," she screamed unable to hold back the pleasure.

He didn't give her a chance to regain her senses, he forced her to bend over and he entered her from the back right there with his massive dick. Two and a half hours later he was still fucking her brains out. In her head, she couldn't believe the things he had her body doing, she never thought her body could be bent and twisted in so many different positions. She lost count of how many times he made her cum after the 10th one, she stopped counting. The only thing she could do now was to ride his massive dick as if her life depended on it. Not knowing how long it would take for him to cum, she started talking shit to him. That must have did the trick because she could feel his dick getting harder and harder the more shit she talked to him. She hopped off his dick when she thought he was just about to cum and put his dick in her mouth. "Cum in my mouth, daddy, make that dick cum, please daddy, cum in my mouth," she begged as she jerked his dick up and down!

Just when he was about to cum he surprise her," baby, I want to cum inside of you...Stop so I can cum inside of you," he said as they switched positions. He was just in time because soon as the head of his dick felt the wetness of her pussy, he started cuming in her. Dizzy from pleasure she looked up into his eyes," baby, what if I get pregnant, we ain't use no protection, you do realize that, don't you?" "That's the idea! Don't sound bad to me; I guess we'll have a little Silas running around here," he said laughing as he kissed her passionately.

CHAPTER 13

JOEY and Malik had spent the last few night's creeping through the hood, posting up in spot's they hasn't been in a minute, like, the first driveway in the Projects'. It was easier than they thought to blend in and keep a watchful eye on Angie's crib for Silas or his runner Philly. However, in their attempt, it proved to be useless and hopeless, from the looks of things, both Angie and Silas had fallen off the radar. Nobody had seen them, and it seemed strange because Angie didn't even stop in to check up on her apartment, that was weird! Philly was the third-wheel, so it wasn't no wonder he was missing along with the other two, but that to told a story of its own. He had a need to get high and the street's was his play ground, and for him to show his face, could only mean that they bounced out of town, probably to re-up.

Joey glanced down at his watch, it was 2:30 in the morning and here he was still in the Projects' like he was still a young-buck. "Dude ain't nowhere in sight. Ain't shit jumpin' out here, I'm about to bounce," he said. Then he looked down the long walk-way and noticed a familiar walk from a female, and that was definitely his cue to bounce," see you'll be in good hands, I'm out," he said nodding in the direction of the approaching female.

Malik didn't look in that direction right away, instead he used this as an opportunity to cast a little joke, "I feel you but I'm chilling. I might just run into something strange that's trying to do something for some change," he said laughing.

"Ain't no need reminding me, I already know exactly how you get down. I need to get out this damn vest, this shit is uncomfortable."

Malik started rapping one of his favorite verses from one of his favorite

Jay-Z songs "You... can't say you'll put the vest away and wear it tomorrow, cause the day after niggaz'll say damn, I was just with him yesterday!"

"A-ight Mr. Jay-Z, junior, just make sure you stay on your ones and keep your eyes wide-open...I'm out," said Joey giving Malik a pound and a hug still looking at the approaching female with a grin on his face.

He walked towards the Run street side and out the Projects', he was hoping to see that pretty little green-eye chick that drives that small gray car, but he knew he wouldn't see her because she hardly ever hung-out, let alone at 3 in the morning.

Malik finally turned around expecting a familiar face from the way Joey was talking and nodding his head. It was Tiffany and she was on a mission walking in his direction. His whole focus was on her firm legs and that walk that made every nigga in the hood want to fuck her, he had to admit it, she still had it, the CRACK hadn't taken her down as it did most people, he thought. He also noticed the closer she got the more she seemed to smile, like she was looking forward to seeing him or something and ever since she got that first pack from Auntie Pam, she's been on a mission to prove something to him. He figured that out when she asked for the second package! They've been working together every night since then, but they kept their business to their selves, only Auntie Pam knew, but she still only knew but so much.

"Hey Malik, what you doing out here in the hood this late, what brings you out," she asked brushing up against him with her firm titties? The look in his eyes told the story and what was on his mind as far as she was concerned. So much so that she had to fight for his attention, punching him lightly on the arm to bring his attention away from her body and to have eye contact. "Get your mind out of the gutter," she said laughing and trying her best not to allow her own mind to think the same thought's he was thinking.

His eyes went from her firm titties down to the gap between her legs, he licked his tongue, embraced her tightly as he whispered in her ear," damn girl, you make a nigga want to bend your ass over right here and fuck the shit out of your sexy-ass!"

"Don't tempt me with a good time," she said with her eyes meeting his with that same lustful look in them. "For real though, I know you ain't out here spying on me, are you?"

His mind was in another world, a world where Tiffany was his sex slave and he could do anything he wanted to do to her. The best thing about his thoughts was that she enjoyed it just as much as he did. All the while, he never heard one word she was saying to him, and she finally caught on by the distant look in his eyes. "Did you hear me...I asked you a question. Now, what are you doing out here like this?"

" Huh...Wh..What you say, Tiffany?"

She placed both of her hands on her waist and stood there in front of him, being ever so careful to allow her double-jointed leg's to poke all the way back giving her the ultimate sexy look," never mind!" She opened her purse and was about to give him the rest of the paper that she owed him on that last pack. "I came up here to get rid of these last 5 dubs I got but it's slow as hell."

Before she got the opportunity to pull the paper all the way out, he stopped her. His mind went to what the connect had warned him about over and over again. The connect had warned both him and Joey not to accept paper out in public no matter how harmless it appeared to be. His favorite words were; 'A picture is worth a thousand words!' In turn, he put his arm back around her and said very calmly," come on, let's bounce...Keep that paper in your pocket-book, we never know who's watching us."

These were the times she cherished most, he always seemed to become a different person when it was just them. In her heart, she knew he loved her and he had his own way of showing it, but more importantly, she wanted him to understand that she knew her position and was willing to play it at all costs. Because she knew her position so well, that's the same reason why she would never allow herself to be out in the streets fuckin' niggaz for CRACK. It wasn't like, she couldn't; niggaz has offered her as much as an ounce of CRACK for one night with her, but every time, and she turned them down...With ease! Like their new venture, she would never fuck-up one red penny of his; she just respected him that much. In the back of her mind, she knew that one of these days, he'd get the message and see her for the woman she really was, and until that day came, she was willing to play her part! By the time they were passing the Rec center, leaving out the Projects', she asked the burning question, "I saw Joey with you but he was walking off before I got there, what are the two of you doing out here? Whatever ya'll are up to, it's not a good look for ya'll to be out here like that. Remember, you never know who's watching;" she asked with her eyes pleading for an answer that her mind knew would never come.

A couple of minutes later they were walking into Auntie Pam's house at 3 A.M., to find her sitting in her favorite spot; at kitchen table facing the front door. He was caught off guard by seeing the other lady everybody called Auntie there with her. What really threw him for a loop was the young chick sitting at the table with a glass dick in her mouth and beaming up to Scotty! It was Jazzy, he ignored everybody else and walked right up beside her, "damn Jazzy, you should've been let me know that you get down like this, I would've been looked out for your crazy-ass, but I didn't know."

Tiffany was equally shocked because she didn't know that Jazzy smoked either, and she really didn't care about it, but that lustful look she had in her eyes was one she did care about. She wasn't a fan of Jazzy or her crazy-ass cousin Amanda, to her; those bitches gave her hell all through high-school. If it wasn't one thing it was the next, she was well aware that Malik had been fucking Amanda for as long as she could remember. It wasn't like they tried to hide it, Jazzy would always throw that shit in her face. It wasn't like she was a punk but fighting Amanda was out of the question, that bitch was crazy as all out doors. Looking at Jazzy suck on that glass let her know that she was new at it; a smirk crept across her face knowing that she was in for a ride of her young life. Instead of sitting at the table with the rest of them, she spoke, but not to Jazzy, and then went to find herself a comfortable spot on the sofa in the living room away from the madness. The only thing that mattered at that moment to her was that she knew that soon enough, her and Malik would be somewhere doing what they do best...Fucking each other's brains out! Feeling some type of way about Malik catching her smoking CRACK, she looked over her shoulder at him and said, "there's a lot of things you don't know about me," as she licked her lips so seductively that everybody and they momma knew what she was trying to do and who's attention she was trying to capture, even Tiffany caught on.

Jazzy had given Malik the response that he was looking for and expecting, he really anticipated her response, for him it was a lock. Instead of entertaining her statement, he turned around and went into the living room and sat next to Tiffany. Knowing that Tiffany was the extra jealous type when it really came down to it, true she played her position, but he knew that to ask her to sit back and watch him flirt with someone like Jazzy was asking a bit much. He snuggled up real close to her laying his head on her firm titties, he caught Jazzy watching him, but she cut her eye in a different direction when he looked at her. He smiled. He decided to let Jazzy know who ran the show and who was the main bitch because he was smart enough to know the best revenge is served on as a cold dish and Tiffany would be the one doing the serving tonight. Plus, nobody ever knew what was going on in Jazzy's sick mind. He winked and tapped Tiffany on the leg, "yo Jazzy, won't you come over here and tell me some of the shit that I don't know about you."

Not wasting time, Jazzy jumped from the table and made her way into the living room. Mistake number one, she turned her nose up at Tiffany like she wasn't anybody. The surprising part was that Tiffany returned an evil stare of her own, but she spoke," hey Jazzy!" Tiffany reached into her purse and pulled out a handful of paper. She laid it all out on the end-table and started counting it. "One-hundred, Two-hundred, Three-hundred, Four-hundred, Five-hundred, babe, here's the three-hundred I owe you plus another two just because I love you so much." Tiffany got up from the sofa leaving Malik and Jazzy alone, she turned back around and looked at him over her shoulder," Malik, let me know when you're ready, I'll be in the kitchen with Auntie Pam." Then she made eye contact with Jazzy," oh, nice seeing you Jazzy!"

When Tiffany got into the kitchen, she pulled out a sandwich bag with CRACK in it; she gave Auntie about what looked like a gram a piece. That was all it took to hype Auntie Pam up, she stood-up laughing," that's right, don't let that bitch come up in here an think she's running shit. That's right, let that bitch know how we get down up in this mutha-fucker," she said boasting and giving her high fives all at the same time. "Auntie Pam, you stupid...And crazy as hell," Tiffany said trying to whisper.

"Ain't no whispering around this bitch, let that bitch know who run the show. If that bitch wants to get down, let her crazy-ass know she gots to go through you first!" Malik made some small talk with Jazzy and became turned off when he got the impression that she was shittin' on her cousin Amanda for no reason. Since Amanda wasn't there to defend herself, he stopped her mid-sentence, if one thing he hated the most, it was fake people...People who smiled in your face and wanted to stick a knife in your back. Jazzy reminded him of such a person, but he had a trick for her!

"Yo Tiffany, come in here for a minute?" When she got in the living room, she stood in front of him with both hands on her hips, knowing that stance turned him on. It made her look like she was on America's Next Top Model and he loved it. "Ahhh, what you think about Jazzy?"

That caused a huge smile to creep onto her face, "see now, all that depends on how badly she wants to see you smile, daddy," she said throwing on the extra charm.

"You already know, my wish is your every command, you know I want to see my daddy smile at any cost!"

That whole conversation with them was starting to make Jazzy feel a little uncomfortable. In her mind, she knew exactly where this was leading to and she didn't want to be bumping no pussys with Tiffany. She didn't particularly like the female action, it was different when it came to White-girl, that was a move to keep her in White-girls' head, but to do it with Tiffany, that shit was out the question. Getting freaky with Malik wasn't a thing, she actually looked forward to it, he had all the CRACK and she knew from how Amanda said his dick game wasn't nothing, to her it was like taking candy from a baby. She was seriously weighing her odds, and one last look at Tiffany, she was impressed and felt moisture between her legs. Tiffany had it going on still, after all of these years. She said fuck it in her head, to her there was really no difference between tricking for powder cocaine and CRACK! She still tried to shoot her shot with Malik," I ain't really feeling this threesome shit you got in your head, I'm down with whatever though. I doubt you'll be able to handle one freaky bitch let alone two of us," she said trying to make fun of his small dick.

"What you think Tiffany," he asked? "Ain't no need asking me what I think because you already know what I think," she said but her eyes were on Jazzy. She was sizing her up in her mind. She was also letting Jazzy know regardless of the outcome, she was the one controlling the shit.

Auntie Pam was in the kitchen listening and decided it was time to show Jazzy where she stood in the scheme of things and who made the rules. She walked in the living room with her stem still in her hand and blowing out a thick cloud of CRACK smoke, "oh, she's definitely going with ya'll, twosome, threesome, fuck it, she's going even if it's a damn foursome. If that's what you want Malik, then that's what you'll get, that is if it's cool with Tiffany. You damn right Pitbull, oh shit, I mean Jazzy?"

She was quick to remind Jazzy that just the other day, Silas was ready to make her suck and fuck a Pitbull for his paper. Jazzy caught on quickly to just what Auntie Pam was referring to about Silas and the Pitbull. She knew he was serious because when he told her over the phone what he was going to do to her if his paper wasn't correct, he had the damn Pitbull in the car when he came to pick-up his paper, so she knew he was serious. 'Lord knows bumping pussys with a pretty bitch ain't got shit on sucking no dog's dick,' she thought to herself. At that moment she understood the price she had to pay and just how deep she was in this CRACK game.

The one thing Auntie Pam knew best about Tiffany and Malik to be true was that they were much better as a team than apart. If they wanted to break a bitch's spirit, they could do it, they did it before and they'll do it again. She recalled the story that Brenda had told her right before she got locked-up. She said it was like a contest between the two of them and she was their subject. Malik would fuck her silly with that King Kong dick of his until she begged for mercy, then Tiffany with her pretty-ass would eat her pussy so long that she couldn't even cum any more. Not to mention that dildo that Tiffany had, when she got tired of eating pussy, Tiffany would strap on that huge black dildo and fuck her in the ass.

The crazy thing was that she said one of them would watch and rest while the other did her in and then they would switch, never once giving her a break of her own. Brenda said they made her feel like a rag-doll the way they handed her back and forth with each other. They fucked her all over that hotel room, from the dresser, on the bathroom sink, with her head out the window and Malik fucking her in the ass as she yelled and screamed out into the night air. They really got a laugh out of that! They didn't stop until she totally submitted to their will and broke down and started crying uncontrollably, she said she literally had to beg them to stop. Ever since that night, Brenda would always leave when they came around at the same time, she said she always felt like they would take her pussy again and she just couldn't handle it.

Auntie Pam had to laugh at the thought because Brenda had called from jail just the other day and retold that story; she said that shit still got her having nightmares to this day! Jazzy was standing there in the middle of the living room looking the part of a dope-boys' wifey. Her Prada sneakers with no socks, her Prada wife-beater, down to the matching Parda jean-short outfit. She had on a nice watch and bracelet, everything was in place, her hair was done, and she looked good. On the outside everything appeared perfect, but on the inside she felt just like a CRACK whore should feel. It was like she was being auctioned off to the highest bidder and it sent chills up her spine. Not to mention bumping pussys with her enemy, she shook her head in disbelief. Her mind was telling her to say fuck it but before she could fix her lips to say what she was thinking, Auntie Pam grabbed her by the arm and pulled her in the bathroom with her.

Auntie Pam didn't say a word, she packed her stem and shoved the stem into Jazzy's mouth," pull real slow, this bitch is loaded," she said holding the fire steady on the tip of the stem while Jazzy inhaled slowly. "Look here lil' momma, this the CRACK game, all that bullshit you use to do fucking with powder, that shit is over. You can't use your pretty looks to control shit, this is a vicious cycle, we use our body to speak for us so get with the damn program," she spit to her with force in her voice. Jazzy blew the smoke out real slow, and her ears were ringing. She was high and ready to take on the world. "Ain't like you don't want to fuck him anyway, I see through that bullshit of yours...Handle your business bitch and make me proud."

All Jazzy could do was to shake her head in agreement to let her know she understood what she was saying. The highly addictive CRACK had not only invaded her lungs and blood stream but her mind as well. There was a sudden feeling of calmness that came over her and she was carefree, ready to get down with the get down.

CRACK was a mutha-fucker! "Thanks Auntie Pam, I really needed that. For a minute I was shook, I didn't know what the hell I was going to do, I almost let a little dick and some sweet pussy scare me away from my piece of pie. I'll be damn if I'm going to let that happen."

Auntie Pam stood there like the proud General she was about to send one of her best soldiers off into the field to battle, "that's the Jazzy I know. Do you bitch, do you!"

Jazzy and Auntie Pam walked out the bathroom, all eyes were on them, Jazzy noticed all eyes were glued to her. She looked at Tiffany, licked her lips and winked at her, next she looked Malik up and down like she was sizing him up. She opened the front door and looked back over her shoulder, "ya'll coming or what? I'm ready to get buck," she said walking out the door onto the front porch!

Tiffany looked over at Auntie Pam," damn you good! You still got it, don't worry, we'll take good care of lil' momma," said Tiffany with the most determined look on her face that any of them has ever saw.

But if you were smart and looked closer, that look was really saying:' Jazzy just made the biggest mistake of her young life!' Jazzy was floating on cloud 9; the cool air had her nipples sticking out like elevator buttons as she stood by the passenger's side of the car waiting to get in.

Tiffany and Malik walked out behind her, she looked at them and she had to force the thought of what was about to take place out of her mind, it was just too much to deal with, at least that's what her pride was telling her. She was about to have a threesome with CRACK head Tiffany as her and Amanda referred to her. However, for some reason, this time it didn't make her feel good to down another female, after all the bullshit that Tiffany been through, she had to give it to her, she never once heard about Tiffany being out there in the streets, or selling her body for CRACK.

If it hadn't been for Amanda, she thought that she and Tiffany would have been friends in school, but since Amanda was her cousin and she had a thing for Malik, she had to roll with her blood. What did Tiffany have that she didn't have? Back when the rumors first started, she use to pray on Tiffany's downfall, just like everybody else in school. It was always Amanda's story, if she could get Tiffany out the way then Malik would be all hers and she and Jazzy hatched some evil plan, now here she was at Tiffany's mercy.

What will everybody say about me being a CRACK head? Will Amanda and White-girl laugh at me the way I use to laugh at Tiffany when she first started smoking? All those thought were going through her mind and she couldn't do anything to derail those evil thoughts; what could she do? Malik hit the locks on the doors and then threw the keys to Tiffany.

'Damn, this nigga got her driving an all that.' All Jazzy could do was shake her head in disbelief, with her sick mind, she thought if she got her little ass by the passenger's side she would be riding shot-gun with Malik, but he tricked her again. Tiffany was beating her at every turn, down to who would drive before Malik could get comfortable on the back seat,

Auntie Pam came out the house on the porch, yelling his name," ahhh, Malik, come here right quick?" He reluctantly got back out the car, "What now? Damn Auntie Pam, what the hell you want?"

"Boy, if you don't watch your mouth...You better." Giving up because he knew he was in a losing battle," my bad, but you see I'm about to bounce, I'm ready to go handle my business, what can be more important than that?"

"Bring yo' little ass on over here and find out!" He made his way back across the street and back up onto the porch, Auntie Pam leaned in close to whisper in his ear. "I wasn't going to tell you, but the chick Jazzy, I had to bail her out of a bind, a huge debt that her ass couldn't pay. She's into us for a couple of stacks and I want you and Tiffany to introduce her young ass into the family in a real special way...In other words, make sure ya'll dog that young bitch, her ass belongs to us and let her know that we know she belongs to us," said Auntie Pam with venom in her voice.

He took two steps back, he had a devilish grin on his face," you don't know? I was going to do that anyway, I don't even have to mention how Tiffany feels about her. I haven't seen Tiffany this excited since ummm yeah, your girl, Brenda and that was right before she got locked-up."

They laughed a wicked laugh together and hugged each other good-bye. They were thinking the same type of thoughts about Jazzy and they both knew it, so no more was needed to be said. When he got into the car, Tiffany was in the cock-pit and ready to roll-out, while checking the rear-view mirror; she winked at him and smiled. He got comfortable in the backseat! Her first stop was at the 7-eleven across from the Days Inn. She came out the store with a bag full of shit: She had batteries, 3 boxes of condoms, several lighters, cigarettes, soda, chips, candles, and whip-cream. She got back in the car and handed the bag over to Jazzy, "hold this," was all she said to her. The night was going to be one to remember.

Auntie Pam strolled back into her house satisfied knowing that Malik was going to lay down the law to Jazzy and Tiffany would definitely put her gansta down, and that was truly music to her ears. Auntie could tell right off the bat there was a slight change in Auntie Pam's demeanor. It was like she was walking on air or something, she couldn't really put her finger on it, but she knew something had changed since she went outside and spoke to Malik.

She had every intention of getting to the bottom of it though," girl, you got that crazy look in your eyes, what the hell you up to?"

"I ain't up to shit; I just feel for that young bitch, she just bit off more than she could chew fucking with Malik and Tiffany!"

"Pam! What do you mean by that? That boy ain't gonna hurt that child is he," asked Auntie nervously?

"Damn right he's going to hurt her, but not the way your crazy-ass is thinking. He's going to hurt her mentally, you know, fuck her pride up and all that type of shit. The boy got a dick as big as a horse and he never gets enough of fucking those bitches, and his side kick, Tiffany, she'll walk through hell with gasoline drawers on. Trust me; they'll have her ass doing shit that's only seen in them XXX DVD's. I'll bet my last penny that when they do finish with her ass, she won't be on that high-an-mighty bullshit no more! She need to be taught the rules of this CRACK game, she need to know and understand that if you fuck somebody's paper up, there will be consequences for your action and oftentimes, those consequences won't be pretty. By them fucking her over and over again I know it's bound to go through her mind at some point that all this is happening to her because she fucked up that paper and that's how you begin to tame them young wild bitches. Pain and Pleasure, that shit's crazy because they both hurt so good, you feel me girl?"

Auntie knew in her heart that Jazzy had made that unfortunate mistake of crossing over from one game to the next. In the CRACK game, there's one very important lesson and most people miss that lesson. It's rather simple to learn and understand, but everybody seems to miss Rule# 1 of the CRACK game and it's as stated: THERE ARE NO RULES IN THE CRACK GAME!

In a sense, Auntie Pam was giving her a crash course in the game, from the outside looking in it may appear that she wanted to see Malik dog her, but the reality of it all is this. There is nothing Malik could do to Jazzy that will compare to what she'd be willing to do to herself for a blast of CRACK, if she doesn't learn the game and fast. Hopefully, she'll always use this night as a learning experience, she'll reflect back to this night as the night she gave up her choice, she no longer had a say as to what she would do or could do, all that went out the window when she dived into the CRACK game head first!

"You know what? The more I sit here and think about it, she deserves everything that comes down that pipe. One thing I do know about you Pam is that you'll make that girls skin as tough as leather! Lord knows it's going to be tough for that chile in this day and time, shit ain't the same as when we jumped in this game." With that said, both of the ole' school vets tapped their CRACK stems together as if they were Champagne flutes. They were making a toast, but not the way normal people made their toast and they both said at the same time, I'll smoke to that!

Malik was itching to ask Jazzy the million dollar question, the one, when you start hitting the pipe thang? Not even realizing it, his mind had betrayed him, even though he wanted to ask her, he didn't want to ask her at that moment, but his voice had a mind of its own and asked her anyway. He shrugged it off and said 'fuck-it' in his head. From the side view, he could see Jazzy rolling her eyes as he asked the million dollar question, she started sucking her teeth.

"Why, what difference does that make, here I am ready and willing to be your sex whore for the night and all you can think about is when a bitch started smoking CRACK. Ain't that about a bitch, Malik the notorious drug dealer worried about how a trick like myself became a trick, oh ain't you special boo, she said laughing at herself."

He cracked open a fresh deck of Newports and continued talking to her," you're absolutely right! I really don't give a fuck to be honest. Just know this; I'll make this a night you'll never forget-Trust that!"

"Yeah whatever nigga! Just see how long you can keep that little dick of yours hard, from what Amanda be saying, this shit should be like taking candy from a baby." Jazzy busted out laughing, she felt like she just killed two birds with one stone; the first being Jazzy saying that he had a small dick and for two, she slid in the fact that after all of these years, her cousin Amanda was still fucking Malik.

Tiffany didn't waste her time addressing Jazzy, she knew in her heart where she and Malik stood, only the guilty would respond. Jazzy would be just like the rest of them bitches, especially once Malik put his dick game down, she knew it took a certain woman to handle that King Kong dick and she was perfect. After Malik fucked most females silly, they either hated him or loved him and to keep it 1-hundred, she had to take her hat off to him, he definitely knew what he was doing when it came to fucking. They almost always conceal how they felt under the veil of hatred because they were either too scared to ask for more of that dick of his or he had them so sprung they didn't know how to take the feeling of pleasure he dished out to them. She smiled because she already knew what the outcome would be! "Where to daddy," Tiffany asked looking in the rear-view mirror at him? She winked and smiled at the same time to let him know she was down with whatever.

"It don't really matter, I'll leave that up to you and our guest...I'm just ready to get this thang jumping."

A few minutes later, Tiffany was pulling into the parking lot of the Marriot Hotel next to Toys' R' Us, when he attempted to hand her paper for the room she turned him down. "I'm good...I got this one daddy." Her voice was so calm and her demeanor only confirmed what he was already thinking. She had every intention of breaking Jazzy's will and her spirit.

Tiffany was always at her best when she thought she had something to prove and tonight was one of those nights for her. Jazzy had over-stepped her bounds throwing Amanda's name all around the place like she didn't know she had a thang for her man. It was a long standing issue between the three of them and right now she didn't need Jazzy's big mouth reminding her of the old days, she was well aware of the competition she had when it came to Amanda. Since she wasn't wild back in the day she felt like she couldn't really compete with the free-spirited Amanda, from what she had heard, Amanda was the type who was fucking grown men when she was still in the 10th grade, and she couldn't compete with that, so she just ignored the fact that Malik was fucking her, it was only a fuck and she was the one who had his heart, so she thought back then.

The way she always thought, it was Amanda always in her way from having the man of her dream's to herself, and it made things worse since Amanda was so popular and fly as hell, she was very pleasant on the eyes, she gave her that. That very fact is what brought her out of her comfort zone and examine the street-life, she wanted to show Malik that she could be 'Hood' to; she wanted him to know that she would do anything he wanted her to do. So when she use to hear Malik talk about how high he was getting, she had no idea that he was only talking about weed, her ignorance lead her to smoking CRACK! She didn't even know what the fuck she was smoking, but all she knew was that if Malik did it, she would get him back by doing the same thing, at the very least she thought it would show him that she was down.

Malik pumped his fist in the air at the mention of Tiffany saying she had the room, "yeah, that's what the fuck I'm talking about, my baby-girl got her own!"

Jazzy took that as a direct blow to her lack of having any paper of her own to contribute to their late night party outside of her body," sorry ya'll but a bitch ain't got no paper to throw in the pot...My bad," she said with a real stank attitude to match her look.

"Don't worry about that Jazzy. You're our guest of honor so your paper ain't no good tonight, the only thing you have to do is be willing to perform at your best."

"Oh, don't worry about that, you'll have your wish one way or another. You'll have two whores at your beck-n-call all night long but the thing is, I doubt you'll be able to hang. We might just put that ass to bed real quick like," she added with her devilish smirk. Immediately she turned up the music so loud in her attempt to drown out whatever it was that Malik was about to say to her. She was tired of all the talking, in her mind, she recalled all the stories Amanda use to tell her when it came to Malik. If Amanda had him busting off real fast, then she knew he wasn't a match for her, she was freakier than her cousin and knew her pussy got wetter. So in her mind, if Amanda could do her thang with him, then she wouldn't have no problem, the more she thought about it, Malik started looking more and more like her own personal lottery ticket.

———————————————————————————

Joey and Terri were up early the next morning despite a late night mind blowing sexapade between the two; however they had business to handle and nothing would come between that for either of them. Terri had looked into some property out in Ruckersville, Virginia late last month and found a beautiful home that was already in foreclosure. She contacted the local bank and learned that the bank wasn't trying to make a profit; all they wanted was recoup their losses from their initial investment.

It didn't take much to convince Joey that it was a good move for them. He had such a tremendous amount of respect for her judgment and ability to hold-down the fort for the both of them, he practically gave her free reign to spend as freely as she wanted, he had that type of trust in her. She gave Malik the once over admiring his suit, "damn baby, you really rocking that Armani suit from head to toe; you look good enough to eat. If we had just a little more time, I'd eat your ass hole," she said playfully, but serious at the same time.

He shrugged his shoulders, he knew the suit was tight, for $8,000, it just had better make her want to eat him whole, "sounds like a plan. It's 7:30 in the morning, I'd much rather crawl back under the covers with your sexy-ass then let you go handle all this by yourself ...Why you need me anyway?"

He stuck his tongue out playing with her, "you know what? You're starting to look like breakfast yourself!" She walked over to him, she wanted to tighten up his tie for him and smooth out his blazer, "sounds good play-boy, however; we have a very important business meeting with the bank at 8:30am sharp. We don't want to start our business off on a bad note by showing up late, you know how long-winded you are when it comes to," she said pointing at his dick.

How about this, we go take care our business, close the deal, end the meeting and then you can have a taste of the sweetest candy known to man," she said smacking her own ass.

"So, let me remind you of your own famous words, remain focused! The big picture is the only picture that counts." Impressed by how much she retains from the jewels he drops on her from time to time, there was no way that he could re-butt anything she just said because he tells it to her all the time, truth needs no support!

"I'll hold you to that. Let's bounce then, shall we," he said holding out his arm like a true gentlemen that he was.

They had a nice Lincoln Town car that they rented just for this occasion. They didn't want to just sound the part; they wanted to look the part as well. Presentation was 80% of the deal, they learned the importance of looking the part, they were ready! I've prearranged to have our broker to deposit $175,000 into our account. The bank is asking for 'a-buck-eighty'," she said trying her best to sound like him when he talks business in the streets. We're going to walk out that bank with that house for the One-Seventy-five, deed in hand, watch, watch what I tell you, she boasted. She had on her game face the moment she got in the car with him and her game face was furious.

It took them all of Four and a half hours to close the deal and they were walking out the bank with smiles on their face from knowing they had the deed to their very own property. They owned it free and in the clear, they didn't owe the bank one red penny and they were proud of it. Phase one of their plans had gone exactly as Terri had predicted," told you baby, we talked them right into a corner," she said smiling. What he didn't know until the meeting was under way, Terri had the ace of spades up her sleeve, just when the bank wasn't willing to budge, she dropped the bomb: 'Excuse me, but are you aware that neither this bank or the previous owner of this property has paid the property tax in the last 2 years?'

Once she dropped that bomb, they ended up giving the bank only a-buck-fifty for the property saving twenty-five grand, what a wonderful day she thought. He had to give her all the props, I don't know nothing about all this shit, I didn't say or do anything to make them listen to me, that was all you baby and I'm so proud of you for that. I was only there for you, after I said good-morning, and nice to meet you, it was over for me, you took over like I knew you would." He winked at her," but what I really want to know is how the hell you find out about the property tax not being paid?"

"That was always my ace in the hole. I knew it the first day I researched the property. I needed you to see me in action and how I get down for our crown. It's my job to put us in the best possible position, so that means I have to know more than they know even though it's their property. When I'm considering spending your money, I have to know these things and it put me in the right mind frame. The bank knew the property tax would be passed down to the next buyer, with the buyer being a young black female, with a dressed up thug on her side, they figured they could get over. However, they couldn't afford us to walk out of there without the deed, another year of missing the property tax and its late fees; they would have been in the red, even after selling the property. They were happy to come up 5-grand short, hell, sometimes in this business; a lost like that is well worth it, but not for us. So how'd you like the show, baby?"

"Liked it? That's an understatement, I loved it and to hear how you had that shit all planned out even before we walked in there, that's some boss-bitch type of shit."

Terri had formed a small Realtor Company using her name and Joey as a silent partner but the major investor. She filed the necessary paper work with the State so she could keep all her investors anonymous that was a little tax trick her professor had taught her. Phase two of her plan really showed how brilliant she really was, the property they just bought was already sold. Terri had sold the house to a family from Florida without actually selling it to them, not without the deed anyway. That's what she would be doing in her next meeting at another bank in Charlottesville at 3 P.M. " Babe, by the time we walk out our next meeting do you realize that we would have made a cool Seventy-Five thousand dollars in a matter of hours?"

Terri was just as excited as a 5 year old on Christmas morning. Malik looked down at his Mavado watch, he wasn't really feeling the next meeting," babe, I get the message. I know you can handle your business; I got mad faith in you. You have to do the next meeting without me, another one of those meetings and that shit will drive me insane," he was saying laughing at himself. She knew he wasn't into all these meetings and all that, she just wanted him there at the first one so that they could always look back on that meeting and say they did it together. She had planned that he would back out on the next meeting anyway, but she didn't' tell him that she knew he would, that would be too much information for one day.

"Okay daddy, your baby-girl can handle things from here," she said with that contagious smile of hers. The more she licked her lips the more he wanted to fuck her right there in the car. "You keep licking your lips like that I'm going to put something in your mouth to lick on!"

With the black tint on the windows of the Lincoln she said," don't tempt me with a good time mister, go ahead, give me that dick," she said stretching over the center console devouring his dick right there in the bank's parking lot. She knew the windows were tinted but she really didn't give a fuck who watches, this was her man and she loved him with all her heart! Like the true woman she was, Terri sucked her man's dick and then gave him a shot of her dripping wet pussy. Her golden rule: Never allow your man out of your sight if he's still horny! She lived by that creed, if she failed at her job; she knew she was slowly inviting trouble into their relationship and that she didn't want.

A man would be a man, but what she wanted was a happy man, when she was finished, she giggled and asked him," where to sir?"

"Drop me off down Page, I got some business to take care of down there with Auntie Pam." Terri was familiar with who Auntie Pam was and where she lived. Secretly, she wished that Joey would walk away from the streets. She had known from the second day of their relationship that he was a hustler, it was in him, from the walk he walked down to the way he talked, but she never mentioned it to him. Back then she didn't think the relationship would go past any-where because she wasn't the type to be attracted to the hustling type. However, Joey proved her wrong at every turn; he wasn't anything like she thought he would be. Joey ran his business like a fortune 500 CEO; he was strong minded, intelligent, focused, handsome and very open to criticism. He won her over quickly and now here she was unable to envision her life without him in it, and if you let her tell the story, she wouldn't have any other way.

"Alright then, call me in a couple hours... Hopefully, later you will return the favor," she said with that sneaky grin on her face and a wink. After several raps at Auntie Pam's door, he let himself in. She was laid out on the sofa still sleep, he wondered why she insisted on them buying that expensive bedroom set when she never slept in the damn bed? He couldn't figure that shit out to save his life.

He tapped her on the arm trying to wake her up as she whispered in her ear, "get up sleepy head, it's almost One O' Clock in the afternoon ...What you doing still asleep?"

She opened one of her eyes to see who it was that was waking her up, but she took one look at the suit he was wearing and jumped up out of her sleep," shit, who's funeral am I missing?"

He laughed at her because she could barely keep her balance from jumping up so fast," come on, get up!"

"The only time I see any of ya'll asses in a suit is for somebody's funeral, so tell me who damn funeral am I missing," she demanded? "Where's Malik, he stayed her last night didn't he," asked Joey ignoring her question?

She started yawning and stretching all at the same time as she managed to get herself together. "Oh shit...I'm still tired as hell...He didn't stay here last night, he and Tiffany left with the young girl that be with Auntie, what's that damn chile's name," she said trying to remember Jazzy's name. "Shit, I can't remember that chile's name, but they said they were getting a room or some shit like that."

Auntie Pam decided to go up-stair's and get herself together, she knew that today was going to be a long day and nothing could start her day off better than a steamy hot shower to wash some of the CRACK smoke from her body. When she got in her room up-stair's, she went to her favorite drawer and pulled out her stem, she had to have her, 'wake-up' if she didn't have anything else. She loved the feeling of the CRACK smoke as it invaded her lungs' and chest; it gave her an instant high. She blew the smoke out slowly and whispered to herself," fuck the bullshit, I'm chasing that paper today!"

By the time she came back down stairs, Auntie had woke-up as well and had the full-court press on Joey. Auntie had wanted to give Joey's young ass a shot of that pussy for some time now but the timing was never right, she figured that no time was better than the present but that got fucked-up with Auntie Pam busting in the living room. "Damn Pam, you sure do know how to fuck up a wet dream," she said eyeing Joey the whole time.

"Your crazy-ass been trying to give that man some pussy since he was knee-high to a grasshopper and he ain't fucked you yet. What makes you think he'll fuck your ole' prune pussy now," said Auntie Pam laughing at her. "Take this instead!" She threw her a gram of CRACK and told her to get her mind right because today was going to be a long day for the both of them.

Joey knew better than to get in the middle of two ole' time friend's, "Auntie Pam, get me a plate, please," he asked pulling out 2 ounces of CRACK. "Auntie didn't wait for Auntie Pam; she jumped up from the sofa," I got it baby, sit tight," passing Pam as she stuck her tongue out at her.

"Yeah bitch, go head, make yourself useful cause that man don't want none of that dried up pussy of yours," said Auntie Pam.

"I guess it's just the two of us this morning because I know Malik and them probably won't be around here until later this evening." Auntie Pam stood in the center of the living room and pointed at her friend Auntie," what, you don't see her or something?"

"Yeah I see her, how can I not see her? But for what I'm talking about, she's already down the block doing her own thang, so that cut her out of this picture, you know what I'm saying?" Auntie came back in the living room just in time to voice her theory," that's a long story Joey, I'm sure Pam will fill you in later but just for the record, I'm here if you need my help…I can definitely use the extra paper," she said giving Pam that, 'I know I owe you look'.

Joey was well aware of the history the two women shared with each other but to him, none of that shit really matter to him when it came time to chasing that paper, and he felt the most comfortable with the team he already had. But the look Auntie Pam gave him made him give in for her sake," a-ight then, I'll tell you what: Go home, take care of your business, you know shower, shit, or whatever else it is that women do to get their shit proper and come back down her in a hour or two; I'll be ready for you by then."

Auntie Pam saw the look in Joey's eyes, she knew he didn't like when people from outside of his comfort zone came in the picture. She in turned gave Auntie the nod and showed her the door," come on girl, go get your shit together and I'll talk to him," she whispered as she led Auntie out the door.

Joey didn't waste any time in tearing into Auntie Pam's ass the moment she came back into the house. "You know damn well that we don't need any new faces around here, we got a good thing going here!"

"Come on Joey, me and Auntie been chasing paper for damn near 20 years together off and on, she's really good people Joey." "Good people? You gotta be kidding me right? Ain't no such thing as good people in this game, especially if you're on the outside looking in. This game ain't built on good people; go tell that shit to all the homeys doing life sentences because they was surrounded by so-called good people. Those dudes ain't never coming home...Never! What makes you think this shit is any different," fired Joey?

He knew that the truth was a hard pill to swallow for her but she needed to realize that this shit was just that serious. He didn't mind having her mad at him for the time being than later have her as his co-defendant facing a Federal Rico trial. His love for her ran deep in his veins, he even felt some type of way about having to talk to her like that but he didn't have any other choice, he needed for her to see the other side and harsh tones were expected. For him the story was always the same, only the players changed, sex, paper, and drugs sends niggaz to prison for the rest of their lives and he wasn't trying to let that happen to any of them.

_____   _____   _____   _____   _____
_____   _____

Not long after they finished bagging up the 2 ounces' of CRACK, Malik, Tiffany, and Jazzy walked through the front door. Anybody who knew Malik could tell that he just had the time of his life, that big kool-aid smile said it all. Tiffany was no different, she had a certain shine about how she walked and looked, and you could tell that she was happy because Malik was happy. Her sole mission in life was to see him happy, regardless of what she had to do, she was on Malik's team and was willing to go to any lengths to prove that to him. From the way she looked at him, you could tell that she y loved that man! It was always a special time for her when Malik spent the night with her, even if they had company. The odd ball in this picture was Jazzy. She looked defeated, her walk was crooked and her hair was a mess. She just looked like she'd be taken advantage of, her facial expression told the story of being the latest victim of the Tiffany and Malik sexapade.

Joey wasn't sure if Auntie Pam had told him that it was Jazzy that Malik and Tiffany had left with, but he was confused. If anything, seeing Amanda wouldn't have seemed strange, those two would do anything for Malik, but her cousin Jazzy? Now, that had to have a story behind it and he wanted to hear it.

"Damn, look what the wind done blew in...Oh shit, I see you're the latest victim Jazzy? Never in a million year's would I have predicted this show...Never," said Joey laughing at how Jazzy looked. Jazzy knew he was throwing shot's at her but she was to tired to respond to the bullshit, she just put her middle finger up and plopped down on the sofa next to Auntie Pam. What she needed was a couple hours of rest but that wouldn't come because the instant she sat down, Auntie Pam passed her a freshly packed stem," get yo mind right because from the looks of it, your body is in pain."

Jazzy wasn't able to see that this life wasn't all about blowing Peru all the time, so she took the stem and took a blast. She pulled long and slow not even caring that she was smoking CRACK right in front of Joey and Malik, in her mind she said fuck it. Especially after what Malik had her doing last night, when she tried to pass the stem to Tiffany, she didn't want it. Jazzy greedily took that as more for her and she took another hit from the highly addictive substance, it bugged her out the way the CRACK melted on the stem with the assistance of fire, or was she high already?

Joey could barely believe his eyes by seeing Ms. Thang smoking CRACK, yet the reality of the life-style didn't surprise him any. This was a classic case of, MATTERS OF THE HOOD', and he's seen more times than he could count how the hood swallowed the best of them whole. Jazzy was no different, she just happened to be the hood's latest victim. "Yo Malik, come up-stairs, I need to holla at you."

Malik followed him upstairs and the first thing Malik said full of excitement was," damn homey, we beat that pussy into submission last night. I wish you could've seen her ass begging a nigga to stop fucking her, but you know me...I fucked her even harder; I even fucked the bitch in the ass while she was eating Tiffany's pussy. The bitch is a professional pussy eater, I'm telling you, and the bitch can eat some pussy. She begged me to cum all over her face, she was licking that shit off her lips, and she loved it."

He would've kept going had Joey not stopped him," spare me the details, I want to know when the bitch start smoking CRACK and how the hell she ended up in our spot?" Malik shrugged his shoulders," the bitch was here when I got here last night. She was with the umm umm the lady Auntie, from down the block. You gotta ask Auntie Pam what the whole story is, she knows more than I know homey, all I did was fuck the shit out the bitch, all that other shit wasn't on my mind. Did you bring that?"

Joey went into the closet and opened the safe; he took out a brown paper bag. "Yeah, this twenty-five thousand. Take it out to your car and put it in the trunk or something, the connect suppose to be calling soon and when he do, we'll be ready," said Joey handing the brown paper bag to Malik. Malik took the bag and flew back down the steps taking two at a time. He didn't take notice that Jazzy was walking to the window as he went out the front door.

Malik was opening his trunk and about to put a brown paper bag in his trunk, two dudes approached him from behind. It looked strange to her because one of the dudes was from Prospect, but since she didn't see no guns' she just watched. Within a split second, what she saw next had her questioning her own sanity. The dude she recognized hit Malik in the back of his head with the butt of a chrome gun, Malik hit the ground hard. She tried to scream, she was telling her mind to scream, but nothing came out her mouth, The only thing she could do was tap Tiffany on the shoulder and pointed out the window, "look!"

Tiffany looked out the window just in time to see one of the dudes kicking Malik in the side of his head as he lay motionless on the ground, he looked dead. Her mind tried to remember if she heard any gun shots, she jumped off the sofa screaming to Joey up-stairs," they killing Malik outside," then she ran out the front door to help her man.

CHAPTER 14

FOR the last couple of weeks Amanda and Silas would handle their business during the day and spend every second they could together at night. It was like therapy for the both of them, they would meet up somewhere, get a room, talk half the night, sex each other as if their lives depended on it. Today was no different as they checked out the Omni Hotel downtown and he dropped her off on top of Prospect.

"So what time will I be hearing from you today," she asked getting out the Caddy? Even after weeks of looking into her beautiful eyes, he was still couldn't help but stare because they were so exotic and different, they even change colors depending on how she felt.

It was easy to lose his train of thoughts but a light tap brought him back to reality," huh, oh, you tell me sexy!"

Amanda rolled her eyes at him," see, that's the shit I be talking about. You think I don't know what you're trying to get at but I do...You want me to call you, huh?"

His grin increased on his face the more she spit the truth as she saw it, but he couldn't argue with her because she was dead-ass, "I'm saying, if that's what you want to do I won't get in your way from calling me when you get ready...Go right ahead and be my guest."

She stood up as she was fixing her mini-skirt, her golden brown thighs aroused him as he locked in for their firmness. All he could think about was the pussy, it was so good, he could never get enough of her, he was tempted to go in the building with her and taste that candy of hers. She was getting thicker and thicker everyday it seemed, he loved it! He attributed it to the fact he convinced her to stop sniffing powder. It surprised him when she took his advice and didn't bother bringing up the vice he had of his own. There really was no reason for her to listen to what he had to say, especially when he was still sniffing dope himself, and not to mention that he didn't have to support her habit, she had her own paper to do her thang. She had her own so he knew she wasn't with him for what he had or who he was in the streets. The way that ass was looking, he knew she was getting thicker and the funny thing is that she knew it to. "I might breeze through later, who knows what the wind will blow your way," he said licking his lips and thinking about a quickie with her.

"So what you're really saying is that you'll come through to check up on me, huh? I see right through that shit," she said laughing. "For-real though, come through, I'll be looking for you; you know I just might have something for you to tighten up for me," she said patting herself on the ass! She gave him a quick peck on the cheek," go head, get gone, you know how hot it is over this way. I don't want them 'boys' fucking with you all day long, you know how they do," she stepped away from the Caddy.

She stood there until the Caddy disappeared down the block, she scanned the area and seen her worker's out there on their grind. She spotted Jacob in the middle of the circle entertaining the crew as the clown he was, since nobody waved her over, she decided to carry her ass in the building and see what was up with White-girl. She was also aware that since she been getting real paper the dudes were jealous because of her relationship with Silas, even though they never said it, it was more so how they looked at her whenever he came around; she was sharp enough to know that a person say saw way more by not actually saying one word, their body language spoke volumes and she seen it in the dudes on top of Prospect. 'Fuck'em', is what she told herself, she was going to do her regardless, and she ran the show not them. She crossed the street and walked down the steps and entered her building using the back door.

The thing about the hood was that shit went on all the time and sometime you were involved and other times you was just guilty by association as was the case with Amanda. She was unaware of the War that was brewing between the Projects and Prospect but she would soon become an unwilling participate. All eyes would be on her because she was the voice of the hood, everybody would look to her for what to do, that's just the ways of the hood, they tend to lean towards the person who's getting the most paper and she was that Bitch! It was already an on-going conversation about how she came out of nowhere and took over the hood without using force or violence. She walked up the steps taking her time, when she opened the door to her apartment, she thought about the bill Jacob owed and almost turned around to go back up there and embarrass him right in front of his little crew, she would've but her body was a little sore, Silas put his gansta down on her all night long. She was exhausted! Her phone started ringing," yeah what up nigga? A-ight, yeah, I seen you up there, I'm walking through the door right now, Come up," she said talking into the phone before she hung up. 'I knew that nigga seen me,' she said to herself talking about Jacob.

Once Amanda opened her front door and stepped over the threshold, the aroma of food invaded her nostrils," damn girl, you got it smelling like Mel's up in this piece, what you over there whipping up," she asked? She shut the door and when she turned back around White-girl was peeping from behind the wall of the kitchen and at the same time that they made eye contact with each other, they both yelled, "eggs, bacon, and toast," they both fell out laughing because that was the only thing that White-girl could cook without burning.

White-girl seemed extra bubbly today as she looked Amanda up and down," girl, you and ya boy Silas been going strong for almost a month now every night, you getting thick in the thighs to ...Don't let me find out," she said eyeing Amanda suspiciously.

Amanda rolled her eyes putting on her game face, but one mention of Silas forced an unwanted shit-eating grin on her face and all she could say was, "I love that man!"

White-girl was caught off guard by what she said, L.O.V.E., not that nasty four letter word. "Not my girl, say it ain't so?"

Amanda didn't say a word; all she could do was to shake her head yes over and over again excited. " All I'm saying is you need to remember that shit you use to tell me about love, and in case you forgot let me remind you. You told me that love doesn't exist in the hood so there's no need looking for it," said White-girl.

"What you need to do is check yourself and keep it pimpin'!" Amanda did her best to ignore the once famous motto she has lived by for more than half her life. She preached and taught that to her most trusted girlfriends and recommended that they follow that motto, now here she was falling victim to what she thought was once impossible. Her heart and mind was on different pages.

Changing the subject," Jacob called right before I walked in the house, he supposed to be on his way up here. I know that paper better be straight," she said avoiding the topic of that dirty four letter word. White-girl put up her index finger," what would we do if one of these dudes tries to buck on paying us, what will we really do? Like for-real, have you ever thought about that shit," asked White-girl seriously? Just when Amanda was about to answer her, there was 3 light raps on the door," who goes there," she asked knowing it was Jacob from the knock?

Jacob twisted the knob and let himself into the apartment, in his head he was thinking about how they never locked their door when they were there. He smelled the food as it made him instantly hungry, then his eyes locked in own Amanda's golden brown thighs. He had lust in his eyes and his voice was husky," what up ladies, I see you still looking good Amanda!"

There goes that fucking look that she recognized right away, it was the look that said, 'I want to fuck you!' But she really translated it as he thought shit was sweet with them because they were females so she decided to play hard ball with him, "that mutha-fuckin' paper is what up nigga!"

"Damn Amanda, it's like that? Whatever happened to hello, hi you or how about something to eat Jacob, glad to see you."

She took two steps in his direction and was nose to nose and spoke slow and calm," this ain't no fuckin' social gathering nigga, this is business and until we handle our business there's nothing worthwhile talking about. But since you're in the mood to be doing the talking, let's talk about this bill you owe me."

He stepped back away from her because he knew she was dead-ass with that straight-razor of hers and he wasn't trying to be her latest victim, she had that look in her eyes. Once he was out of striking distance and comfortable he looked her in the eyes and said, "I had to throw that shit last night. I ain't got no paper, shorty, now what," he had a sneer on his face. He then looked at White-girl and then back at Amanda, shrugged his shoulders, " I ain't got it shorty."

Amanda's reaction and response was to slow because White-girl whipped out a chrome .38 long, it was trained on Jacob's mid-section. "Now...If you don't have that paper, I'd say you picked the wrong two bitches to try and play. I'll put that head to bed for fuckin' with our paper and guess what? The funny thing about all of this is that it wouldn't be nothing for me to kill yo' ass, call the police and tell them that you was attacking her when I walked in so I shot you. Look around nigga, I'm the only white bitch in the hood, so they won't think nothing of the fact that I'm visiting my dearest friend, I'm going to get a fuckin' award for killing your dumb-ass! So I suggest that you unass that paper you got in them pocket's because I know you got it, matter of fact, I know you got more than what you owe us. You did just come off on a heist didn't you," she said through clenched teeth?

The gun, the story, and his heist was all true but what he couldn't figure out was how the hell did she know about the heist, it just happened? She could definitely kill him and get away with it and never do a day in jail. He raised his arms in surrender and smiled to let them know he was just playing," ease-up shorty, I was just fucking with ya'll," he said nervously. "Whatever you do, just don't shoot me...Please don't shoot me," he begged.

Amanda didn't act like she was surprise by White-girl and the gun she was holding, instead, she started talking to him, "shut your bitch-ass up," she demanded. She began going throw his pockets and found a huge wad of cash, more than what he owed them. "How much is this?"

"Listen to me for a minute Amanda...I was bullshitting, you see I got paper and if I wasn't going to pay ya'll I wouldn't have even came up here, I would've just ignored you. You know how I do it! I got nine thousand on me right now, I came up here to fuck with ya'll and then tell you that I wanted to spend all this paper with you, I'm down with you Amanda, I'm down with you! Let me spend my paper with you."

"Fuck that shit nigga, you think we some lame-ass bitches don't you? Who the fuck are you to be coming up in here giving us some type of litmus test on our gansta? But see, this the type of shit I've been waiting for my whole life, I never knew if I was going to be ready when it presented itself, I knew this shit was coming, that's why I got this," she said walking in his direction and holding the gun higher in the air. When she got close, she hauled off and came crashing down on the side of his jaw with the butt of the gun. Then blow sent him crumbling to the floor in pain!

Amanda looked on in a daze, she couldn't believe what White-girl had just done but she didn't try to stop her. The timid little White girl she met months ago was gone. She was drunk off the power that came with seeing major paper, she was forceful, and direct, from the looks of it, she looked like this was her normal lifestyle. Amanda liked it!

"So you still trying to spend that paper with us or what," asked Whitegirl with the gun at her side as she stood over him?

He was struggling to keep his consciousness when survival kicked in, he looked at White-girl and saw murder in her eyes, it literally scared him. He wasn't ready to meet his maker, that look she had made him have a renewed respect for her.

He shook his head yes and threw the rest of his paper at her feet. "Get yo' dumb-ass up off the floor and get the fuck outta here! I'll bring that shit to you on top of the hill...For the record, you might want to know, we don't keep no more than a ounce in the house at a time. Just thought you might want to know before you went and did something stupid," said White-girl helping him to his feet.

She let him out the door and before he was all the way out, she smacked him on his ass and said," if you be a good little boy, I might just let you taste this sweet pussy tonight," as she laughed wickedly and slammed the door in his face.

She leaned against the door staring at Amanda. She exhaled real loud and whispered, "I'm not going to apologize for my actions, he was testing us. If he thought we was weak and could get away with it, he would've beat us for our paper and everything else we got in here. Fuck that, we work to hard for that bullshit to go down like that!"

She walked closer to Amanda to see if she could detect any fear in her eyes but she didn't," I had to let him know that we're 100% serious about this shit, don't let the skirts fool you because fucking with us the wrong way and you can easily lose your life!"

"Girl, fuck Jacob, he deserved that shit. You just surprise me, that's all. What I want to know is, where did you get that gun and why you didn't tell me about it," asked Amanda as she went in to hug White-girl?

"It's just me and you girl!" "It's always been you and me, It'll always be me and you. I'm just happy that you ain't mad at me."

"I ain't never mad at you; you're my sista from another mother! Why you tell him that we only got one ounce in here, where's the rest of the work," she asked nervously?

These were the times that Amanda showed a weakness in her armor. 'How can she not know why I told him that?' White-girl looked closer at her, 'she really doesn't know.' It was clear to her now that Amanda hadn't been on her A-game since she's been running around with Silas every night, but she didn't say it to her, it fell right into her plan. She didn't mind being the Captain of the ship if Amanda wanted to do something else.

"My sista...My sista...I'm going to tell you this: The CRACK game that we are playing brings out all the crazy people and we can't get comfortable. If those dudes out there really knew what we were holding up in here, the both of us would be dead within the hour. I'm certain of that! We seeing major paper over here and sooner or later, them stick-up boys will come snooping around. From the way we doing shit, we serving dudes right out the front door like we got a license for this shit, it's only a matter of time before shit blow up in our face, either the stick-up boy's or the detectives will be enjoying the fruits of our labor and I don't like the sound of that either way. We need to start throwing these dudes off our trail; we have to find us a stash spot. We can have one spot for the drugs and another spot for the paper, that's the only way we'll stay alive to enjoy all this."

Amanda couldn't believe her ears, White-girl was definitely on point and she couldn't agree with her more. If White-Girl wasn't her best friend and didn't know her story, she would swear that White-girl was a born drug-dealer with CRACK spots all over the city. But she knew better and witnessed firsthand how scared she used to be, but that girl is long gone, she was learning on the job and learning fast.

"You keep impressing me every day, where's that little scared white girl that first came around here? All I know is wherever she is; leave her there! I love the new and improved White-girl; she's strong, focused and ain't going for the bullshit...WOW! I love it," laughed Amanda.

"You know what? Everything you're saying, Karma told me this same shit, she said that a day would come when I was going to have to take my game to the next level and that time is now thanks to you. It sounds so much more truthful coming from you than when she said it. So let's get it then, I'm with you!"

They spent the next two hours or so, gathering and counting their paper. When they were finish counting they had over thirty thousand in cash and nine ounce's of CRACK left. Setting aside the six thousand they owed Karma, they were still straight. White-girls' plan to find some stash spot's made a lot of sense now that she was looking at all the paper at one time. "I never took the time to actually count this shit, thirty thousand, that's a lot of paper we got," declared Amanda.

"I know and that's why we gotta get this shit outta here. Between the stick-up boys and the detectives, somebody's bound to come through these doors wanting a piece of what we're building here and if that happens either way we'll be fucked."

Amanda took her time thinking about a nice spot to stash the CRACK, she learned from her cousin Blacko that the best place to stash anything illegal was to stash it outside. You have to eliminate the risk of somebody seeing you when you do it and you have to make sure that your spot was close by and easy to get to even in the dark. White-girl licked her lips and said to the young boy, "you can hit this soon as you get your paper up, right now you're light weight, you hustle for me so how the hell am I going to be fucking the help? I'm a boss bitch and you're a runner, so tell me, how's that going to look," she asked blowing the young boy off?

The young boy was put in check by Jacob, he didn't want the young boy experiencing what he just went through with that crazy White bitch, that would fuck up everything and right now, he needing both White-girl and Amanda, especially after what he done to the boy across town! All the dudes could do was watch as White-girl and Amanda walked off down towards Bailey road. They found a nice spot to stash the CRACK and decided to walk through Johnson Village to call a cab. The cab took no time to get there, and before they knew it, they were on their way down 10th street on their way to Madison.

As they passed Auntie's house on Page, Amanda said, " I wonder What Jazzy been up to lately?"

"Fuck that girl, she ain't worried about what we been up to because if she was she would've been called or something. What we need to be doing next is going to the Auction to buy us a little hooptie so we ain't gotta be fucking with these cabs like that no more, you feel me," said White-girl?

CHAPTER 15

JOEY damn near broke his neck rushing over to the window to see what all the commotion was about. Jazzy was downstairs screaming at the top of her lungs about Malik being robbed out front and he couldn't fathom the idea of his homey being robbed, let alone right in front of their spot. With Malik having just left his side on his way downstairs to put the paper in the trunk, he shook his head in disbelief, what he saw when he looked out the window took his breath away! Malik was stretched out on the pavement almost in the middle of the street. He grabbed his 9mm and his .40 Caliber off the dresser and raced down the steps. Meeting Tiffany at the door, he almost ran her over trying to get out the door, both of them was in a race to help save someone they loved dearly. Once he got out the door, seeing Malik laying there on the pavement motionless and with his legs and arms in an awkwardly position, sent chills up his spine. He quickly tried to recall had he heard any gun shots? Not able to remember if he had, he reached down to see if Malik had any visible injuries to his body, a good sign was that he wasn't lying in a puddle of blood. There was no blood on his clothes, so he breathed a sigh of relief for the moment.

"Malik...Malik...Wake-up homey," shouted Joey and Tiffany as he began smacking him lightly on the cheek. Joey's eyes began scanning up and down the block to see if he could catch a glimpse of who had done this to his homey, but whoever done it was long gone just like the brown paper bag that had the paper in it, everything was gone! " Yo Malik, you ain't hit are you?"

Malik was slowly regaining consciousness, his eyes were glassy and his facial expression indicated that he was in a great deal of pain. You could tell because his eyes were searching for answers and it look like he was also trying to figure out exactly what happened to him. All the while, Tiffany had propped his head up onto her lap as she sat flat on the ground trying her best to comfort her man! When his eyes finally focused and noticed Tiffany and Malik, he smiled. He knew he was in good hands' no matter what with them two taking care of him, then, he took notice of the two guns in Joey's hands. Auntie Pam and Jazzy was standing on the porch not to far away looking on, they both had a concerned look on their faces. He made a fetal attempt to get himself up but the pain and dizziness forced him back down into Tiffany's lap.

"Take your time Malik, get up slow," whispered Tiffany in his ear.

"I'm good...I'm good, my damn head hurts like hell but I'll live, so help me up."

Joey was able to smile knowing that his homey was going to be alright after such a scare. He knew for the type of paper he got robbed for, most dudes in his position didn't live to tell the story! A few bumps and bruises wasn't nothing that Malik couldn't handle, he was tough!

"Tiffany, take these in the house while I help Malik up." She looked at Joey like he was crazy but she took the guns from him nonetheless. It was widely known that she hated gun's, but since Malik was in the equation, she shoved one of the gun's down in her waist-band like she'd seen Malik do countless of times.

"I got the gun's, but make sure you be careful with him...I'll not going in that house until ya'll make it in safely, I'll cover your back," she said raising the .40 Caliber," this is our protection and I have every intention on protecting ya'll, so go ahead," she said dead serious. The fear in her face was gone and it was replaced by the sight of pure determination, Joey took notice and didn't waste any time getting Malik up from the pavement.

He made sure to walk Malik slowly and carefully back into the house with Tiffany on his flank like a secret service agent! Jazzy looked on in disbelief and sheer confusion, she couldn't believe what she had just witnessed. 'That was Jacob from Prospect,' she said in her head. She watched Joey carefully as he aided his homey to safety, she admired the loyalty they showed one another, even Tiffany assumed a very important role. She thought she would hate Malik after last night and use that to justify being happy that he got robbed and beaten up, but her heart was telling her something totally different. With each stolen glance at him, she felt her pussy get moist and then it started throbbing for that special touch that only Malik could do. Hating to admit it, but she loved the way he was so hard and aggressive, down to the way he man handled her last night. With all of these conflicting thought's going through her mind, she decided that this wasn't a good time to tell any of them who it was that she saw while she was looking out the window. It would only complicate matters and she couldn't stand for that to happen at this moment. The flip side to that problem was that she knew that if Malik didn't see who done that to him, that information would certainly come in handy in due time and she could use that information to buy back her freedom if need be. In her position, leverage was everything. She was fresh out of luck and ideas so she decided to hang onto what she saw, even if it wasn't long. She walked over to where Auntie Pam was and whispered in her ear, grabbed 4 dubs off the table and left out the front door. Nobody seemed to mind that she was leaving at such a hectic time, and that was because everybody except was hoping that she had sense enough to leave and let the family have some privacy.

With all the commotion, Auntie Pam was glad to give Jazzy the CRACK to get her ass away from them. She waved Jazzy off so fast that Jazzy almost didn't want to leave, she sensed something big was about to happen, but her addiction was calling and she had the CRACK in the palm of her, she bounced. Auntie Pam went into the kitchen and returned with an ice-pack and told Tiffany," put this on his head!"

Tiffany was one of the calmest of all, and that was because she was counting her blessing, she knew that Malik's situation could have been worse, she was just thankful that it wasn't. He could very well be at the University of Virginia's emergency room on his way to the Trauma Unit with gunshot wounds throughout his body. For her to hold that ice-pack on the back of his head was nothing to her, she'd fight God to make sure Malik was comfortable. The only thing that bothered her was the fact that Malik kept trying to close his eyes and trying to go to sleep.

"Malik, you can't close your eyes or go to sleep," she said forcefully!" Open your eyes, if you have a concussion the worst thing for you to do is go to sleep baby, you gotta stay woke."

Joey was sitting on the arm rest on the chair right next to Tiffany and he needed to know so he asked," did you see who did this to you?"

Malik tried his best to shake his head no, but the pain was unbearable, he felt like his brain was being tossed all over the inside of his skull. "No, I didn't see them niggaz, wish I had. I feel like they hit me with a bat or something, my head is throbbing."

Joey tried to put things in perspective for not only him but everybody as well, "see, that's what happens when the real paper start coming in. Do you want us to take you to the hospital?"

"I'm good, I got Tiffany here to take care of me and I can't deny her that. You know she wanted to be a doctor, don't you?"

Everybody looked at her, they knew it was her dream to become a doctor before the CRACK became a part of her everyday life. She had the biggest smile on her face, she told Malik she wanted to be a doctor the first day they met back in the 9th grade when he was trying to holla at her. She never knew he remember that conversation since it was so long ago. Her whole life was planned on becoming a doctor but reality smacked her in the face, life dealt the cards from the bottom of the deck and the cards she had been dealt was that of a CRACK addict!

"Since you don't want us to take you to the hospital, you have to promise us that you'll stay awake and you won't try to go to sleep on us, can you promise us that?"

She sent Auntie Pam to get her purse and grab the Tylenol 3's she had. Joey looked on," Tiffany you can't give him them, they'll definitely make him sleepy," he said looking at her take the pills out her purse. "I know! They ain't for him, they for me," she said swallowing 2 of the pills dry. " Malik, make sure you don't go to sleep," demanded Joey."

"I got him! You know I ain't gonna let nothing happen to him, he's my entire life and then some...Ain't no way I can let nothing happen to this boy," boasted Tiffany.

Joey knew business still needed to be handled, the robbery was their problem. This is the life they signed up for, you win some and you lose some. Violence was just as much a part of the lifestyle as Cocaine and Baking Soda, they went hand in hand, you can't have one and not the other. "Yo, I gotta meet dude in about an hour, stay put and get yourself together homey, I got this," said Joey.

Auntie Pam had heard enough and she stepped in. More than any of them, she knew the importance of Joey making it to this meeting and used that as a spring board," I know that's right, Joey! We got Malik, you already know that. Me or Tiffany ain't going nowhere, you just make sure you leave one of them pistols here with us just in case I gotta bust a nigga in they ass."

"Joey, what about the paper, what you're going to tell dude?" Malik knew that the connect would want what belonged to him come rain, sleet, or blizzard, a bill was due and the connect was expecting his fair share. He didn't want Joey having to tell the connect the paper was fucked up by himself, that didn't sit well with him, anything could happen!

Joey knew exactly what Malik was implying but he didn't want his sweating it, he had it covered," that shit ain't nothing homey, that wasn't shit! Trust me, I got this shit covered, he'll get his, don't worry about that. I gotta go take care of something before I go holla at dude, but I'll come back and check on you before I go," said Joey as tear's were welling up in his eyes. He had to get out of there, he needed some air. He needed to be alone and time to think. He wanted to put the pieces together to this puzzle that stood in front of him.

He took Malik's car and drove around thinking about what happened and how it could've happened right under their nose. It wasn't like Auntie Pam's spot was their stash spot and everybody knew, they barely kept any real cash their anyway and nobody but him knew he was going to be there with that type of paper, nobody! That's when it hit him, niggaz been trying to tell him all along that something was going on but he was hard-headed and didn't want to believe that shit was going down like that. They must have been watching the crib and just waiting for the right opportunity, and when Malik came out the house with the brown paper bag, they took that as their opportunity.

He had to call Terri just to get his mind off the day's events plus, he needed for her to stop and get more paper if she didn't already have it on her. Hoping her meeting with the bank was over, he contemplated hanging up by the third ring, but she answered," hey sexy, how's things going, where you at right now?"

She told him that she was coming down Main Street and he told her to meet him over on Madison Avenue in 5 minutes. She was happy to have him call her much happier that he wanted her to meet him. As she was still talking, she realized that he had already hung-up on her in mid-sentence. She whispered a, ' I love you too.' Replaying the conversation over again in her head instinct kicked in, there was something strange in his voice, she stepped on the gas, she had to get to their meeting place as quickly as possible. It took her all of 4 minutes to get on Madison and as she was pulling in, she noticed the headlight's of Malik's car flick on and off at her. She pulled her car over and got in with Joey! She seen that stressful look on his face and she had to ask," What's wrong baby?"

"How much cash you got on you right now?"

" I... I...I just cashed that check from the people from Florida; it's like a lot, why you ask?"

"Grab me twenty-five grand, I need it for something," he said staring out the window the whole time never once looking at her. The way he was acting it scared her, but she did what he wanted.

She got out the car with him and went to her own trunk where the paper was stashed under her spare tire. She took her time counting out just what he asked her for, she briefly looked over at him in Malik's car but she couldn't see him because the tint was so dark. All she could do is hope he was looking and she smiled! Joey eyes were scanning the area as he replayed the day's events in his mind.

At one turn he was winning with Terri and their new business but at the next, he almost lost his brother to violence. He immediately noticed a cab turning onto Madison, he was on it. His alert level was raised higher than the U.S. code RED, he clipped the safety off his .40 Caliber. Terri was still counting the paper in her trunk when he looked at her, he wasn't really worried about her because nobody from his life style knew she even existed but sitting in Malik's hot ass car there was no telling what or who wanted to see him. As the cab cruised past, he was happy for the tint because he could clearly see Amanda and White-girl in the cab, Amanda was breaking her neck to try to see who was in the car but she couldn't because of the tint. 'What the fuck they doing over this way,' he questioned himself?

By the time Terri got back in the car with him, she noticed that his focus was in the rear-view mirror looking at the cab that passed by them. He was crouched low in the driver's seat and she was beginning to get nervous, "baby, what's going on, you're starting to scare me?" She tapped him lightly on the thigh, "you know if I didn't know any better I'd feel some type of way about you watching 2 females in a cab, but I know better," she said laughing trying to cheer him up!

"So you saw them too, huh? You're sharp girl, ain't nothing getting past you."

"That's right, I'm your wifey, I'm supposed to be sharp and I also know when something's bothering you, I just don't know what it is...Yet!"

After not been having a single thought about Malik since Silas had come into her life, she almost broke her own neck twisting and turning trying to look into his car. A curse word escaped her mouth as she struggled to see, it was useless because of the dark tint on all of his windows. In her mind she tried to remember the last time she had even seen Malik, it's been a minute! Silas had taken over not only her body but her mind as well and she never had the opportunity to think about Malik, but now she was wondering if in fact she really missed him? At the sight of his car she got excited and her heart beat a little faster as she thought of the possibilities if Malik was in the car.

"Ain't that your boy Malik's car right there," said White-girl as she poked her in the arm and pointed at the parked car all at the same time? She keened in on how Amanda's demeanor had changed once she saw the car so she thought it wise to urge her to pursue the young baller," won't you call him, girl."

Amanda turned her nose up at the thought of having to call Malik, her status had grown since the last time they were together and she knew that she didn't need his paper or his drugs, so she spit," I ain't calling him! What the fuck we gotta talk about?

White-girl ignored her little and told the cab driver where to park. They got out and walked across the parking lot to grandma's house.

Joey was still looking on from a distance, something told him to sit there and wait, he didn't know why but when he saw the duffel bag, his spider senses went into overdrive. He looked over at Terri," babe, let's drive your car!" He used the opportunity to switch car's when he seen White-girl and Amanda disappear behind the screen door of the old lady who opened the door. He made a mental note of the old lady's address, the cab was still waiting outside so that told him that they didn't plan being to long. From his intel of the streets', he was well aware of the rumors surrounding Amanda and her partner White-girl and how they were getting paper over Prospect. It was rather hard for him to believe what he had heard because he knew how much Amanda loved to get her nose dirty. However, the hood had a way of taming the wildest beast when in pursuit of the great American Dream, CASH! What he couldn't get out of his mind was even if everything he's been hearing and then some were true, what the hell were they doing over on his side of town and on Madison at that, so close to one of his stash spots? Everybody in the game knew that the Project niggaz ran everything from Main to Madison, so what the hell were they thinking?

He looked down at his watch, knowing he had to meet the connect soon, he decided to give the connect a call; hoping the number he had was even in service. He was lucky because the connect answered on the second ring and he started talking," yo, I'm going to be about an hour late...Something came up and I have to handle it. I got my wifey with me too, will that be a problem? He was shaking his head up and down," a-ight then, see you when I get there!"

His conversation was over just in time to see Amanda and White-girl coming back out the house, this time Amanda was carrying a brown paper bag just like the one Malik had earlier. He dismissed that as his mind playing tricks on him because every store and every hood nigga used brown paper bags for one thing or another. "Follow the cab when it goes pass us, but don't pull out until it turns off of Madison." Terri didn't know what was going on, she was a little nervous but she listened to what he told her to do, not because she feared him or anything, it was more so her being curious about what his lifestyle was really about. She had an idea that whatever was on his mind was related to the two females in the cab.

Joey placed another call, this time to Auntie Pam's house, Terri could hear their conversation and she strained to listen, under normal circumstances she would have blocked them out, but she wanted to know.

"Was just about to call you, Malik's feeling better, he wanted me to call you and tell you that he was going with you and for you to come by and pick him up. He's up-stairs right now taking a bath, Tiffany's in there with him, I thought she was suppose to wash him or whatever but from all the moaning and screaming, I know he's gotta be feeling better now," said Auntie Pam laughing as she relayed what was going on in her bathroom.

Terri heard it all and she already put together that something had happened to Malik. It all made sense now because Joey didn't seem like himself when she got in the car with him and now they were following a cab to god knows Where, all she knew was that if something happened to Malik she had to be there for the man she loved and she intended to do just that. "A-ight, good! Shut the shop down, don't nothing move until I say otherwise...I'll be there in a few, I'm caught in the middle of something and soon as I get through, I'll be back down there," he said right before he hung up.

For the first time in her entire life, Terri was starting to feel like a Bad Girl, all the following and secret phone conversations between Joey and whoever he was talking to reminded her of some 007 shit, except this shit was real life! The look on his face told her that none of this was a joke and she was willing to give her right arm to see to it that he was safe. She refocused and forced those images of what she saw on television escape from her mind, it was time to put on her game face. She maintained a safe distance all the way down 250 By-Pass, down by the Tennis courts and all the way back up to Main Street.

The cab finally turned up 7th Street and Joey knew they were on their way back to Prospect. He told her to park in the cut near the step's but still on top of the hill to be able to see everything. Amanda was the first out the cab, brown paper bag in hand, she walked straight over to one of the youngin's standing out here and handed him the brown paper bag. Now, that only confirmed that they didn't have nothing to do with the robbery because ain't nobody in the hood going to hand-over twenty five thousand to some little nigga on top of Prospect. He still knew that he had to do it; he took out his cell phone and took several pictures of Amanda and the youngin she gave the brown paper bag to. He got solo shots of them and shots of them together!

Amanda got back in the cab and the cab went down towards Bailey. Satisfied with what he had, he said to Terri who was looking on as the confident wifey," come on baby, let's bounce, go back across town to Page."

"To where," she asked confused? He knew he made the mistake soon as the words left him lips, she wasn't very good with the street names, she was better with associating places with the people who be there," go to Auntie Pam's house," he said simply.

They rode back across town in silence; Joey was to deep in thought to say a word. Terri wasn't the type to ask question after question knowing that whatever was on his mind had to be very important because he let her ride along with him. Problem solving was one of her strong points and she intended to use her skills to help her man. Joey had never let her get this close to his lifestyle and that told her all she really needed to know. She reached over and touched him on his thigh," you know I love you, right?"

He looked over at a smiling Terri and returned the warm concerned look," I know, but you have to understand that I'm not the same person out here in these streets as I am when I'm with you and I didn't mean for you to be with me following people around Charlottesville...You know what I'm saying?"

All she said was," I know that!" She had witnessed that first hand in such a short period of time being with him. His attention and focus was on his surrounding and not on her as it usually is but what she really wanted him to understand was that she didn't care who he was when he was out in the streets. All she cared about was his safety and how he treated her, where was never less than royalty. She parked her car a couple houses down from Auntie Pam's and turned off the engine. She sat there not knowing what to do because she'd never been on the inside of the house. Joey chambered a round of his .40 Caliber and it sent chills up her spine.

He got out and had to peep back down into the car," come on, make sure you lock all the doors," said Joey not even trying to hide the gun in his hand. She didn't know if the sight of the gun should have made her scared but it didn't, she was more so excited knowing that Joey would do anything to protect her life. She unconsciously grabbed the duffel bag off the back seat and hoisted it over her shoulder like it was her over-night bag and she was spending the night with him. At least she did hope the last part about spending the night with him was true. He looked at her crazy with the duffle bag over her shoulder and she said, "Every woman needs a thug in their life," giggling the song.

Her smile, singing and her wink let him know that she was comfortable with what was going on. She lead the way as Joey followed closely behind, he was definitely her bodyguard and she enjoyed it. When they walked in the house, Tiffany was sitting on the sofa with an icepack still on Malik's head. "How you're feeling homey," asked Joey looking from Auntie Pam back to Tiffany?

"Other than a slight headache, I'm good," said Malik making it to his feet. He embraced Terri," hey stranger! Can't believe he let you come up in here like this," he said making fun of how Joey always kept her away from the family. She looked from Malik over to Joey and then back to Tiffany with a warm smile on her face, "okay, and how are you doing stranger?"

Joey jumped in and began introducing everybody to her, "everybody, this is Terri, my better half ….Baby, this is Auntie Pam, and that's Tiffany."

_____ _____ _____ _____ _____
_____ _____

Silas was on his way over to the rooming house on Dale so that he could pick Philly up. When he pulled up in front of the rooming house he decided to call Amanda, playing around he switched his voice and asked, "hello, may I speak to Ms. Amanda please?"

"Stop playing with my boy, this is me, you acting like you don't know my damn voice or something," she spit into the phone.

"Now is that a way to speak to someone you care about?"

"Oh, you got games huh, and you're trying to cover up the fact that you miss me already and you just had to call me? Listen, where you at anyway," she asked?

"I'm on Dale waiting for Philly to come out the house, why?"

"Well ...Since the both of us was thinking about each other, I was just about to call you to, but you called me first, I need a small favor." When he didn't say anything, she got a little nervous; it's nothing like you're thinking. I'm not that type of girl" she said laughing.

"What is it then and how you know what I was I was thinking?"

"Just listen because we're getting off track. Me and White-girl are on our way out to Airport Cars and we want to buy a car so we don't have to be catching all these damn cabs all the time but the problem is we don't want them taking advantage of two females. We need a man to come with us so we can get this best deal, you know how them people is, they'll try to get over on us in a minute," she said exhaling loudly.

"That's it? Where ya'll at now?" "We're going down Preston; we just passed that park over this way."

"A-ight, go to the Cookout and wait for me there. Sit tight babe, I'm on my way right now."

"That will definitely earn your fine-ass some brownie point's with me," she said laughing right before she hung-up.

"I shouldn't...", was all he was able to get out realizing that she had already hung-up on him.

_____ _____ _____ _____ _____ _____ _____

Malik managed to get up from the sofa without too much hassle, up and ready to go handle their business. Joey wanted him to stay off his feet and get some rest but Malik wasn't hearing any of what he was saying. "Let's bounce so was can take care of that, I'm glad you didn't bounce without me; where partners now how would that look," asked Malik dead serious?

Joey pointed to Terri who had found a nice spot in one of Auntie's Pam's recliner. "Since you ain't trying to hear nothing I gotta say, I still gotta get her out of here, but come upstairs I need to holla at you for a minute." While they were upstairs, Joey filled him in on what he had seen with Amanda and White-girl. He told him all about the duffel bag, the brown paper bag, and the dude she gave the bag to on top of Prospect. Then he showed the pictures. "Yo' do you know him," asked Joey curiously?

Malik took several good looks at the pictures of Amanda and some dude, but he didn't notice the dude by name. "From what I've been hearing about Amanda, she's handling her business over Prospect, I don't know how but they say she's ballin' real-hard. As for dude, I don't know him personally but his face is familiar, I've seen him over Prospect a few times but I never had any words with him. All I know is something gotta be up with her and her crazy ass cousin Jazzy, shit don't make alot of sense. You got Jazzy over here smoking CRACK and all that dumb shit while her cousin, her best road dog, is over their way getting all the paper; now that's some bullshit if I ever heard it. Those two bitches been tight forever and now all of a sudden they don't even hang no more," said Malik as he took one more picture of Amanda noticing how fine she looked.

She was always fine to him but the drugs always played a part in her downfall, but from what he was seeing, it looked like she had her shit together! Not knowing who was responsible for the robbery was starting to really rub Joey the wrong way, he was very angry and wanted answers to all the questions he had running around in his mind. "Everybody's suspect and I mean everybody, Jazzy, the bitch who brought her down here, Auntie, Amanda, and this dude whoever the hell he is, he's suspect to. The streets has a way of talking and I'm going to find out just who did this shit and when I do, it ain't gonna be nice," spit Joey!

Malik cut him off before he could go any further with what he was saying, "don't sweat it, when we do find out it's on, I'm shooting in broad day light, I ain't got no mercy, so you ain't even gotta stress yourself about all of that. Fuck that shit for now, let's go handle our business with the connect, this shit can wait until we get back."

When Joey got back downstairs, the ladies were talking, laughing, high fiving each other like this was just another normal day for them. Terri was so involved in their conversation she didn't notice Malik and Joey come back. She looked comfortable, like she's known Auntie Pam and Tiffany her entire life. Auntie Pam was the first to notice them as they stepped back in the living room cutting the girly conversation short," speaking of the devils, here they come now," she said laughing and tapping Terri on the leg.

"Terri, come here, I need to talk to you," said Joey. She got up and winked back at Auntie Pam and Tiffany and followed him in the kitchen.

"I gotta go and handle some business with Malik, so I need to know where you want me to drop you off at?" Terri's eyes lit-up because Auntie Pam had told her that this was going to happen, but she wasn't mad at all, she had a backup plan and now all she had to do was to run it by Joey.

"Well, since you had me thinking that I was going somewhere with you and now I'm not, you're kicking me to the curb, I thought that maybe I'd take Tiffany with me so that we can go and get our nails and toes done. That's if it's cool with you, is it," she asked in her best voice?

"That's cool, but there's one condition, I need to drive your car and I'll drop ya'll off at my car that's parked up the block on West street." With everybody in agreement even Tiffany; they dropped the ladies off on West Street. It was music to Tiffany's ears when Malik told her that he'd be back rather late but he was coming and expecting for her to be there when he got there. She didn't care as long as it meant that she could spend more time with him. Terri was also feeling some type of way about Joey allowing her to have a glimpse into his world!

"Ya'll be careful," said Terri getting out the car and kissing Joey on the lips. As soon as they pulled away from the ladies, Joey took the opportunity to jump into Malik's business," why you smiling like that?" Malik casually shrugged his shoulders and said," I don't know what you're even talking about, homey. And for the record, I wasn't smiling."

"Whatever! If don't nobody else know, I know and I think it's Tiffany, she's working on you, ain't she?"

He exhaled, "only if she could get her shit together, then who knows, but damn, she's a CRACK head Joey!"

"Won't you be the one to help her then; you already know she'll jump through hell for your crazy-ass. We got the paper, won't we get her into one of those rehabs the stars be going to or some shit. Fuck how much it'll cost us, she's definitely worth it, she's family too!"

It was strange hearing Joey talk about sending Tiffany to a rehab because he was thinking about the same shit; he just didn't know how to go about asking her if she wanted to go. Deep down in his head he had serious feelings for her but the fact remained that she was a CRACK head and he wasn't about to wifey no CRACK head regardless of how he felt about her. He could only trust her but so much, is what he kept telling himself, but even that didn't work because she wasn't your average CRACK head, she didn't act like one, didn't dress like one and she most definitely didn't treat him like all the other's treated him. He thought about that all the way to meet the connect. His thought's wrangled with what his heart wanted him to do, and this was exactly what he didn't want to have to deal with, it was to much!

It had taken them a little over twenty minutes before they pulled into the driveway of the connects mini-mansion. They were greeted by two big black Africans, the Africans were heavily armed and that seemed odd since this was such a respectable neighborhood. Joey eased the car right next to the Lexus GS430, again the Lexus brought back memories but he just couldn't place the car from nowhere! Getting out and following the two Africans to the back of the mansion, they stopped in their tracks noticing the connect engaged in a conversation with a very beautiful Spanish female. She was top notch, she'd give J-lo a run for her money on her bad day, that's how fly this chick was. The connect waved and spoke," Malik...Joey, won't you have a seat at the patio table, I'LL be with you in just a couple minutes." They watched as the Spanish chick and the connect embraced as they said their good-bye's, Joey could tell that whoever the Spanish chick was she wasn't the connect's girl, there was a certain level of respect he showed her. Joey and Malik couldn't help but watch the Spanish chick shake her well developed ass out the backyard and disappear behind the same fence that they came in by. The connect walked right up on them while they were still lusting over the Spanish chick," she'll murder the both of you if she knew what you were up to. Never allow the little head to get the big head in trouble, gentlemen," said the connect as he embraced both Joey and Malik. The truth was stunning and they both knew personally someone who literally lost their life behind a female, a decent shot of pussy could have the average man thinking about things he wouldn't ordinarily think about doing to someone. Entire countries have been destroyed over one shot of pussy, Joey knew the stories of history all to well, it was Malik who wasn't sold on the idea! They both embraced the connect and they sat back down at the patio table.

Joey didn't waste any time, he got down to the business at hand: Malik being robbed! The more details he gave the connect about the robbery or the lack thereof, he had to admit the smoothness of their execution of the robbery. The connect sat there patiently listening to the whole story, he couldn't help but smile at the way Joey told the story. In Joey's head he couldn't figure out why the fuck the connect smiling while he told him about the robbery? He decided to make a brave move, he threw the brown paper bag onto the table in the direction of the connect, "here's the twenty-five we owe you!"

"You guys never cease to impress me! Here you are telling me the story of your life about a robbery that took place just hours ago and you still able to pay the bill you owe, like I said before, that's very impressive," said the connect nodding at the bag on the table and then nodding at one of the Africans. As one of the Africans reached in to take the bag, the connect looked over at Malik and said," I'll assume it's all here, right?"

Malik didn't like the way the connect was looking at him, actually he didn't care too much for the connect at all but it was in the spirit of business that he sat there listened and observed the whole conversation. He was familiar with all the connects movements, each one would get a reaction out of one of the Africans.

"Now that you guys have been robbed, I want to know what you plan to do about it." Malik couldn't pass up this opportunity, he had to say something, so he began to speak slow and clear choosing his words very carefully.

"The first thing we're going to do is to find out who's responsible and once we figure that part out, let's just say, we'll show them no mercy!"

"Malik, have you ever killed a man," asked the connect? Malik tried his best to maintain eye contact with the connect but he lowered his gaze. He knew he had never killed anyone, his body count was on zero and he wasn't proud of it. He shook his head no feeling defeated. The connect quickly took control of their conversation and came unexpectedly to his young soldier's defense, "Malik, any fool can kill a man so don't ever forget it! However, I personally handpicked you and Joey on your ability to trap paper. The loyalty you two show each other can't be found in this day and time, it's rare, so whatever you do, don't lose that about yourselves. Neither of you were killers when I first approached you and I don't intend to make killers out of you, that's an advantage that you'll never understand until you become a killer. So don't be looking sad over there because you've never killed a man, don't feel no type of way about being robbed, use it as a learning experience, pick your head up, you have a lot on your plate and I'm going to need for you to be the strong and intelligent team that you are, and that's the only way you'll win in this game," he said patting Malik on the back.

Shaking his head confused, Malik said," I don't get it? We're supposed to act like this shit never happened...Is that what you're telling us?"

"Usually I'd step in and use my resources, but I have a tremendous amount of respect for you two and I won't get in this one, not right now anyways. You guys are very smart, I'm confidant you'll make the right decision when the time comes. Now, let me ask you a question, is twenty-five thousand worth going to prison for and perhaps the rest of your lives?"

For the first time since explaining the story, Joey spoke up, "twenty-five thousand isn't nowhere near worth doing one day in prison let alone a life sentence! But what I do know is that the next twenty-five thousand or the one after that might be! I'd much rather nip this in the bud now before the streets start talking and knowing the streets, the truth will come out in due time."

The connect had that wicked grin back on his face," you're exactly right Joey! But I want ya'll to understand this: To kill a man ain't shit, any fool can pull the trigger and kill somebody. The tricky part is this, try killing a man while he's still breathing; now that's saying something! I'll make ya'll an offer that you shouldn't turn down; you find out who did this and bring them to me. Let me handle them and we'll call it an act of good faith on parts, yours and mine." The connect stood to leave, his next meeting was about to take place in the next 30 minutes and he had to get these two out the way to usher in the next two, "I doubled-up the pack this week, let's get it while the getting is still good, remember, the Sun don't shine forever."

Silas weaved in and out of traffic on his way to meet Amanda and White-girl. It dawned on him he was suppose to pick Philly up at the rooming house, that was crazy, he was parked right in front of the rooming house, once he started talking to Amanda everything on his mind had went blank. He had to laugh at himself; he was falling and falling fast for her. She was on his mind now, every moment he shared with her made him feel like a new man, her beautiful eyes and she had the type of body that you would die for. It only took him God- minutes to get there; he spotted the cab parked near the pay phones. He pulled right next to the cab and jumped out his car and went to the driver's side of the cab. He paid the cab what the girls owed and nodded towards the Caddy, both Amanda and White-girl got out the cab giggling like two high schoolers sneaking around.

"Hey Silas," said White-girl barely able to conceal her laughter as she slid in the back of the Caddy! Amanda was happy to see him and she snuggled in very close to him and kissed him passionately. "I miss you," she said pulling herself away from his warm embrace. Licking her lips and wiping the corners of her mouth, her look and aggressive approach said it all. She wanted him and he knew it! The way she was looking at him was just enough to make his manhood rise and come to life. Had White-girl not been in the back, he would have gotten them a room and showed her exactly how he was feeling about her. The animal deep down in his soul was begging to be released but the timing wasn't right for him so he switched the subject," so what ya'll trying to buy?"

"I want a truck," blurted out White-girl from the back! "And you my dear... What do you want," he asked staring Amanda in her beautiful eyes?

"Why? You buying or something," she asked playfully? "For-real though, I don't really care what we get. I just want the damn thang to run, I don't want to lemon. I can even do certain hooptie's but the fucked-up ones, I ain't doing it, I'm too fly for the bullshit," she said throwing her long silky hair back behind her ear. The way he was glancing at her she couldn't help buy grin, he had that type of affect on her body, and not just her mind, but down between her legs something was going on because she was wet as hell. She couldn't shake her sexual thoughts of him driving his dick in and out of her soaking wet pussy. Saying fuck it in her head, she reached over the center console and started playing with his dick through his jeans. She was mentally torturing herself because she wanted his dick in her mouth more than she ever wanted a dick in her mouth.

White-girls phone brought her out of her sexual daze," hello," said White-girl answering her phone. "Yeah, a-ight, I got you. You gotta give me about 2 hours, I'm not in town right now but I'm on my way," then she hung-up before the dude on the other end had the opportunity to ask her anything else. She tapped Amanda on her shoulder, "that's them dudes from down Tonsler Park, we gotta holla at them in 2 hours." "How about you go and handle that while I go and handle this," said Amanda pointing down towards Silas dick!

Two hours later and they were driving off the dealership lot with a Dodge Durango. Everything was put in Amanda's name, White-girl's idea because she said that that would be the only way to park the truck inside of prospect without it being towed. She also convinced the young black dude who sold them the truck to fix the paper work because they paid the entire Thirteen thousand in cash in exchange for a late night romp between the sheets with her. White-girl was off the chain, but the reality of the situation was convenient for all parties. With the Country in a huge recession the car dealer was just happy to sell the damn truck, so what he had to alter the paper work just a bit, that wasn't nothing they didn't do on a normal basis. In this day and time the object of the game was to get the sell, he not only got the sell, he was also lucky enough to be able to get some tender white pussy.

That milky white skin him thinking of all types of positions he wanted to bend her body into, he wondered if he was flexible? To him, the greatest thing about the recession was that it benefited those who had cash on hand, nobody questioned the cash or where it came from. They were saying that America was in its worse financial disaster since the 1929, fall of the stock market, that's bad! Now here were two young females who had cash in hand and wanted to buy a vehicle, what was he to do, not fix the paper work? Deny himself a piece of that young white pussy? He kinda guessed they were hustlers by the car they drove onto the lot.

Nonetheless, all the smart drug-dealer's benefited from the recession and then you had people who the young salesman worked for, under normal circumstances he'd wouldn't have approved of the altered paper work, but today, he signed off on the paper work right away, they were willing to turn a blind eye on the whereabouts of the cash. Thirteen thousand dollars brought the crook out of an otherwise law abiding car dealer, and he didn't even have to think about what he was going to do! Walking out the office, White-girl had the keys and Silas was out front looking at a later model version of the Caddy he was driving.

She got in the truck and pulled up next to Silas and Amanda," yo, the first thing we gotta do is get these damn windows tinted," said White-girl laughing.

"That ain't no problem, I know a dude down Garrett, who tint windows for a little bit of nothing...I can call him now if you want me to?"

Amanda butted in," you can do all of that as soon as you take care of this," she said pouting and pointing down between her legs!

"I'll tell you what, break my girl off, give me dudes number, I can holla at him on my own, you know me, a small promise goes along way, and I might just get the windows tinted for free! Right now, I'm bout to bend these 4-corners and go holla at them dudes down the park, I'll catch up with ya'll later," she winked and had that devilish grin on her face.

"Here," he threw her a piece of paper with dude's number on it. "Sounds like a plan, she might make it late tonight but don't look for her before eleven and that's if she's even able to come out to play then got something special planned for my boo," he said looking over at White-girl in the truck laughing at the way he was talking.

White-girl pulled out the parking lot leaving Silas and Amanda still looking at the older model Caddy, she started talking to herself,' you can keep her ass out all damn night as far as I'm concerned, who really gives a fuck? Not me! Nope not me!' In her mind, Silas had proved more useful than she originally planned, she only had to make a minor adjustment and that was nothing to her, she thought turning on the radio to the local station. The station was playing one of her favorite songs, 'Lil' Kim and Junior Mafia's, Get Money!' She smiled and began singing along with Lil' Kim, then she shouted,' this white bitch got game... You better watch out,' she shouted over and over again.

Silas was almost unable to handle Amanda's advances, she was all over him. He could barely drive, she was sucking and licking on his neck and making circles with her tongue in his ear, she was ever biting his dick through his jeans. With her free hand she went under his tee-shirt and played with his nipple, he was doing everything not to run a red light or crash into anything, she was good at what she was doing and it made him feel good.

"Baby, I want you to fuck me all day long, I don't want you to stop, can you please fuck me all day, daddy," she begged as she sucked on his finger? "If you don't stop, I'm going to pull this damn car over right here and fuck the shit outta you on the side of the highway," he said playfully as he pushed her hands away from him. What she said next made him want to make good on his promise of pulling over right there, she said to him in her most serious voice," you can fuck me wherever you want, just fuck me! I want you to man-handle this pussy like you own it and once you fuck me, I want you to slow down and make love to me over and over again!"

Amanda knew by the huge bulge in his jeans that she was getting the best of him, she smiled at her handy work, but at the same time, her pussy was soaking wet! Her juices were escaping and beginning to drip down her leg, every movement sent electric shocks down to her pussy. Every time she touched herself she moaned and licked her lips, the friction from her clothes and her hand had her on the verge of cuming right there as she starred at Silas. He had her about to cum and he never laid a finger on her, un-strapping her bra and sliding it off through the sleeve of her shirt, she exposed her titties to him. She got her nipples rock hard and made her tongue make track circles around her nipples and they got harder than they ever been in her life. He stopped at the first Hotel they came to and it was the Double Tree, he made the right turn into the parking lot speeding to the entrance. He handed her two hundred dollars," get the room, I'll park the car," he said pulling up to the entrance!

She jumped out the car fixing her clothes and looked back in not taking the paper, "remember, I got my own paper, daddy! All you need to do is hurry up and park and meet me in the lobby!" Silas didn't waste any time looking for a parking spot, he drove all the way to the back of the parking lot deciding to jog back, and it'll be quicker than him searching for a spot up close. When he entered the lobby, Amanda was standing there waiting on him by the elevators, "come on daddy, I already got the room!"

She jumped into his arms the moment the elevator doors closed and their tongues danced around each of their mouths playing chase. Amanda was clearly the aggressor, she couldn't get enough, she put her hand down his pants and found his rock-hard dick, and she played with the pre-cum coming out the head of his throbbing dick. She knew what she wanted and was determined to get it! She forced herself to pull away from him, for what she had in mind the elevator would work perfectly," baby, I need you! I want you to fuck me right now, just stick the head in, I need you," she said as she turned her back to him and pulled down her clothes giving him access to her body. As he began rubbing the head of his dick up and down her clit, it slide in with ease and she gulped for air, "ahhh, damn baby it feels sooo hard."

Just as he was getting into the pleasure of her warm and wet pussy, the bell notifying them that the elevator will be stopping at the next floor was enough for him to pull out and get himself together. "What are you doing," she asked looking back over her shoulder? She hadn't heard the bell indicating the elevator was stopping at the next floor; she was immersed in the way he made her feel. "Hold-up a minute, the elevators about to stop on the next floor," he said helping her get herself together. From the way she was looking in his eyes he could tell that she wasn't pleased that they had to stop. Their floor was the next stop as another couple got on the elevator, Amanda didn't stop playing with his dick as she kept her back to him, the other couple was a younger couple so she figured they would understand the love they shared between each other, but all they got was wicked stares as if they were animals.

They got off, she looked back over her shoulder and said to the couple," lighten up, I love this man with all my heart and I can't seem to ever get enough of him," then she giggled like a school girl in love!

They ripped off each other's clothes the moment they broke the threshold of room, barely able to keep her away from him long enough to make sure the safety latch was on. Even at the height of sexing his boo, their safety came first. Her body was steaming hot and there was no mistaking what she wanted and she wasn't going to be denied now that they were alone. "Bring that dick over here, gotta taste it and feel it inside of me," she demanded! She took a seat on the edge of the King size bed as she flicked her tongue in and out of her mouth as she made her tongue ring do tricks he's never seen her do before with it. He walked over to where she was sitting with his dick at full attention; her mouth was only inches away from his dick. She smiled wickedly and opened her mouth wide as she hungrily accepted his offerings. Licking and sucking on his dick as if it was truly the last supper, her loud slurping sounds combined with the performance she was putting on could only be matched by that of one of the hottest porn-stars of this day and age. "That's right daddy, that's right, fuck my face. Ohh shit baby, your dick is so big, fuck my face daddy, make that dick cum all in my mouth, I want to taste it...Please give it to me daddy, give it to me," she begged over and over again. She had only one goal in mind and that was to make him cum harder and longer than he has ever cummed in his life. She was jerking, licking and sucking all with the same motion, she needed for him to cum in her mouth, that's all she thought about. She had one trick left up her sleeve that she hadn't done to him yet and she figured that now was as good a time as any. She looked up at him with those beautiful eyes of hers and said to him," Silas, Silas, look at me damn it, look at me while I suck your dick," she said through clenched teeth and never missing a beat while still sucking his dick. She began sucking and jerking even harder the more he stared back down at her! She was lost in her own lust.

Those beautiful hazel-green eyes of hers proved to be too much for him to handle. His body began to get stiff, "oh shit...I...I'm a--about to fuckin' cum," he said through his own clenched teeth trying his damnest to fight a battle he wasn't going to win. With both of his hands on the back of her head, he began fucking her face so hard that she was gagging and coughing damn near chocking but never stopping.

The pain she felt in the back of her throat felt so good, she managed a wicked smile while he tortured her mouth. With her mouth filling up with cum, she swallowed and only let just a bit escape from the corners of her lips. She was able to get even the little that escaped by wiping it with her finger, then licking the remaining cum off her finger. He loved the fact that she was nasty and freaky; she even loved it when he called her a nasty bitch, something about that saying made her pussy wet instantly! What she brought out of him made him feel like he could fly, her beauty was intoxicating, her sex-game was top of the line, and not to mention that she was a ride or die type of chick with her own paper! Life couldn't get any better he thought. He looked her in the eyes," lay your sexy-ass back, it's my turn now," he said getting down on his knees as she was still on the edge of the bed.

He started his handy work at her big toe as he traced the outline of her tonnail and the sexy red polish she had on all her toes. He flicked his tongue over every toe and sucked on the little one just long enough to hear a moan escape her lips. By the time he got to the bottom of her feet, she was giggling as she tried to pull her foot back away from him, he moved up to her calf muscle where he drew a smiley face with his tongue causing her body to flinch and retreat from the warm and wet pleasure of his tongue. Her body was again on fire! He spent close to 2 minutes licking the back of her leg and calf, she could barely take the pleasure he inflicted upon her body and he hadn't even yet touched her dripping wet pussy. "Damn baby, it feels so good I don't want you to ever stop," she moaned. "Slide all the way up on the bed and keep your eyes on me," he demanded. "Make sure you keep your eyes open the whole time, to!"

Eagerly slid up on the bed not wasting a second of doing what she was told. She watched as his tongue began tracing the outline of her entire body, his warm tongue made her drunk with pleasure. His hands massaged and caressed her firm body, paying special attention to her hard nipples. Her perky nipples were standing at full attention the same way she had his dick standing while she was sucking it. He bit down lightly on her nipple stretching it as far away from her body as he could without hurting her, again she moaned out in pleasure. Her moans were corning at a constant rate even without her consent because she was trying her best to keep her mouth shut, but she couldn't, his tongue was just too much for her. He took notice that her right hand had traveled down to her love tunnel. He started spelling his name on her collar bone with his tongue, warming up for the big deal. With her pussy dripping wet and on fire, she couldn't help but run her finger across her swollen clit lightly, she closed her eyes and moaned again but he caught her," didn't I tell you to keep your eyes open and look at me?" He removed her hand from her swollen clit," I got this, you just make sure you keep your eyes on me!" Leaving a wet trail down the middle of her stomach, he didn't stop until his breathing and tongue was at the opening of her love-tunnel. He flicked his tongue out and ran it up and down the length of her pussy as he pressed lightly against her swollen clit. "You want me to eat your pussy," he asked her?

With her eyes wide and her eyes more green now than hazel, all she could do was to shake her head up and down continuously, then all of a sudden her mouth opened," yes ...Yes ...Please daddy, eat my pussy, please make this pussy cum, I can' t take it no more, please daddy, eat me," she begged him. Spreading her pussy wide open he watched as her swelled clit peeped out back at him, it's hood was shelled and hard. He knew she was ready for the taking but he wasn't ready, he inserted his middle finger deep into her love-tunnel as he sent another electrical shock throughout her entire body. "Oh shit, don't stop that, right there, finger fuck me, oh shit that feels sooo good."

He continued to finger fuck her, he had another plan for her, he started spelling his name with his tongue on her clit. With each letter he spelled out with his tongue, her pussy got wetter, with his finger sliding in and out of her pussy with ease as she bucked her hips up and down off the bed, she was now possessed. He inserted 2 more fingers and applied more pressure to her clit, she went crazy and gasped for air as his 3 fingers went to work with his tongue.

"Oh shit daddy, daddy, my pussy is about to explode, daddy, I.. I..I'm cuming," she said as she grabbed his head with both of her hands and began bouncing up and down off the bed fucking his face with the same intensity that he had when he was fucking her face.

"That's it! Right there, that's it. Oh my fuckin' God, I. ..I. ..I'm ,Ahh, Agg, Ahhh, fuck meeee," she screamed with his face buried between her legs sucking on her clit as she came in his mouth!

Even before she could regain her senses he had the head of his dick positioned at the entrance of her love-tunnel. Her pussy was still throbbing and wet as ever. He slid in her with ease but she almost lost her breath," oh shit, go slow to get it all the way it, damn it," she growled from the pain of his big dick.

Deep in his own thoughts and agenda, he didn't pay her no mind, instead, he shoved his whole dick inside her wet pussy and started fucking her hard, deep and fast. He had the entire bed rocking as her head was bouncing against the head-board. It was hurting for a minute then the pain went away and she couldn't believe what she was feeling," Silas, Silas baby, I'm cuming again, yeah, fuck this pussy," she cried to him!

He wasn't taking on prisoners; he flipped her over with her face down and her ass up as he entered her from the back. He bit down on his bottom lip as he held her by her hips and rammed his dick in and out of her pussy with everything he had in him to give. "Whose pussy is this," he asked?

"You know this pussy belongs to you. It's all yours daddy," she wined back to him. "Look at me then, didn't I tell you to look at me," he demanded?

Even on all fours she listened to what he told her, she looked back over her right shoulder and screamed out loud," this your pussy daddy and you can do whatever you want to your pussy, so fuck this pussy as hard and as deep as you want to!" The way she was throwing that pussy back at him and those green eyes of hers was again to much for him and he couldn't hold back another second," oh shit baby, I'm about to cum. Shit, I'm cuming and I can't hold it," he said through clenched teeth as he bit his bottom lip.

"Don't take it out, cum in me, I want to feel it, cum in me baby."

He was caught off guard because she had never let him cum in her, she was to fearful of getting pregnant, she would let him cum in her mouth before she let him cum inside of her, however this time it was different. He had to pull out of her and when he did, she didn't give him a chance, she went to work cleaning off his dick with her tongue. She would suck his dick every time it got soft and he would eat her pussy to catch his breath and then they would fuck each other's brains out that lasted most of the day until they were exhausted. They lay in each other's arms and talked.

"Do you want children," she asked?

"Yeah, of course I want children. But do you?"

"I want four kids, two boys, and two girls! The only thing, I want all my kids to have the same father, I ain't with all that different baby daddy bullshit, that's crazy."

"That sounds good, but for me, I gotta be out this game before I have any children."

"I can't tell," she said smacking her lips. "Not from the way you just shot about 10 gallons of cum all up in me, that was enough cum for 10 kids," she said laughing.

"Suppose I get pregnant, then what?" "We get all the paper we can real quick, get out the game, go down south beach and get married."

"You think you got it all planned out huh? Well, suppose I don't want to get married, mister, and then what?"

He got serious," if you're having my baby, you don't have a choice, we're getting married and that's that, I got it planned out if you plan on getting pregnant," he said getting up to use the bathroom.

———— ———— ———— ———— ————
————

Terri had taken Tiffany with her to get her nails and toes done at her favorite salon. At first, Tiffany was hesitant but she convinced her to come anyway. Terri knew right off the bat that Tiffany was a drug addict but she could also tell that she was very beautiful. She had a sense of raw beauty that she was hiding behind all the stress and pain of her life. Tiffany kept putting her head down whenever she spoke and that told her that her self-esteem was down or even lost. With Terri being the type of person she was, it was natural for her to extend a helping hand to Tiffany, loyalty begets loyalty, and that was something she didn't learn in a class room, she learned that from Joey! There was a daily war Tiffany fought in her head that nobody knew about. Being a drug addict wasn't easy, with her need to fit-in and stay close to Malik is what got her into this trouble in the first place. By the time she looked up and saw where she was at in life, it was damn near to late, she was a functioning addict! Her whole life was surrounded by Malik and there was nothing she wouldn't do for him, and that's the thought process that caused her to lose herself. With all that she did and was willing to do for him, she forgot to appreciate who she was as a woman.

"Terri, I really appreciate you bringing me with you, I ain't had my nails or toes down in a long time."

"Don't mention it. You looked like you needed a friend with all that's going on with them two men in our life, so here I am."

With her head down, Tiffany said barely above a whisper, "I want to get out this lifestyle so bad but I don't know how...I don't know what to do," she said as tears escaped down her cheek. "Tiffany you can do anything you want, you just have to put your mind to it and be determined," said Terri!

Auntie was just getting out the shower when Jazzy strolled through the front door. "What's wrong with you," she asked?

"Malik just got robbed in front of Auntie Pam's," said Jazzy as she plopped down on the sofa. "And I saw the whole fuckin' thang!"

"What you mean you seen it?"

"I...I was looking out the window when I seen the dudes coming from the side of the house. They hit him in the head with the gun and kicked him a couple of times," she said like she was struggling to tell the story. Auntie could tell that from what she saw, it had affected her a great deal. But it was more than just seeing the robbery, then it hit her," you know who did it, don't you?"

Jazzy shook her head up and down as she loaded her stem," yeah I know who did it."

"Did you tell Joey or Auntie Pam about it?" Shaking her head no as she blew out a thick ring of CRACK smoke from deep down in her lungs," how was I going to tell them that?"

Auntie hurried up and got dressed," come on here, we gotta go back down there and tell Joey who it was you saw that robbed Malik!" "They left, they went somewhere, "said Jazzy with a blank look in her eyes. "Here smoke this," she said throwing a dub at her. Snatching up the dub, Auntie reached for her phone, " I gotta call Pam first, I gotta tell her we'll be down there," as she dialed the number.

CHAPTER 16

JOEY and Malik were on their way back to Charlottesville from Lake Monticello after their meeting with the connect. With all that had happened thus far, Joey wanted to do a little sightseeing. He looked over at Malik and said," I wouldn't be surprised if the connect already know who robbed us, shit; he knows everything else we do, so he should be the one telling us the story. Who, What, and Why!"

Malik was usually the one feeling some type of way about how the connect knew so much about them, but this time it was Joey and he felt that if the connect did know, he should tell them who was responsible. A tight lipped grin crept across Malik's face as he spoke, "you right! That shit wouldn't surprise me either, and if he doesn't know, I bet by this time tomorrow he'll know everything. That's why we gotta figure this shit out on our own...If we put our minds to it, we can figure this shit out."

"Ain't no question about it, but for me I'd feel much better if we could put some metal to this niggaz mind," laughed Joey lightening up a little. "You know me, I'm definitely wit that! We should be letting the streets' know that ain't shit sweet when it comes to us. The only thing about all that is that, we gotta be smart about it! Twenty-five large is a nice piece of change, but no matter how you look at it, that shit ain't worth doing a life-sentence for and I don't care how you flip it or turn it, that shit ain't worth going to prison."

For the first time in a long time, Malik had assumed the role usually reserved for Joey and he knew it. He felt like all his talks with Malik was starting to sink in and he couldn't do nothing but smile and agree with him. "You right Malik! You're definitely right on this one, ain't nothing out here in these streets worth doing a life-sentence for. The flip-side for us though is that we're out here playing this game and if our street respect ain't where it's suppose to be, we can cancel it. None of these dudes out here really fuck with us, I see the way some of these dudes be looking at us, they look at us like we some little niggaz who got a nice plug. They deal with us because they have to, a nigga can see right through that bullshit. Even before we was getting real paper, some of these same dudes only dealt with us because we had that fire weed. All I'm saying is this, If niggaz really knew what we were holding, they'd be trying to murder us everyday all day! We're missing that level of fear that's always present in dudes in our position and I know it, you know it and these dudes out here know it. We gotta lay down the law on this one, we gotta let these dudes know that we ain't to be fucked with, that's all I'm saying."

Malik put his free hand under his chin and started rubbing it as he looked back over at Joey, "so you're telling me you're ready to get busy out here in these streets?"

"This all I know, when those niggaz was out here running with Safee' and them, they wasn't going for shit! Wasn't all that out-of-town shit jumpin' off unless they said so, point, blank, period. How the fuck we let this nigga Silas set-up shop right here in the hood and do nothing about it like we the shit or something? Tell me how we come to this? I know he thinks we pussy, I know it."

Joey wasn't just venting to his homey about some shit that was behind his control, he was starting to change before his very eyes and it was like he knew he was changing but he couldn't stop himself even if he tried. One thing he knew about what he was saying was that every word that came out his mouth was the truth, whether he liked it or not. He wanted to get off the interstate at the 5th street exit because he wanted to ride through Prospect. He wanted to see what he could see and something in his head was telling him that Amanda had something to do with what happened to Malik but he didn't know to what degree or why?

The streets had been talking about her the last month or so as it is, she came up outta nowhere getting paper and her spot in Prospect was the only spot that hadn't been affected by them selling dimes. Everywhere else had to shut down shop or come buy from them, but not Amanda, she was able to continue to sell her shit with few problems. She wasn't selling dimes like they were but her dubs were bigger than normal and that kept the fiends from having to walk all the way across town like the fiends from the other different neighborhoods were doing, and her cocaine was just as good as theirs. How can that be? As they were passing Amanda's building Malik looked over in that direction and he almost flipped out his phone to call her but his pride wouldn't allow it. He knew of her new found fame in the hood and deep in his heart he was happy for her, she deserved it if you let him tell the story especially after all the dick she sucked on pennies. Despite her new found fame, he was still the infamous Malik from 10th Street and there was no way that he was calling her. He also noticed the few young hustlers out there, they wasn't nobody, only mall hustlers; they posed no harm. Joey was looking as well; he only nodded his head to the beat of the song playing in the car!

Joey was deep in thought and his chest was poked out, he was feeling himself. He felt strong, confidant, and sure of whom he was on the streets of Charlottesville! With the 2 bricks of pure cocaine stashed in the stash compartment in the car, he wanted to make a pit stop down at the barber shop on Cherry. Malik looked over at his comrade as he made the right turn at GoCo's instead of keeping straight towards they hood. "You gotta be kidding me, you do know what we got in the stash box don't you?" Joey acted like he didn't know what Malik was talking about, but he'd gotten his information first hand from the connect that the best K-9 unit in the Country couldn't smell inside the stash-box and he was willing to give it a test in case they happened to get pulled over. He parked the Camry next to the all White Mercedes Benz 600 V-12. Malik fell in love over and over again every time he saw the car," damn, every time we stop down this spot, they always here," he said pointing at the Benz.

Everybody from the Projects knew the Benz belonged to Mann, him and his partner Ru, they were hood legends; wherever you saw Mann, bet your last dollar that Ru wasn't far! Mann was sitting on the hood of the Benz talking on his cell, his 40" cable Platinum piece was hanging low, soon as he seen Joey, he hung-up.

"Joey, Malik, what's good homey," asked Mann embracing the both of them smiling?

"You know what it is, homey! Same shit, different day," answered Malik.

"If I had ya'll hand, I'd throw mines in," joked Mann.

"I ain't up to shit, we about to bounce soon as Ru get done, we're going to Miami tonight to fuck with some bitches," said Mann strongly! Joey caught a glimpse of a few dudes from Prospect in the Barber Shop and walked in. He was still feeling some type of way about how things went down and for some odd reason, Prospect left a bad taste in his mouth. He spotted his favorite barber doing what he do best, " yo J.Y., what up? I need a quick line-up."

J.Y. looked at the dude who was already sitting in his chair getting his hair cut and nodded for him to get up. The dude couldn't believe what was happening and looked at J.Y. and then over at a smiling Joey. He was holding a crispy one-hundred dollar bill in his hand giving it to J.Y. for the round up.

"Yeah homey, he's a regular; I know you know something about that, being you're in the distribution business," said J.Y. making a play on the young hustler's mind? "Don't sweat it; your cut is now on the house!"

Dude reluctantly got out the chair with the barber's cape still on, for what Joey was getting he didn't need the cape, he barely even needed a shape-up. It took J.Y. all of 5 minutes to finish Joey's shape-up and watched him walk out the barber shop. The way Joey was eyeing the youngins from Prospect told J.Y. he was feeling some type of way about them, but it wasn't his place to speak on it, he watched closely.

Joey knew the Prospect dudes would resent the fact that he made one of them get out the chair so he could get his shape-up and that would become the new hood gossip, and for once he entertained the thought that the hood would be talking about him. Right before he left the shop, he turned and gave the Prospect dudes one last look; he had that evil smirk on his face!

Malik was still out front engaged in a conversation with a sexy young chick that Joey had never seen before. He was busy getting her number for him to even notice Joey walk up behind him. The sexy chocolate young chick was looking at Malik like he was something to eat as she said to him," you better call me too! I'm eighteen now so I ain't trying to hear all that bullshit you use to kick to me when I was a shorty... I'm grown now and I want to do some grown-up shit with you tonight," she kept saying with her seductive voice.

Joey's ringing phone is what caught Malik's attention as he turned around to see Joey looking at him smiling. He couldn't say nothing because Joey had already answered his phone," what up baby?" It was Terri on the other line of his phone and she could be heard without him having to put the phone directly on his ear," nothing! We just got our nails and our toes done. You back yet," she asked?

"Yeah, I'm back, why? I'm on my way back to the spot, but why you ask? Is everything alright with you?"

"Yeah, I'm good. Tiffany's good. Listen, I'll be there when you get there, there's something I need to holla at you about and I think you'll like it." Knowing that Terri was on her way back to Auntie Pam's without him didn't sit well with him; he waved Malik over so they could leave. It didn't take him long to get the short distance back to his side of town and when he entered the house, Terri, Tiffany, and Auntie Pam was deep in a casual conversation. To his surprise, Terri looked extremely comfortable and even calm to be sitting in a CRACK house. He didn't know if he was impressed or thought he made a bad decision!

"Speaking of the devils, here they come now," said Auntie Pam cracking up with laughter. "I'm glad ya'll here, I got a message for ya'll. Auntie called me a few minutes ago and she told me to hold the both of you here until she gets here...She said that's it's very important, so stay put," she said with force!

Tiffany wasn't paying much attention to what Auntie Pam was saying her only concern was Malik and how was he feeling? She walked right up to him and asked," you need anything? Is your head still hurting?" If you looked closely, you could see Malik turn his head because he was smiling so hard. He took a seat on the sofa opposite Terri as he cut his eyes over at Auntie Pam to see if she had seen him smiling. "I'm good, I'm a little tired but I'll live."

"You want something to eat then?" Terri sat back on the other sofa observing how Tiffany interacted with the man of her dreams. She had learned over the last few hours that Malik was the love of her life and was familiar with the history they shared with one another. She knew of Tiffany's struggle's with her addiction to CRACK and all the other demons she had to face on a daily basis out in the streets'. It truly amazed her that despite Tiffany's shortcomings that her supreme focus, desire, attention, and her heart belonged only to Malik. She felt a sense of loyalty to Tiffany and she barely knew her but her loyalty and determination is what drove her to see if she and Joey were able to help her. "Ain't that cute," laughed Terri pointing at Tiffany as she tended to Malik. Tiffany barely looking up or taking her attention off Malik said back to Terri," shut-up girrrl, you crazy!"

Joey had enough of watching Terri all up in their business and they he remembered that she wanted to holla at him about something so he wanted to get to it," what's up baby, what you wanted to holla at me about?" Just as Terri was about to talk to him about what her plan was in walked Auntie and Jazzy. The look that Auntie had in her eyes told Terri she had better wait until she knew who these people were before she started talking in front of them. Auntie waved the guys over to her," Malik...Joey, I need to holla at ya'll about something real important," she said eyeing the stranger in the room.

She shot Terri a look that said,' who the fuck are you?' But she dared to say what her mind was thinking and also she wasn't willing to say anything that the Commonwealth could play back in court! Joey sensed what was happening so he was the first to speak up for his boo, "everybody in here is family so you don't have to beat around the bush as to what you can and can't say in here!" Then he walked over to Terri and kissed her in the mouth letting everybody who wasn't certain about her know that she was his people. Looking into Terri's eyes he simply said," we'll finish that later!"

Auntie making sure Jazzy was still standing next to her nudged her in the ribs so that she could take the floor. Jazzy took a deep breath and kept her eyes on the floor as she spoke but she hesitated and Auntie wasted no time," she's got something to tell ya'll about what happened this morning."

Jazzy could feel the temperature rising quickly throughout her entire body as the eyes and all the attention was on her. She looked up briefly and made sure to keep her eyes planted on the floor, she couldn't bear to look Malik in the eyes, with her mind telling her to get out of there, and she couldn't, not at this point. If she was to turn and leave now, everybody would swear that she was a part of the robbery, and since she knew the position she was in, she had to focus and put everything in its proper perspective. She still fought with herself as to how does she really tell them? And how much of what she saw does she tell them? Those were just a few thoughts going through her head and what could happen if she didn't say anything at all? With all those thoughts going through her head, there was one single thought that propelled her to tell what she saw and that was: CRACK! If she didn't know anything, she knew that once Joey and Malik found out that she didn't have anything to do with the robbery they would break her off something proper, so she lifted her head slowly and made eye contact. The first person she made eye contact with was Tiffany and the look she had was one of hatred, pure evil. She took another breath and then made eye contact with everybody else except Tiffany.

"This morning when you went outside Malik, I was at the window watching you. I saw everything! I saw the 3 dudes come from the side of the house with guns in their hands, I wanted to say something but I was so nervous that nothing came out. I wanted to scream, holla, bang on the window, anything, but it was happening so fast that I couldn't. I seen the one who hit you on the back of your head, it was Jacob from Prospect and then I seen him snatch the brown paper bag from your hand, then they ran back the other way. I'm sorry Malik, I'm sorry but I didn't know what to do," she was now in tears and everybody in the living room bought her story. Hook, line, and sinker!

Malik, he jumped off the sofa and smacked the shit out of her and was nose to nose with her with lightening speed. "You knew them niggaz the whole time and didn't say shit? Bitch you gotta be crazy! Then you bring your ass in here like you can't get it or something, what you think we soft?" He was fuming with anger and spit was coming from the sides of his mouth, he looked over his shoulder at Joey," this bitch is crazy!"

Joey pulled his cell phone out and began scrolling down until he found what he was looking for. He walked over to Jazzy and showed her the picture from his 'phone "who's this?" Jazzy's eyes got wide and her heart started beating a little faster. She couldn't believe her eyes, there was Jacob and her cousin Amanda on top of Prospect. The crazy thing about all this was Amanda was handing Jacob a brown paper bag.

"That's him right there! His name is Jacob and I know him real well, but I can't understand what the hell is Amanda doing with him?" That's all Joey needed to hear, he was ready to get busy," come on Malik, let's bounce. I know that little nigga on top of Prospect somewhere.

Malik turned to Joey and put his right hand on his shoulder as he whispered," not right now homey! If we make a move on this clown right now, we'll be putting everybody in this room in harm's way one way or another. Even Terri would be at risk and she ain't even with this type of shit...You know what we gotta do; we gotta play a sucka to catch a sucka," said Malik releasing his firm grip from Joey's shoulder. He shot Jazzy a murderous look then went to take a seat back on the sofa with Tiffany. Joey was locked in his own thoughts, rage and anger almost consumed him. It seemed that he was having an out of body experience, he heard Malik clearly but he was unable to respond. His only thought was hurting Jacob! There was a picture of him and Malik sitting on the mantel piece of them when they were 9 or 10 years old, he couldn't take his eyes off the picture. That picture represented to him the love and loyalty they shared with each other and for the first time in a long time, he wanted to hurt those who hurt Malik. The more he stared at the picture, the question came back to him; is twenty-five grand worth putting himself in harm's way? Or worse, doing a life sentence?

Terri was experiencing for the first time, the other side of who her man was, and what he really did to earn his paper, the strangest thing was that she wasn't afraid or scared. She was more so drawn even closer to him, she admired the loyalty he showed Malik and it made her feel comfortable and safe in their presence. Nevertheless, she knew Joey was at a cross roads and she needed to do something to bring him back to who he need to be to survive in those mean streets. She was aware that one false move she could very well lose him forever, she understood that all too well. She slowly walked over to him as he continued to stare at the picture on the mantel piece, she stood directly in front of him blocking his view and put her arms around his neck," baby, I know you're up-set right now, and rightfully so, however, I need for you to be smart about this! I can't live without you, I need you baby, you're my entire world," she said before kissing him passionately. She knew she had his attention because his tongue was dancing around in her mouth as they played tongue tag. She opened her eyes and his stare was intense, she knew at that moment that his heart belonged to her and her alone.

"You right! Malik's definitely right on this one," he said as he eyed both Malik and Terri, the two most important people to him in the room at the time. "I need the both of you as well!"

"No question, we know what we gotta do. If Amanda's down with this shit I'll find out, she's only a phone call away," insisted Malik.

Jazzy felt the need to speak up for her cousin Amanda, "I doubt she has anything to do with this. She's my cousin but this ain't how she gets down with hers, the bitch is green as grass when it comes to shit like this, trust me I know," she said recalling how nervous Amanda was when she clipped Jacob for his CRACK.

"Bitch, that's your mutha-fuckin' cousin so of course you'll say some bullshit like that. You don't want a nigga getting at her so you'll say anything to keep a nigga up off her ass...As far as I know, both you bitches suspect! What the fuck you doing on this side of town anyway," questioned Malik as he got back up and was nose to nose with Jazzy once more?

The old Jazzy came alive, "nigga, if I had anything to do with that shit I wouldn't be here now telling your silly ass who it was who robbed you! Think nigga. Think. You right, she's my cousin and to keep it one-hundred, you think that if we were in this shit together that I would be helping you? See, that's where you got the game fucked up, if my cousin had something to do with this shit, I wouldn't tell you shit, blood is always thicker than water all fuckin' day. So what you need to do is think real hard and make your next move your best move because I am," fired Jazzy.

Auntie Pam sat on the sideline allowing Joey and Malik to work this thing out as best they could but at the same time she knew Jazzy had just over-stepped her bounds with them two and if she didn't gain control over the situation somebody would get hurt. "Malik, I gotta tell ya'll this because you have no idea what's going on with Jazzy and her cousin Amanda. Jazzy haven't spoke to Amanda in over a month or so, they fell out over some bullshit but that's neither here nor there."

Auntie stepped in as if this shit between her and Auntie Pam had been scripted," I know that this girl wanted to tell ya'll the moment she saw what happened but she was nervous as hell. I know for a fact that she hasn't spoken to Amanda just like Pam said; she's been with either me or Pam everyday all day. Can't anybody in here speak for Amanda but Jazzy, she ain't have shit to do with what happened."

Auntie Pam was listening closely and observing everybody's comments and now it was time for her to add her two cents, "Joey...Malik...The first thing ya'll need to figure out is who knew about the paper and go from there. I doubt that this chile had anything to do with it so don't use her as an escape goat, now if ya'll know something I don't know, please let me know."

There was only one person in the room who knew about the paper and that it was going to be there and that was Joey. He bought the paper there himself and he almost spoke up a little to fast. He decided to hold his tongue until he figured out who else was involved and how this shit happened. He knew the CRACK game brought out the worst in everybody, the seller's and user's alike! "Yo, Malik let's bounce, we got some business to handle!" Malik pointed to the duffel bag on the floor, he wasn't riding around Charlottesville with 2 bricks of cocaine in the car. "What about that," he said still pointing at the duffel bag?

"You feel like cooking," asked Joey looking over at Auntie Pam? She rolled her sleeves up and looked at him like he was crazy," do I feel like cooking? That's what the fuck I do...I cook! Let's get it, ain't no mutha-fuckin' robbery gonna stop us from doing what the fuck we do." She had a wicked smirk on her face," I say we turn this shit up a notch or two and the next cock-sucka who come around here on that bullshit, I'm sending they ass to South 1st Street my damn self!"

He knew she meant business when she said that and knew that she was right. They had no choice but to turn it up a notch or two and he knew exactly how he was going to do it. He almost emptied the contents of the duffel bag right there on the floor, but Terri was right there watching his every move. "Terri, come up-stairs with me, I gotta talk to you about something."

Terri wasted no time in falling in step behind Joey as they made their way up-stairs and into Auntie Pam's bedroom. She was sure to close and lock the door behind them, "what's up baby," she asked in her most innocent voice? If you could look into her eyes you could see the lust!

"Listen, I got a lot of thangs to handle and I can't do it with you hanging around here like this. I need you to go back to the room and chill, I'll call you later when I'm on my way." As he watched her body movement, he was briefly confused by the way she was looking back at him. He didn't know what she was thinking until she opened her mouth to speak. She leaned back against the locked door and took a deep breath.

"I knew this was coming and I don't have a problem with it and I will leave. This ain't my lifestyle and you know that, but at the same time you're my responsibility. I have one condition and you're going to have to agree with me before I tell you what it is…Okay?" " A-ight, but what is it?" Terri walked over to him with her eyes locked in on her target," you have to let me suck your dick right here and right now!" She didn't wait around for him to respond to her request; she dropped down to her knees and slid his dick into her mouth. She was determined to ease some of the tension in his mind and she sucked and sucked his dick as if his life dependent on it. It proved to be working because before either of them knew it, she had him cuming all in her mouth. She looked up to see that big smile on his face, knowing she had done her job," baby, you were really stressed out and you needed that," she said giggling. "I can't have my baby out here in these streets trying to conduct his business all stressed out, nope, not me, I'm going to take care of you, and don't ever forget it Joey!"

Joey couldn't believe her reactions and what she was saying but at the same time, he knew she was correct in her observation of him and there was arguing that point. "Damn baby, you're right, I needed that. I feel better already, but that's just round one, it's your turn, I want some of that pussy!" He was just like her, not really waiting for her to respond, he spent her around roughly, her back was to him he, reached around and unbuckled her clothes. He made sure to drop her pants down to her ankles and bent her forward over the bed with her hands holding her for support. He slowly spread her ass cheeks and stuck 2 fingers in her dripping wet pussy.

Barely able to control herself she whispered, "I almost came sucking your dick....Put that dick in me baby, please put it in." He slide his monstrous dick into her as she gulped for air, he entered her love-tunnel slow and deep. She was forced to rise up on her toes trying to ease the pain that felt oh so good to her. She wanted more but she had to take her time with the size of his dick. She learned her lesson a long time ago with him, it didn't pay rushing. She was moaning softly. Joey couldn't hold back, he wanted to fuck her and fuck her really hard. The harder and faster he fucked her, the louder her moans became. He started smacking her on the ass," whose pussy is this?"

"Ahh, damn baby, this your pussy, it's always been your pussy daddy," she screamed at the top of her lungs! She turned to look at him from over her shoulder and saw the look and concentration he had on his face she decided to add fuel to the fire," oh my god...Ahh, shit you're fucking the shit outta meee, come on daddy, fuck your pussy harder," she begged through clenched teeth. The more shit she talked to him the wetter her pussy got and the harder he fucked her.

She was clawing at the sheets and anything else she could hold onto but there was nothing else there for her to grab. Then it hit her, she was about to cum and started screaming at the top of her lungs without a care in the world," Jesus...Jesus, oh my fuckin' god, help me, oh shit baby, I.. I..I'm cuming right fuckin' now," she screamed over and over as she released some bent up tension of her own! He was cuming at the same time as she was and he was glad for that because that meant nobody heard his faint moans of pleasure as he called her name over and over again.

They both collapsed onto the bed with his hard dick still deep in her love-tunnel. She looked at him from an odd angle," damn baby, why you do that to me?"

They busted out laughing at the same time knowing that they had just fell even deeper in love in that moment. "Shit, I needed that," he managed to say in between catching his breath.

"Now, what's that one condition?"

"I don't even have to answer that because you just did it and did it well might I add. Oh, for-real though, I want to take Tiffany with me if that's okay with you?"

He smiled and impressed with her even more," that's cool with me! I think she needs a friend like you, maybe something will rub off on her, but I don't have to tell you that." Making a pit-stop in the bathroom to tidy up as best they could before they had to go back downstairs to face the crowd.

When they hit the bottom of the steps, everybody was staring at them with a smile on their face. Terri knew at that instant that they had heard them up there but she didn't feel no of way about it, actually it made her feel good! She returned each and every stare as she fanned herself trying to cool down. She not only surprised Joey but everybody else as well," ya'll know a woman will do whatever it takes to keep her man happy even if it means she'll be the center of attention…As for me, there's no limit I won't go for him," she said pointing at Joey!

Auntie Pam was the first to break the silence with her loud laugh," I knew it was something about you that I liked…That's right momma, handle ya business fuck the bullshit." Terri walked over to high-five her and Tiffany down to Jazzy and Auntie, but she stopped short at Malik," that's a woman's thang and you're my brother so I gotta leave you out on this one." She whispered into Tiffany's ear and Tiffany was smiling like a little girl," come on girl, you're bouncing with me, the fellas got business to handle," said Terri disappearing out the front door with Tiffany on her heels.

Auntie Pam got busy in the kitchen cooking the cocaine into the highly addictive substance called; CRACK! She had so much CRACK, she had to use 2 pots to cook. With the CRACK still wet, Joey took out his digital scale and put on ounce to the side next to him as he used the scale to weigh out each package. He looked up, " everybody listen up, we're about to change this mutha-fuckin' game forever...We're now selling .3's for Ten dollar's and this is what the new dimes look like," he said holding up the small baggy. Jazzy and Auntie both said at the same time," shit, we can easily get twenty for them all day long." Joey jumped down their throat," if I say we selling these for Ten fuckin' dollars then we're selling them for Ten fuckin' dollars and not a penny more. If you two can't do that, there's the damn door, I suggest you use it," he said pointing at the door!

It took them all of 3 hours to finish cooking, weighing, and bagging up much of the CRACK they cooked. There was still more that needed to be cooked and bagged but Auntie Pam was getting frustrated and tired. "I need a fuckin' break from this shit, come on ya'll we're going up-stairs to get our minds right," she said grabbing an 8-ball. Joey jumped in her path laughing," you ain't gotta go up-stairs, we're about to bounce." He handed her 4ounce's," just make sure ya'll bag that up for later, the whole city is going to be over here trying to get these dimes...Watch what I tell you." Auntie Pam took the CRACK," same deal? We'll be done with these before midnight," she said proudly. "Same deal Auntie Pam, we wouldn't have it any other way," said Malik from all the way in the living room laughing.

CHAPTER 17

JOEY and Malik were making their normal rounds of dropping off CRACK and picking up their paper, it's been nearly a month since they started selling the dimes and they were doing well. They extended their territory from not only the Projects' and 10th Street area to clear across town down to Garrett. The decision to expand was a conscious and well calculated on their part. Since the boy Silas hadn't been seen in the Projects' in awhile they decided to go to his backyard and see what they can see, they really wanted to bring the drama where he was known to get paper but it wasn't working as planned.

    Down Garrett, they hooked-up with Dre'. Dre' was one of the many dudes from Jersey who made Charlottesville their new home. He had been in Charlottesville for like...Forever! He was a good dude at heart and easy to deal with because of his up-front and straight approach to life. Dre' didn't pose a threat to their situation, he played his position to the tee, it also helped that he wasn't your big time hustla, his greatest asset was his mouth piece and his ability to captivate his troops! He was always in the company of a handful of local cats, he made sure they did all the dirty work and in turn for what they did for him, he painted a picture for them in which they could believe. His war stories were legendary, it didn't hurt that he was a natural comic enabling him to be able to keep everybody relax and calm in the most of ill situations. Now, the thing that really set Dre' apart from everybody else was that he wasn't just a slick talker, he made shit happen and not only for himself but his troops as well. Anybody trying to set-up shop in Garrett would eventually have to go through him and it could be your choice or by force, either way, he would win the battle. That was the perfect situation for Joey and Malik, they sought him out based solely on his ability to get the job done. They needed to get the drop on Silas and Dre' would help them do that for a couple of dollar's. Once they turned into Garrett they went straight to Dre's apartment, Joey knocked on his door. His ole' lady answered," hey Joey...Malik! Dre's in the bathroom but I know he said he was waiting on ya'll to come," she said ushering them into the apartment. The living room was full of dudes from down Garrett, Joey and Malik both only nodded their heads at the guys, no conversation was necessary. Most of them was either drinking on ole' school 40 ounce of 'old-gold' or playing madden on the PSP.

It was especially difficult for Malik because ever since the robbery, he hated crowded with different dudes. His mind would sometimes get the best of him; it would have him thinking that one of them dudes could have been the other two who were involved in the robbery. Joey was more at ease but he kept his Glock .40 ready and as he looked over at Malik, he was doing the same with his Glock .40. Trust was non-existent to them these days; they came to the conclusion that the only thing the streets seemed to respect was, Violence! The dudes in the living room thought the world of Dre', they also knew who Malik and Joey was. If you let them tell the story, they would say that Joey and Malik were there to buy their drugs from Dre' and not the other way around as it really was. Malik hated the idea of letting them dudes think that they were hustling for Dre'. With each passing day since the robbery, Malik had given every out of towner he came across, hell; it became something of a legend how he treated them. It was Joey who convinced him that it was for the best to have them dudes to think just that. Without ever admitting it, Malik felt Dre' was different anyway, but he would never tell a soul how he felt. Tired of waiting on Dre', Joey and Malik got up and went to the bathroom door, three soft raps and they let themselves in. "What up family," said Dre' standing over the tiny sink hand washing his socks? Dre' lead them into the bedroom, "damn, I ain't even know ya'll was here...How long ya'll been here?"

Dre' walked over to his closet and went through a few shoe boxes until he found the one he was looking for then he pulled out a stack of paper. He threw the stack onto the bed in Malik's direction. "That's you family!"

"Do I need to count this shit," asked Malik seriously? Dre' looked at him like he was crazy," family, you been coming over here 2 or 3 times a week for a month now, and every time you ask me the same shit. I've never short changed you one red penny, not one, so you should be asking yourself that question."

Joey knew of the tension between the two and usually he always kept his mouth shut and out the way while they went back and forth about something that the both of them got off on. Power! However, there were more pressing issue's he wanted to deal with. "Dre' what's the word on dude, you seen him yet," asked Joey?

Dre' quickly separated the work that Malik had given him in exchange for the paper he just spent. Most of the CRACK went into the same shoe box that contained the paper, while the rest went into his pocket, and then he looked back over to Malik, "yo, your paper is straight! You don't have to ever have to worry about that...Never, business is business and I got a good thang going here, so I ain't trying to fuck it up," he said firmly!

Dre' found a comfortable spot on the bed and lit his cigarette. He inhaled deeply as he blew the smoke out slowly before he shifted his attention from Malik back to Joey. " I...I..I knew I had something to tell you...The word on the street is that your boy Sosa came through yesterday. Silas wasn't with him, ain't nobody heard nothing from dude, it's like he's not even out here no more, and if he is, he's doing a helluva job staying on the low." He took a few more puffs off his cigarette and then continued, "I do know Sosa and Tasha been moving all their shit out off and on for like a whole month or two. For some reason, they don't seem to be in a rush to get it done. That bitch came through here stuntin' in a 600 Benz and all Sosa did was shoot a little dice with the homeys. I sent a few troops his way to buy some work but he wasn't doing nothing. All he kept saying was that he was chillin' and that's not like him at all. I don't know what's happening but something is real strange with them two, I don't know what to tell you, but all I can do is when I do see son, I'll let you know."

Joey and Malik had gathered all the information they were going to get for one night and now it was time for them to be on their way. They took the scenic route back over to the Projects; they wanted to see what they could see. Every since they converted to selling all dimes, they not only had the Projects jumpin' but other spots like Garrett as well. With their goal being to lock down the entire Charlottesville, their plan was really starting to see some day light; with each passing day it looked better and better. Now, with the new spots came new people, gansta's, and killer's alike wanting a piece of what they had. It seemed everybody wanted in on their operation or just wanted to get down with them for no reason.

Malik had been trying to contact Amanda with no luck. When he finally got her on the phone, she told him that she was to busy to talk and whenever he called back, she didn't' answer her phone. She was avoiding him and it made his think that she had something to do with the robbery. He was certain she played a part, an instrumental one at that, he just didn't' know to what extent it was. If it hadn't been for Joey convincing him to stay the course, continue to play stupid about the robbery, he would've been handled his business with her; no question about it. Joey didn't want him doing anything until he at least had the opportunity to sit down and talk to her, get a vibe from her reaction, however, that was getting harder and harder as each day passed.

Joey tried everything to keep him humble and calm and the only thing that seemed to work for a while was having Malik count all the paper they generated from their new dime spots. The dime spots made the twenty-five grand look like chump change. Nevertheless, that was like putting a band-aid over a gunshot wound, the situation with Amanda would demand his attention in time. Malik wasn't happy at all as to how things were coming along so he did his own investigation. He quickly enlisted the help of one of his best CRACK customers; Star! She was now his eyes and ears out there on the streets, especially over Prospect. He had learned through Star that Prospect was the only spot in Charlottesville that hadn't been affected by the sell of their big dimes. Somehow, White-girl and Amanda stayed stride for stride with them. The weight they generated over Prospect was just enough to keep their customers from coming across town to seek out the famous dimes. She had told him that there was no question about it, White-girl and Amanda had Prospect on lock-down and they were running Prospect with an iron-fist! Malik really wanted to get at them now because he felt that they were using his paper to support their operation and hold Prospect down. They were competing with them to lock Charlottesville down and he didn't like it one bit.

Joey on the other hand had his own opinion of Amanda, it was all that much different from Malik because he to felt she had something to do with the robbery and he was also hearing how they had Prospect on lock-down. He figured that they used the paper to find a nice connect to keep the business going. What bothered him and kept him focused was that why Jacob would let Amanda and White-girl have all the shine while he continued to hustle on the strip? With Amanda giving Malik the cold shoulder, it was apparent that Silas had become their new connect. He was definitely capable of getting cocaine cheap from up-top and then sell it to Amanda and White-girl for a much cheaper price and that's why he hasn't been seen lately.

Silas seemingly had fallen off the planet at the time of the robbery, shit was starting to come together. He was also aware that Amanda and the boy Silas was now a couple and that further convinced him that all of them were in on it... Even White-girl. The other thing that bothered him about Amanda and Silas was that if he was so much in love with her then why would he have her out there on the front line like that? Then he remembered, typical out of town character... Use a bitch to show you around! Since they were out and about, Joey decided to bend the 4-corner's and drive through all the hot spots, even Prospect. Making a right onto Prospect from Bailey he drove slowly. Passing the bus stop he spotted a group gathered around apparently gambling. He didn't pay the dudes much attention until what Malik saw would forever change their lives as they knew it. "There he go right there...That's Silas over there in the middle of the crowd, pull the car over, pull over," demanded Malik!

Joey smiled, he asked Malik a question that he really already knew the answer to," you strapped?" And you know it homey, I stay strapped, vest and all, said Malik pulling out his glock .40 chambering a round! Joey was already planning their escape route as he drove slowly down Prospect. He knew with the amount of people out there, their get-a-way had to be swift. Bending a left near the Park, he decided to park there so it would leave them 30 seconds or less to get back to the car but far enough not to be spotted until it was too late. Let's be smart about this homey, there's a bunch of people out there already and best believe they'll be testifying against us if we get caught," said Joey killing the engine and chambering a round in his gun. "Fuck with me, all them mutha-fuckers will be corpses, fuck the bullshit! I counted at least 8 dudes out there so we'll assume that there's 8 hammers out there with them so be easy," added Malik checking to make sure his vest was completely strapped-up.

As Joey and Malik got closer to the dice game a few unsuspecting eyes locked in on them, yet they were blind to the fact of what was about to take place. For all they knew, Malik and Joey was there for the dice game, however, Silas was in the center of the circle crouched down on one knee watching the dice dance for him as he rolled for his point. The entire crowd was captivated by his dice skills he had long spotted both Malik and Joey when they drove by the first time. Without anybody noticing, he flipped the safety off his .45

Dessert Eagle, the sight of Malik and Joey left a sour taste in his mouth and he wasn't taking any chances. Had it not been for Amanda, he would've been gone over the Projects' to straighten Malik for all the constant calls to her phone. When she asked him to let her handle her own business on her own terms he reluctantly agreed, as long as he didn't have to actually deal with or see Malik on a regular basis he was cool with her handling it on her own. They were spending every waking moment together so he wasn't worried that she was playing him because she reminded him each and every night that her pussy belonged to him and him only! 'What the fuck is this little nigga doing over here,' he wondered?

Malik didn't waste a moment making his way into the center of the dice game meeting each harsh stare with one of his own. His murderous glare matched his murderous attitude, the robbery didn't sit well with him, and he wanted some get back! Charlottesville was just big enough to stay out of each other's way but at the same time you wouldn't have a problem finding someone if you knew where to look. All the dudes on top of Prospect either knew or heard of who Malik and Joey was through the way they were handling their business all over Charlottesville. They were quickly becoming hood legends and everybody knew it. Malik wasn't only known for the big weight he sold in the dimes but by the way he treated out of towners of late was something to really write home and tell momma. He became the talk of the city in no time. "I got a hundred the dice lose," said Malik dropping a crispy hundred dollar bill on the pavement.

Silas didn't bother looking up or taking his eyes off the dice, he spoke slow and calm," all we shooting is Ten dollar's big time," laughing at his own joke.

"Ain't nobody ask you what you was shooting, I said I got a hundred the dice lose, from the looks of it, you got the dice so miss me with that slick shit.

You out here beating these little niggaz for they re-up, but if you're scared to lose a few dollars...I'll definitely understand, small time," spit Malik kicking the hundred dollar bill closer to Silas. "Fuck it, if you need some paper to shoot with, keep that hundred. There's plenty where that came from," he said pulling out a stack of Ten thousand in hundreds smiling.

He was certain to show the whole crowd that he was holding some real paper for the dice game and now it was Silas turn to make a move. Nobody except Joey had seen Amanda who was standing about 20 feet away doing her own thang when she heard a familiar voice coming from the crowd. It was a voice she knew well, a voice she use to love to hear. She wondered how the hell he managed to walk right past her.

She was dressed in all black, black jeans, black hoodie, black Jordans, standing between two parked cars in the driveway. If you didn't look close she would fool you into believing she was one of the fellas, but if you looked closer, her beauty gave her away to who she really was.

Joey watched her ease over to the crowd, he watched her watch Malik! She knew Silas hated Malik because she didn't make it a secret that she used to deal with him on that level and it didn't sit well with him. Plus Malik had been calling her even when she told him that she didn't want to be bothered. It was hell for her but she managed to make it happen, she finally convinced Silas Malik was a distant memory of her past life. She sucked and fucked her way into Silas mind letting him know that she had no intentions of reliving her past with Malik! She watched from a safe distance as Silas humbled himself and accept Malik's offer to shoot dice for a hundred a game. To her it seemed that Silas wasn't just shooting dice against Malik, he was shooting dice for the love of his life as he poured his everything into the game. They were left to shoot head-up, nobody else bothered to get in their way; they wanted to see what the outcome would be. Amanda looked up and that's when she saw Joey, they locked eyes but neither smiled. She seen a look in his eyes that she's never seen before and hadn't it not been for Silas being out there with her, she would've been scared.

The dice game started out going back and forth, Malik would win a few rolls and Silas would come right back and do the same thing. Silas remained silent,

Malik talked big shit whether he hit his point or crapped out. When the time came back around for Malik to roll the dice he decided to up the ante dropping 5 crispy hundred dollar bills on the pavement. He was tired of going back and forth with the small change; the hundred dollars was only bait to get him where he really wanted him. "Shoot Five," he said scooling the dice!

Silas dropped his Five to the pavement with no problem. Malik's next roll was a seven, he won! He then left the entire pot on the pavement," shoot the grand!" He must've felt it because he was now on a roll; he hit his next 8 points, winning on the come-out half of the time. Never picking up the paper, he had a nice stack on the pavement at his feet as he went into over drive and clowning Silas at the same time.

"Somebody better get'em, I'm ready to break this nigga for everything he got, re-up and all! Bet two grand nigga," spit Malik! He hit his point within 3 rolls.

For the first time in a long time Silas was on the losing end of a dice game. Losing six thousand to Malik didn't sit well with him; he only had two hundred left on him. He looked over at Malik and said," I'll be right back, I gotta get more paper," getting up from his one knee.

"Yeah...Yeah, you do that nigga. Matter of fact, bring your whole stash out here, I'll be more than happy to talk that shit off your hands since you don't know what to do with your paper." Malik took 5 hundred dollar bills at a time and started throwing them in the crowd of onlookers. He did that three times then said firmly, "niggaz from the Projects' always look out," then he started laughing uncontrollable.

"Miss me with your bullshit little nigga," said Silas getting frustrated! Amanda saw his nostrils flare-up and knew he was mad, she had to do something. She stepped from behind the crowd and walked over to him," hey baby," she said kissing him on the lips. She handed him a stack that looked just like the one Malik started out with, "do you baby," as she fell back in the shadows of the crowd.

The look on his face seemed to be getting worse than before she handed him the paper and she couldn't figure out why? "I'm good Ma'," he said grabbing her by the arm before she got to far away from him.

"Damn, if it ain't Ms. Prospect All-Day, and All-night, Amanda," said Malik as he invaded her personal space attempting to hug her.

She moved quickly to evade his touch, "don't put your fuckin' hands on me, Malik," she spit with venom in her voice!

Malik took two steps backwards and smiled, "oh, my bad, how can I forget?" He took out two more hundred and tossed it on the pavement at her feet, "time is paper for you, there you go, now bring yo' ass over here and let me see you bitch, with them damn sexy devil eyes of yours," he said still laughing.

The moment Silas heard him call her a bitch it sent him into a rage that he couldn't control; he wanted to get at Malik, "don't call her out her name no more!" By doing to much talking, he made the fatal mistake of getting too close to Malik as he tried to get between him and Amanda. He put his hand on Malik's midsection trying to stop him from getting any closer to Amanda.

He missed the slight grin on Malik's face because he was too busy thinking about what he wanted to do. Malik hit him with what them Project dudes call a 'fast-ball.' It's a classic one-two combination to the chin, the power from the punches sat Silas flat on his ass in a daze.

He fought the temptation to go out, he couldn't figure out for the life of him how he ended up on the pavement when just a second ago he was standing protecting his ole' lady?

The crowd was now in an up-roar and that's what brought him around to what happened, the crowd was saying,' Malik got'em another one...He knocked his ass out!'

He never saw the punches coming, when he looked over at Amanda, the look she had on her face let him know what he had to do to even the odds. He reached into his jacket ready to pull out his pistol from its shoulder holster when he felt a cold piece of steel on the left side of his temple. It stopped him from trying to draw his pistol, he knew what was happening, then he heard a voice," I wouldn't do that if I was you." The voice sounded like Malik but he was still standing in front of him laughing and looking down at him. He cursed himself for not following his gut feeling, something told him that Malik wasn't alone but since he couldn't spot anybody who didn't look like they belonged in the crowd he let it ride. His mind went back to the passing car,' shit, it was two of them in the car!'

Amanda started screaming at the sight of Joey with a gun to Silas temple," Malik, you's a pussy...Why you had to steal'em? You a pussy, you and your boy with the gun, ya'll pussy. This man up here by himself and ya'll go jump him like that," she continued to scream louder and louder. She wasn't anybody's fool, the louder she got, the closer she came to Malik as she slipped her straight razor from her forearm under her hoodie.

By the time she figured she was close enough to strike, the distance was perfect. She swung a lazy right at Malik's face ready to rip it to shreds; she knew she had him because he was caught up in the ruckus and still laughing at Silas while he tried to gather himself. Catching her out the corner of his eye he ducked right in time able to miss the damage of the straight razor. His reaction forced him to throw the same fast-ball punch, catching her square on the button. Unlike her man Silas, her small frame collapsed to the pavement, she was out cold before she hit the ground landing right on Silas!

"Bitch, stay in your place," said Malik spitting on her. Silas had to do something, the rage in him forced him to reach for the pistol but Joey caught him two times with the butt of his pistol sending his body crumbling back down next to Amanda! He was sleep and snoring before he even knew what hit him, again. Malik saw the opportunity, he walked over to Amanda and pulled all the cash she had on her from her pockets and spit on her again. Stupid bitch, I bet you won't be stealing from me no fuckin' more!"

Joey wanted to know why Silas kept reaching in his jacket and for caution, he slid his hand inside the jacket feeling the pistol in a shoulder holster, he relieved him of his pistol. He didn't touch the two hundred that was still on the ground next to him, when he looked up, a police car was screeching up the block from Bailey. "We gotta bounce," he said to Malik as they walked off as if nothing had happened. When they got to the car, Joey jumped behind the wheel headed back across town to the Projects. You know we just started something, don't you," grinned Joey?

"We ain't start shit! We just answered the call...Fuck it, I'm glad it's on. Next time I see dude, I don't have to hesitate, him, Jacob, or the bitch Amanda...It's shoot first, shoot second and then shoot some more until they gone," said Malik feel good.

Joey drove across Main street and down 10th Street before he said a word, "you know I'm with you, regardless! Shit gotta change though, all that hanging out for nothing has to stop. We take care of our business with caution but other than that, we gotta be on our P's and Q's!"

The police pulled-up near the crowd that had gathered around Silas and Amanda as they were being helped up. The officer was trying to be over friendly, "excuse me young lady, are you okay," he asked looking over at Silas? Amanda rolled her eyes at the officer as she and Silas made it to their feet. She eyed the officer with contempt and if he wasn't the police, she would've tried him with her straight razor, but she knew she didn't have a win.

They walked across the street arm in arm helping to balance each other," I can't believe that he hit me like that, he hit me like I was a nigga." Silas got the both of them ice packs when they got inside, "put this on your mouth," he said looking at her injuries. They reminded him of how that rapper who was in that bad accident talked and she was swelling fast. He couldn't make eye contact with her because he felt like he let her down. He was steaming mad on the inside; there was only one thing that could cure how he felt, Murder! It was all his fault and he didn't protect his ole' lady, that was unacceptable to him and to make matters worse, he allowed another dude to knock her out. Having Malik almost knock him out too, that shit depressed him. He was already thinking of getting his revenge, often serve best cold! Instinct made him pat for his gun but it was gone. Realizing that either Malik or his partner had taken his pistol, he really felt embarrassed now...That's almost the worst thing that could happen to you in the hood outside of being murdered, getting knocked out and having your pistol taken.

He watched from the corner of his eye as Amanda lay back on the sofa, she was obliviously in a great deal of pain, she could barely let the ice touch her face because it was so sore. "Baby, you want to go to the hospital?"

Amanda slung the ice pack across the room in frustration, "the hospital? You gotta be kidding me right? I'm ready to murder this nigga, that's what the fuck I want to do!"

Silas hung his head low because he knew that everything that happened to her was his fault, "you don't mean that, you're just angry. You can't take murder back, once it's done your fate will change," he said looking into her eyes. His stare met his and he saw something in those beautiful eyes that he's never seen before. It was the same murderous look he used to see in Sosa's eyes when they caught their first body. "You're serious ain't you?"

She shook her head up and down," yes! I dead serious and I'll make sure that I get that nigga if it's the last thing I ever do, he's going to pay for that shit."

White-girl and Jacob were on their way back from the country from making a run for Amanda and Silas when they got the call from one of the youngins from on top of the hill, he was also in on the robbery so he knew how to contact Jacob with ease. Jacob listened closely as the youngin told him all the details about the run in between Silas and Malik, the youngin didn't leave out anything! "Did they say anything about the robbery," asked Jacob as he continued to listen and shake his head up and down occasionally?

"Good, is she a-ight? What about dude, what he do? Word! A-ight, so they in the crib now. I'm on my way over there now, make sure you stay low and out the way, I'll holla at you when I get back to Prospect...One!"

White-girl was behind the wheel driving but all of her attention was focused in on what Jacob was talking about and she wondered who he was talking to.

Straining to hear their conversation, she couldn't hear but so much because the music was a tad to loud, she turned it down some. She figured whatever was being said had to be important, his body language was uneasy and he kept his answers short and to the point. She knew him all to well, something bad had to have happened, she was sure of her ability to have him spill his guts to her in due time; that's just what she did! When the timing was right, she would trick him into telling her everything, even without her having to ask the most direct questions.

From her observation of Jacob, she learned quickly, he couldn't hold water. She's been letting him fuck her every now and then, so she knew what she had to do to get the information she desired, she just did it a couple of weeks ago. She tricked him into telling her about the robbery with Malik, she played her part perfectly. She acted liked she didn't already know what happened, from that moment, she knew she had him eating out the palm of her hand. What really let her know that she had his mind was that she could make him suck her pussy for hours and never let him stick the head of his dick inside of her…She had him! He was her little whore and didn't even know it, she allowed his to think that he was blowing her back out and that's why she gave him free CRACK or cheaper prices, however, she had her own agenda but she needed him to pull this off.

He reclined in the passenger seat as he ended his call, he had to close his eyes in order to think clearly. She cut her eyes over at him briefly but she didn't bother him, she wanted him to feel important, she knew her advantage was; Patience! That was something he lacked and she was sure of it.

He was mentally going over the possible outcome with what happened between; Joey, Malik, Amanda, and Silas in his head. He knew for certain that Silas wasn't pussy, he wouldn't let that shit ride, now all he had to do was make sure that he was the last man standing. Somebody would definitely get bodied, some will go to prison, and the others will walk away from the life style because of the trauma inflicted upon their minds and bodies. He believed that he could ease in the number one spot if this played out the way he was thinking and if it did, he could take over both the Projects and Prospect at the same time.

Charlottesville would be in an uproar if the cocaine dried up, it was an opportunity that he couldn't' pass up. Unknowing, a smile crept across his face! "What the hell you're over the smiling about baby?" she asked placing her hand on her hand on his dick.

"Huh? Oh..I...I was just thinking about your fine ass, that's all," he said making her hand get a firm grip on his dick! She looked away and in her mind she was saying,' here it comes!' It didn't take 2 minutes before he started talking and spilling the beans, "my little youngin told me that Joey and Malik just got into it with Amanda and Silas on top of the hill."

That's wasn't what she expected to hear, she knew that a run-in like that couldn't have ended up good, she took out her phone and dialed Amanda's number, "damn, what the fuck happened? Fuck the bullshit, I gotta call my sista," she said looking away from him. "Hey girrrl, what's going on up there," she asked?

Joey's first stop when they got back across town was down on Page to check on Auntie Pam. From the looks of things, things were moving smoothly, Auntie and Jazzy was standing out front directing all the traffic and Auntie Pam was on the side of the house meeting the CRACK demand. It appeared to be at the very least 25 cars parked back to back and another group of people walking, all there to get that big dime, now commonly referred to as, 'Pig-nuts!'

"This bitch is jumpin', I see mutha-fuckers' from all over Charlottesville, Waynesboro, and Gordonsville. It's some mutha-fucker's I don't even know," said Joey.

Malik shook his head at the sight of all them people, "it's all good as long as the sun is shining but at the same time, this shit got us sticking out like a sissy in a locker room." Joey was impressed by the way Malik was turning into a much better thinker and wasn't so gun-ho as he use to be. He was calm, cautious, and poised all at the same time. He was starting to get spoiled by the paper in a good way, it was now starting to matter to him and he wanted to hold on to it for as long as he could.

Time was limited in this game and they both were aware of that fact, everybody pays the piper at some point. For them, the paper was only a means to the end, however, with the recent events, the scales were beginning to tilt against them and Joey knew it. All eyes were on them as they got out the car, especially Jazzy. Since the robbery, she had proven herself over and over again through her many sexual favors for Malik. She was all smiles and happy to see him, he'd been fucking her almost every night for the last month. He smacked her on the ass real hard and said, "get that paper for daddy!"

"And you know it, I wouldn't have it any other way," she said beaming with pride.

Joey's phone started ringing and he looked down at it noticing that it was Terri calling, he put a little pep in his step as he made his way up on the porch, into the house. He was able to answer by the forth ring.

"Hello, yeah, what's up baby?" he asked adjusting his phone on his shoulder.

"Umm yeah, he's with me now. A-ight, give us about an hour, for real, one hour and we'll be there," he said laughing into the phone. Malik came in at the end of his conversation with her and he just had to ask, "we'll be where?" Joey didn't answer his question he kept doing what he was doing, then Malik said, "yo, we gotta do something about Auntie Pam and them. We can't just leave them over here like this, they'll be sitting ducks."

Joey was already packing a duffel bag full of shit, a scale, CRACK, paper, baggies, and a few other items they would need. As he looked down in the duffel bag he thought about what exactly was in the bag, it screamed one of two things: You're a dealer or a User! "We're shutting down shop, give Auntie Pam one ounce so she can do her with it and ask her where she wants to go because she can't stay here. She can get a room or whatever, I ain't really worried about nobody doing nothing to her as long as she's not here, so the choice is hers, but we gotta go anyway...Terri want us to meet her at the Double-Tree in an hour." It took close to twenty minutes before everybody was ready to leave Page at the same time, Auntie Pam, Jazzy, and Auntie jumped in a cab while Joey and Malik drove off. The entire ride to the Double-Tree was in silence, each locked into their own thoughts of the events that have taken place over the last few hours.

The one thing that the both of them thought about was that they were going to play this game to win by any means necessary!

Recalling his conversation with Terri, Joey thought she sounded like she was pressing him to get to her as quickly as possible, had she used their code word for emergency he would've been ready to run up in there with 2 guns blazing but she didn't use the code word. However, she still sounded unlike herself, something wasn't right but he didn't have a clue as to what it was if anything? Pulling into the parking lot, his eyes began scanning the area for danger, when he drove around the parking lot several times; it was now time to go up-stairs. He braced himself as he entered the room expecting the worse, his eyes immediately searched the room for a surprise but there was none. He finally exhaled once he saw a smiling Terri looking beautiful.

Tiffany was on the side of the bed, out of sight from Malik and Joey, and once they closed the door behind them, she jumped out and screamed," surprise!" Malik broke out with the biggest smile ever, he couldn't believe his eyes. He hadn't seen her for 5 weeks since she been in rehab. No visits, phone calls, or mail from her while she was away. When she went in she told him that she wasn't going to contact him until she got her shit together and from the way she was looking and the way he looked at her, she had her shit together. She ran and jumped in his arms. "Damn baby, you look sooo good," he said not wanting to let go of his embrace. He pushed her away from him so that he could get a better view of her body; he turned her in a complete circle. With both hands on her hips she smiled and said," oh, that you Malik, I gained about 15 pounds but that's not the most important thing that I've gained….I've regained my self-respect back," with the proudest look on her face. She was really happy; she had accomplished a lot in such a short period of time.

Malik couldn't take his eyes off of her only to glance over at her and mumble a silent, 'Thank-you.'

"Damn Tiffany, you're beautiful, I'm so happy for you, I feel like I went away and accomplished something. However, I do have one question for you; what made you do it? You know, get clean?"

She looked at Terri, pondering over that question since her second day in rehab, in her mind, she knew the reason, but telling Malik why was a whole other story. She knew him so well she knew that question was going to come once she left rehab and that's why she's been thinking about it for so long. How would she tell him? Although she had rehearsed her answer over and over in her head, she even practiced in the mirror once or twice. Yet, nothing could prepare her for the real thing, even when she told Terri what she would say it was easier. Terri nodded for her to proceed with what she had to say. This was by far one of the hardest things she's ever had to do in her life, her palms were moist and it felt like her knees were shaking, her heart was beating a million miles per second. She closed her eyes and then opened them only to stare Malik in his eyes as she exhaled real slowly.

"Before I even get to your question Malik, I want to thank you Terri for believing in me and helping me see who I was when I couldn't see myself...Thank you from the bottom of my heart, but you already know that! And thanks to you Joey for even allowing me to hang out with your wifey when I was fucked up, because quiet as kept, had you said you didn't want her around me one time, none of this would've happened to me, so thank you my brother."

She walked over and hugged both Terri and Joey as she made her way back over to Malik. She kissed him lightly on the lips. "Now, for the love of my life, that's a very good question. I knew you would ask me that, I even told Terri you would. I've practiced over and over how I would answer your question but none of that's working, I'll just tell you the way it is. Malik, I'm pregnant, I'm 8 weeks and I couldn't continue harming myself much less my baby, I just couldn't do it," she said as she put her head down as if she had been defeated.

"Now, before you even ask me, it's definitely your baby, you're going to be a father Malik, this baby is yours," she said crying. To say he was blindsided by the news would be an understatement, he almost fell out.

He also had a smile bigger than the one he had when he first saw her on his face, and it was growing by the second. "Come here girl and give your baby daddy a kiss," he said laughing real loud. "I love you girl, always have."

White-girl had remained calm as she got the details from Amanda about what happened on top of Prospect. From what she was hearing kinda matched Jacob's body actions and non-response to her questions. It was cool with her because it gave her a reason to drop him off without having to take him back up to Prospect with her.

Jacob sat and I listened to the details that Amanda was willing to give up on the phone, he could hear her clearly, however, Amanda was smart, she wasn't saying but so much on the phone. There was no way that he was getting in the middle of this thing between Amanda, Silas, Joey, and Malik, it was just something he couldn't afford to be a part of. His only hope was that this Silas character would go on a mission killing both Joey and Malik, that way it would I keep him from having to murder either one of them because he knew for certain that if they I found out about the robbery, he wouldn't have any other choice but to kill one of them or I be killed. When she told him that she was dropping him off that was music to his ears, he quickly told her that he wanted to be dropped off down Tonsler Park. That way he was far enough away from Prospect and close enough to the Projects', both spots was within walking distance for him.

"I'm cool with that, you can drop me off down the park," he said looking over at White-girl smiling. "Tell Amanda I hope she's alright!" White-girl rushed up the steps into the apartment hoping that the image she had of what she thought Amanda looked like wasn't accurate, for once she was hoping that she was wrong about how bad thangs was.

She found Amanda in her bedroom lying on her bed, "Amanda! Do you need to go to the hospital or something? What happened? Where's Silas? What can I do to help," she said firing question after question? She managed to get all that out without missing a beat!

Amanda was clearly happy to see her girl, however, when she tried to smile, the pain was too much to bear, moving her jaw was now becoming impossible.

The pain was excruciating! "I'm good girl, my damn jaw hurts like hell, but I'll live," she said as she kept trying to open and close her mouth.

White-girl found a comfortable spot on the bed next to her, "so what's the deal? What are we going to do about this shit," asked White-girl needing to know what was up with her man Silas? She knew that he was a man of pride and if he was in love with her the way he always was claiming, she knew he would have to react.

On cue, Silas came out the spare room to answer her question first hand, he looked at her with a strange look in his eyes but she didn't pay him no mind. "I got this! Ya'll sit back and let me handle this shit, this is what I do," he said standing to leave. He bent down in front of Amanda and kissed her on her forehead, "I love you girl!"

Amanda knew this super-man bullshit was coming and she wasn't really trying to hear it," there you go with that shit, I told you a million times that I'm a big girl, I can take care of myself. I'm not sitting around here waiting on you to do something that I can very well do for myself. It's either we do this shit together or you go your way and I'll go mines," she said looking him dead in his eyes to let him know how serious she was!

Silas felt himself getting more frustrated by the second but he had never had to make this type of decision before, he didn't know how to really react to what she was saying. In his mind he knew she was serious, but the problem with that was he's never had another partner outside of Sosa, and to him murder was a tough thing to digest. How could he deny her the opportunity to have her revenge? He wondered if she could really do it and live with herself after the fact. The killing wasn't the problem; most people got caught because they couldn't stand the nightmares that came with that game. Will she go and spill her guts to the authorities when it gets rough? Those were just a few thoughts he was having, what he had in mind for Malik and Joey involved much more than putting a bullet in their head, he wanted to torture them for days until they begged him to kill them. Can she handle that?

The one thing he had to admit was that she has proven herself to him countless of times with her self-driven character and her willingness to do whatever the situation called for, she wanted to be the top dog and she knew it came with making life or death decisions. He tried his best not to allow his personal feelings and emotions cloud his vision, this was the CRACK game and rule number one; there are no rules!

Amanda was sharp, somebody had schooled her along her travels, she was fully aware one slip could cost her her life, who was he to make such an important decision for her? The major conflict was not even her, but rather her partner White-girl, over the last couple of days he watched her closely. When he first met Amanda, White-girl was green as grass but lately, she seemed to be the brains and the driving force behind their operation. That puzzled him. The more paper they got, the more White-girl called the shots! He didn't want to be the one to throw shade on their party, and he knew Amanda needed her road-dog by her side now more than ever.

She was always at Amanda's beckon call, but what was her motivates? To much was going through his head, he needed some time and air to think about all of this. "Babe, I'll be back in a couple of hours, I gotta go check on something, call me if you need me," he said walking out the room.

She closed her eyes and shook her head back and forth, she was also frustrated. She was tired of how he was acting and she had enough of him for the time being. Without having to say it, she was happy to see him leave; she wanted to talk to her girl in private anyway. "White-girl, I'm telling you that something was real strange about how Joey and Malik just happened to pop-up over here tonight. That shit ain't like them at all, they ain't built like that! Malik's a fighter, I'll give him that, but where the gun-play comes in at? Joey's too smart to be walking around Charlottesville strapped and he's damn sure not letting Malik's crazy-ass do it. When he hit me, that shit hurt like hell, he thought he knocked me out but he didn't, I knew I didn't have no wind and if I just stayed down I was hoping that he wouldn't stomp me out. I heard him talking about I stole something from him and then I could feel his ass going through my pockets, he took some of my paper too! The funny thing is that Joey's gun came out way before Malik's and he's the calm one. Something bought them over here, they was ready for war, now I have to find out why they were over here? Regardless of why they were here, that nigga punched me in my face like I was a dude and he's going to pay for that! If that's the last thing I do in life, that nigga gonna know that that was the biggest mistake of his life." She was more determined than she's ever been in her whole life!

White-girl sat there at the end of Amanda's bed holding her hand and listening to her tell her story. She had to admit to Amanda was on point, however, she remained silent. It took a patient ear to listen and not say what was on her mind. She saw no need in mentioning the fact that Jacob was introduced to a female friend of hers who planted the idea in his head to rob Malik, it would be meaningless and pointless! The one thing she hated most about what she was doing was to do something counter-productive to what her original plans were. Knowing that Amanda was sharp and on point, she knew with the proper amount of time, Amanda would soon come to figure things out and piece this shit together on her own and that's why she would make her next move her best move.

Silas pulled onto Run Street in the Projects' so that he could stop and holla at Angie. It's been a few days since he's last spoken to her, but his real motivation was knowing she was able to get some information and use her house at the same time to creep around the Projects' without being noticed to much. His mind was set when the time came if he was to see either Joey or Malik, it was kill on sight! He walked through her back door and she was at the kitchen table, she smiled, happy to see him. "Hey stranger, haven't seen your sexy-ass in a minute, she said. She got up from the table to give him a big hug as well. Even though she wanted to ask him a million questions she didn't, she played her position to the tee! Come sit down and try this shit, it's bangin', she said passing him a bill full of dope. He observed the dope on the bill, the off-white substance looked good to him, it was something he needed at that point, he sniffed once, then twice and looked back at her," where you get this?"

CHAPTER 18

MALIK and Tiffany were beginning to settle into their room at the Double Tree, the funny thing about the two of them was that they were unable to take their eyes off the other. Malik couldn't keep from smiling, for once in a long time; his life seemed to start making sense. He sat back and listened to her as she talked, he was in a zone from how her body had transformed in such a short time, he loved it! Even before she went to rehab he thought she looked good, but now that was an understatement. Her face had gotten fatter, her hips and ass was incredible; he couldn't take his eyes off her ass. Deep down he loved himself some Tiffany, especially now that she's gotten herself together. She caught him staring at her ass on more than one occasion since they got into their room. His eyes would dart away from her ass up to her chest and back down to her ass. She was wondering if he could really see the difference in her body because at first she couldn't tell herself and doubted that she was really pregnant. However, she was met with that famous lustful look in his eyes that she had grown accustomed to, but for some reason, they looked even gentler. It was now clear that he wanted her and she didn't mind him wanting her, she wanted him as well,' damn that man looks good,' she said to herself. She had to focus her mind on what was in front of her because he was starting to look like something to eat to her, her mind was in the gutter and she knew it but there was nothing she could do about it.

"So, tell me about rehab," he asked?

She was happy to be talking about rehab, anything to get her mind out the gutter," it was cool! They had us taking all kinds of test, right off the bat they tested us for everything you could imagine. HIV, Aids, breast cancer, you name it they tested for it. Shit, they even tested us for sugar," she said laughing at herself.

She couldn't take it any longer, the counselors in rehab had told her not to rush into having sex even when she wanted it, they said not to start any serious relationships for a while, 90 meetings in 90 days! She could hear them in her head as they explained why wait, but she had her own agenda, plus, Malik wasn't a new relationship, he was her baby's father, that had to count for something. She walked over to him and held his face in her hands as she spoke slowly to him, "when I had to take that last test, the pregnancy test? I was scared as hell, something in me was already telling me I was pregnant but I didn't want to believe it but I knew. I thought back to us and how we never used protection, I was begging for a reason to get out of getting high and I knew that being pregnant would be that reason, I like to believe that I wished it into being," she said smiling.

"When they told me I was pregnant, well, my first thought was how could I explain to you not just that I'm pregnant but you're the baby's father? You know with me out here getting high and all that, that's what really scared me," she was saying rubbing her stomach!

For some odd reason, he had a doubtful look on his face but in his head, he knew he was the baby's father; he could hear Auntie Pam in his ear now. She saw the look to, and wanted to address it but he said something that would change everything. The look she had was so intense and he hasn't seen that look in such a long time that he knew he had to be there for her no matter what the outcome would be. "You ain't gotta worry, I got you baby!"

"I didn't know how you'd react. You know, with me getting high and all that shit, but the reality of my life started playing right in front of me. Everything I've ever done, every major decision I've ever made has involved you, and you're always the driving force behind everything I do in my life. I've done a lot of stupid shit to gain your attention, and I would have done anything to see you smile, even now, but the only difference now is that you're no longer number one in my life. Sorry, you'll have to take a back seat to our baby, you're a strong number two, but my life now has to be centered on this baby and not just you! I love you with all my heart, but my life is no longer mines to live recklessly, there's a life growing inside of me and this life is bigger than you and me. I will do everything in my power to make this baby's life easier than our life. No more CRACK for me, EVER, she said with force in her voice! She had to gather herself, stepping away from him and sitting on the edge of the bed fighting back tears that she refused to shed. She wanted him to say something but there was nothing for him to say, she had spoken and laid down the law. He just sat there and stared into her eyes. His intense stare was too much for her, she folded under the pressure and the flood gates to her tears flowed freely down her face.

He was frozen stiff by her powerful choice of words, he knew her pain fist hand, he even agreed that mostly all the pain she felt and inflicted upon herself was to make him happy all the While abandoning her own feelings. He made her jump through all types of hoops to be with him and every time she jumped and jumped higher and higher, and he admired her for taking the first step in the right direction. There was no way he would leave her now. Who was he to place judgment on her life? "Tiff, don't cry baby, I'm here for you and my baby, I'm here every step of the way," he said kneeling down in between her legs. He wiped her tears away," they say that a journey of a thousand miles starts with the first step, and I must say that you've definitely taken the first step, now let's take the rest of them together!"

She embraced him tightly, her heart fluttered, "Malik, we need you, I've always needed you but I'm telling you right now, I will not compromise the health of this baby growing inside of me. Not for you and definitely not for me, not now and not ever." His phone started vibrating on his hip just as they kissed each other. He had the mind to ignore the vibrating phone but his instincts told him otherwise. He looked at the number and at first didn't recognize it, but then figured out that it was Star's number. He had to answer now! "Yeah, what's good? I hope you got something good for me at this hour. Word! Keep that on ice for me, I'm on my way as we speak," he said before hanging up.

Everything about him had just transformed before her very eyes, he went from smiling to putting his game face on and that's when she knew that whoever was on the other end of the call had something if now everything to do with his business in the streets. He quickly stood-up strapping on his bullet proof vest as he grabbed his twin .40 Calibers'. "Babe, I gotta go, get yourself some rest. I'll be back later," he said bending down and kissing her on the forehead.

Just like that he was gone, the streets were calling and he had to respond. She just looked at him and could only hope that the lord will protect him! He was banging on Joey's door like he was the police. He wanted to hurry, that was the call he's been waiting for. Joey opened the door to see his comrade dressed and ready for war, "what's wrong, homey?"

Malik smiled, "it ain't what's wrong, but rather what's right! I just got the call; we got the 411 on your boy Silas. He's in the Projects' right now; he's at Angie's spot. If he's in the Projects' you know what that shit means, he's even asking questions about us. I say we go and handle this dude before he gets a chance to know what's happening."

Joey shut the door leaving Malik standing in the hallway. It took him all of 4 minutes before he returned fully dressed in his war gear: black on black everything! His black on black P89 Ruger's even matched his outfit. "You right, we gotta go handle this fool, ain't no way we can allow him in our hood and asking questions about us! If he's looking for us in the Projects, that can only mean one thing. You ready for this Malik, ain't no turning back after tonight, "said Joey making sure his own vest was tight?

Before he could close the door good, Terri was on the phone dialing Tiffany's room to check and see what she was doing. She welcomed their new sista-hood, she now had someone she could really talk to other than the girls she went to school with. She didn't have to pretend when she was with Tiffany, the fear was now gone and she didn't have to worry about revealing her man's business. "Hey girl, I'm on my way down there," she said into the phone even before Tiffany could object! Truth be told, Tiffany was sitting there thinking about whether or not she should call her but Terri beat her to the punch. She didn't want to intrude on her personal business since Terri has already done so much to help her, but she was happy that she called, she didn't want to be alone.

Opening the door she greeted Terri with a hug, "I see he got Joey to leave with him, huh? I'm sorry Terri; Malik does that all the time."

Terri gave her another hug," girl, what they do together ain't your fault or mines, that's just what they do! I'm use to it now, even before I was supposed to know what he did to earn his money, he would up and leave. I never got in his way then and I didn't have you then, so I'm definitely not getting in his way now. Just remember, and you know better than me, we signed up for this shit," Terri said laughing! "I know that's right," said Tiffany giving her a high-five! "You hungry? We can hit up the Pancake House if you want?" "Hungry? Girl, I stay hungry. Let's bounce," said Tiffany rubbing her stomach!

———————————————————————————————————————

Silas sat back on the sofa sniffin' dope like his mind was gone bad, uninterested in what was going on right in front of him. With Angie and Star in the 69 position butt-ass naked with Angie munching down on Star's pussy like it was the last supper, his thoughts were on Amanda. He was beating himself up pretty bad about what happened. He wished he handled the situation differently, had he done something before they approached the dice game perhaps he could have avoided the mental embarrassment of being knocked-out, having his pistol taken and having his ole' lady receiving the same treatment. With the loud and persistent moans coming from both Angie and Star it forced his to look. Angie had 4 fingers in Star's pussy with her thumb in her ass-hole. Star looked like she was in heaven! Star knew from Angie's bragging about his dick size that she really wanted to give it a try and see what he was working with," bring that monster dick over here and fuck my face," she managed to say. Angie had another plan for her, she started fucking her pussy rough and Star couldn't take it much longer, the pleasure was just too good. Oh shit, Angie, Angie, I'm fuckin' cuming right now, ahhh, Lord Jesus, Jesus, Jesus; stop it. Stop it, you're killing me," Star begged, drunk from the pleasure Angie was causing to her body!

"Shut the fuck up bitch! I'm going to make this pussy cum over and over until he tell me to stop, she managed to say with a mouth full of Star's pussy as her cum flowed down her throat. Angie wouldn't stop, she now had damn near her whole hand inside of Star's pussy stretching it beyond belief. I said make that pussy cum again," she said forcefully.

Watching as Star's eyes roll in the back of her head from the pleasure she was receiving from Angie's tongue, she almost regretted being there and agreeing to this situation. She almost forgot how good Angie ate pussy. She looked over just in time to see Silas get up from the sofa and head up-stairs. That was her cue to get Angie to take a break, because she was punishing her pussy. Up-stairs Silas found what he was looking for, his Desert Eagle .45. He was happy that he decided to stash a pistol over there, now all he needed was his vest, but he left that over Amanda's apartment. Now, he had to slightly alter his plan to roam around the Projects', he had to use caution without his vest. The show was good and under normal circumstances he would've joined the pair, but not tonight, he had something bigger on his mind and it didn't involve sex. He had to get out that house!

He came back down-stairs just in time to see Angie and Star trading positions, now since the tables were turned, it was Star causing Angie to scream and moan in pleasure. Star had her legs spread wide with a huge double-head dildo with half the dildo in her pussy and the other half deep in her ass-hole. Now Angie was begging but she wasn't begging for her to stop, she wanted Star to stick the dildo in deeper and fuck her with it even harder! That was enough to catch his attention as he watched Angie's ass-hole swallow a good 9 inches of the dildo. With the dope starting to take affect he caught himself nodding right there at the door, he was forced to lean against the wall to gather himself. With all that was going on right there in front of him, he couldn't stay; he had to get out that house. Knowing that Amanda was over Prospect banged-up pretty good he couldn't enjoy the show. A month or two ago yeah, he would have quickly dismissed his thoughts of Amanda but tonight he couldn't. He was in love!

The only thing that he had to look forward to was getting back at Joey and Malik for hurting her, but at the present he would settle for just roaming the Projects', it was always live and reminded him of back home in Newark. He needed something to take his mind off of Amanda without having to feel guilty about it and involving himself in a threesome was out the question. His best hope was to catch Malik or Joey out there slippin, that was a long shot but he's seen worse odds and come out on top. Relaxed and confident, he was ready to catch some reck as he eased out the house into the warm night air. The change in climates caused him to call Earl after his first 3 steps outside. 'Damn, I'm high as a mutha-fucker,' he whispered to himself. For him being high only meant that he was that much more on point than if he wasn't so he didn't hesitate going about his business. He really welcomed the intense high of dope. Easing a Newport out, he took a long drag blowing out the smoke, he got light headed for a second.

Sticking a piece of big red gum in his mouth, he was now feeling good and ready. He added an extra bounce to his step, extra up-top style his walk said, Fuck You!

There was a group gathered at the top of the first driveway, it was evident to him that a dice gaming was in progress. 'Not another dice game,' he thought as he felt the comfort of his Desert Eagle. With his eyes darting all over the place, he scanned every face in the crowd, relieved that none of those there was either Malik or Joey, he relaxed abit. When he noticed a familiar face he really relaxed, it was Jacob from Prospect. He knew he was good; at least one person would be on his side in case something went sideways. Having an ally was something he needed. He took another long drag off his cigarette as he blew smoke rings into the air as he stepped off the curb ready to cross the driveway and holla at Jacob.

He wondered if Jacob had seen either Malik or Joey. Just as his foot hit the pavement of the parking lot he had to cross 3 shots rang out in succession. One of the bullets found its mark hitting him in his shoulder sending him spinning 180 degrees. Instinct kicked in, he cursed himself for not having his vest. He went to pull his pistol but the pain in his right shoulder was too intense, he couldn't lift his right arm.

He turned to run back towards Angie's and away from the shots, more shots followed him barely missing his head. The missed shots were plunging into the bricks sending dust everywhere, whoever was shooting was trying to murder him, he thought. He had to see who it was because he could hear foot-steps running behind him, he quickly glanced back over his shoulder and locked eyes with Malik.

He was closing his distance; Malik had an evil smirk on his face. "Don't run now nigga" yelled Malik as he sent 4 more shots almost hitting him in his cabbage. The distance between him and Malik was about the same for him to make it to Angie's front door but it wouldn't leave him any room to get into the house. There was no way he could make it into the house without Malik filling his back with bullets', he decided his only hope was to out run him. Hopefully he could make it to his car that was parked a short distance away on Run street. He tried once more to lift his right arm to get his pistol because that would be the only thing that could give him an equalizer and buy him some time, he was unsuccessfully. It proved to be useless; the bullet in his shoulder had damaged his nerves in his arm. He was running faster as he passed Angie's house making sure to keep his distance at a safe pace. The shooting seemed to have just stopped but he wasn't wasting any time to look over his shoulder, he was running for his life! At top speed he left Malik in the dust, he was almost at his car and safe. As he bent the corner of the last building 10 feet away from his car, he ran into Joey with a shot-gun aimed at his mid-section. "Oh shit," was all he got out as he tried to stop and change directions!

"Joey stood up-right from between two parked cars, his 12 gauge shotgun aimed at his mid-section," where you going so fast homey," he asked with a smile on his face? Joey aimed the shot-gun down at his knee-cap and pulled the trigger.

The blast sent Silas entire knee-cap hurling into the White fence. He stumbled but caught his balance with his left hand, Joey aimed at the hand that was balancing him and keeping him from falling and pulled the trigger once again. Boom! Then the next shot caught him square in his chin knocking it completely off his face. He crashed to the ground with his eyes twitching. He wasn't dead yet.

Malik eased around the corner and walked over to him, "you really thought you'd be alive to see another day, huh," laughed Malik?

He looked up, the pain was so severe that he knew the end was near for him, "fu-fuck your country ass, Nigga fuck…" was all he got out. Malik shot him 6 times in the face before he could finish his sentence. Two more rounds to his chest, Silas had taken his last breath!

Jacob popped his head up from the dice game like an ostrich rising from the sand; the gun fire that was coming from behind him was deafening and noticeably close. He stayed calm and low to the ground as he forced his eyes to focus on where the shots were going. A short distance away from him he saw Silas body spin 180 degree's. His cigarette went in one direction and his body in the other direction. He knew right away that Silas was hit, since Silas reaction time was so quick he thought he had on his trusted bullet proof vest. What he saw next caused him to pull out his own .380 pistol, Malik ran right pass him giving chase behind Silas firing from two guns. He had a clear shot at the back of Malik's head but didn't want to take the shot, not yet anyway!

The crowd ran in the opposite direction of all the gun-fire, Jacob slowly trotted at a good distance behind Malik to hopefully to see Silas murder him. With the lead Silas had on Malik, he knew Silas would get away, from the looks of it, Malik was giving up on chasing him, and he looked tired. Silas turned the corner onto Run Street, Malik was still in the Projects' just passing Angie's jogging. A couple seconds after Silas turned the corner, Jacob heard loud shots. The shots were the loudest he's ever heard, he stopped dead in his tracks. Malik on the other hand seemed to speed up at the sound of the loud gun-fire. Instead of running to keep up with Malik, he decided to walk at a quick pace, he turned the corner, Malik and Joey were standing over Silas body giving him a lead shower! Without ever looking up to see him in the distance, Joey and Malik walked off as if nothing happened. He crouched between the cars, Silas body was still shaking violently, he wanted to help but there was nothing he could do. Plus, he didn't want to become victim number two, he stayed put until Joey and Malik disappeared in the distance.

It didn't take a rocket scientist to figure out Silas was dead. He stared down at the lifeless body; his face was one big glob of blood, brain matter, bone and displaced hair from the top of his head. If he didn't witness that it was Silas, there was no way that the body could be recognized by looking at his face, there was nothing left! A closed casket would be needed. By the time the paramedics arrived there was nothing they could do for him, another young black male, dead on arrival. The arrogant white detective was now on the scene looking for a helping hand as usual. "Alright guys, no need moving the body, he's fish bait! This here is my crime scene, please step this way. "We don't want to contaminate any potential evidence, do we" he asked with a smirk on his face?

The white detective walked over to a nervous Jacob," hey buddy, did you see who killed this young fella?" For a second, he almost slipped and blurted out that Joey and Malik were responsible for killing Silas but thought better of it. Becoming a snitch wouldn't help his case in taking over the CRACK trade in the Projects, at least not yet. He shook his head no as he stared at the body and what would have been Silas face," no, I don't know what happened. I came around the corner and here he was, I've never seen this guy a day in my life detective!" The detective shook his head because whoever this guy was nobody seemed to know his name, he took his card out and passed it to Jacob," okay buddy, take this, if you happen to hear anything or remember anything, and I mean anything, give me a call," he said with a wink. He turned back to the body," it's a shame that ya'll murder each other like animals," then chuckled and left.

Jacob had to take one last look at the body, he saw a long yellow glob seeping out where his temple should have been, he choked and almost called Earl. In his mind, he wanted to get as far away from that body as possible. He eased through the crowd of on-lookers as he tucked the detective's card into his pocket for a later date. Perhaps some time later that card could come in handy and take the detective up on his offer. If Malik and Joey were willing to murder Silas in the middle of the Projects with people watching, he knew what they would do to him if they found out that he was responsible for the robbery. He couldn't allow that to happen, he loved himself too much for that! He was going through his mental rolodex thinking about what actually lead up to the robbery. He was at the Waffle House with White-Girl late one night when she pointed out this white chick who she said was eyeing him real hard. He never caught the other chick watching him, but when she urged him to go holla at her, he did.

With White-girl proposing a possible threesome, he had no choice but to try his hand. If hadn't been for White-girl offering a threesome, he would have never approached the white chick, he wasn't really into the average white girl, they were too silly for his liking. Come to find out, the other white chick use to be one of Malik's fuck-buddies and he had her spilling her guts by the end of the night. Up-set that Malik had cut her off, she was down for anything, well almost anything, she didn't' want to have a threesome with White-girl, but she didn't mind going to the room with him and fucking the shit out of him. He had to give the girl that, she was a monster in the bed, she done all kinds of tricks with her pussy that he's never seen outside of a porn movie!

Their relationship was short lived, a week or two, three at the most before she told him she was returning back to either North Carolina or South Carolina, he couldn't remember Which one but it was one of them. When she mentioned that it was easy to catch Malik slippin', he didn't pay her much mind because she was mad at him for cutting her off so he knew she would say anything for attention. In the back of his mind though, that robbery was sounding real sweet to him and that's when he went to holla at him little homey's about doing the robbery. Just so happen, the day they went to scope out the house, they caught him coming out with the brown paper bag and it paid off. So, the chick he was fucking didn't even know that he actually went through with the robbery, she was long gone, so as it stood, the only people who really knew about the robbery was two homey's and White-girl!

He crossed over the tracks on his way to Mel's, he wanted to get out the Projects and Mel's was his best bet, he took his cell out and called White-girl. "Yo, pick me up at Mel's, they just killed Silas over here in the Projects," he said into the phone.

"Huh? Huh, what you say? Who, Who did what," she asked?

"Look, just pick me up at Mel's, I'll tell you all about it When you get here. I saw the whole thing!"

"Stay right there, don't fuckin' move, I'm walking out the door as we speak."

He picked-up on the fact that White-girl didn't tell him that her and Amanda were on their way, she said she was on her way and that sounded strange to him but he shrugged it all as White-girl being White-girl. Picking up his pace crossing the train tracks, it was a bit to dark out there for him to be taking his time, Malik or Joey could be lurking anywhere. He wouldn't feel safe until he got back across town to Prospect where he was most comfortable. White-girl decided against waking up Amanda, not yet anyway. No need in stressing her out until she found out exactly what happened to Silas out there.

She needed to be alone when she spoke to Jacob, she tip-toed pass Amanda and out the front door. When she got outside in front of the building she took a deep breath and looked to her right and then to her left just to see who was watching her. Jumping in the truck wasting no time, the pedal to the medal. She didn't bother braking as she crossed the train tracks and even ran the red light on

Main Street as she made a sharp left and a quick right and there she was in Mel's parking lot looking at Jacob.

He was standing on the side of the building puffing nervously on a Newport. She could tell he was jittery as she watched; he took 3 or 4 back to back drags off the cigarette as he looked around like somebody was following him. The closer she watched him, she began to almost get nervous herself as she scanned the parking lot herself, for a second she thought he was trying to set her up. She clutched the .38 special that sat on her lap under a towel. She nodded him over but from the looks of it, he didn't see her but he was looking right at her. She rolled her window down and hollered, "Come on boy, get your crazy-ass in this truck!" Jacob was standing on the side of Mel's puffing hard on his Newport; he wasn't taking any chances. Malik or Joey wouldn't sneak up on him, not tonight anyway. He knew if by chance he spotted either of them he wouldn't hesitate to squeeze off every shell from his .380. With his back against the wall he knew at the very least, he could see it coming, he was well protected, he had his own back so he thought, and then White-girl's voice brought him out of his dream-like state. He had slipped just that fast, and he knew it.

He jumped into the truck, the moment he was safely inside, White-girl bombarded him with question after question "What the hell happened? Who shot who? Is he really dead? How you know? When did it happen? And where the hell were you when all this took place?"

He had to put his hand up to stop all the questions; she was firing them like she was interrogating him. She asked all those questions without even taking a breath of fresh air," slow the fuck down, damn!" The whole mood changed the instant he told her to, shut the fuck-up. She didn't like for him to tell her what to do, she had to tighten her lips before she said something she would later regret. "Look, just tell me what happened and how it happened," she asked real calm?

He wiped his face with his bare hands and looked out the window. The one thing he knew about her was that she was a fiend for information and he decided to exercise his temporary power over the situation. Silence was his power! He took his time and when he finally looked over at her, he caught the chrome barrel of her .38 special pointed directly at his mid-section. He was thinking, 'this bitch is crazy for-real.'

"I don't really know what happened, I was over there shooting dice and the next thing you hear is: Boom! Boom! Boom! Boom! I looked up from the game and there is Malik coming out of nowhere shooting and chasing behind Silas. You know me; I sent a couple shot at Malik to give Silas some time to gather himself. So many people were out there that I had to get low, you know how niggaz run their mouth, I ain't want no part of that bullshit, I ain't got time to be going to court for some stupid shit. That's those dudes turf and I busted my gun and got low. They started chasing Silas down towards Run street, I tried to keep up, but by the time I caught up with them Joey and Malik was standing over top of him. They dumped so many bullets in that boy's face they almost knocked his head off his shoulders. I couldn't help him, he was gone and I bounced!"

She picked up on his nervousness; it was the way his eyes kept scanning back and forth. It was evident that whatever really happened, Joey and Malik spooked him! 'This nigga pussy for-real,' she thought to herself, but she kept watching him from the corner of her eyes. She knew he would come in handy in the near future so she allowed him to have his say and tell the story the way he sees fit, she wouldn't cast shade on his prime time moment, not yet anyway. "A-ight, A-ight, we have to eventually tell Amanda what happened to him, however, we'll leave out the part about you being there and seeing the Whole thing. She'll want to know why you're still alive and her man's dead, she question your loyalty! But, you don't have to worry about all that, you let me deal with that part of the story, plus, I know best, you know that right," she said patting him on his thigh!

He looked over at her like she was crazy at first but the harsh reality of having to explain to Amanda why he was in the Projects' in the first place and then him actually being there When Silas was murdered, that was to much for him, he liked White-girl's way better. He knew he needed to have and keep White-girl on his side, especially if he wanted to take over both Prospect and the Projects', "you're exactly correct! Amanda doesn't have to know all that, it'll be too much for her. She love dude to death, you do know what's best," he said winking back at White-girl. "Good. We'll just tell her that somebody else told you and you told me because you couldn't get in touch with her. She's still sleep," she insisted.

Having had enough of him, she dropped Jacob off down in Orangedale, "stay low until I call you," she said pulling in the driveway of his baby mama's house. She took her time turning around in the circle of the dead end, she knew she had to get ready and put her game face on well before she delivered the news to Amanda about Silas. One thing about that relationship, Amanda loved the ground Silas walked on and the news of his untimely death would certainly devastate her.

Trying to fake her own surprise of his death would be the hardest thing for her because she really didn't give a fuck about the dude. As far as she was concerned, Silas was only a casualty of the vicious cycle of the game he played. Some lived. Some died. By the time she walked through the front door, Amanda was on the sofa sleep. She contemplated not even waking her up but she knew she would never hear the end of it; she had to wake her up.

Grabbing Amanda by the arm she started shaking her," Amanda, Amanda, wake-up girl, wake-up," she insisted. Still groggy and sleepy.

Amanda tried to gain her senses and focus on White-girl's face," huh, huh, huh, why the fuck are you shaking me like this. Bitch you crazy?"

"Amanda, they say something bad happened to Silas over the Projects'." She sat straight up at the mention of his name and bad in the same sentence, she lit a Newport and allow those thoughts to pass through her mind.

"Now, what's so fuckin' important that you had to come and wake me up like this," she said blowing the smoke out her mouth? Then it hit her again, it was when she blew the smoke out that she felt the pain in her jaw, putting two and two together," did you say something bad happened to Silas?"

_____ _____ _____ _____ _____
_____ _____

Joey and Malik made their way up to Paoli Street to stash their guns and get into the whip they only used for emergencies. The cold black on black Ford Mustang sat in the backyard under a cover. It was the perfect get-a-way car, with 260 on the dashboard; they could out run any police car with no problem. Getting the Mustang was Joey's idea, he was certain that one day the car would come in handy and that day was tonight. Malik took a quick look over his shoulder as he put the guns in a hole they had already buried behind the shed, " I think we're good, ain't nobody really see shit," he said covering the hole and getting in the Mustang. They rode back to the Double Tree Hotel in complete silence. Each of them knew and understood that their original plan of using the CRACK game as a stepping stone for something bigger was now over. The hood would eventually start talking about the murder and make the connection between what happened on top of Prospect to what happened in the Projects'. It was the part about being involved in another murder of a young black man that didn't sit well with Joey, but at the same time he knew it was either Silas or him or Malik could very well be dead! The lifestyle of a drug dealer has a way of sucking you in deeper and deeper no matter what your real agenda may be. Before you look up, you're face to face with your own untimely death, and that was something they were trying to avoid. "Yo', this shit is crazy, I know that what we did was something that we had to do, make no mistake about it. It was either him or one of us and I ain't going out like that. You know what I mean, homey? But I got the strangest feeling, even with him being dead, why don't I feel like the beef is over?"

Arriving back at the Double Tree Hotel, they precede going straight to Joey's room. When they opened the door, Terri and Tiffany was sitting at the table eating, playing cards, and laughing their heads off drinking orange juice. Tiffany looked up, she rolled her eyes at Malik at first glance; she definitely gave him that baby momma drama look. She didn't acknowledge him or Joey; she went right back to discussing what she was talking about to Terri. Terri was unable to hold back like Tiffany was doing, Joey was just on a different level, so she thought. She felt like this was what she signed-up for so there was no room for her to complain, even more so now-a-days. When she looked up, she had a welcoming smile on her face, unlike Tiffany. "Hey baby, I got you something to eat, I know you're hungry," she said going over to where the bag of food was sitting on the mini-bar.

Malik nodded at Terri but didn't speak, looking at the back of Tiffany's head he headed for the door, "come on Tiffany let's go," he said existing their room on his way to his own room. Safely behind closed doors of their own room, the first thing she said was," you killed him didn't you," as she looked him up and down?

"What the hell you're talking about now? Kill who?" he asked trying to avoid what she was asking him.

"Malik, there's blood all over your sneaker's, your socks, and the bottom of your pants leg. That shit wasn't there when you left. What you need to be doing is getting rid of that shit. All of it, bury it, burn it, do something with it but just get that shit out of here," she said staring him in the eye. "Oh, by the way, we love you just that much and we can't lose you now so handle your business!"

_____ _____ _____ _____ _____

_____

Amanda started screaming, clawing, and sobbing uncontrollable as White-girl told her what she heard about Silas getting shot. After a long and agonizing scream, Amanda tried her best to collect herself as she exhaled slowly. "Take me to the Projects'," she said looking White-girl square in the eyes. White-girl had a blank look on her face and it was hard for Amanda to read her thoughts. "I said take me to the fuckin' Projects right now damn it" fired Amanda still calm but forceful!

White-girl remain locked in her own thoughts, wondering but determined to stand her ground, but with a loss for words, she faltered under the pressure. "Amanda, the police are over there, I don't think that's a good idea, we should.

Amanda cut her off before she could finish her sentence, with tears rolling slowly down her face freely, "and tell me just how the fuck you know all that when your dumb-ass is over here with me, tell me that bitch? How the fuck you know what the police are doing if you're here with me?"

White-girl knew at the tone of Amanda's voice that she had over-stepped her bounds. At the present moment she knew the only thing she could do was to take her to the Projects'. "You right! Calm down, get your stuff together, I'll drive you over there," said White-girl defeated.

Amanda managed to wipe the tears away, "you know if he's dead, I have to identify the body. They won't know who he is. He never carries I.D. and I can't allow my baby to go out like that, he ain't no John Doe and I have to make sure they take good care of him. I love him way too much to sit back and do nothing," she said breaking down once again. She looked at White-girl again," you sure they said it was him?" White-girl nodded, she didn't want to say anything to up-set her, she has never seen her this emotional and knew by her actions that she was suffering from a broken heart. "That's what they're saying. They say it was him!" They walked out the building and Jacob was standing in the parking lot next to their truck. He spoke softly as Amanda walked pass him, she didn't even look up at him. "I'll be here when ya'll get back," he said more so to White-girl than Amanda.

White-girl smiled, she wasn't happy, just glad that he had sense enough not to jump his dumb-ass in the truck with them. "Yeah, you do that. Hold down the fort until we get back," she said instead of saying what she really wanted to say to him. If she had her say, she would've said something like; "Your scary ass ain't going back over the Projects', you're too scared of Joey and Malik for that, you wack-ass nigga!' Yet, she maintained her cool, her mind was going a million miles a minute but you couldn't tell by looking at her.

Handling Amanda wouldn't be hard if she stayed focused on the bigger picture. Amanda was in a daze, she was completely silent. She just stared out the window as they made their way across town to the Projects. As they came down-10th Street, the police had Run Street blocked off. They went all the way around and came into the Projects' from Page Street. Amanda had her stop at the first speed bump beside the mail boxes.

"We can walk from here, looks like all the police are over there," she said pointing in the direction of all the police. As her and White-girl got closer, she could see them just about to put his body in the coronary's van. She spotted his Prada sneaker's he was wearing sticking out from under the white sheet that covered the rest of his body. She ran through the yellow tape screaming.

"Wait! Wait! That's my finance' in that van, you gotta let me see him," she begged the two officers putting him in the coronary's van! The same White detective who spoke with Jacob earlier walked over to her because of the commotion she was causing. "May I help you," he asked her?

"Yes! That's my finance' right there, you gotta let me see him," she said but not waiting for him to answer her. She was only feet away from him, she made her move and snatched the sheet from his face, and the sight of what she saw caused her to let out a scream that could be heard throughout the Whole Projects.

She barely recognized him; his face had been disfigured from all the shots sustained to his face. Nevertheless, she bent down and whispered in his ear that she loved him with all her heart, then what she did next, crept everybody out. She kissed him right where his lips were supposed to be, but it was only a big glob of bone, blood, and brain matter. The White detective almost went in to stop her but he wasn't fast enough. Once he heard that scream, he realized that she loved this dude and wasn't about to come in between that. He knew better! He also knew that she could be more help to his investigation if he allowed her to say her good-byes and pay her respects. She already proved helpful by giving him the name and age of his victim; he was no longer a John Doe.

"Ma'ma, I'll give you a couple of minutes alone with your finance' before we have to take him away," he said patting her lightly on her shoulder. It didn't take her long, a minute or two and she was done, she walked away from the love of her life. The tears were all gone, and there was no longer the look of helplessness on her face, it was replaced with a look of sheer determination, rage, and revenge. That was her driving force! There was nothing else left for her to do, she looked the detective in the eyes and said," Please take care of my baby!"

Just as she turned to walk away, the detective stopped her again, "ma'ma here's his personal belongings; I thought you'd want them, a ring, watch, chain and his cell phone. He also had close to five thousand in cash on him," the detective winked at her. "Call me if you have any questions!" "Thank you officer," she said turning quickly and walking away with her hands full of Silas things. She was looking at the ring because it was a woman's ring and she's never seen it before. It was clearly an engagement ring, sitting in the truck, she tried the ring on. It fit her finger like a glove. She took the ring off, look inside of it and it read,' Amanda, I love you!'

White-girl had to ask her was she alright because of the look she had on her face. She couldn't read Amanda and that wasn't normal for her, she could always at the very least tell if she was angry, mad, or sad, but not this time. Amanda slipped the ring back on her finger, looked over at White-girl and said, "Joey and Malik did this shit, I know they did it! Malik always use to say to me that if he ever had to shoot somebody that he'd shoot them in the face so they could have a closed casket funeral. They shot my baby's face off!"

She shook her head in disbelief," after that shit that happened tonight over Prospect, I know for certain that they did this shit; I can feel it in my gut. I know one thing, I won't rest until I get their ass, and I mean that shit." White-girl got the message, murder was in Amanda's eyes and it couldn't be mistaken for fear, this was the real thing. "So what you wanna do then," she asked? Amanda looked at her like she was either crazy or stupid, "where's the gun? That's all I need to know. Fuck the bullshit!" "It's there in the glove box."

Amanda opened the glove box and pulled out the gun. She sat the gun on her lap and every once in awhile, she would flip the gun over and over staring at it as it sat in her hand. She checked the bullet's, unloading and wiping all the shells off then reloading the gun. She did that several times before returning the gun back into the glove box. White-girl kept cutting her eye at over at her while she played with the gun. She was wondering what was on her mind, but she didn't bother to ask her. Her thing was, as long as Amanda didn't do anything stupid with the gun, she was cool with whatever she was doing. People mourn in different ways and if this was going to help Amanda in the long run, she wanted to give her all the space she needed to mourn properly. It helped that she was entering the last phase of her own agenda and didn't want to attract the wrong type of attention from Amanda. "Amanda, you hungry? Let's go to the Waffle House and get something to eat. I know you might not want to go, but you gotta eat, you haven't eaten in a while," said White-girl eyeing the ring on her left finger.

Amanda was deep in thought about Silas, she was wondering if he was going to ask her to marry him? Would she have said yes? Is this how true love felt? Those were just a few of the thoughts going through her mind; she flipped his cell phone open and started scrolling down his phone book. When she came across his homey Sosa's number she was about to call him and tell him of the bad news but thought better of it. She didn't want to be the bearer of bad news; she figured she'd call when she had something good to tell him about Silas death. Unconsciously she hit the send button but when she realized what she had done, she ended the call just as fast. 'I'll call him later,' she whispered to herself.

Getting comfortable in their both at the Waffle House, Amanda was just about finish her meal when she was forced to rush from the table and run to the bathroom. She called Earl just in time as she ran into the stall by the door. Everything she ate was coming up; she couldn't hold it down even if she tried. Her stomach was in an up-roar, she attributed her sickness with all the stress of the day and evening. It was enough to drive a sane person insane yet, she was still standing strong. She felt as if she didn't have a choice in the matter, she had to represent not only for herself, but the man of her dreams as well! She stood in front of the mirror staring at her own reflection as she rinsed her mouth out. She washed her hands and her face. When she looked at her reflection once again, she got it. For the first time she seen what Silas had been trying to tell her for the last two weeks, her face was getting fat! Shaking her head as if she was in disbelief, however, she couldn't have been happier. 'I love you Silas,' she said barely above a whisper, she took his cell phone out her pocket and found Sosa's number and dialed it!

CHAPTER 19

MALIK was up early the next morning despite Tiffany laying down her gansta on him, she had 30 or so odd days of bent up stress she released on him. Tiffany sexed him over and over until he was forced to tap out due to her appetite for his dick. He was up and ready to move around, he was on the edge of the bed and turned the television on in time to catch the report about Silas murder and their investigation of that murder. The News Anchor was telling the public the detectives handling the case needed their help and there was a Ten thousand dollar reward for the information that led to the arrest and conviction of those responsible.

He couldn't help but smile knowing that he had gotten away with the ultimate crime, Murder! Knowing the streets all to well, he knew in due time the streets would start talking, especially since the beef with Silas on top of Prospect but it didn't bother him to much. The one thing he wasn't going to do was hid out and having them people looking for him, he wasn't going out like that; he knew the best thing he could do was to allow his face to be seen. If the streets wanted to know something about him, he would be right there to answer the call. He was going to the hood, his whole street rep depended on it, plus he knew hiding out would only make him look that much more guilty, so he got dressed in record time.

It didn't take him long at all to end up on Page Street sitting on the rock wall reading the Newspaper and drinking a quarter water. He felt good being out there on the block and his focus was on his surrounding even though he was absorbed with the sports' section of the newspaper. He spotted Star leaving out the Projects from the Run Street side but he didn't acknowledge her at all. Star was coming out the Projects' when she spotted Malik on the corner of 10th and Page Street reading the newspaper, from the looks of it he was engrossed in the paper, and she shook her head in disbelief knowing that he'd just killed somebody the night before. In her mind she thought the young boys wasn't built like the dudes from back in the days when she first got in the CRACK game, but at the same time, that was their business, she had only one thing on her mind as she approached him. "A man like yourself shouldn't be caught slippin' out here like this, it's a cold world and a dangerous neighborhood," she said standing only inches from him. "If I was your enemy, I could've had you," she said laughing!

He raised his brow unimpressed," is that so? What were you going to do about that," he said pointing to the red dot on her white-tee at the center of her chest? "Every closed eye ain't sleep; I thought you would understand that by now." She caught him slippin' he had his Desert Eagle trained on her chest, not to mention the beam he had on her, he couldn't miss with the beam. At that moment she realized that she made the correct decision when she got on his team. Still playing around, "so what's good? I know you heard what happened out here last night, didn't you?" He shook his head no as he looked in her eyes," I ain't heard, won't you tell me about it since you seem to know so much."

With both of her hands on her hips she smiled," shit, if you ain't heard about it I'm sure you will by the end of the day. I ain't the one to be broadcasting the news, it don't involve me or you, so it ain't much to talk about. Fuck the bullshit, you got something for your girl or what?"

Pointing across the street towards two parked cars, a McDonald's bag was sitting on the ground between the cars. "You know I got you, you're a legend around here! Where would the hood be if it wasn't for you," he said smiling. "That's your McDonalds' bag over there!"

"Good looking Malik! Where Pam at," she asked walking across the street to the McDonalds bag on the ground? Before she walked off, he had to ask her something that he's wanted to ask her since he was a shorty on the block. "Yo Star, let me ask you something: Do your ass ever sleep?"

"Hell to the fuckin' no! How can I sleep with all this good shit ya'll got running around here? Fuck the bullshit, I'll sleep when I die, right now I'm trying to get my mind right," she said dead serious. In his mind he knew she meant every word she spoke. Since he could remember, she was always on the scene, even way before he stepped off Auntie Pam's porch he use to see Star running around doing her thang. He watched her closely as she picked up the bag and walked down the street clutching the McDonalds' bag tight.

His phone started ringing, he thought it was Tiffany calling until he looked at the number, it was Joey. He answered on the second ring, "yeah, yeah, word, I'm on 10th and Page now why? A-ight, I ain't got no problem with that, I'll be right here or down on Page chillin'." Malik started playing a game on his phone after he hung-up with Joey. They were on their way to come pick him up, the girls wanted to go to Kings Dominion for the day and he didn't mind. He shrugged it off and thought that might be a good idea. Then he asked himself a simple question,' what the hell are you doing on one of the hottest blocks in all of Charlottesville with Desert Eagle after a murder in the hood last night?' That lone thought causes him to get his ass up and move down the block away from the corner. As he stood up to leave a nice little truck sped pass him, he was too caught up in his own thoughts to pay the truck much attention.

Amanda and White-girl had just driven past him on the corner! "Shit! There go Malik right there," whispered Amanda as if he could actually hear her from inside the truck. She even leaned back in her seat so that he couldn't see her. It wasn't like he could see her even if he was looking, the triple black window tint made it impossible to see inside the truck. Take the right on Paoli Street," she said to White-girl. She couldn't believe her luck, barely getting enough sleep last night she was up early because White-girl wanted to take some paper to the stash house on Madison Avenue.

Silas had invaded her dreams all night long and they seemed so real to her, she even prayed to God that he would change things but she knew nothing could bring him back but she still tried her hand. In her dream there was one thing that he kept saying to her over and over again. He said,' be careful, enemies are everywhere!' The last time he said that to her in her dream, White-girl had tapped her on the leg awaking her from her beautiful dream and that's how they ended up on 10th Street. "White-girl, pull up over there. You gotta listen to me; all you gotta do is make a right at the end of this street and go down to the stop sign and park. I'm going to go through the cut and sneak up on him, he won't see me coming, and when you hear the shots come around the corner and pick me up. That's all you gotta do, can you handle it?"

Amanda eased her frame out the truck on Paoli Street, one street over from Page. She was going to use the trees and bushes to conceal her from being seen by Malik While she got close enough to shoot him. She turned around and gave White-girl the thumbs-up. 'You ready,' she asked herself. She even nodded her head yes but she was still nervous. Her legs were wobbly, sweat was running down the CRACK of her ass, and her hands were moist from sweat. She dried her hands off on her jeans as best she could, When she watched White-girl drive off she knew there was no turning back now, not even if she wanted to she couldn't! This was bigger than her, this was about revenge for the man of her dreams and since Malik took that from her, she intended to take his life from him. Fair exchange wasn't robbery in the hood! She closed her eyes and said a soft prayer, 'Silas my love give me the strength and accuracy to kill this mutha fucker.' She took one more deep breath and exhaled slowly, 'come on, let's go girl,' she coached herself. Taking her time as she eased through the bushes and using the trees for protection, she came out the alley behind the big white house at the entrance of the Projects'.

Lucky for her Malik had moved down from the corner of 10th and Page when she first seen him, this would be easier than she originally imagined. His back to her, only about 40 feet away, in front of her. The 40 feet wasn't far and she thought she could make it before he knew what was happening, her only problem, there nothing between him and her that could protect her if he looked behind him. She remained crouched behind a tree watching him and she figured out a way to make this happen and she live to tell the story to her child. One thing she had in her favor was that whatever he was doing with his phone he was deeply into it because he had yet to look up, not even to see what's in front of him as cars passed him. 'Only if I could get closer!' If she didn't know anything else, she knew that the element of surprise was in her favor and she couldn't lose that, it would be the difference between living and dying. He had a clear shot of her once she made her move if he looked, the open field provided her no protection. She envisioned shooting him in his face the way he shot Silas, that was all it took to get her blood boiling and ready to attack!

With her palms now dripping with sweat and her legs feeling like they were going to betray her, she composed herself and got ready. Malik looked up briefly at a passing car that blew its horn at him but he was back to his phone in no time. She stood-up, 'it's now or never girl,' she coached herself as a single tear streamed down her right cheek. She rose up from her crouched position and broke out into an all out sprint towards Malik. She was at top speed quickly as she took aim at the back of his head without having to slow herself down, 'a little closer, closer,' she told herself.

The first shot rang out when she was only 10 feet away from him and it caught him in his upper shoulder blade knocking him forward. He hit the pavement hard but didn't stay there; he looked-up over the little wall just in time to see her charging at him with murder in her eyes. Without having to think, his reaction time was perfect, he eased his Desert Eagle out sending a wild but lucky shot in her direction. The shot was low but it ricocheted off the ground and grazed her thigh. She stumbled but caught her balance and returned fire. She was driven by the rage she had for him that she didn't even feel the bullet graze her thigh. Using her country girl skills, she took her time as she had Malik in the cross-hairs of her gun before she pulled the trigger. She wanted this shot to count and the bullet found its intended target; she hit him in the center of his chest knocking the gun out his hand from the impact. That shot stretched his ass out, he was laid out on his back on the pavement with his pistol 5 feet away, he couldn't make it to his pistol, his chest was burning too bad. She continued forward as she jumped off the wall landing only inches away from him. She had the devil in her eyes!

Her anger had finally gotten the best of her, by now she was crying and screaming in a language that he couldn't understand.

"Why, why, why, why Malik, why you have to kill him like that?" She aimed her gun towards his right foot and pulled the trigger shattering his ankle bone and causing tremendous pain to his leg. Then she shoot his knee cap completely off, "answer me nigga! Answer me, he was all I had and and killed him. Why you do it," she continued to ask over and over as she screamed loud.

He was in a great deal of pain by his facial expressions as he starred back at her not knowing what to say. He knew she was going to kill him from the evil look in her eyes so he was content on going out like a soldier. When he saw her raise her pistol up towards his face, he knew this was the end. She was going to be the last face he ever saw, he was waiting for his life to pass by in his mind but it never came. With tears blurring her view she raised the pistol from down by his knee and shot him near his dick, one bullet went clean through his hand as he tried his best to protect his dick, the second shot went into his thigh as he moved his leg just in time. He'd had enough of her playing with his life, he looked up at her and said real calm," go ahead and just kill me you nasty no good bitch!"

She raised the pistol to his eyes, the Whole time she was shaking her head up and down, he was trying his best to time her, and as luck would have it, he moved his head as she squeezed off another shot. She missed him but the bullet still skidded off the pavement into the side of his head. She missed, a car horn caught her attention, she forgot that she told White girl to pick her up, she heard the shots. It seemed like forever but it's only been a minute or so since she fired the first shot. When she finally looked-up, that proven to be her biggest mistake, it wasn't White-girl who was blowing the horn, it was Joey! She almost lost it but White-girl was also on the scene, she was only a few feet away and closing in with the door to the truck already open. She let off a single shot towards Joey; he returned his fire from his riot pump shot-gun almost knocking sparks from her small frame. She knew she was no match for the shot-gun, she ran to the truck. White-girl was now shooting at Joey forcing him to take cover giving Amanda the necessary time to get to the truck safely.

White-girl threw the truck in reverse and sped backwards all the way down Page until she got to 8th Street and a safe distance away from crazy-ass Joey before she straightened up the truck. "Damn girl, where the hell you learn to drive like that," asked Amanda?

Tiffany jumped out the car and ran over to where Malik was laying out on the pavement. His face was bloody along with his legs, his hand, and his chest. He didn't look good to her, he was barely conscious. She was having a hard time trying to prop his head up into her lap as_ she cradled his head. His eyes closed and she thought she lost him. "Malik, Malik, Malik, you gotta wake-up baby. I'm here, please wake-up," she begged through her tears!

Joey took one look at his comrade and knew there was no need waiting for the ambulance; he picked Malik up and put him in the back of the car. "Tiffany, put this on where he got shot, make sure you stop the bleeding," he said handing her a towel. She sat in the back with Malik trying her best to stop the wounds from spurting out blood, but every time she thought she stopped it from bleeding she found another hole. She started talking to him, "please baby, wake-up for me, Malik, hold on baby, we're almost there. Hold on." "Keep that towel on the bullet wounds," yelled Joey from the driver's seat! "Shit, I'm trying but that bitch shot him so many times that I don't know where the blood is coming from. I'm trying Joey, I'm trying but it's just too much for one towel.

Joey drove like he was a man on a mission, not stopping at the Red light at the top of 10th and Main Street, he crept through making sure he wouldn't cause an accident. Blowing his horn as he crossed over, he was only a minute or so away from the emergency room he pulled into the front ready to get his brother in to be seen. Time was his enemy and he knew it, but the best thing about the University of Virginia was that if you could get there alive your chances were very good that they'll save you! Luckily for them a nurse was standing out front smoking a cigarette ready to haul the wheel chair back inside, he flagged her down and they put Malik in the wheel chair.

The nurse didn't blink or waste a second, she jumped into her zone as she yelled coming through the doors," Black male. GSW (Gun Shot Wound). Head Trauma. GSW to the chest cavity, shot in his hand, leg, and other apparent injuries. He's unconscious, his pulse is weak. Breathing is shallow." The nurse was quick and very impressive; Joey felt a sense of relief knowing Malik was still breathing when he got him to the emergency room. It was widely known that the University of Virginia had some of the best Surgeons in the world. His chances were very good; he had a good shot of living. Looking over at Tiffany with all the blood on her clothes, if he didn't know any better he would've thought she had been shot as well. "You alright," he asked her?

She immediately broke down and cried in his arms," why Joey, why is this happening?" He let her cry on his shoulder but after a few minutes he knew he had to prepare her for what was to come, "Tiffany, you gotta be strong, the police and Detectives are gonna be here soon and they'll want to speak with you. You gotta get yourself together! We don't know anything and we have to convince them of that, can you remember that?" "I know that Joey," she whispered as she wiped her eyes.

The nurses and doctors immediately prepped Malik for surgery, with the head nurse coming back out to speak with them once Malik had been stabilized. "He's ready and prepped for surgery; we have some of the best medical minds in the world, the best neurologist and surgeons so he's in great hands. Form what we can tell so far is that he's been shot several times from a small caliber weapon at close range. We're very concerned about the shot to his head, the X-rays is showing some swelling on his brain, we'll have to drain the blood to stop the swelling. We won't know the extent of that injury or what impact it'll have on his facilities down the road. We have to take this minute by minute. Right now all we can do is allow the doctors to do their jobs, we'll let you know how he's doing the moment he comes out of surgery. You guys will be able to see him once we get him into recovery, until then, you know, it's like I said, it's a minute by minute situation."

"Thank you ma'am, please do whatever you have to do to keep him alive, I'm pregnant and we're going to need him. Please save my husband," begged Tiffany! Joey stood there looking, and listening, he knew already that he's done the best thing that he could do for Malik; He got him to the hospital alive! Everything else was now in God's hands. He wanted to leave the hospital but didn't want to leave Tiffany alone. He had business to handle and Amanda was the only thing he thought about. However, he couldn't leave Tiffany at the hospital alone in her condition, with Terri having to handle something, he was forced to call her and give her the news about Malik and a few other details. He went outside the emergency room so that he could talk to Terri as he scanned the parking lot. Giving her the details and instructions, he was done talking to her within 5 minutes. She wasn't far away, thinking that she was still meeting them down on Page Street; she still wasn't but a couple minutes out. Hanging up with her, he slammed his cell phone down on the pavement breaking it into a million pieces. He picked-up the larger pieces and walked down to the end of the parking lot throwing the different pieces in different directions throughout the parking lot!

By the time he got back up to the emergency room, Terri had just pulled up. Tiffany was also standing out front with an unlit Newport dangling from her hand as she starred up at the sky. Terri got out the car and walked over to him," "babe, everything you asked me to get for you is in the trunk, your new phone is on the passenger's seat," she said glancing over at Tiffany and the unlit cigarette. Let me get over there with her," she said nodding her head in Tiffany's direction as she kissed him on his cheek. "Be careful!" Terri walked over to Tiffany and hugged her real tight," we're going to get through this; you have to stay strong for both Malik and the baby." She looked Tiffany in her eyes and then said," The baby don't need that, you've come too far to give up now," pointing down at the unlit cigarette. At the mention of Malik and the baby in the same sentence it seemed like she transformed right before her eyes. Tiffany threw the unlit cigarette to the ground and stomped on it as it was already lit. "You right, Malik will be fine, I can feel it and I know my baby needs for me to remain strong," she said wiping the tears away and standing up straight.

Joey watched the exchange between the two of them and then walked over and hugged them both. "Here comes the detectives, Terri don't say anything, let Tiffany do all the talking, she knows what to say to them, I'm out." He got into Terri's car just in time to hear the detective ask Tiffany do she know who shot Malik and why. She nodded her head no and grabbed Terri by the arm telling the detective," sorry, but we have more paper's to fill out for him, so if you'll excuse us," she said with a smile on her face. She left him standing there with an out stretched hand still holding his card with his information on it. She didn't want any parts of whatever he was offering and pretended as if she never saw the card he was holding.

From the comforts of the car Joey smiled as he pulled-off. He had a list of things he needed to do with the first being to place a call to the connect and inform him of the shooting and Malik's condition. Next, he had to go down Page to Auntie's house where Auntie Pam was staying. He knew Jazzy was there and he wanted to get a feel for her first hand being that she was Amanda's first cousin! "Amanda, we gotta get you to the hospital, you've been shot," said Whitegirl as she drove down Main Street in the direction of the hospital. "No, I'm good, it's only a flesh wound, it didn't go through, it only grazed me, I'm good!" "Put that back in the glove box then," said White-girl pointing at the gun in her hand. Amanda was a little nervous and in some pain but at the very least she managed to get Malik back for killing Silas, they were now even as far as she was concerned. It actually brought a smile to her face," I got his ass; I shot him in the face just like he did to Silas. I know he's dead because I shot him at least 6 times, I got his ass, White-girl." "Let's go down the country to your peeps spot then, I can take you down there until this shit blow over. Once I take you down there then I can come back up here and get our things from over Prospect and bring everything back down the country. You know the police might be looking for you, I did see some old lady sitting on her porch when I picked you up, no telling what she might say to the police, plus Joey and Malik's girl Tiffany seen you. What will they say if he's dead, you said they ain't built like that? We gotta be careful Amanda!" "I ain't going down there, take me over 1st Street, my cousin Blacko will know what to do in this situation," she said finally putting the gun in the glove box. That sounds good too, I'll go and get rid of the guns and clean out the house over Prospect.

White-girl went straight to Prospect after dropping Amanda off at her cousin's Blacko's spot on 1st Street. She carefully put the guns in Amanda's closet in one of her many show boxes and put the other gun in her waist band. She put a half of brick of CRACK , 2 ounces of powder cocaine, and 15 X-pills along with eleven thousand dollars in cash in a separate shoe box. She arranged everything just as neatly as she first found it, the other 2 bricks that they just had got from Karma yesterday, she put them in her duffel bag along with the paper they were taking to the ole' ladies on Madison. In all, she had over 200 thousand in cash plus the 2 bricks of CRACK. She took her phone out to call Jacob. "Yo, where you at? Good. Meet me at Amanda's apartment right now." Jacob was down inside of Prospect so she decided to walk outside and meet him; she wanted to see if anybody was watching. She saw him walking slowly up to the building, he looked nervous as he kept looking over his shoulder. White girl motioned him to follow her into the building and out of sight of any on lookers.

Inside the building the first thing he said to her was, "yo, I heard Malik just got shot over on Page, you heard that?" White-girl put her game face on, "no I ain't heard nothing, who told you that?" "Where's Amanda?" "She had to take care of something, she'll be gone for a minute, but I didn't call you up here to talk about her. Who told you Malik got shot? Who did it? Where you said it happened," she said firing question after question. She knew he couldn't stand a lot of pressure so she poured it on thick. This was the time she loved the most because she got the opportunity to play the stupid little white girl who doesn't know jack-shit about the hood. That role has gotten her this far and one last role wouldn't hurt anything. Just as she thought, he started talking. "Little Stevie from the Projects' called me and told me what happened. He said ain't nobody see shit and if they did see something they ain't saying who did it or nothing." She took two steps closer to him and whispered," well, that's what happens when you do crutty shit in the hood. What goes around, comes back around to bite you in your ass, you gotta be careful out here." Then she grabbed his dick through his sweat pants. It didn't take her no time to get his dick hard, it was rather easy for her. She pulled his dick out right there in the hallway and dropped down to her knees as she slowly licked all over the head of his dick before deep throating it. Once she heard him let out a soft moan, she stood back up.

"You know what Jacob? My pussy is soaking wet and throbbing to be fucked, can you do anything about that for me? I need to be fucked and fucked good," she said batting her cold blue eyes at him?

"Can I do anything about it? You kidding right? Damn right I can do something about that for you, you know I love that pussy," he said cupping her firm titties with both of his hand and squeezing her nipples'. She began walking up the steps and then turned back around and looked over her shoulder at him and said," if you can't punish this pussy I'll have to find somebody who can. But, if you want to fuck me you can, I have only one condition; I want it rough, I want you to fuck me like I stole something from your black ass, can you do that for me?" She made a point of giving him a good look at her ass as she went upstairs. She stopped dead in her tracks almost causing him to run head first into her ass, "oh, by the way, I've never let you fuck me in my ass but today's your lucky day. I will let you fuck me in my ass as hard as you want." Then she giggled," The harder, the better."

You could have bought him for a penny as he stood there with his mouth wide open, "not yet I haven't but best believe, I'll make sure you get exactly what you're asking for," he said determined to fuck her in her ass as hard as he can. He couldn't believe his luck with her, even though he's fucked her before it wasn't nothing like she was asking him to do to her today. He's only heard the stories about how freaky she really was now he was going to get his opportunity to see firsthand.

"Bring that big black dick up these stairs, I got a lot of stress that I need you to take care of for me, I gotta release it and I don't know of any better way than have you fuck it out of me." He walked into the living room and watched as she undressed herself, he was so excited that he got out his clothes well before she did. He helped her remove her bra and panties. His dick was rock hard and standing at attention poking her in her back side as he took her bra off. They didn't waste any time. She bent over right there in front of him and said," spit on your dick and stick it in my ass nigga!" He did just what she told him to do; this was one of the few times he didn't mind the white girl telling him what to do. He made sure to spit on his dick and guided it into her ass-hole just like that. It slid in, but he knew she felt it because her whole body tensed up from the pain and she was biting down on her bottom lip.

"Ahh, that's right, it's in my ass," she moaned. "Smack my ass as you fuck me nigga, smack it real hard," she demanded as she tried to help spread her own ass cheeks. He knocked her hands away. "I got this!" He said to her finding her ass-hole extremely tight. He was taking his time because he knew that a woman who allowed you to fuck her in her ass didn't want you to just bang her up, so he went slowly despite what she had told him at the start. "I said fuck the shit out of me and stop making love to me, if I wanted somebody to make love to me I would have found somebody else, she barked through clenched teeth. Jacob pulled his dick almost all the way out of her ass, with only the tip of the head still in, he rammed in dick into her ass-hole so hard that he made her bite her tongue as she let out a loud scream. "That's what the fuck I'm talking about. Fuck meeee!"

He didn't take no mercy on her ass-hole, if she wanted him to fuck her, he would make sure she begged him to stop. He had an evil grin on his face as he continued to pound her ass-hole over and over. What he heard her screaming next really made him feel like he was the man. "Oh shit Jacob, your big dick is about to make me cum, damn it, damn it, I, I'm cuming," she moaned. He fucked her even faster and harder, sweat dripping from his chin onto her red ass, it was red from all the smacking he was doing but he didn't care he was in a zone now.

She managed to get him to stop long enough for her to lie back on the carpet with her legs up on his shoulders; she guided his dick into her pussy. "Now beat the pussy up the same way you fucked me in my ass you black nigga!" She knew the more she called him nigga the harder he would fuck her and that's what she wanted. He plowed into her pussy, his dick kept slipping out because her pussy was so wet and wasn't as tight as her ass-hole. As she was looking up at him she said to him, "Choke me." He knew that he heard what she had said but he wasn't really with that shit, it wasn't until she yelled it to him'" I said choke me nigga, and if you can't do that take your dick out of me and get the fuck out, I'll find somebody else who will fuck me the way I want to be fucked." The next thing he knew was that she reached up and smacked the living shit out of him making him dizzy for a second. "Don't look at me like that, grow some balls and smack me back...You a man or a mouse," she asked with that evil smirk on her face?

He didn't have a choice and he knew if he didn't do as she said that she would definitely make him get up and get out, he was having too much fun to leave now. He smacked her in her face turning her face fire engine red and to his surprise; she smiled and licked her lips. "That's right, smack the cowboy shit out of me, you hit like a little bitch, nigga!" His next smack sent her head flying to one side of her body as the blood trickled down her lip this time, again she smiled. "That's the one but you're still a no good, low life, black nigga who's afraid of this white pussy." She took both her hand and racked them down his chest drawing blood, but he surprise her, he didn't yell out in pain. Instead he grabbed her by the throat and began choking her and fucking her even harder until he noticed her eyes rolling back in her head. He stopped choking her and she gritted her teeth together and out of breath, she said to him," please don't stop fucking me, you're about to make me cum, I need to cum Jacob do whatever it takes to make this pussy cum. Ahh...Ahh, that's it, beat this pussy up, oh Jacob fuck meeee," she screamed at the top of her lungs as she started cuming like she's never came before.

Her body went limp from her cuming so hard but he was still fucking her and now enjoying it, he was on the verge of cuming too so he demanded of her,

"I'm going to cum in your mouth so when I tell you to open your mouth you do it, a ight?" She nodded her head up and down letting him know she understood what he wanted her to do. He was now more excited than ever as he continued to fuck her real hard, hearing her soft moans really made his cum," open your mouth bitch," he demanded as-he was cuming all in her mouth. She swallowed every bit of his cum and even licked his nuts once he drained him dry of all his cum. Their sexathon only lasted 30 minutes but they got a lot accomplished in that short amount of time. With both their bodies battered and bruised, they were tired, at least he was. His chest was on fire, he had scratches from the top of his chest down to the bottom of his stomach. She continued smiling at him, "you'll never forget this pussy will you," she asked? "How can I ever forget something like this? You're the freakiest bitch I know, you'll do anything," he said stretching out on the sofa.

She got up and got dressed," I gotta go and get Amanda but I want you to stay here until come back, that way I ain't gotta be running around looking for you, I got 4 ounce's for you when I get back." He shrugged his shoulders," bet, I'll be right here when you get back. You drained me anyway, I gotta rest, I ain't got nothing left, it's all in your stomach," he joked her.

"That's only round one, we'll finish up later, I gotta have some more of that black dick, she said walking out the front door." Oh, I almost forgot," she said pulling a chrome .45 from her purse. This for you, that's if you want it?"

"You damn right I want it, this a pretty mutha-fucker," he boasted admiring the pistol! She smiled knowing that he would like the pistol, she was happy to make him happy. She foolishly bumped her shoulder into the door frame as she was leaving out causing a bad bruise to her shoulder. It didn't matter much because it only matched the rest of her bruised and battered body. Her drive back across town to Madison was one she was looking forward to; she smiled the whole time as she dropped the duffel bag off at the old lady's house.

From Madison she took her time and cruised up towards Main and to the hospital where she walked into the emergency room. She walked up to the nearest nurse and whispered to her," excuse me miss, can I talk to you a minute? You have to help me...I...I was just raped!"

The nurse looked into her defeated eyes and saw the marks all over her face and neck, she knew this young girl needed her help," oh my god, come with me sweetie." The nurse took White-girl in the back with her and pulled the curtain around so nobody could see them," I'm going to have to perform a rape kit on you...You'll have to undress, here's an evidence bag, put all your clothes in there," said the nurse handing her the evidence bag.

White-girl started crying uncontrollably as she slowly took her clothes off, from the looks of it; it looked like it hurt her to take her clothes off in front of a stranger. The nurse swabbed her skin, her mouth, and her vagina. Next, the nurse took lots of pictures of all the bruises. She found immediate damage to White-girls' rectum and her hymen, her insides were swollen and beat red from the damaged inflicted upon her body. Sniffing and still crying her eyes out, White-girl had one last thing to tell the nurse, "he, he...He made me...me open my mouth while he came in my mouth," then she broke down and fell to the floor!

It's okay baby, he can't hurt you no more. I'm going to have to ask you a few standard questions and I'm also going to have to notify the proper authorities. I have a detective here right now who will be more than willing to help you with this. Would you like that?"

She was playing her position to the tee, everything sounded so perfect and her body language was on point. The nurse bought her story hook, line, and sinker. "He...He, said that he'll kill me if I said anything to anybody."

The nurse handed her another gown, "put this on so it'll cover the back of your body, I'll be back in one second. The detective is going to have to ask you a few questions and I have to go get him, the faster I go get him the quicker this monster who done this to you will be off the streets." Three minutes went by and the nurse came back with a white detective by her side. "This is the detective I was telling you about." "What's your name young lady," asked the detective?

Happy to see the detective, White-girl had to put on her best performance, "my...My name is Elizabeth Klean and I'm a student here at the University. My parents are Mr. and Mrs. Klean of the Science department and my father is the head Dean over at Darden Law School. My address is: 77 Farmington Place, but you can't tell my parents, they'll kill me," she said crying again. She knew that by giving them all that information that the detective would start treating her different right away, for one she was a white female and for two, she was the daughter of two very important Professors at the University of Virginia.

"Do you know who did this to you?" She shook her head yes," his name is Jacob but I don't know his last name."

"Where did this happen, where were you?" She thought that was the stupidest question that the detective could ask her, he asked her the same question twice. Wanting to tell him how stupid he was but she couldn't, if she wanted this to work she had to maintain her position.

" I...I was visiting a friend of mines over in Prospect and when I knocked on her door, Jacob answered. He told me that I could wait there until my friend got back she wasn't supposed to be gone but a few minutes, but she never came back. I even talked to her on my way over there and she told me that she was on her way and that Jacob would be there to open the door for me." "Where," asked the detective again? He had to be certain that he heard her correctly," where did this happen to you at?"

There he goes again with this two question bullshit, she thought. "Prospect, she said a little louder! He raped me in Prospect and he raped me over and over for well over two hours and he beat me when I wanted him to stop, he said he'll kill me if I ever told anyone, and he put this chrome looking gun to my head... He said he would kill me."

"Then what happened?"

"What do you mean what happened?"

"I need to know how you got away from him, did he just let you walk out the door or did you have to fight him to get away?" "Fight him? Are you crazy, he had a gun to my head, I couldn't fight him? He simply fell asleep and I escaped while he was still sleeping on the sofa." "Is he still there now," asked the detective?

He's gotta be crazy, I'm here with him how the hell do I know if he's still there, she thought to herself. She shook her head yes figuring that that's what the detective wanted to hear, "yes, I think he's still there but you can't go there, he's got a gun and said he didn't mind using it, he's crazy," she said looking him deeply in his eyes.

"You said his name is Jacob, correct? And you also said that you were visiting a friend at 777-G Prospect, correct? And you said that he has a weapon, correct?" She shook her head yes to every question and then the detective was ready to leave, "the nurse will take care of you from here, I'm going to arrest this Jacob character, he has to be taken off the streets before he does this to any other female, I can't let that happen on my watch. "Are you willing to file charges, aren't you Elizabeth," asked the nurse helping the detective?

"Yes, but you can't tell him where I am. Please, you can't tell him where I am," she begged!

"Don't worry yourself about all of that Elizabeth; we'll take care of you. But, I have to contact your parents, their probably worried sick about you."

"I know their worried about me, I haven't been home in some time, but you can call them for me," she said sounding defeated.

It took the detective all of ten minutes to secure a valid search warrant for Amanda's apartment and assemble two strike teams as he notified the drug task force. He asked the drug task force to focus on Amanda and her whereabouts and they could probably find her somewhere on South 1st Street. White-girl had given him all the information that he needed and the full extent of Amanda's drug ring she was running in Prospect. The case was getting bigger and bigger by the second. Amanda had proven to be very elusive and able to operate and run her gang of street thugs' with a lucrative profits right under the nose of the drug task force. The drug task force had been trying to do for the last month or so was to bring her down, they were unable to get close to her. None of their informants knew anything but hearsay and she wasn't selling drugs to anybody personally, she was incredibly smart, very secretive, and extremely careful how she conducted her business. The drug task force was able to locate several pictures of her and White-girl on top of Prospect, the whole scenario was starting to come together and make sense to them. Elizabeth must have been in debt and Amanda put Jacob on her sending her a message and that's why she never returned back to her apartment, thought all the detectives. Elizabeth even told them about a shooting in which Amanda was bragging to her about this morning, she said something about somebody killing her boyfriend and then she killed them this morning. The white detective put two and two together with the help of the drug task force, Amanda was the same female that he gave him a name for his John Doe and now she was his number one suspect in a different shooting in Charlottesville. He couldn't have that, not in Thomas Jefferson's town, 2 shooting within a 24-hour period? With one strike team dispatched to South 1st Street and the other to Prospect, everything was a go as they spoke to each other via head sets.

"Police, Jacob Jones ...Don't move, put your hands were we can see them," shouted the leader of the strike team! Jacob was still half asleep and thought he was dreaming for a second until he felt the cold steel on the side of his head. When he finally focused his eyes, there were 8 brawly white men stand over top of him in full riot gear and guns pointed directly at him, beams and all. The strike team was stressed in all black and have the impression that they were willing to killing his black ass if he made one false move. He froze. They cuffed him and sat him up on the sofa, he was still wearing only his boxers, the rest of his clothes were scattered throughout the living room floor where he first undressed. The strike team started searching the entire apartment once he was secured and cuffed. For starters, they took the Chrome .45 sitting on the end table next to him. From there they went straight into Amanda's bedroom and to her closet where they found several guns, a large amount of CRACK, X-pills, powder cocaine, a few used straws, half a pound of purple haze, and well over Ten thousand in cash! Everything was right where White-girl had told them it would be. They laid all the items out in front of Jacob as he sat in the living room not really sweating what they found. His eyes deceived his thoughts because they were as big as saucers.

"We really got your black-ass now, you won't see the light of day for a good number of years. When we finish with you, you'll be doing football numbers." "That shit aint mine, you seen where I was when ya'll busted down the door."

He started laughing, "I was in here sleep, and for the record, I don't live here. You know damn well I'll beat this shit in court," he said boasting and sticking his chest out.

The strike team didn't say much, they let him run his mouth as they took him downstairs and put him in the back of one of the detective's car. Jacob sat in the back still smiling because he knew it was only a matter of time that he'd be right back out there on top of Prospect doing his thang. He wasn't at all worried about those charges, he's seen many dudes beat them with the same type of charges. However, as the detective pulled into the emergency room parking lot, that when his smile faded away, he didn't know what the hell was going on. "What the fuck we're doing here," he asked from the back?

The same white detective he seen last night when Silas was murder met them at the entrance, for a second Jacob felt relieved, he knew he had an ace in the hole, if it came down to it, he was willing to tell the detective who murdered Silas and that's what he figured all this was about. They were going to let him walk as soon as he told them what they needed to know to close their case. The detective led him inside and straight to the back of the emergency room and into a small room. "Mr. Jones, I'm sure you remember me, but right now I'm going to need your permission to do an examine on you, well, I won't be doing the examination, the nurse here will perform the examination. Do we have your permission?" Jacob didn't know what to say, at the same time he didn't want to get on the detective's bad side, one thing he knew for certain was that he wasn't at the jail so there was still a chance for him to walk away from all of this, so he foolishly consented to the examination. "Do what you gotta do, but what's the examination for anyway?" The detective took several pictures of him, with his clothes on and then with them off. Then the detective left as the nurse performed the examination.

When the detective returned to the room, Jacob's whole world would change, "Mr. Jacob Jones, you're under arrest for rape, assault, and malicious wounding on a one, Ms. Elizabeth Klean, possession of a fire-arm while in possession of a controlled substance, Possession of 50 or more grams of CRACK cocaine, possession of cocaine, possession of a dangerous substance while in possession of a fire-arm."

He couldn't believe his ears, for some reason the only thing that continued to play over and over in his head was the charge of rape and who was Elizabeth Klean? He wasn't buying it; this had to be a big mistake. They white girl he fucked almost 2 months ago popped in his head for some reason because she was the only female he fucked that he couldn't really account for, he didn't even remember her name. "Who the fuck is Elizabeth Klean?"

When the detective showed White-girl several photos of six black males she picked Jacob out within 2 seconds, there was no doubt in her mind who he was and what he done to her, she had all the evidence to prove it. The detective went on to tell her all the stuff they found inside of Amanda's apartment and when he asked her did she know anything about all those drugs, her eyes went straight to the floor.

"Do you know anything about all those drugs Elizabeth, if you know anything you can tell me and I'll help you?"

As seasoned detective and he already knew the answers to his questions he just needed her to validate what he was already thinking. He's seen this type of thing before; they were using her to handle their dirty work and took full advantage of her drug problem. It was easy for a bright young girl like her to get caught up with some very dangerous people and that's why he would do any and everything in his power to help her walk away from this type of thing with her dignity still intact.

"Listen to me Elizabeth, if you have a drug problem, let me know right now. Those people were taking advantage of you but that's no reason for that monster to have raped you. All you have to do is be honest with me and then I can help you... Will you be honest with me?" On the inside White-girl was smiling from ear to ear but she couldn't allow the detective to pick up on how she was feeling. She was exactly where she wanted to be at that very instance. She shook her head yes to the detective as she slowly began to give the detective her version of the story.

"It all started about 5 months ago; I met Amanda at the mall in the bathroom. She walked up on me when I was in the bathroom sniffing powder cocaine, I forgot to lock the stall and she walked right on in on me. She offered me more cocaine and told me that I could come and hang out with her at her apartment. I didn't have any more money so I decided to go along with her. Once I got to her apartment in Prospect we got real high, well I did anyway and before I knew it, she had me having sex with 7 or 8 different dudes for more powder cocaine. The more I had sex with them the more cocaine she would give to me and after a while, I just got use to it and started hanging with her every day because I knew I would get high hanging with her. I just wanted to be able to fit in and that's what I had to do to fit in with them, all I had to do was let the dudes have sex with me. After a while I started driving her anywhere she wanted to go, I didn't have to have sex no more for the cocaine, she just gave it to me, cocaine was everywhere. When I called her this morning she was bragging to me about how she shot somebody and told me to wait for her at the apartment, she made me promise that I would wait there for her, and I promised her that I would wait for her there. But when I got there, Jacob raped me because I didn't want to have sex with him like I use to do before Amanda told me that I didn't have to do that anymore, my debts were paid," she started crying uncontrollably again as she told him all the things they made her do over there.

"Do the drugs belong to Amanda," asked the detective?

"They belong to Amanda and Jacob, from what I seen, they work together with the drugs and she tells me where to drive her." "Have you ever seen Amanda with a gun?" "She keeps more than one gun at her apartment and carries one on her at all times. Amanda is very violent, she said she didn't mind using her gun on anyone.

After interviewing Elizabeth, the detective quickly relayed that information back to the drug task force team who were already familiar with Amanda and her operation in Prospect. They obtained several major arrest warrants for her after finding large amounts of illegal substances in her apartment along with Elizabeth's story; they finally had enough to arrest her. They were going Federal with this one! It didn't take the drug task force long to locate Amanda on South 1st Street. She was sitting in a car of a known drug dealer from over there. The strike team jumped out on her and surprised her, her first thought was that they were arresting her for Malik's murder.

"What the fuck? Why ya'll putting these damn hand-cuffs on me so fuckin' tight," she fired? The lead detective spoke up for the entire group, he was rather happy to be able to deliver the news to her, "well, for starters, you're under arrest for possession with the intent to distribute 50 grams or more of cocaine base, possession of a fire-arm in furtherance of criminal enterprise, and that's just the beginning," he said laughing. "That's enough for us to get the cuff's on your fine ass."

The drug charges were music to her ears, since she wasn't under arrest for the murder of Malik there was a chance for her beating this bullshit, she figured. She looked the happy detective dead in his eyes and said, "a-ight then, come on, let's get this shit over with...I'm trying to make bond," she said walking herself to the patty-wagon.

The detectives asked the magistrate judge not to issue her a bond based on other violent information they obtained from a witness, however, the magistrate set her a bond anyway. "Bond is set at One hundred thousand, cash or property."

Amanda smiled knowing that the hundred thousand was only a phone call away and she would be out within the hour as soon as she contacted White-girl and have her post her bond for her. "I'll be out in thirty minutes, soon as I call my girl she'll be here before I'm even processed." After getting her processed, she used her one phone call to call White girl's phone but she didn't' get an answer, instead she left this message for her. "You won't believe this shit but I'm locked the fuck up, my bond is a hundred grand. Get that dick out your mouth and bring your ass down here and bail me out," she said laughing into the phone.

That was 5 hours ago and she was still sitting in the holding tank, it was just her luck that the holding tank didn't have a phone and she used her one phone call, it wouldn't be until the morning before she got to another phone. She asked the officer what time it was and when he told her it was after 10:30 p.m. she decided to lay back and get some rest. Then the thought hit her, suppose White-girl is in jail to and that's why she hasn't come to bond her out yet, she had to be locked up, she thought. Had she listened to Blacko, he told her to call him because he would be waiting for the call but she already used that call to call White-girl. She smacked herself upside the head for being so stupid, it was oblivious that if she was in jail on all those drug charge's then it's only right that White-girl be locked-up just as well, they were partner's and that's why she didn't answer her phone. She closed her eyes and thought about Silas, a smile crept across her face, and that's the last thing she remembered before she was off to sleep. This would become her nightly ritual, the first of many nights in a lonely jail cell. The end was near but she had no clue!

CHAPTER 20

A few days after Malik got shot, all Joey could think about was the doctor telling him about the bullet lodged in Malik's head. Unsure of the damage, it was too early to tell if his wounds would have significant impact upon his life, for now he was in an induced coma to allow his brain to heal itself. He was well aware that Malik could never return to his normal self, he could stay a vegetable, be paralyzed, or any of the other not so good endings, he was wondering if it was worth it? He knew and understood the risks well before he took his first package from the connect because he went over them in his head over and over again. They couldn't blame this on ignorance or lack of understanding. All of this was by some strange and fucked-up way, brought on by no one but him and Malik! He was trying his best to chalk it up and charge it to the game but his mind wouldn't allow him to do that, not without difficulty anyway. His mind flashing over the scene as he saw it the day Amanda was standing over Malik and the look she had in her eyes told him that it was over for his homey, that evil smirk on her face told him that he was to late, but when he saw Malik move his arm he jumped at the opportunity to save his brother and never hesitated for a second. Was there anything he could have done to save him.

Terri sat on the opposite end of the bed watching Joey get dressed, the shooting had affected him. For the last couple of days, he hadn't been his normal vibrant, happy-go-lucky self, he changed. There was also one single thing about all of this that made her realize something: It could very well have been him sitting in that hospital bed and not Malik! The writing was on the wall and it was her duty to bring the writing to life and have Joey read it for himself that was her mission. From the classes she took and personal experience, she was smart enough to know nothing in the CRACK game lasted forever, especially the good times.

She continued to wrangle with the thought of how can she convince Joey to walk away from the CRACK game and the whole lifestyle? What she knew she would be fighting against was the fact that Joey would eventually want to get some revenge since he knew exactly who shot his brother, how can she advise him to let it ride and just walk away when this was the life he chose to live and revenge was just as much a part of that lifestyle as breathing? She had to deal with the fact that she didn't have a problem with it when she first found out about what he really did to earn his paper, how can she convince his without appearing to pushy? Was it even possible for a guy like Joey to walk away from something he's been doing for so long? Would he need help? Deep down in her mind, she knew he wasn't the average hustler, he had dreams and was already putting his paper in a position to make him a very successful businessman in the near future, so that told her that he was looking past the CRACK game. Or did it? This was damn near one of the hardest things she had to consider in her young life, her entire future was hanging in the balance and she was aware of that fact. Can she maintain perfect balance?

The brief ride to the hospital only lasted 6 or 7 minutes, Joey had gotten them a room at the Hampton Inn on Main Street so they could be close in case something happened and had to get to the hospital quick. The only gesture that Joey did that showed her she was important to her was when he hugged her, he hugged her extra tight and his kiss seemed to last a life time to her. It made her more determine to have her man and the life they deserved, how would she do to make that a reality?

They walked into Malik's room, Tiffany was asleep on the cot the hospital provided. She slept with a smile on her face and her right hand on her stomach, Terri took notice of that and almost decided against waking her up, but she had to.

"Hey sleepy head, how's my sister doing," asked Terri as she lightly rubbed Tiffany's arm waking her up? Tiffany opened her eyes to a smiling Terri and a very concerned Joey, she was happy to see the both of them. "Hey girl," she said stretching and yarning as she got herself together. "I gotta brush my teeth and wash my face," she managed to say making her way into the bathroom.

Joey was standing over Malik just staring at him. The first thing she did was kiss him on his lips," you know he would kill me if I kissed him and didn't brush my teeth," she said to Joey trying to get him to laugh. "The doctors told me that he can hear us when we talked to him. You can talk to him Joey," she urged him. She walked back over to Terri," girl, when the doctor told me he can hear me, I talked his damn ear off last night. I had too, I love him so fuckin' much but I don't know what to do," she said breaking down and starting to cry.

Terri walked over and whispered in Joey's ear "I'm going to take her downstairs to get something to eat, take your time and talk to him, tell him what's on your mind if you don't tell nobody else, tell him baby," she said hugging him like her life depended on it. Come on girl; let's get you something to eat because I know you haven't eaten nothing!"

In the hallway Terri could sense she was starting to break down, she stopped right outside the room and hugged her tight letting her know that she wasn't alone. "Everybody knows and understands how much you love him, you don't have to convince that to nobody, even he knows it...He'll wake-up soon, I know he will, but until he does, I'm going to need a favor from you. I'm going to need for you to remain strong don't stress yourself out, you have to remember, and everything that you do or think will have a direct impact on this baby's life. Every feeling and emotion you have, the baby will experience the same thing."

It seemed like every time somebody said something about the baby it instantly changed her state of mind, no matter how she was feeling. "Thank you girl, I needed to hear that. I..I don't know what I'd do if it wasn't for you, you've done so much for me in such a short time. I don't want to place a burden on you but I need you, I can't get through this without you." Terri grabbed her by the hand and pulled her towards the elevator," don't worry about it, we're family and family has each other's back. I never said this, but we both know, that could have very well been Joey up there, we gotta have each other's back...You feel me, my sista," said Terri putting on her best ghetto voice.

By the time Terri and Tiffany got back up-stairs to the room, they were different, they had a relaxed attitude to what was going on and Joey noticed it right off the bat. He was sitting down watching the news as a picture of Amanda and Jacob flashed across the screen. The volume was low, he rushed to turn it up. He already heard about her apartment getting raided but nobody knew much about what she was charged with or what the drug task force found if anything. The news anchor was saying that there was a large amount of CRACK cocaine, guns, and cash seized from the apartment. In the next frame it showed the entire drug task force standing behind a table full of drugs, weapons, and money. The lead detective began talking about an attempted murder charge against Amanda and a rape charge against Jacob. The rape and attempted murder charges caught his attention, in his mind he was saying no, he didn't want them to go out like that. He was waiting to see White-girl's picture come across the screen but it never happened, he wondered what happened to her? She could be on the run or anything, but something seemed strange and odd, rape isn't something most hustlas take part in and Jacob was a hustla. Despite how he felt about him, he needed to know more about this charge of rape and the attempted murder.

"What the fuck? This shit is crazy, who the fuck did Jacob's dumb-ass rape and who is Amanda charged with attempting to murder," he questioned looking back over at Tiffany and Terri?

Tiffany caught the look right away and addressed him, shutting him down even before he got started, "Joey, don't look at me like that! All this shit is news to me as it is to you, I don't want to see that bitch in nobody's jail, I want to see her ass 6 feet deep! Ain't shit changed with me Joey except that my family is more important to me, and in case you've forgotten, ya'll all the family I got," spit Tiffany growing frustrated with Joey!

Terri sat back and observed the exchange between the two; she knew not to involve herself one way or another. What they were discussing had nothing to do with her or how she got down. She wasn't in the streets or was she a part of their lifestyle. She admired the way Tiffany stood up for herself, It was a definite show of strength, and for Joey, it only reflected the endless cycle of the lack of trust one had for any and everybody involved in that lifestyle.

"The State charges against these two defendants, has just been dropped and the Federal Government has taken over this case with hopes of more arrest to come, Amanda and Jacob have been remanded to the custody of the U.S. Marshalls service," said the news anchor.

Everybody's eyes were glued to the television that they almost didn't hear Malik coughing, all three of them all turned in his direction just in time to see him pulling the tubes in his nose and mouth, trying to pull them out, his eyes were open but they were blood shot red. He looked confused. Tiffany broke her neck getting to the side of his bed as she screamed for the nurse. Terri stepped out the room and went to the nurse's station and told them what was going on, the nurse's rushed past her and into the room. "We're going to need everybody to wait outside, we have to stabilize him, shouted the head nurse!"

"I ain't going nowhere," demanded Tiffany holding Malik's hand. She wanted to make sure the moment he regained his senses that her face would be the first person he saw.

White-girl was on the fifth floor of the hospital since the day she walked through the doors, they had her in their drug treatment program. It was time for her to say her good-byes. Her hardest adjustment was getting use to having them call her by her real name, she's been going by White-girl for so long and now when she heard her real name called, took her a minute to realize they were talking to her. White-girl was not only a name for her; it became a way of life!

White-girl had became a permanent character whom she learned to become, mind, body, and soul. In her sick and twisted mind, she was feeling some type of way about having to give the role up, she loved it so much, but she also knew it was time to now move on to her next project, and that brought a smile to her face. Lucky for her, her parents had somehow convinced the detectives she didn't need the thirty day in-patient program in Richmond. With Richmond being bigger than Charlottesville it was more of an opportunity for what she had in mind.

It had to be placed on the back burner, she was enrolling back into the University of Virginia. Her entire stay on the fifth floor, the television stayed tuned into the news every time it came on, everyday there was something about Amanda and Jacob, and it forced a wicked smirk on her face every time she saw their faces'. She wondered if Amanda realized she was behind it all. From the messages that she had gotten her cousin to leave on her voice mail she must not because he kept saying that she needed to holla at her, but she had no intentions of ever speaking to either of them in this life time or the next. It was her grind, her hustle that separated her from them, 'charge it to the game, bitch,' she whispered to herself!

She had one last obstacle to face before leaving the hospital, the detective was on his way up-stairs to speak with her on her way out, the nurse had already told her. She squeezed into her smallest and tightest shorts, they were meant for this occasion. Her wife-beater was hugging her firm titties and if you looked closely, you could see her nipple's because she didn't wear a bra. In her mind, she could get any man she wanted even a seasoned detective. Her training in the concrete jungle taught her that! Throwing on the finishing touches to her make-up in the bathroom she could hear him entering her room. It was his hard bottom shoes that gave him away. She walked out looking and smelling like she was ready to be fucked and sucked to heaven and back and she knew it more than anybody else.

"Hello Elizabeth, how are things going for you here? I see you're on your way out of here, I'm proud of you, you deserve it, and you've been through so much. I might as well get to the business at hand; I just wanted to let you know that we got both Amanda and Jacob. From what we believe, Amanda is the master-mind behind a very profitable drug empire; she's going to be charged with the attempted murder of a rival drug dealer from across town. We haven't had the opportunity to speak with him just yet; he's still in a coma. We found the gun in her apartment; it appears to be the same weapon fired into this guy's head. Her finger prints are all over the weapon, all we're waiting for now is the ballistics to return. You're a very lucky young lady, no telling what those monsters would have done to you had you not walked in here and told us what happened to you, which took a lot of courage to do! Jacob, well, he's singing a beautiful song as we speak, he's going away for a very long time with the rape conviction. He's doing the best he can to save his ass on the drugs and weapons charges, somehow, he keeps telling us that you're involved, but hey, that's normal, he's looking to save his own ass and he's willing to say and do anything to help himself even if that means he has to lie. He'll be gone for a very long time, we really don't care what he has to say about the drugs', the rape will give him so long in prison that your great, great, grand-children will be safe from that monster. All you have to do now it get yourself together, stay clean, testify, and all of this will eventually blow over, you'll do great things in life, I'm sure of that," said the detective looking in her eyes.

She put the sad and lonely look on her face; she looked down at the floor before inhaling and then exhaling real slow. When she finally looked back up at the detective his eyes were now glued to her rock hard nipples. That brought a slight smile to her face, "detective, I understand that I'm a very lucky girl and I appreciate everything you've done for me. Believe me, I've learned my lesson and I'm definitely ready to get this behind me, but I still feel like there should be something that I can do to pay you back for all you've done for me, but I don't know what I can possibly do to show you my appreciation," she said smiling and biting her finger nail.

"All you have to do now is testify, that's all you need to do. I'll be in contact with you well in advance, but that's it. "You do that," she said licking her lips as she turned her back to the detective picking up her bag on the floor beside her bed. With her shorts being so short one of her juicy pussy lips jumped out catching the detective off guard. He swore he could see the moisture glistening on her pussy from where he was standing. He forced himself to look away, he checked his wallet for his card that was all he could do. She stayed bent over long enough to accomplish just what she wanted because when she finally looked back up, the detective was fidgeting through his wallet in search of something, she didn't know what he was looking for until he retrieved a card. She glanced down towards his dick and his little pecker was poking right through his pants', she stared into his eyes. When he looked away, she knew he had an eye full of her wet pussy, on the inside she smiled but maintained eye contact. In her head she was saying,' a thin waist and a pretty face will get them every time.

The detective brushed the beads of sweat from his forehead and handed her his card," make sure you call me, you can call me anytime," he said stressing the anytime.

She moved in to give him a hug, she pressed extra tight against his chest with her as she whispered in his ear making sure her lips grazed his ear," thank-you detective, I'll be sure to call you!"

They parted ways as the nurse took her to the back of the hospital where her sister was waiting for her in their parents new Mercedes Benz. She walked down the few steps and handed her sister her bag. "Hey Elizabeth, how you doing bitch," asked the sister laughing?

"Fantastic bitch, what the fuck you thought. That damn detective creeps me the fuck out. He wants to fuck me but he doesn't know exactly how to ask for the pussy...I might help him out with that in the future, he'll come in handy," insisted White-girl. Leaving out the parking lot White-girl got right down to business, "did you get all my stuff from Madison?"

"Yeah, I got it, I even cleaned the house out. You already know my nosey ass looked all through you shit, you got a lot of money and drugs, what's next?"

"You mutha-fuckin' right that's a lot of shit I got. It's well over three-hundred large in them bags, and a whole gang of CRACK. What's next? Bitch we're on to our next grind, but right now take me to my dorm room, I'm starting to miss it and I'll tell you exactly what we're going doing next."

Amanda and Jacob stood beside their attorney's ready to hear the long list of bullshit charges they were facing. She smiled at Jacob; she hadn't seen him since they got locked-up. He didn't smile or even look at her, he was in his own zone.

"The Commonwealth of Virginia moves to dismiss all charges against Amanda Smalls and Jacob Jones," said the Commonwealth's attorney. Amanda was shocked the charges were being dismissed; you looked back over at Jacob, "I knew this was some bullshit!" She was ready to have the hand-cuffs taken off her but that didn't happen.

"Your honor, the Commonwealth will be turning these prisoner's over to the services of the United States Marshalls, these offenses will be addressed in the Federal court in the near future," said the Commonwealth's Attorney with an evil smirk on his face.

Amanda felt her legs give out on her as she almost fell to the floor; her stomach was on fire, it felt like somebody was sticking a knife in her stomach.

Her attorney had to catch her from falling. The judge started speaking," well, this was supposed to be a bond hearing, however, the Commonwealth has dropped all charges against the prisoner's and therefore, I no longer have jurisdiction to hold a bond hearing in this court at this time. These prisoners are released from the custody of the Commonwealth of Virginia and remanded to the custody of the United States Marshall's service taking effect immediately," he said before banging down his gavel on the large desk.

Amanda thought about trying to make a run for it but there was nowhere for her to go, all exits were blocked off. Two huge Marshalls ushered Jacob out of one door and she couldn't understand why he wasn't putting up any resistance, it made her head spin! The remaining Marshall's took her out the other door. What she came to realize later was that Jacob was taken to the regional jail in Orange County while she remained housed at the Albemarle/Charlottesville Regional jail. On her ride back to the jail, the Marshalls was joking her about her making bond in the Federal court, they knew it was damn near impossible unless you cooperated with them and that was something she had no intentions of doing. Still not giving up all hope, White-girl was still out there somewhere; she figured that White-girl was just waiting for things to blow over before contacting her. She knew that she was holding a nice piece of change so making the bond wouldn't be the issue; the issue would be getting the Federal government to give her a bond. However, from what the Marshalls were telling her, she damn near gave up making bond even before she got back to the jail. Every day since she's been in the jail she barely ate anything, and when she got back for lunch it was no different. She had more shit on her mind and food wasn't one of them. Every time the trays with the food on them came, the smell would cause her to run to the bathroom and call Earl. She didn't give her sickness thought, but the ole' head was watching her every move from a distance. She needed to take a nap, the lunch trays had her feeling sick again and with all that court shit, she wanted to close her eyes and dream because that's when Silas would come to her, she needed to see his face and hear his voice. Climbing up on the top bunk, she said a prayer and closed her eyes trying her best to count backwards to a hundred; she was out before she got to fifty!

By the time the dinner trays came, Amanda was still in her bunk asleep, the ole' head watched closely to see if she was going to get up but she didn't. The ole' head walked over to her and woke her up, "trays," said the ole' head softly. Amanda rose up just enough to see who it was that was tapping on her bunk, when she seen the ole' head she simply said," You can have it, I'm good," and turned over to get more sleep. The ole' head walked over to the other side of her bunk and began whispering in her ear," chile, you's pregnant and that's why you're so sick and all that. You haven't eaten much of anything since you've been here, if I didn't know any better, I would think you were trying to kill that baby in your stomach...Now get yourself up out that bunk and eat something because if you don't, that baby don't stand a chance." For some reason the thought of being pregnant forced Amanda out the bunk, soon as her feet hit the floor, she lifted her shirt to examine her belly. There was a bulge there, she tried her best to recall the last time she had her cycle but she couldn't remember. She looked at the ole' head, "you might be right. Thinking back, her body had been in disarray since she been locked-up, she had to be pregnant. "Damn, if I am pregnant they might give me a bond or something...Maybe even probation on these bullshit charges, right?" The ole' head looked her in her eyes and choose her next words carefully," let me tell you something, there's going to be a hundred niggaz and bitches jumping on your case in exchange for a time cut, these crackers don't give a fuck about you or that baby you're carrying. All that CRACK they got out your house, the paper, the guns, and not to mention that crazy-ass co-defendant you got. He's running around raping University of Virginia students, and she's suppose to be white, you're apart of all of that. You tell me, you still think you'll get a bond? I'm sorry I had to throw shade on your parade but those people don't give a shit about none of us unless you're in bed with them. The only important thing in your life right now is that baby you're carrying."

Before Amanda had a chance to say anything the C/O came into the pod and told Amanda she had an attorney visit and that she should be ready in 5 minutes. Her and the ole' head locked eyes but neither said a word. Amanda followed the C/O out the pod and towards the front of the jail where an attorney was waiting for her in a small room.

"Miss Amanda Smalls, please to meet you. Have a seat," said the attorney. She took a seat opposite the attorney, keeping her mouth shut she wanted to see what the attorney had to say before she opened her mouth. In her mind she was thinking this visit couldn't be good news because it was too early for that, her case had been turned over to the Federal government. "Do you know what's going on with your case," asked the attorney? She looked at the attorney like he was crazy, "do I know? Ain't that your job, you are the lawyer, right?" She forced herself to calm down and take a deep breath, she promised herself not to jump out the window until she had a good enough reason.

"Listen, all I know is what their saying about me isn't true. All those drugs they got out my apartment, well if they got them out my apartment, they must have put them there because I know I didn't! We should beat this shit, I ain't put any of that shit in my apartment, I might look stupid, but I'm far from it," she insisted.

"To answer your question, yes and no. There's a lot going on here, from what they tell me, the United States attorney will be seeking a superseding indictment in the near future against you and your co-defendant Jacob Jones, you know him don't you? Right now, they're saying you're a Queen-Pin and mastermind behind an extremely large CRACK cocaine ring. You'll be indicted under the RICO law, and to be honest with you, that's one helluva charge to beat! As for your co-defendant Jacob, well, he has even more serious charges. For starters, he's giving a detailed statement against you as we speak with the United States attorney's office in exchange for his rape offense. He's charged with raping a white female who was a student at the University of Virginia and her parents are very important people in the community. She's also claiming that you were her drug connect and that you forced her on more than one occasion to have sex with multiple guys in your apartment for drugs, here's a picture of her, we're not suppose to have this photo but I had my investigator dig it up," he showed her a picture of white-girl.

Amanda's mouth fell wide open, and her head started spinning, "you gotta be kidding me, this is White-girl, she's my fuckin' partner! Ain't no way Jacob raped her, he's been fucking her for well over two months now," shouted Amanda in disbelief.

"Here's the thing, that's not what she's saying and with Jacob already making the deal of his life with the United States attorney's office, that makes you the lone suspect in a major CRACK cocaine ring. Now, they also have a gun that seems to match the bullets they retrieved from the body of a rival drug dealer that everybody's saying you shot because a dispute. Your finger prints are all over the gun, now, the victim himself, well, he hasn't said anything, he's in a coma right now. Miss Smalls, these charges are very serious, the mandatory minimum is a life sentence, that's what you're facing and this is just the beginning. The government is willing to offer you a one-shot deal, you give them your connect and testify, as a professional, I say take the deal," said the attorney.

Amanda sat back in the jail issued chair and crossed her arms as she watched the attorney intently. This was one of those times she wished like hell she had her straight razor so she could slice his face wide open. She had to use her mind instead of a piece of metal. She knew a set-up when she seen one, this attorney had have come from the Government, to hem her ass up in a situation she wouldn't be able get out of. He was definitely a Government henchman. In her mind nothing he said made sense, except the shooting that she did do!

However, she wasn't admitting shit to this cracker, not now or not ever. Why would Jacob have to rape White-girl when she was practically throwing her pussy on him every chance she got? And more importantly, who told them he raped her? Even if he did rape her, which she couldn't believe, why hasn't she been charged with the drugs along with her? Something wasn't adding up, too many pieces were missing and she intended to find out what was really hood with her case. Again, she forced herself to remain calm, she knew the attorney wasn't on her side, it was best listen and then react later.

The attorney saw that look in her eyes, he knew she didn't trust him, he's seen that look a million times in his past but she had the game fucked-up, he couldn't tell her that, not at the moment anyway. "Listen to me, later this week, the Government will return a superseding indictment against you and don't be surprised if your name is the only name on the indictment. If you're willing to cooperate with the government, that's different story. Just keep in mind, you can possibly receive a life sentence for these crimes you're charged with, that's a lot for a young lady like yourself to think about."

"Okay, tell me, how much time I am looking at right now, "she asked seriously?

Between 10 to 14 years, but come next week with the superseding indictment, you'll be facing nothing less than a life sentence."

"You're saying that if I snitch I'll get anywhere less than the rest of my natural life, is that what you're telling me?" She couldn't help the little chuckle that came out her mouth.

"Miss Smalls, the Government doesn't call it snitching; they use the term, substantial assistance. If you help them, I know for certain they'll help you. If you tell them about your connections who knows, if it's good, you may just walk away from all of this with a few bumps and bruises, nothing you won't ever recover from," he insisted. "I think that's something you should consider, do you want to tell me who your connections are," he asked searching her eyes for any information that will tell him that she was ready to break and tell everything but he saw nothing.

She stood-up from the small table and looked the attorney dead in the eyes, "you got me fucked-up, I'm not your average bitch you see, that was mistake number one. I ain't nobody's snitch, if I did it, I'll claim it, I'm not bringing nobody else down for something I did. I'm sure the Government sent your pretty ass down here to sell me up the fuckin' river but guess what? A bitch like me has been swimming upstream with no paddle all my life. This shit ain't nothing new to me…Tell the Government to go fuck they self," she said in a low, calm voice. She turned around at the door and looked back at the attorney," "by the way…You are fired," she said as she banged on the door to be let out by the C/O.

The attorney had a wicked grin on his face, he was happy to hear those words coming from her mouth, too many times do a young black male or female crumble under pressure. "Miss Smalls I'm sorry but you're not able to fire me because you're not the one who hired me to represent you in this matter. And for starters, the worst thing you could do right now is walk out that door, I'm sure Karma wouldn't like that very much," said the attorney smiling.

" Karma, what the fuck you talking about?"

" Listen, I had to come down hard on you like that, Karma sent me to represent you on this case but we first had to find out if you was either working or going to work with the government to give her up, I'm sure you can understand her concerns about that, can't you?"

Amanda shook her head in disbelief, finally someone who really was on her side. "I think we should get down to business, would you like to come back over here and sit down?"

"Before we go into anything, I need to know where the hell White-girl and what's the deal with this rape bullshit?"

This time it was the attorney who sat back in his chair and crossed his arms, "everything that I've said to you about your case is true, the rape, the drugs, the superseding indictment, all of that is true but as for your girl White-girl, she set you up real good. From the looks of it, she's behind everything." He pushed a huge stack of papers her way, "this is called your discovery, it's everything the government is going to use to try their best to convict you of everything their charging you with. They will employ the help of local snitches, jail snitches and anybody else willing to lie on you. Take this back and read it, I'll be back tomorrow. Oh, here's a number you can call anytime, the person on the other end doesn't know me or Karma, but you can use the number to make three way calls or whatever," said the attorney as he got up to leave.

She had one last question for the attorney, "so what are my chances for bond? I guess it wouldn't really matter being White-girl stole all my money, maybe you know, maybe, Karma would spot me the money if you talk to her for me, I just want to get out of here."

" Right now it's very important that you read everything I've given you so that you can help me with your case as much as possible, the reality of your situation is that the Government doesn't give a shit about you or your situation. I'll set something up in the near future, however, here's how it works: I was telling you about the superseding indictment the government will be seeking in the next week or so. If I got youa bond hearing tomorrow and you were successful in that attempt, the Government will only revoke that bond using the superseding indictment as a weapon. I say we wait until the Government has charged you with everything they're going to charge you with and we'll move from there," said the attorney looking very serious.

Amanda walked back to her pod in a daze, all that information she learned from her attorney blew her mind. She had a migraine! Jacob snitching? White-girl snitching? Who would be next, she thought to herself? She went straight to her bunk and didn't pay much attention to all the eyes that were focused in on her and her movement. For the time being, she only wanted to lie down and process everything, she wasn't even able to read what her attorney had given her, not yet anyway.

The ole' head was the main one watching, but she watched from a distance, it was in Amanda's body language that told her the most. She was familiar with walk and same body language, Amanda was her some years earlier. She had that same look and walk after her attorney visit; it was that first visit that told you who was who. She knew exactly who Amanda was and not only from watching the news, Amanda had gotten herself caught up in a deadly game played by our trusted Government. It was evident that our Government was out to destroy the lives of young black men and women alike! It was the same old story: White folks would get 2 years for trafficking millions of dollars while the young black male or female were handed sentences with football scores and even life sentences for selling CRACK cocaine.

Our Government will attempt to make a deal with some while destroying others with that deal, and if you don't take their deal, you can pretty much count on doing at the very least the next 20 or so years in a Federal prison. That's exactly what happened to the ole' head some 11 years ago, even in her situation, the people who testified against her were higher than she was on the food chain and our Government knew all about it, however, they played the game because it looked good on paper. With our Government, it's either you take the deal or deal with enhancements, there's no in between with our Government. The younger generation of today coming into the system by the thousands doesn't have a clue or idea of their consequences when they put that highly addictive substance called CRACK into their hands. She has seen the system turn friend against friend, brother against brother, father against son, daughter against mother, with the help of our government, this has turned the Black family upside down. For this reason alone, the ole' head was more determined to help Amanda with her case, she couldn't sit by and watch another young black female be used as a tool or a fool for the government.

She let Amanda sleep until the trustee came and went with hot water, she fixed them a prison meal, after all she had gotten use to making the best with what she had to work with. It was time for her and Amanda to have a serious talk and with it being later in the evening; they could talk without to many people in their mouth. She walked over to Amanda's bunk and woke her up," Amanda, wake up girl, I made us a swell, come on and eat," she insisted.

"I ain't hungry, I just want to sleep," said Amanda still half asleep! Naw sista, we went through this shit once today, you don't have to get up for yourself but you better get up for that baby. I know your young ass go hard, but I'm telling you right now, you're going to have to kick my ass to get me away from this bunk, so come on because either way, you're going to have to get up."

The ole' head was still standing there smiling When Amanda finally turned back around to face her. This time Amanda got out the rack, washed her face, her hands, and brushed her teeth. When she got back over to the ole' heads bunk, she passed Amanda a large envelope. "Read this, I'm sure you'll find something in there you can relate to."

Amanda's first thought was that did everybody pick today to give her something to read? She was mentally drawn to open the envelope for some reason, she began reading and then re-reading the ole' heads' transcripts from her trial. To her it seemed like she was reading exactly what she was charged with, the big difference was that this already happened 11 years' prior. The ole' head was 11 years' in on a twenty year sentence. All that information made Amanda feel sick all over again. "Damn, they did you dirty!"

The ole' head look at her, "that's my point, that's what I'm trying to get you to see. You're in the same position as I was, you don't have to make the same mistakes that I made. So, what are you going to do," asked the ole' head looking at her closely?

"If you're referring to snitching, I'm going to tell you just like I told that lawyer today; I ain't nobody's snitch. Fuck it, twenty, thirty years', I'm going to do mine," boasted Amanda sticking her chest out.

"What you tell the lawyer when he said that?"

Amanda smiled, "whoever said it was a he and not a she? Anyway, I fired his ass on the spot and walked my black-ass out of there." She thought it a good idea to spin the whole situation, she wasn't sure who's side the ole' head was really on so until she found out, she would spin her every chance she got and if it turned out that she had her best interest at heart she wouldn't mind in the end.

Seventy-two hours after Malik had come out the coma, Tiffany was in the room packing the rest of his belongings. He was to be released from the hospital after his miraculous recovery. 98% of her time had been spent by his side, she had begged, pleaded, and bargained with GOD to spare Malik and for his complete recovery. At this moment, she believed her prayers' had been answered. There was nobody with her to take Malik home and that's the way she wanted it. She hired a limo, they would be leaving the hospital in style, and she knew Malik would get a kick out of that. She had even more news to tell him, she wasn't just pregnant, she was pregnant with twins. She would tell him on their way down to Auntie Pam's where everybody was waiting on them for his surprise welcome home party!

"Come on baby, I'm ready to get out of here," said Malik sitting himself in the wheel chair.

White-girl and her sister were outside her dorm room bringing in the rest of her things when they were approached by a well dressed and fine brother. "Hello ladies, may I help you with your bags, I'm going in this building myself," asked the fine brother?

White-girl's sister could see the lust in her eyes and that was her que to get gone," a-ight sis, you don't need me any longer, these are the last two bags of yours, I'm out."

White-girl waved her sister off as she stared into the eyes of the stranger. He was sexy as hell, just the way she liked them. He wasn't as street or hard as she was use to, but from the print in his sweat pants, that was all that mattered to her at the moment.

"Of course you can help with the bags; I'd like that very much. So, what's your name," she asked not really caring what his name was, she was going to fuck him if his name was god, she didn't care.

The stranger took both of her bags and began following her up the stairs and into her dorm room on the first floor. She asked him his name again as she went into the room, she thought he didn't hear her the first time. "Oh, my name is Sosa, and yours," he said dropping her bags on the floor.

She noticed he had on gloves; she was going to ask him was he riding a motorcycle or something but her pussy was getting wet, she wanted that dick inside her throbbing pussy. She was picturing herself sucking his black dick; it was something about a black dick that she couldn't resist. "So, do you go to school here," she asked stepping even closer to him?

For some reason his smile was so intense that she was forced to look away, and when she looked back at the stranger, fear over-took her. Sosa was standing inches away from her with a black .38 special with duct-tape on its handle. The gun looked just like the one she had given Amanda to shoot Malik! With the .38 special trained on the center of her forehead, he moved even closer, she could smell the peppermint on his breath he was so close.

"I'm sure you remember my brother, his name is Silas, you remember him don't you? Well, I have a little message from your road dog, Amanda! You remember her to don't you?"

White-Girl was about to scream and when she opened her mouth; Sosa put the silencer in her mouth and pulled the trigger five times before he stopped. "That's for the both of them you stinking white bitch!"

——————— ——————— ——————— ——————— ——————— ———————

———————

Malik was happy as hell to have everybody surprise him, he was happy to see everybody. They were his family and that was the most important thing to him, Auntie Pam called him into the kitchen.

"Malik, some girl is on the phone for you, she said it's really important."

He took the phone from Auntie Pam," hello, who this?"

"Malik before you hang-up, hear me out, it's Amanda..." There was a brief silence on the other end; she thought he had hung-up on her," Malik, you still there?"

"I'm here, what the hell you want and how you get this number?"

"I need your help but you know I can't really holla like I want to because of my situation...I just need to know what you're going to do?"

"I'm not the one you gotta worry about, I'll see you when I see you but you won't be seeing me in no court room," he said hanging up the phone!

THE END...